W9-DBY-933

Praise for **LINNEA SINCLAIR**

"Linnea Sinclair beautifully blends SF and love stories to make some of the most exciting and satisfying romance novels being written today." —Jo Beverly, author of *The Rogue's Return*

"Fun, fast and sexy! Linnea Sinclair always delivers a great read." —Robin D. Owens, author of *Heart Thief* and *Heart Duel*

"With her trademark snappy dialogue, smart characters, and sizzling romance, Linnea Sinclair has readers flipping the pages at light speed." —Susan Grant, author of *The Legend of Banzai Maguire* and *Your Planet or Mine?*

"One of the brightest new voices in science fiction romance." —Catherine Asaro, author of *Schism* and *Skyfall*

"[Linnea Sinclair] has the knack of intriguing with romance and delivering a solid story too." —Jacqueline Lichtenberg, author of *Dreamspy* and *Those of My Blood*

"Linnea Sinclair brings her own dimension to the world of sci-fi/fantasy romance. Her richly textured novels are to be cherished first page to last." —Patricia Waddell, author of *Whispers in the Stars* and *True Blood*

Praise for **FINDERS KEEPERS**

Award of Distinction for Exceptional Merit from *Heartstrings Reviews*

Winner of the CataRomance Reviewers Choice Award for Single Title Sci/Fi, 2005

Finalist for the 2006 RITA Award for Best First Book

Finalist for the 2005 RIO Award for Best Sci-Fi/Fantasy Romance

Winner of the 2001 Sapphire Award for Best Speculative Romance Novel

Winner of the 2001 PEARL Award for Best Sci-Fi Romance

Romance Reviews Today Perfect 10 Award

"*Finders Keepers* is romance, but also science fiction in its truest form. Ms. Sinclair creates a complete and fascinating universe." —*Romantic Times BOOKreviews*

"A Perfect 10 . . . a riveting, tightly written, edge-of-your-seat tale that pulls the reader in from page one, never letting go until the poignant finish. . . . I highly recommend this to readers of all genres, and hope like heck there's a sequel!" —*Romance Reviews Today*

"The author's sure hand with characterization makes each twist of this emotionally laden story line as suspenseful as any well-wrought battle scene. . . . With peppy, laugh-out-loud dialogue, an outstanding cast of supporting characters and a big serving of adventure in the mix, *Finders Keepers* is guaranteed to show readers a pleasant and thoroughly entertaining time." —*SciFi.com*

"Would I recommend *Finders Keepers* to hard SF fans? Definitely! Would I also recommend it to romance fans? Absolutely! Linnea Sinclair is obviously a versatile author with a wonderful imagination, which enables her to take readers along for the ride." —*Novelspot*

"Has the wow! factor in spades...The plot and characterizations are detailed, dynamic and deeply immersive and make this super-charged sci-fi release twice as interesting as anything this reviewer has come across before....Well-developed and wonderfully imaginative, *Finders Keepers* has 'exceptional merit' written all over it." —*Heartstrings*

"*Finders Keepers* is a great ride from start to finish....A delight to read...Sinclair delivers a story balanced nicely between space opera adventure and emotion-centered romance—not the easiest thing to find anymore. Thanks, Linnea!" —*Speculative Romance Online*

Praise for **GABRIEL'S GHOST**

Winner of the 2006 RITA Award for Best Paranormal Romance

2003 Prism Award, 2nd place (tie with *An Accidental Goddess*), for Best Futuristic Romance

2003 RWA Windy City Choice Award, 2nd place, for Best FF&P Romance

Winner of the 2002 Affaire de Coeur Award for Best Futuristic Romance

2002 Sapphire Award, 2nd place (tie with *An Accidental Goddess*), for Best Speculative Romance Novel

2002 PEARL Award Honorable Mention for Best Science Fiction Novel

Romance Reviews Today Perfect 10 Award

WordWeaving Award of Excellence

"Brilliant plot, strong characterization, fast-paced action." —*Romantic Times BOOKreviews*

Five Stars! "With nonstop action and a heart-felt love story, *Gabriel's Ghost* is a must buy." —*CataRomance Reviews*

"Both an exciting sci-fi adventure and a warm romance, with deep characterization and meaningful relationships. Highly recommended." —*Romance Reviews Today*

5 Ribbons! "Ms. Sinclair does a perfect job of blending sci-fi, technology, world-building, and romance in *Gabriel's Ghost*.... Not one to be missed." —romance junkies.com

"*Gabriel's Ghost* is a high-flying sci-fi romance for a number of reasons—not the least of which is the sense of euphoria it will give readers craving credible science fiction as well as a complicated-but-fulfilling love story. There isn't a shadow of a doubt in this reviewer's mind that Bantam Spectra has a bona fide interstellar star in this author. Prepare to be starstruck, dear reader." —*Heartstrings Reviews*

Five Moons—Outstanding Cosmic! "Who said there is no good way to blend sci-fi and romance? . . . What we are looking at here is the next incarnation of the genre. It's deep, visceral, and more human in that it's emotionally and—yes—sexually intense. Sci-fi has never been better!" —MystiqueBooks.com

"Readers have come to expect the extraordinary from author Linnea Sinclair, but *Gabriel's Ghost* still exceeds all expectations! With the vision and texture of a poet, the heart of a warrior, and the skill of a master, Sinclair creates a world of psychic gifts and shape shifters, of dangers beyond imagination and love beyond question. . . . A tale so entrancing, so mesmerizing that readers will be absolutely blown away." —*Midwest Book Review*

"Sinclair writes an intriguing blend of science fiction and romance, with lots of action-adventure, great dialogue, a sneaky sense of humor that won't quit. . . . A much richer, more emotionally demanding tale of suspense that . . . starts off fast and furious and never lets go." —NoveLists/EBSCO Publishing

"*Gabriel's Ghost* may be the best synthesis of science fiction and romance fiction yet, appealing to two readerships that once seemed to have nothing in common. Both the dramatic tension and the sexual tension are there from the first chapter, and they never let up.... The whole novel combines grittiness of character with grittiness of science fiction background in the tradition of C. J. Cherryh." —John J. Pierce, author of *Imagination and Evolution*

"A non-stop thrill ride with a pace that never slows down, *Gabriel's Ghost* is enthralling.... The sexual tension crackles and the love scenes are positively incinerating. Combine all of this with fascinating supporting characters who are never quite what they seem and a hard look at prejudice, genetic engineering and the ease with which the truth can be twisted, and you have an intellectually and emotionally satisfying book." —*Sime-Gen Reviews*

"How can a review do justice to a book that sweeps you away from the very first page? ... *Gabriel's Ghost* is a phenomenal book and one that deserves its place on keeper shelves all over the world.... Linnea Sinclair has managed to mix religion, politics, adventure, science fiction and romance into one of the best reads of the year. A true winner!" —*Interludes Magazine*

"An adventure a minute, with one revelation after another developing and deepening the relationship between hero and heroine, even as they threaten to tear them apart. I don't know if there are any more stories in this universe, but I'd sure like to read them if there are." —Gail Dayton, author of *The Barbed Rose*

Praise for *AN ACCIDENTAL GODDESS*

Finalist for the 2005 RIO Award for Best Sci-Fi/Fantasy Romance

Winner of the 2003 RWA Windy City Choice Award for Best FF&P Romance

2002 Sapphire Award, 2nd place (tie with *Gabriel's Ghost*), for Best Speculative Romance Novel

2002 Romantic Times BOOKreviews Award Nominee: Best Small Press Futuristic

2002 PEARL Award Honorable Mention for Best Science Fiction Novel

Romantic Times BOOKreviews Magazine's 2002 Gold Medal Top Pick Award

Gold Medal, Top Pick! "This is exquisite storytelling that combines delicious romance, a spellbinding plot, and vivid characters into a powerful drama that transcends genres." —*Romantic Times BOOKreviews*

"Linnea Sinclair's fertile imagination scores another winner.... Combining science fiction, fantasy, adventure, romance, and wry humor, *An Accidental Goddess* can't help please any reader looking for the ultimate in escape from the mundane. Well written and riveting...make a place for it on your keeper shelf." —*Romance Reviews Today*

"*An Accidental Goddess* is lots of fun. Sinclair's future world is nicely fleshed out, and Gillie and her partner, Simon, a sentient entity who's not exactly a computer or a person, are well-developed, engaging characters.... Entirely entertaining." —*Contra Costa Times*

"Proves once again why Sinclair is one of the reigning queens of science fiction romances...This is a book readers can hand to non-SF fans and say, Try it. You'll like it. And they will...provided they enjoy bright, attractive characters, an interesting plot, action, adventure, humor and romance." —*Starlog*

"A quirky, humorous, fast-paced saga of deception, passion, trust, and risk...Linnea Sinclair's innovative and entertaining story will captivate the reader and provide hours of laughter, suspense, and adventure." —*Fantasy Book Spot*

"A great, great story with a fabulous romance and I loved every minute of it. No wonder Ms. Sinclair is a double RITA finalist with *Gabriel's Ghost* and *Finders Keepers*." —Gail Dayton, author of *The Barbed Rose*

Praise for *GAMES OF COMMAND*

"Linnea Sinclair just gets better and better! *Games of Command,* her latest science fiction romance, features not one but two sexy, dangerous heroes, along with two strong, capable women and two fabulous furry furzels. Sinclair whips her characters through a story that is as exciting and action packed as it is passionate. *Games of Command* is not to be missed!" —Mary Jo Putney, author of *Stolen Magic*

"Fascinating, fabulous, fast-paced, with one of the best heroes ever! I've been waiting for *Games of Command* and what an incredible story! Wow!"
—Robin D. Owens, RITA Award-winning author of *HeartMate*

"Excellent, strong feline companions. Four paws up!"
—Zanth, hero of *HeartMate* by Robin D. Owens

"Heart-pounding action, compelling characters and taut suspense make *Games of Command* a must read!"
—Patti O'Shea, author of *Through a Crimson Veil*

"In *Games of Command*, Linnea hits it out of the park—hell, out of the galaxy!—pairing my favorite kind of hero with my favorite kind of heroine in a rip-roaring adventure with enough twists and turns to leave even the most jaded reader guessing until the very end." —Susan Grant, author of *The Legend of Banzai Maguire* and *Your Planet or Mine?*

"If you enjoy adventure romps, romance novels and space opera, you'll get them all in this book. . . . This is fun science fiction beach reading. Enjoy." —SFRevu.com

ALSO BY LINNEA SINCLAIR

Finders Keepers
Gabriel's Ghost
An Accidental Goddess
Games of Command

The
Down Home
Zombie Blues

LINNEA SINCLAIR

BANTAM BOOKS

THE DOWN HOME ZOMBIE BLUES
A Bantam Book / December 2007

Published by Bantam Dell
A Division of Random House, Inc.
New York, New York

This is a work of fiction. Names, characters, places, and incidents
either are the product of the author's imagination or are used
fictitiously. Any resemblance to actual persons,
living or dead, events, or locales is entirely coincidental.

All rights reserved
Copyright © 2007 by Linnea Sinclair Bernadino
Cover illustration © 2007 by Stephen Youll
Cover design by Jamie S. Warren Youll

If you purchased this book without a cover, you should be
aware that this book is stolen property. It was reported
as "unsold and destroyed" to the publisher, and neither
the author nor the publisher has received any payment
for this "stripped book."

Bantam Books and the rooster colophon are registered
trademarks of Random House, Inc.

ISBN 978-0-553-58964-1

Printed in the United States of America

Published simultaneously in Canada

www.bantamdell.com

OPM 10 9 8 7 6 5 4 3 2 1

With heartfelt thanks for their suggestions and input: authors Robin D. Owens, Susan Grant, Stacey Klemstein, and Anne Aguirre, and my reader/crit partners Nancy Gramm, Donna Kuhn, Michelle Williamson, and Lynne "Liberry Lady" Welch.

As always, to Daq and Doozy, *fur* all your help. And to Jaime Bernadino Warren—one of the first people to "meet" Theo Petrakos—and her dad, Rob Bernadino, who after all these years still find me amusing.

Acknowledgments

This author gratefully acknowledges the assistance of:

Sergeant Steve Huskisson of the Plantation (FL) Police Department; Detective Sergeant Scott Peterson of the Collier County (FL) Sheriff's Office; Joel Reyes, former Hialeah (FL) Police Officer; and Deputy Sheriff Bob Cooley (VA), Valor55, GoDirectly2Jail, and other law-enforcement personnel on the Officer.com and RealPolice.net forums... who answered an author's constant questions with such detail, patience, and good humor. Their assistance has been invaluable. Any sense of law-enforcement authenticity in this book is fully their doing, and for that I'm grateful beyond words. Any errors in police procedure you may find are no reflection of their expertise but rather of the author's stubbornness to have the characters and the plot go her way. God bless you all, and keep you and yours safe out there. May guardian angels always watch your six.

Author's Note

Greek phrases used in the manuscript have been transliterated for readers of English. *Efcharisto* to author Tori "Sofie Metropolis" Carrington for the corrections and additions!

Author's Playlist

Juno Reactor: *Komit, Conga Fury, Swamp Thing, Kaguya Hime, Children of the Night*

Theo Petrakos's Playlist

Traveling Ed Teja: *Blue Light, Blue Dime, The Down Home Zombie Blues, The Down Home Divorced Guy Blues, Jorie's Sigh—* www.geocities.com/edteja

Every time you hear on the news about people running away from a crazed gunman, remember that someone's son or daughter in a police uniform is running *toward* that crazed gunman.

—From *What Cops Would Like You to Know,* author unknown, posted on various law-enforcement sites on the Internet

DOWN HOME ZOMBIE BLUES

Lyrics by Linnea Sinclair & Ed Teja
Music by Ed Teja (ASCAP)

G
Found myself wondering why so many people die
        G7
Nothing left inside them but two useless eyes
 C7   G
Staring out at this cold, cold world
    D7   C7 G
They got them down home zombie blues

Say, baby, baby, hear what I say?
You see a zombie pass by today?
She ain't talking; hell, she ain't even breathing
She's got the down home zombie blues

Now I'm way past Jupiter, in the middle of the stars
Cruising past asteroids, just me and my guitar
We're hunting down a nightmare, tracking fast and
 sure
Ain't got no time to waste, got them down home
 zombie blues

Got a ship that's fast, gets me on my way
Got a laser pistol in case those zombies wanta play
We're hunting down a nightmare, tracking fast and
 sure
Ain't got no time to waste, got them down home
 zombie blues

My gal's a sharpshooter, and she kisses mighty fine.
Not much we can't handle hunting zombies side by
    side
We're hunting down a nightmare, tracking fast and
    sure
Ain't got no time to waste, got them down home
    zombie blues

Say, baby, baby, hear what I say?
You see a zombie pass by today?
She ain't talking; hell, she ain't even breathing
She's got the down home zombie blues

©2003–2007 by Ed Teja & Linnea Sinclair

DOWN HOME DIVORCED GUY BLUES

words by Ed Teja & Uncle Steve
music by Ed Teja

A
Going home alone, watching my life go by
D   A
Maybe, maybe not give love another try
E   D7   A
I got them down home divorced guy blues

Taking my time getting out again
I still like the women but I don't know when
I'll be over these down home divorced guy blues

Eating my dinner right out of the can
Why mess up a kitchen for just one man
I'll be eating right again when I'm over these divorced
    guy blues

Wanting a life that will be for two
But I'm still gun-shy
Got these divorced guy blues

Taking my time getting out again
I still like the women but I don't know when
I'll be over these down home divorced guy blues

© Ed Teja & Uncle Steve, 2003

The
Down Home
Zombie Blues

1

Another dark, humid, stinking alley. Another nil-tech planet. What a surprise.

Commander Jorie Mikkalah cataloged her surroundings as she absently rubbed her bare arm. Needle pricks danced across her skin. Only her vision was unaffected by the dispersing and reassembling of her molecules courtesy of the Personnel Matter Transporter—her means of arrival in the alley moments before.

The ocular over her right eye eradicated the alley's murky gloom, enhancing the moonlight so she could clearly see the shards of broken glass and small rusted metal cylinders strewn across the hard surface under her and her team's boots.

Another dark, humid, stinking, filthy *alley.* Jorie amended her initial appraisal of her location as a breeze filtered past, sending one of the metal cylinders tumbling, clanking hollowly.

She checked her scanner even though no alarm had sounded. But it would take a few more seconds yet for her body to adjust to the aftereffects of the PMaT and for her equilibrium to segue from the lighter gravity of an intergalactic battle cruiser to the heavier gravity of a Class-F5 world. It wouldn't do to fall flat on her face trying to defend her team if a zombie appeared.

She swiveled toward them. "You two all right?"

Tamlynne Herryck's sharp features relaxed under her short cap of dark-red curls. "Fine, sir."

Low mechanical rumblings echoed behind Jorie. She shot a quick glance over her shoulder, saw nothing threatening at the alleyway opening. Only the expected metallic land vehicles, lighted front and aft, moving slowly past.

Herryck was scrubbing at her face when Jorie turned back. The ever-efficient lieutenant had been under Jorie's command for four years; she knew how to work through the PMaT experience.

Ensign Jacare Trenat, however, was as green as *liaso* hedges and looked more than a bit dazed from the transit.

"Optimum," replied Trenat when Jorie turned to him, straightening his shoulders, trying hard not to twitch. Or fall over.

Jorie bit back an amused snort of disbelief and caught Herryck's eye. A corner of Herryck's mouth quirked up in response. They both knew this was Trenat's third dirtside mission, perhaps his sixth PMaT experience.

After eight years with the Guardian Force, Jorie had lost track of how much time she'd logged through the PMaT, having her molecules haphazardly spewed through some planet's atmosphere. She'd seen stronger officers than the broad-shouldered ensign leave their lunch on the ground after a transit. The itching and disorientation would drive him crazy for a few more trips.

At least it was a standard transit and not an emergency one. Even she was known to land on her rump after one of those.

"Are we where we're supposed to be, Lieutenant?" she asked as Herryck flipped open her scanner. The screen blinked to life with a greenish-yellow glow.

"Confirming location now, sir."

Jorie glanced again at the scanner she'd kept in her left hand through the entire transport, power on, shielding at full. If it beeped, her laser would be in her right hand, set for hard-terminate. Recent intelligence reported the chilling fact that some zombies had acquired the ability to sense a Guardian's tech, even through shields.

That's why she and her team were in this stinking filthy alleyway, on this backward, nil-tech planet the natives had aptly named after dirt.

They were hunting zombies.

Because zombies were on the hunt again.

"Confirmed, Commander." Herryck squinted at the screen with her unshielded eye. "Bahia Vista, Florida state. Nation of American States United."

A subtropical area, according to the Guardian agent on active hunt status here for three planetary months. An agent whose reports had ceased without explanation two days ago. Jorie knew from experience what that could portend. She'd seen it before with agents and trackers who thought they could solve a rogue-herd situation alone. One tracker against one zombie had a chance. An agent with basic tracker training might live long enough to escape. But if there was more than one zombie or if the agent was caught unawares . . . It was the latter she feared.

She'd known Danjay Wain for more than a dozen years—he was one of her older brother's closest friends and had flown as her gunner on her last few missions with the Interplanetary Marines during the Tresh Border Wars. For the past three years on the *Sakanah,* he'd worked as Jorie's active hunt agent a half-dozen times. In spite of his teasing, prankster ways—he and her brother, Galin, were so much alike—he was a conscientious man with a quick mind and an insatiable curiosity about tracker procedures.

She dreaded now that, during their many sessions over a wedge of cheese and a brew in the crew lounge, she'd either taught him too much about her job—or not enough.

"Think he's alive, sir?" Herryck's quiet question echoed her thoughts. No surprise, that. Danjay Wain was Herryck's teammate, her friend as well. The jovial agent's sudden silence bothered Herryck as much as it bothered Jorie.

She huffed out a short breath. Even as a marine, Danjay could be impetuous. But she'd never thought him stupid. "I hope so. Any response from his transcomm?"

Herryck squinted at her screen, tapped the query code again, then shook her head. "Still no answer."

Damn. She so wanted the problem to be one of distance, of the ship in orbit, atmospheric interference. Anything but what her gut told her might be true: Danjay's impulsive hotshot streak might have finally won out over his common sense. "How far are we from his last signal?"

"Twelve point two marks, sir."

Twelve marks? Jorie directed a scowl upward, even though there was no way the PMaT chief on board the *Sakanah* could see her. *All right. I can deal with another stinking alley,* she railed silently at the chief. *I know we can't materialize anywhere we want without setting the native nil-techs on edge. But, damn your hide, Ronna, twelve marks? On foot? Let's forget the fact that this is a time-critical mission. Let's forget the fact that we have an agent missing. Do I look like I'm dressed for sightseeing?*

She was in standard hot-weather tracker gear: sleeveless shirt, shorts, knee-high duraboots, socks, and a right-arm technosleeve so she could multitask her units if she had to. Two G-1 laser pistols were shoulder-holstered left and right. A Hazer micro-rifle slanted across her back. In the side of her right boot rested a sonic-blade. Not to mention her utility belt with her MOD-tech—her Mech-Organic Data scanner—and transcomm. Her headset with its adjustable ocular and mouth mike striped her hair like a dark band. She'd need that to target the zombies once a warning sounded.

Hot-weather gear notwithstanding, she was definitely not dressed for a leisurely twelve-mark sightseeing stroll.

"Sir?"

"We have to acquire transportation." She took a few steps toward the alley's entrance, then stopped. Ronna needed to recalibrate her tiny seeker 'droids to provide landing coordinates better suited to humanoids.

As for Trenat... "Relax, Ensign." In the light of the almost full moon overhead, she could see the stiff tension in the young man's shoulders under his tracker shirt. He hadn't taken his hand off his G-1 since they arrived. "There's not a zombie within fifty marks of this place."

Yet. But there would be. There were close to three hundred on the planet, per Danjay's last report. It was the largest herd the Guardians had found to date. The zombies' controller, their C-Prime, had to be straining its capabilities to direct all the drones.

That also meant the zombies' sensenet was large. They'd probably already detected the energy from her team's PMaT and were alerted to an off-world transport. But PMaT trails faded quickly. As long as her team's MOD-tech stayed shielded, they should be safe.

"Transportation." Herryck thumbed down Danjay's data on her scanner screen. "Land vehicles powered by combustion engines. Fossil petroleum fueled. Local term is *car.*"

Jorie had read the reports. No personal air transits—at least, not for internal city use. Damned niltechs. A four-seater gravripper would be very convenient right now. She resumed her trek toward the alley's entrance, waving her team to follow. "Let's go find one of those cars."

"City population is less than three hundred thousand humans," Herryck dutifully read as she came up behind Jorie. "The surrounding region contains approximately one million."

In her eight years as a Guardian, Jorie had worked cities larger and smaller. Six months ago, Kohrkin—a medium-size city on Delos-5—held seven hundred thousand humanoids. A herd of eighty zombies reduced the population to three hundred fifty thousand by the time the damned council heads alerted the *Sakanah*. Jorie, Herryck, and two other commanders went dirtside with a full battle squadron. Their mission was successful. But the lives of those she couldn't save still haunted her.

She thought she'd seen death as a pilot with the Kedrian Interplanetary Marines fighting in the Tresh Border Wars, ten years past. That was civilized warfare compared to what the Guardians faced with the zombies.

Unless you were a pilot taken prisoner by the Tresh. Jorie's fingers automatically rose to the long, bumpy scar just below her collarbone as Herryck continued to recite the facts Danjay had provided. And, as always, Jorie's stomach clenched. A memento—a very special one she couldn't afford to think about now. She had other problems. Serious ones, if something had happened to Danjay.

The stickiness of the air and the sharp stench of rotting garbage faded. Jorie paused cautiously at the darkened alley entrance, assessing the landscape. The street was dotted with silent land vehicles, all pointing in the same direction, lights extinguished. Black shadows of thin trees jutted now and then in between. The uneven rows of low buildings were two-story, five-story, a few taller. Two much taller ones—twenty stories or more—glowed with a few uneven rectangles of light far down to her right.

Judging from the brief flashes of light between the buildings and tinny echoes of sound, most of the city's activity appeared to be a street or so in front of her. At least Ronna's seeker 'droid had analyzed that correctly. Materializing in the midst of a crowd of nil-techs while dressed in full tracker gear had proven to be patently counterproductive.

A bell clanged hollowly to her left. Trenat, beside her, stiffened. She didn't but tilted her head toward the sound, curious. As the third gong pealed, she guessed it wasn't a warning system and remembered reading about a nil-tech method of announcing the time.

She didn't know local time, didn't care. Unlike the Tresh, humanoids here had no naturally enhanced night sight. It was only important that it was dark and would continue to be dark for a while yet. She and her team needed that, dressed as they were, if they were going to find out what had happened to Agent Danjay Wain.

The bell pealed eight more times, then fell silent. A fresh breeze drifted over her skin. She caught a salty tang in the air.

"...is situated on a peninsula that is bordered on one side by a large body of water known as Bay Tampa." Herryck was still reading. "On the other..."

Gulf of Mexico, Jorie knew, tuning her out. Data was Herryck's passion.

Zombie hunting was Jorie's.

But first she had to appropriate a car and locate Danjay Wain.

"Trust me, this is truly weird." Ezequiel Martinez's voice held an unusual note of amazement.

Homicide Detective Sergeant Theo Petrakos followed his former patrol partner through the cluster of crime-scene technicians poking, prodding, and prowling around the living room of the small bungalow a few blocks from Crescent Lake Park and downtown Bahia Vista. The *whir-click* of a digital camera sounded on his left. He recognized Liza Walters, her blond head framing the familiar piece of equipment.

Zeke stopped and pointed to a nearly shredded green plaid couch. "There."

Theo stepped around overall-clad Sam Kasparov, who was diligently dusting a broken lamp for prints, then came to a halt in front of a body next to the couch.

"Well?" Zeke looked at him expectantly. "Weird, right?"

Theo shoved his hands into the pockets of his slacks and nodded mutely in answer. He wasn't sure *weird* was sufficiently descriptive of the dead, withered body of the man sprawled faceup on the floor. His skin looked like crisp parchment that had been shrink-wrapped over his bones. His T-shirt lay loosely on his frame; his sweatpants seemed overlarge. His red hair, though, was thick, full, and healthy. Not sparse, like the mummy the dead man resembled.

Worse, his eyeballs were still moist. They bulged

from his face like two large, wet, dimpleless golf balls.

Theo had never heard of a mummy with wet eyeballs. But then, this man was no mummy. Mummification of a body took at least a couple of months under normal circumstances in Florida's warmer temperatures. Yet the landlord had last seen the deceased—one Dan J. Wayne, according to the documents Detectives Zeke Martinez and Amy Holloway had found in a kitchen drawer—alive and well two days ago.

Theo had heard of spontaneous combustion. But spontaneous mummification?

He made a mental note to make sure Zeke checked the Centers for Disease Control database. Judging from comments by the crime-scene techs, they were puzzled too.

They couldn't even definitely say that this was a murder.

All they did know was what the landlord—an affable, ruddy-faced French-Canadian who lived next door—had told Zeke and Amy: he was walking his rat terrier after the six o'clock news when he noticed the broken front window on his rental property. He peered in. Then, voice shaking, Monsieur Lafleur had called the police on his cell phone. The first officers to arrive on the scene found clear signs of a struggle in the overturned, broken furniture and torn draperies.

But the struggle didn't seem to leave any corresponding injuries to the dead man on the floor. And there was no evidence of who—or what—he struggled with. If anything.

For all Theo could tell, the dead man had run around like a whirling dervish, demolishing his own living room before falling to the floor in a mummified state.

That would fit with the pattern of shattered glass from the window. The window hadn't been broken by someone coming in but by something—which included a portion of a wooden end table, from all appearances—going out.

Theo hunkered down on his heels next to the body and snagged a pair of protective gloves from a nearby evidence kit. Carefully, he plucked at the neck of the man's T-shirt, then the sleeves.

"Maybe you shouldn't get too close to Mr. Crunchy." Zeke leaned back as if Theo's touching the corpse might cause it to burst, sending lethal chunks splattering against the guayabera shirt that was Zeke's trademark outfit. Tonight's selection was navy blue with a wide white strip up the front. "Might be some kind of virus. Contagious. A new SARS strain or something."

In the fifteen years that he and Zeke had worked for the Bahia Vista Police Department, Theo had seen the wiry man fearlessly dodge any number of flying fists, speeding cars, and even, a few times, bullets. Diseases, however, were another issue entirely. Zeke was probably the sole reason local vitamin stores made any profits. How he stayed married to a doctor was a source of continual speculation.

Theo continued his examination. "SARS is respiratory, not dermatological."

"So what do we got?" Zeke asked. "Some Satanic

cult that thinks the Christmas holidays are Halloween, killing people by draining their blood?"

Zeke might think of Halloween, but Theo's upbringing resurrected another image: the *Kalikantzri*, evil goblins who appeared during the twelve days before Christmas, according to Greek legends. But this was Bahia Vista, not Athens. Theo frowned, then looked up. "Not sure. Hey, Liza, you see this?"

The stocky blond crime-scene photographer squatted down next to him with a grunt. "You mean those marks on the side of his head?" she asked.

"Yeah. Got those when Amy rolled him."

"They line up. Almost like a large pronged vise grabbed him."

"Like this?" She pulled off her hair clip and clicked it in his face. It was a plastic half-moon curve, spring-loaded with rows of teeth.

He took it, turning it over in his hand. "Like this, but big enough to cover his head."

"Saw that happen on a construction site once." She retrieved the clip, twisted her long hair into a bun at the back of her head, and clamped the clip over it. "Guy's skull was crushed. Lots of blood, gray matter. Don't have that here."

No, they didn't. Not even a puncture. Just some barely discernible bruises.

"How are your holidays so far, Theo?" Liza was still squatting next to him.

"Fine," he lied. "Yours?"

"Kids are up to their eyes in toys they don't need, as usual. And they can't even get to the ones under the tree until Christmas." She nudged him with her elbow and grinned. "My husband's cousin Bonnie is in town. She's a couple years younger than you, thirty-four or thirty-five, single. Real cute. Like you." She winked. "You're clocking out for vacation, right?"

He nodded reluctantly. He'd wondered why she asked about his schedule when he ran into her at the courthouse yesterday. Now he had a feeling he knew.

"Why don't you come by the house tomorrow night, say hi to Mark and the kids, meet Bonnie?"

He rose. She stood with him. Liza Walters was, as his aunt Tootie liked to say, good people. But ever since he'd divorced Camille last year, Liza had joined the ranks of friends and coworkers trying to make sure Theo Petrakos didn't spend his nights alone.

"Thanks. I mean that. But I've got some things to do."

"How about next week, then? I'm sure you'll like her. You could come with us to the New Year's concert and fireworks at Pass Pointe Beach." She raised her chin toward Zeke. "You too, Zeke. Unless Suzanne has other plans?"

"New Year's Eve is always at her sister's house." Zeke splayed his hands outward in a gesture of helplessness. "Suzy doesn't give me a choice."

Liza briefly laid her hand on Theo's arm. "Think about it. You need to have some fun. Forget about the bitch."

He smiled grimly. Forgetting about the bitch wasn't the problem. Trusting another woman was. "I'll let you know, but I'm probably scheduled on call out."

"That Bonnie sounds real nice," Zeke intoned innocently as Liza went back to photographing a splintered bookcase. "Thirty-five's not too young for you. I mean, you're not even fifty."

Theo shot a narrow-eyed glance at the shorter man. "Forty-three. And don't you start on me too."

Zeke grinned affably. "So what *are* your plans for tomorrow night, old man?"

"I'm restringing my guitar."

"Alone?"

Theo only glared at him.

Zeke shook his head. "Still singing *The Down Home Divorced Guy Blues*? Man, you gotta change your tune."

"I like my life just the way it is."

"When's the last time you got laid?"

"If you focus that fine investigative mind of yours on our dead friend's problems, not mine, we just might get out of here by midnight."

"That long ago, eh?"

"I'm going to go see what I can find in the bedroom," he said, ignoring Zeke's leering grin at his choice of destination. "You take the kitchen."

Zeke's good-natured snort of laughter sounded behind him as he left.

"Nice work, Trenat." Jorie laid both hands on the vehicle's guidance wheel and, looking over her shoulder, offered the young ensign an appreciative smile. He had done *very* nice work locating a well-concealed storage area of land vehicles and using a combination of mechanical and technical skills to override a series of locks and security devices. All in under ten minutes. Hopefully, determining Danjay's status and returning him and his critical T-MOD unit to the ship would go as smoothly.

Trenat all but beamed at her from the rear seat, most of his earlier unease gone. "This power pack," he said, holding out a thin box slightly smaller than her hand, "will create an ignition sequence and activate the engine."

She followed his instructions as to placement and tabbed on the power. The vehicle vibrated to life, a grumbling noise sounding from its front. "No aft propulsion?"

"No, sir."

No antigravs either. Well, damn. But when in Vekris, one must do as the Vekrisians do. She draped the headset around her neck and studied the control panel with its round numbered gauges. Other gauges had symbols like those she'd seen on signs as they walked the short distance to A-1 Rental Cars. Danjay's reports noted that the local language was similar to Vekran, which Jorie spoke along with three other galactic tongues. The two languages shared a similar—though not identical—alphabet, which explained why many of the signs she saw didn't made sense.

As to why the local language was similar to Vekran, she had no idea. That was out of her area of expertise, and Danjay's. His report had noted it and had been forwarded to the scholars in the Galactic Comparative-Cultures Division of the Guardian Force.

Jorie was just happy the locals didn't speak Tresh.

Tam Herryck, rummaging through the vehicle's small storage compartment on the control panel, produced a short paper-bound book. "Aw-nortz Min-o-al," she read in the narrow beam of her wrist-beam on her technosleeve.

Jorie leaned toward her. Tam Herryck's Vekran was, at best, rudimentary. "Ow-ner's Min-u-al," she corrected. She took the book, tapped on her wrist-beam, and scanned the first few pages. It would be too much to ask, she supposed, that the entire universe be civilized enough—and considerate enough—to speak Alarsh. "Operating instructions for the vehicle's pilot." As the engine chugged quietly, she found a page depicting the gauges and read in silence for a few moments. "I think I have the basics." She tapped off her wristbeam, then caught Trenat's smile in the rectangular mirror over her head. "Never met a ship I couldn't fly, Ensign. That's what six years in the marines will teach you."

The vehicle's control stick was between the two front seats. She depressed the small button, eased it until it clicked once.

The vehicle lurched backward, crashing into one parked behind it.

"Damn!" She shoved the stick again and missed a head-on impact with another parked vehicle only because she grabbed the wheel and yanked it to the left.

Herryck bounced against the door. "Sir!"

"I have it, I have it. It's okay." Damn, damn. Give her a nice antigrav hopper any day.

Her feet played with the two pedals, the vehicle seesawing as it jerked toward the open gate.

"I think," Herryck said, bracing herself with her right hand against the front control panel, "those are some kind of throttle and braking system. Sir."

"Thank you, Lieutenant. I know that. I'm just trying to determine their sensitivity ranges."

"Of course, sir." Herryck's head jerked back and forth, but whether she was nodding or reacting to the vehicle's movement, Jorie didn't know. "Good idea."

By the time they exited onto the street, Jorie felt she had the nil-tech land vehicle under control. "Which direction?"

"We need to take a heading of 240.8, sir." Herryck glanced from her scanner over at the gauges in front of Jorie, none of which functioned as guidance or directional. "Oh." She pulled her palm off the control panel and pointed out the window. "That way."

They went that way, this way, then that way again. Jorie noticed that Trenat had found some kind of safety webbing and flattened himself against the cushions of the rear seat.

"What do you think those colored lights on their structures mean?" Herryck asked as Jorie was again forced to swerve to avoid an impact with another vehicle, whose driver was obviously not adept at proper usage of airspace.

Jorie shrugged. "A religious custom. Wain mentioned that locals hang colored lights on their residences and even on the foliage this time of the year. Nil-techs can be very supersti—hey!" A dark land vehicle appeared on her right, seemingly out of nowhere. Jorie pushed her foot down on the throttle, barely escaping being rammed broadside. There was a loud screeching noise, then the discordant blare of a horn. A pair of oncoming vehicles added their horns to the noise as she sped by them.

"Another religious custom," she told Herryck, who sank down in her seat and planted her boots against the front console. "Their vehicles play music as they pass. And they're blessing us."

"Blessing us?"

Jorie nodded as she negotiated her vehicle between two others that seemed to want to travel at an unreasonably slow rate of speed. "They put one hand out the window, middle finger pointing upward. Wain's reports stated many natives worship a god they believe lives in the sky. So I think that raised finger is a gesture of blessing."

"How kind of them. We need to go that way again, sir."

"I'm coming up to an intersection now. How much farther?"

"We should be within walking distance in a few minutes."

"Praise be," Trenat croaked from the rear seat.

Jorie snickered softly. "You'd never survive in the marines, Ensign."

Zeke Martinez let out a low whistle as Theo led him and Liza into the bedroom. "Damn. Looks like some kind of computer you'd find in a sci-fi flick. It was behind that dresser?"

"The dresser's a fake." Theo shoved the chest-high piece of furniture farther away from the wall. Liza moved in front of him, digital camera whirring. "Drawer fronts are glued on. Inside's hollow."

"Looks like Mr. Wayne didn't want just anyone to find this," Liza said, adjusting the camera's telephoto, zooming in on the object on the floor. The blinking unit resembled an overlarge black metallic mouse pad with a thin lime-green monitor.

"Maybe it's a new kind of laptop?" Zeke asked.

"Not sure," Theo answered honestly. "The screen's a strange color. And the keyboard"—if that's what that long dark area was—"doesn't have keys."

"Touch-pad system?" Liza ventured.

Theo shook his head. "Maybe." He knelt in front of the greenish-yellow screen, pointed to the symbols splattered across it. "That's not ASCII and it's not HTML. But it looks somewhat like both."

Zeke squinted. "Hey, it's all Greek to me." He smacked Theo playfully on his shoulder. "Get it, Petrakos? Greek?"

"It's not Greek. You know damned well I can speak—"

"I know, I know. I just thought it was a good line."

"Suzanne can't possibly love you for your personality."

Zeke arched one eyebrow. "Actually, I'll tell you what my little Suzy loves about me."

"Spare me." Theo shoved himself to his feet as Liza headed back to the living room to ask Sam Kasparov to dust the unit for prints. "I put a call in to the techno squad. One of their geeks should be here in about," he glanced at his watch, "thirty minutes to pick this up. Maybe there are e-mails or documents, an Internet trail. Something that will tell us what happened to Mr. Wayne out there." Noises behind him made him turn toward the living room. The body snatchers had arrived with gurney and body bag.

"Come on." He tapped Zeke on the arm. "Let's go see what the ME has to say."

Jorie hunkered down in the thick foliage bordering the structure, with Herryck on her left and Trenat on her right. A cool breeze now and then ruffled the leaves, tickling the sweat dripping down her neck. The ground under her boots smelled musty. If the blossoms poking through the branches had a scent, she couldn't detect it. They were tightly closed, drooping slightly in the darkness.

Two dark-colored land vehicles sat, power off, at the edge of the street. Two more green-and-white ones—POLICE in gold letters on their flanks—were on a short graveled stretch of yard, a larger boxy vehicle parked at an angle behind them.

Humanoids, some wearing identical green pants and white shirts that were obviously a uniform, moved between the vehicles and the structure. But none of the humanoids appeared to be Danjay Wain.

"Any sign of Agent Wain?" Jorie asked Tam Herryck in a hushed tone.

"Scanning, sir. I'm picking up our tech, but there is some distortion. It's even jamming our PMaT signal. I'm trying to pinpoint the source."

That was not good news. Without access to the PMaT they were essentially stranded. And this was supposed to be a nil-tech world, without the expertise to jam the frequencies the Guardians used.

"It's very localized," Herryck said, as if reading Jorie's concerns about transporting back to the ship. "But I get a clear signal twenty-five maxmeters from here. This can't be the reason why Agent Wain ceased contact."

No, it couldn't. Danjay, like Jorie, had been trained to work around dead zones, natural and artificial ones.

Jorie studied the structure again. There were far too many nils coming and going. That—along with Danjay's silence—did not portend well. Perhaps he'd been seized, removed to a security compound by nils ever-fearful of the unknown.

That would explain his silence. It would also require her to assemble an assault-and-infiltration team, further eating into the time and resources they had to deal with the zombie problem.

Captain Pietr would not be happy.

A shaft of light cut into the night as the front door of the structure opened. Personnel in unisuits appeared, flanking something on a wheeled gurney. Jorie felt Herryck tense beside her. Trenat's hand moved to the G-1 on his hip.

Data suddenly danced across Herryck's screen. "Sir, I've a lock on a biosignature. But it's...damn. Negative state, sir."

She knew, but she had to ask. "It's Wain, isn't it?"

"Yes." Herryck's voice was still a whisper. "Signature discharge indicates death by zombie attack."

Hell and *damn*. She'd hoped—*prayed*—there would be some other explanation for his silence. She liked Danjay. Just before his latest mission, she and

Herryck had shared a pitcher of ale with him in the crew lounge. Danjay always had such wild stories.... She watched his body as it was trundled into the boxy land vehicle, her heart sinking.

Herryck let out a short sigh. "I can't believe this happened to him." There was a slight tremor in her voice, then she ducked her head in embarrassment. "Regrets, sir. I—"

"It's okay, Tam." Jorie gave Herryck's shoulder a quick squeeze. After all Jorie had been through, death of a teammate should be easier. Or at least less painful.

But it wasn't, and she knew that Herryck—who hadn't been a marine, who hadn't seen what the Tresh could do—was feeling worse. "He was my friend too."

Trenat peered around Jorie at Herryck's screen. "You still reading his T-MOD?"

"Only partially. And our PMaT is still out of range," Herryck said, and Jorie could see that, see the spikes in the T-MOD's pattern, see the null icon for the transporter. What in hell's wrath *was* happening here?

Recovery of the T-MOD was critical. It would have recorded the attacking zombie's movement, its stats. And—if Danjay had been toying with the unit to lure the zombie, as she suspected he was—it would also provide important data about the herd.

"Commander Mikkalah." Trenat shifted his weight slightly. Branches rustled. "I volunteer to infiltrate the structure and—"

"Down!" Jorie yanked on Trenat's sleeve as she threw herself onto the dirt, feeling Tam bump her leg as she did the same. Footsteps suddenly moved toward them, beams of lights crisscrossing the ground.

Her hand crept along her side, her fingers curling around the grip of her pistol. She peered over the leaves and twigs at the approaching figures clad in the green-and-white uniforms, recognizing utility belts on their waists and what most likely were armaments hanging from their sides. Her heart pounded. Every muscle in her body was taut.

No escape. She couldn't engage an emergency PMaT transport. The signal was dead.

And if those nils took one step closer, she and her team were too.

2

Theo followed the body snatchers to the front door, where he caught up with Zeke. His former partner had spent the past ten minutes talking to Monsieur Lafleur, while Theo was briefed by the ME. "Mummification, cause unknown until the autopsy," Theo told Zeke, summarizing in six words the ME's five-minute lecture. "Was the landlord able to give you anything more?"

"Not a thing." Zeke stepped inside. "Neighbors on the east are snowbirds. Don't show up until January. The house behind is vacant. Amy and a couple uniforms woke up every neighbor across the street. Nothing." Zeke turned his wrist. "Damn. It's after midnight. I haven't even started the paperwork—"

The trill of Theo's cell phone cut off Zeke's complaint. He flipped it open. "Petrakos." The nasal voice of a cyber-squad technician filled Theo's ear as he walked back into the living room, Zeke trailing behind. Some crazy driver on Fourth Street side-swiped the guy they'd sent to the scene. No, no injuries, but his car had two flat tires and a possible bent axle. The only other technician available lived in Tampa and was off duty.

"We'll wait here until one," Theo offered. "If you can't reach her by then, someone can pick up the laptop from evidence tomorrow."

"One?" Zeke asked as Theo closed the phone. "Oh, man. That's forty minutes wasted. I have to start the report on Ol' Crunchy here."

Liza stepped up behind Zeke. "Thought you guys were finished."

"I am," Zeke said. "Sergeant Kind and Generous isn't."

Theo motioned toward the bedroom. "We have to wait for the cyber-squad tech from Tampa. Unless you want—"

"To take custody of that thing?" Liza snorted softly. "The good state of Florida wants their techs to unscramble hard drives and such. Not us little local CSIs."

"So we wait until the good state of Florida decides to arrive," Zeke put in. "It could be hours, if bridge traffic's backed up because of holiday parties and all."

"Both of you don't have to wait," Liza said. "Where's Amy? You rode in with her, didn't you, Zeke?"

"She went back to run ID on the deceased. I told her I'd catch a ride with Theo."

Liza looked up at Theo. "Want me to drop Zeke back at the station so he can start the paperwork?"

"Fine by me," Theo said.

"Liza, *mi amor*. You're a lifesaver." Zeke grabbed her hand, brought it to his lips.

She tugged it back, laughing. "You really don't want to kiss that. You don't know where it's been. Or rather, I think you do."

He dropped her hand, his eyes wide in an expression of horror.

She wriggled her fingers in his face. "C'mon, big boy. Let's get you back safe and sound before the bogeymen come out."

The front door closed behind them. A moment later a patrol officer pushed it open. "Sergeant Petrakos? Detective Martinez said you're waiting for the cyber squad. Want me to run over to the 7-Eleven, get you a cup before I leave?"

Theo appreciated the offer and said so. He fished in his pocket for two singles and handed them to the officer. "Black, one sugar."

The front door creaked closed again. A few seconds after that, a car door slammed, followed by the grating noise of tires over gravel. Then silence descended upon the small bungalow. Theo went back into the bedroom, peeled off his tan cotton blazer, and tossed it over the footboard of the neatly made bed. He stared down at the greenish-yellow screen.

Coded symbols continued to dance across it. He hadn't found a power source or wi-fi router. His initial tapping on what he thought to be the keypad didn't stop the flow of symbols, so it was more than likely not a screen-saver program. But the computer was obviously doing something.

With a start he realized he had no idea how to turn it off. He really wished the tech from the cyber squad would get here, because if his attempt to shut down the laptop resulted in data loss, it'd be his ass—as squad sergeant—on the line, even though Zeke was primary on the case.

He glanced at his watch. Twelve-forty. Technically, he was now on vacation—seven days of sleeping late, playing his guitar, and, if he got up the energy, trimming the oleander bushes that threatened to overtake his backyard.

Zeke and Amy knew where to find him if something broke in this case. At the moment, there was no good news: no witnesses, nothing taken—as far as the landlord could tell. No motive for homicide, if that's what this was. The landlord said Wayne had been a quiet but likable guy. Right now, they had little to go on. It could be days, even weeks, before the ME's lab analysis, along with information from the usual feelers Zeke and Amy put out, would come back.

He wandered back to the living room, straining his ears for the sound of the tech's car. The clock on the wall said quarter to one. He shoved his hands in the front pockets of his pants, rocking back on his heels. He hated blank time like this, with nothing to do but listen to his own thoughts. He wished he had his guitar. It was an old 1962 Martin OM, beat up after almost fifty years of being carted around and played by its previous owners, but he loved it, loved its sound. Messing around with some of Traveling

Ed Teja's blues tunes would keep him occupied so he didn't start thinking about Camille again, didn't start thinking about what he'd thought was a wonderful relationship that was, in reality, a sham....

He shut his eyes. It all made sense now. Her encouraging him to work overtime. Her erratic schedule at the restaurant. Their constantly depleted checking account. And her moods: wild and intense one moment, deep and despairing the next.

He was a cop. He of all people should've known his wife was a cokehead.

But he hadn't. He hadn't even caught on that she wasn't really Camille Starlton. Out of jail after convictions on drug charges in Alabama, she stole another woman's identity and lived under that name until she met him. Marrying him gave her a new last name, a new identity. The fact that she was also marrying a cop was evidently her idea of a private joke.

Ripping his heart out had been one hell of a punch line.

Damn it, Petrakos, stop it!

He ran one hand over his face. He should never have agreed to wait, but he thought he'd have Zeke to talk to. Zeke with his amateur comedy routines and leering grin. A walking encyclopedia of herbs and vitamins. Madly in love with his wife, who also was madly in love with him.

Lucky bastard.

The sound of a car engine caught his attention. He opened the front door, stepped out onto the porch, and watched the white headlights swing his way. The green-and-white patrol car returning. The officer, cell phone to his ear, nodded to him through the open window, then held out a capped paper container as Theo approached.

Theo accepted the coffee with a smile, then retreated inside.

He should have brought his guitar.

At twelve fifty-five, his cell phone trilled again. No, they hadn't reached the off-duty technician. It was Christmas week and she must be out of town. But, yes, someone would pick it up from the evidence room late tomorrow afternoon—three o'clock, maybe. That was the earliest they'd have a tech available.

"Just for the record, I have no idea how to shut this thing down. There's no keyboard, no mouse."

"You sure it's a computer?"

"Looks like a laptop, yeah. Has a screen."

"Hold down the power button until it shuts off."

"There isn't one." Not one he could find, anyway.

"There's *always* a power button. If you don't see it next to the keyboard—"

"There's no keyboard."

"—check the sides."

Theo turned the unit around and upside down. "Nope."

"It's running on batteries. Look for a panel on the bottom."

"The bottom and the sides are solid. No panels, no buttons. No keyboard," Theo repeated. "Just a screen and a touch pad that does nothing. It's like the screen saver is stuck. I can't even get a cursor."

He envisioned the tech raising his gaze heavenward

in exasperation. "Fine. Close the top. It'll go into hibernate mode. Don't worry."

Easy for you to say, Theo thought as he tabbed the phone off. He grabbed his jacket and pulled it on. *You're not dealing with a dead man who looks like a thousand-year-old mummy and a computer that looks like it's from a couple hundred years in the future.*

He pushed the screen down until it was flat with the unit, then gave it one more gentle shove. He waited a few seconds. No grinding noises like when his hard drive was unhappy. No warning beeps. Nothing.

With a shrug, Theo tucked the laptop under his arm and, juggling his half-empty cup of coffee, locked the apartment's door with the one of the keys the landlord had provided and headed for his car.

The armed nils had walked right by them, lights casting left and right, but Jorie couldn't take a chance bliss luck would surface twice. She moved her team deeper into the shrubbery.

So she didn't know someone had appropriated a key piece of Guardian equipment until Tam Herryck poked her and pointed to the data—still annoyingly erratic—on her scanner screen.

"Hell's wrath, he's taking the T-MOD!" Jorie's voice was a harsh whisper. She pushed the leafy branch shielding her face down another minmeter or two as a tall male in a tan jacket and dark pants loped across the lawn. Now she could see him clearly through the enhanced view of her ocular. He had

Danjay's unit firmly tucked in the crook of his left arm.

"But not Agent Wain's scanner or transcomm." The glow from Herryck's scanner reflected eerily on her face. "I'm still getting readings from them inside the structure."

Double hell's wrath! She had to recover the unit— over and above the fact that it was Guardian tech on a nil world, it was the only clue they had about Danjay's death. But they needed the scanner and transcomm as well in order to be able to synthesize all the information on the herd and its movements. She didn't think they had that many more hours of darkness left.

"Could be worse," Trenat posited in a hushed tone. "The armed security personnel could have appropriated it. This nil's not in uniform. I don't see any obvious armaments. We should be able to recover the unit without a problem."

"Good observation, Trenat." Jorie had come to the same conclusion. A civilian. Probably a delivery person, low on the hierarchy, untrained in defense or combat.

Herryck shifted her scanner in Jorie's direction. "Sir, the T-MOD's definitely leaking."

Which meant a zombie would track and kill that defenseless human too, in the same way one had killed Danjay. Jorie studied the nil with her unshielded left eye as he stepped into the wide glow of a streetlight almost directly in front of her team's position. Male, human, with a medium skin tone and short dark hair. Straight nose, clean jawline. She switched to oc-view on her left, zoomed in on his face. Not young like Trenat, but not old. Younger than her brother, Galin, definitely, though his dark eyes were bracketed by squint wrinkles, his mouth by smile lines. He looked to be within a couple of years of her own age.

Far too young to die. Especially in the jaws of a zombie.

She made a quick decision. "We need that unit. Herryck, I'm on the nil male. You and Trenat access the structure, get the transcomm and scanner, and bring them back to the ship. I'll transit up when I have the unit."

Herryck nodded. "Understood, sir."

"Trenat?"

"Understood, Commander."

"Remember, no direct contact with nils unless absolutely unavoidable." She added the reminder more for Trenat's sake than Herryck's. Tam knew the difference between a tracker—a hunter of zombies—and an agent, whose sole assignment it was to infiltrate and utilize the local cultures so that the trackers could come dirtside and do their jobs quickly and efficiently. But this was Trenat's first tour. His technical talents notwithstanding, he had a tendency to gawk.

Two heads nodded at her. She turned, catching the man's form out of the corner of her eye. "I'm moving now."

"Sir." Herryck's hushed voice stopped her as she straightened, twigs and branches poking into her neck and back. "The land vehicle, sir. Have a care. They don't appear to navigate very safely on this world."

"Recommendation noted, Lieutenant. You both have a care too. See you back on board."

Theo plopped the laptop on the Crown Vic's threadbare front seat, turned the key in the ignition, then reached for his container of coffee on the dash. The sedan's back tire clipped the curb as he pulled away, jostling his hand, and he spilled lukewarm coffee down the front of his shirt and on his right pants leg.

Oh, hell. He gripped the wheel as he pulled up to the stop sign, aware of the damp sensation on his skin and the sickly sweet smell of stale coffee. He wasn't that far from his house. He could kill two birds with one stone if he took five, ten minutes to stop there, change his clothes, and pick up the portable sound system that Lieutenant Stevens wanted to borrow. He could drop the laptop and the sound system off, sleep late tomorrow.

Sounded good.

He tapped his blinker and turned left.

They definitely didn't navigate very well on this world, but fortunately ground traffic was sparse as Jorie followed the man in his vehicle. She'd worked enough surveillance to know how to keep her quarry in her sights and yet stay out of his. Her scanner on the seat beside her—functioning properly now that she was out of the dead zone around Danjay's structure—tracked Danjay's T-MOD and would alert her to any sudden departures from his current heading.

At the eight-minute mark, he turned again. Two

minutes after that, he slowed considerably. So did she, dropping back under the cover of darkness, her vehicle's running lights extinguished. This was a locale of small structures, most likely personal residences, many adorned with small colored lights. His wasn't, she noted as she cruised past. The aft end of his land vehicle was just visible around the back corner of his structure.

The narrow road curved around a small park intermittently bordered by a low wooden fence. She guided her land vehicle onto a grassy area, disengaged the power pack, and tucked her scanner into place in her utility belt. Her rifle was on the floor. She looped the strap over her head, flipped her oc-set in place, and, hugging the shadows, trotted back toward his residence.

The night air tickled her bare arms and legs like a flirtatious lover, alternately warm then cool. The foliage scraping her skin had a strong yet pleasant scent. It reminded her of Paroo, whose tropical islands were renowned for huge blossoming trees and sweet sand beaches. She'd been there with Lorik. An error she didn't intend to repeat.

If Lorik had been the one in possession of the T-MOD, she might well have let the zombie get him first, clamping its serrated jaws over Lorik's fine-featured dark face, chewing on Lorik's pale hair—which at one time had reminded her of the color of starlight—as it sucked the life essence from Lorik's damned brilliant mind. Then she'd retrieve the unit. The thought momentarily cheered her. Other than Danjay's death, things had been going well on this mission until the critical Guardian tracking equipment was separated. Now they were losing precious time. The herd had to be moving, or else Danjay would still be alive. That was his second mistake, after not keeping scrupulous watch on his shields. A herd moved because the craving set in. And the youngest, being on the outside of the hierarchy, moved first, taking individual kills, creating scent trails, drawing the mature herd drones and eventually the powerful C-Prime—the controller of the herd—to them.

A good tracker could almost instinctually feel when the craving started to build. In her thirty-two active hunts, she'd never failed to spot the first signs of a craving.

Danjay may have failed, but his data would not. Jorie skirted along a high hedge in a half crouch. She was at the residence and cover was slim. She glanced down again at the scanner secured to her belt. Shields at max. No intruders. And the T-MOD...

In the structure? No, still in the land vehicle, according to her scanner. Bliss luck! She wouldn't have to wait for the man to fall asleep and risk waking him as she appropriated the unit. She didn't want to hurt a defenseless nil. She wasn't sure what stun setting on her G-1 would be effective with the least amount of soft-tissue damage on this type of humanoid.

She squatted down, listening to the world's odd night sounds—shrill chirps and resonant grumps—as she organized the items in the small pods on her utility belt. A standard desensitizer for any security systems the vehicle might have, then a wide-range sonic lockbreaker like Trenat had used to appropriate their vehicle. She didn't know if she had the young ensign's delicate touch—she decided she would file a nice report on him when she got back to the ship—but she'd get inside. She always did.

With one last glance at her scanner, she rose.

And froze.

Light stabbed the green expanse before her.

Biting back curses, she flattened herself on the ground. The rear door of the residence swung open. The man stepped out in the bright glow of a small overhead illuminator. He no longer wore the jacket he had earlier but was clad in a gray short-sleeve shirt and lighter blue pants. A long black box—not the T-MOD—was tucked under one arm, with two small square boxes nestled in the other. His grip on the smaller boxes wasn't as secure. They jiggled as he plodded toward the vehicle.

He hesitated at the pilot's door, then, evidently changing his mind, he moved toward the vehicle's front end.

Damn! Damn! If he turned even the slightest bit, he might see her under the shrubbery. Her gaze glued to his movements, she levered herself up mere minmeters on one arm and slowly plucked one of her lasers from its holster. If he spotted her, she'd have to stun him. She had no choice.

His attention, however, seemed to be on the vehicle's interior. She had a sinking feeling that she knew what he was looking for. Danjay's T-MOD. The boxes he carried must be some kind of decoder.

He put the smaller boxes on the vehicle's roof, touched something to the side of the door, then a moment later pulled it open. The grinding, creaking noise it made sounded like a barrage of strafer cannons to her ears. The doors on her land vehicle didn't sound at all like that. Was this some kind of auditory security measure?

The rear cargo door of the vehicle suddenly flew open. But no weapons turrets protruded, nothing lethal emerged. She slowly let out the breath she hadn't realized she was holding and watched him transfer the small black boxes to the rear cargo area. The long box went in too. She was considering how to take him from behind when—damn! damn!—he stepped back to the door on the navigator's side, bent over, and came out with the T-MOD in his grasp.

There it was. She had to take possession of it now. It shouldn't be difficult. He was a nil, a civilian. She was an expertly trained military commander with the element of surprise.

She rose in one smooth, swift, practiced movement.

And her scanner screeched out an intruder alert.

Zombie.

So much for keeping a low profile.

"Run!" Jorie screamed at him, her heart pounding in her throat as she tabbed the laser in her right hand up to hard-terminate. "Run!"

She grabbed her other laser and barreled across the lawn. "Drop the T-MOD! Run!" A sickly green glow formed in the night gloom off to her left. She laced the spot with both her lasers, aware that the stupid nil was still standing there, T-MOD in his hands, staring at the expanding portal.

Just as she reached him, the green cloud erupted into hard form maybe two maxmeters away, about level with the top of the high hedge. Its diameter was small. Bliss luck, she'd done some damage but she hadn't stopped it. Yet. She fired off three more bursts, then swung around to face the nil, bringing her micro-rifle across her chest as she did. "Drop the unit, damn you!" Her breath came in hard gasps. "That's a zombie. It'll kill you!"

The man stared down at her. And then Jorie remembered: the entire universe did not speak Alarsh.

But that was the least of her problems. The zombie had arrived.

She swung back as it slithered like molten green liquid out of the hole in the night sky. The man behind her uttered something guttural. She could feel his breath against her hair, could feel the hard tension of his body against her back.

"What in hell is that?" she heard him rasp—in passable Vekran—as the zombie snapped into solidification. Its serrated jaws gleamed in the moonlight and its three sunken opticals pulsed red, strafing the darkness in all directions. Four clawed appendages, long and multijointed, clicked. Energyworms undulated and writhed over its tall, angular body.

"Zombie," she said, her breath still harsh. She shoved her pistols back into the holsters and whipped her Hazer micro-rifle forward. "Okay, big boy. Now we play rough."

She fired as it lunged for them, the rifle's energy almost blinding as it crashed against the void substance of the energyworms. She squinted her left eye closed, viewed everything through the filtered ocular on her right.

The zombie howled, slashing at her with its upper claws. But it stopped advancing.

Swinging the rifle down, she strafed its legs with a blast. The grass around it immediately blackened. The zombie tottered for a moment. She aimed for its topmost eye, but missed as it jerked sideways. "Damn!"

It lashed out with its lower right arm. She caught the movement almost too late. "Down!" she screamed in Vekran. She dropped to her knees, prayed the man behind her understood and copied her movement.

The zombie's long arm snaked out, ripping through the roof of the land vehicle, sending jagged metal hurtling across the lawn. Damn, this one had extenders. She hadn't seen that mutation in a long time. She'd have to adjust her attack, especially as neither Herryck nor Trenat was there to help create a diversion or watch after the nil.

The nil. Another worry. The vehicle behind her was still shuddering, clanking from the contact. "You alive, nil?" she shouted over the noise.

"Yes!"

"When I say run, you run. Understand?"

"No, wait!" He spoke quickly.

She couldn't follow his strange version of Vekran, couldn't catch all the words. She fired another blast at the zombie. "I do not understand all you say. Listen to me. I say run, we run."

"No. Gun! Give me a gun!"

"Gun?"

He slapped at the pistol on her right side. He wanted the G-1. He wanted to help.

Could he? She popped off two more blasts, quickly cradled the rifle in the crook of her arm, and yanked her pistol out. A G-1 was easy to operate. A nil should be able to do it. She shoved it into his large hand, closed hers around his as best she could, aimed, and pressed his thumb against the activator. A steam of laser fire streaked down the zombie's side. "Yes?" she asked, praying her quick lesson was sufficient and he didn't shoot himself in the foot.

Or her in the back.

"Yes!" His mouth curled into an oddly attractive, feral grin.

Damn, she liked that. She grinned back. "Good! Kill!" She lifted her rifle, sighted, and fired, and hoped he mimicked her movements.

He fired in a line next to her. *Good nil!*

"Legs!" She told him, aiming for the same. "Opticals!" She raised her rifle and, this time, took one optical out.

His laser fell silent. Oh, damn, it was too much for him. She was on her own again. Then all of a sudden shots streaked out, and—*pow! pang!*—the remaining two opticals exploded.

She jerked her head around, stared at him in unabashed admiration. "Damn!"

"Thanks." His face was sweaty, streaked. But he still had that delicious—there really was no other word for it—grin.

She swung back, concentrated on the zombie's arms. Blinded and howling, the zombie thrashed wildly, advancing then retreating. It could still sense the leaking T-MOD but, without opticals, couldn't hone in on them for a kill.

It used its extenders instead. Shrubbery flew, tree branches crashed. She yanked on the man's arm. "This way." She pulled him away from the vehicle, away from the T-MOD. Closer to the zombie.

"Arms!" She fired at the coiling extenders. He did the same. Good. She sprinted away from him, ignoring whatever it was he yelled. She was almost to the zombie. She had to duck three times to avoid its claws, but she finally sighted its white heart, just under its grinding jaws.

Almost, almost . . . now! She fired.

The zombie exploded, silently, in a cloud of bright green gas, then disappeared.

Jorie stood, shaking, exhausted, bliss running through her body in galactic-size doses. But only for a few sweet seconds. Then reality hit. The leaking T-MOD. More zombies would come.

She whirled and headed for the gutted vehicle. The man sprinted, catching up with her. He grabbed her arm, frowning. That delicious smile gone. His eyes were dark, intense. She shook him off, then at the last moment remembered he still had her laser. "I need that." She pointed to the pistol in his hand.

"Who are you? What *was* that thing?"

"I don't have time to explain. I need that and my agent's T-MOD. Then I have to get back to my ship."

"You're not making sense."

She frowned at him, not understanding.

"You talk crazy," he said.

No, her Vekran and his were somewhat different. "No time. No words now." She kept it as simple as she could. "Mine." She pointed again to the pistol he'd yet to relinquish. "Mine." She pointed to the unit.

He hefted the pistol in one hand, mulling his options, obviously. As if he had any. She sighed, raised her own pistol, and this time pointed it at his head. "Mine."

He handed her the pistol.

"Thank you." She tucked both back into their holsters, then turned and strode the few steps to the T-MOD. She bent toward it. Hard, muscled arms wrapped around her waist, lifting her up.

Damn, the nil was strong. She wrenched out of his grasp and stared in surprise at the business end of her laser pistol. The one he'd just returned to her. His other hand was clamped on the T-MOD. And that feral grin was back.

"You're going nowhere, lady, until you explain."

She didn't know how he'd managed to get it, but he could keep the G-1, though she'd face the captain's hell-wrath for losing it. She tried to jerk the unit out of his hand, but he wouldn't let go.

"You. Don't. Understand," she said through gritted teeth. "No time!"

"Explain," he demanded, the pistol aimed at her head. A pistol—thanks to her—he knew how to use. She still had her other G-1 but knew she'd be dead if she made a reach for it.

Her scanner emitted one shrill beep. Portal forming. Another zombie honing in on the unit.

She had no choice. Death by zombie, death by laser, or . . .

She jabbed the transcomm on the side of her utility belt with her right elbow and issued a terse order into her mouth mike in Alarsh. "Emergency transit. Engage PMaT. Two life forms. Now!"

The nil-tech world called Earth blinked from her sight.

3

The first thing Theo realized was that he itched all over. The second was that somehow—in the blink of an eye—he'd gone from a horror movie in his backyard to the middle of a *Star Trek* set. He was on a platform facing a bank of computer screens and a short console. In front of the console were a group people in green-and-black uniforms. Two were clearly not human. One looked a bit like a short, curly-haired Wookiee. No, that was *Star Wars*. Wrong movie. The other was...His vision hazed. His head spun. His body tingled relentlessly. He knew with sickening certainty he was moments from passing out.

Not good.

He locked his knees. Someone grabbed his arm, steadying him as he sucked in a deep breath. Something slid through his fingers. The laptop. He turned, then let it go, because now, in the bright lights of this science-fiction movie set, he couldn't stop looking at the woman who took the laptop from him.

He saw her—or thought he saw her—in the uneven glare of the porch light over his back door. A teenager in some mismatched slam-jam outfit running toward him, hollering. He thought she was in trouble, needed help. The whole neighborhood knew he was a cop. He intended to grab her, try to calm her down, when suddenly two beams of light burst from her hands.

That's when he noticed the big green glowing hole in the night sky about twenty feet away.

Seconds later she was braced against him—her lithe, muscular body draped in odd equipment. Some kind of lens covered her right eye. He quickly discarded his initial impressions of teen and slam-jam. She looked like a member of a futuristic SWAT team.

And then he saw the—what had she called it? The zombie. *Cristos!* Worse than any images of the *Kalikantzri* from his childhood Christmases.

He went on autopilot after that. He hazily remembered damning himself for not putting his hip holster and gun back on immediately after changing his coffee-soaked clothes. He somewhat more clearly remembered taking some kind of gun from her. But mostly he focused on that towering abomination with glowing eyes and metal skin covered with crawling, writhing worms.

Understandably, he wasn't focused on her, or what she looked like. Until now. She was sweaty, grass-stained, dirt-streaked. And she was unequivocally gorgeous. Exotic. Medium height, five foot five or so, and slender but not skinny. Her skin color reminded him of honey. She had muscles. She had curves. Nice curves. His gaze traveled up from her cleavage to a heart-shaped face with dark-lashed eyes. And lips any Hollywood actress would pay big bucks to own. Lips he'd love to—

He blinked, hard. *Slow down, Petrakos. Slow down.*

Sounds, voices filtered back into his ears, making him aware he'd been temporarily deafened. A tremor shook his body, subsiding as quickly as it had appeared. He was suffering from disorientation, delusions. Too many nights on call out resulting in lack of sleep, that's all this was. In a moment it would all disappear and he'd be back in his kitchen, popping the top off a nice cold can of orange soda he'd left standing on the counter. He intended to finish that off before heading back to the department with the sound system and Mr. Crunchy's laptop.

He drew in a deep breath, then another. The itching sensation on his skin abated to a mild annoyance. But when the scene before him didn't morph back into the familiar brown and yellow tones of his kitchen, reality began to stealthily creep in.

And it wasn't a reality he liked. He unstuck his tongue from the roof of his mouth and tried to speak. "What happened?" His voice sounded rough. Not surprising, given what his body felt like.

She glanced his way. She was a few feet in front of him, talking in a strange language to a woman with curly red hair who was clad in the same kind of shorts and odd one-sleeved shirt but minus all the hardware. A short spate of more unintelligible words, then she handed the laptop to the woman and stepped back up onto the platform.

"Mine." She reached for the gun he still held in his hand.

His cop senses kicked in. Instinctively, he stepped back, raising it.

A pale-skinned man and that Wookiee-looking one reacted, silver weapons appearing in their hands. Aimed at him. Tension laced the room. Another man and a dark-skinned, yellow-haired woman turned from their consoles, hands on the weapons at their hips.

"Mine," the woman in front of him repeated.

He was outnumbered. He might be able to take two, three of them out, but his stomach was still doing somersaults. Even if he could somehow convince his legs to run, he doubted he'd make it as far as the door alive. Unless, of course, this was some kind of elaborate practical joke. In which case, if he reacted with deadly force, innocent people could get hurt.

Every good cop knew there was a time to act and a time to wait, gather information. This, clearly, was not a time to act.

Gritting his teeth, he lowered the gun. The woman plucked it from his fingers. The weapons aimed at him disappeared into holsters. The low hum of conversation resumed.

The woman said something he couldn't understand.

"What?"

"No concerns. You're safe here."

Safe? Where *was* here? Hell, he was a detective. He should be able to find out that simple answer.

"Where am I?" he asked, putting some firmness in his voice this time. At least, he thought he had. His head still wobbled. He shook it. *Wrong move, Petrakos.* That didn't help.

"*Sakanah.* Ship," she said.

He listened for a moment to the other voices around him. Hers was the only one in the room he could understand. "Where?"

"Come."

Well, hell, why not? his brain said, as it completed yet another looping circle. It wasn't like he had anything else to do. Still wobbling, he followed her off the platform, scratching at the prickling sensation on his arm.

A long gray *Star Trek*–looking corridor, a right turn, then another. She said nothing, guiding him with a slight touch on his arm when his feet—still numb and clumsy—stumbled in the wrong direction. Blocks of lettering on the walls looked like HTML code. Or ASCII. Like the lettering on the laptop screen.

For some reason he felt that was significant, though he couldn't remember why.

She stopped before a recessed doorway, touched a small pad on the right. The door slid open, silently.

And the galaxy opened before him like a vast black sparkling maw.

This time his knees did buckle.

He grabbed for the door frame. She grabbed his elbow, guided him in. "Sit."

A ready room. That's what it was always called on the space shows. A conference table ringed by chairs. He dropped into one at the corner of the table as sweat beaded on his brow. The wall in front of him was all window. All black space, sprinkled with stars.

It could be a projection, a movie screen, but somehow he didn't think so. Damn.

She came to the table with two tall clear glasses and pushed one in front of him. "Drink. It will help settle the body after the PMaT."

Peemat? He had no idea what she was talking about but picked up the glass, sniffed it. Smelled like water. He realized he was parched.

She took a long draft of hers, licked her lips. "Water." Her voice rasped slightly.

Sweet Jesus and Mother Mary help him. She was gorgeous, totally gorgeous in a way that seized him right in the gut and didn't let go. Not fashion-model gorgeous—her features were too irregular, her mouth too wide, her nose too broad, her chin a bit too narrow. And not movie-star gorgeous. He'd dated women like that. Hell, he'd married Camille. Camille was so beautiful, men would turn in the street and stare when she walked by.

Though he never did. He knew she was beautiful, but he never had that turn-and-stare reaction to her. He liked looking at Camille, but he always was able to stop.

Not like this.

He took a mouthful of water, swallowed. Then another. Some of the fog hovering in his brain started to clear. Maybe it was thinking of Camille that did it. The itching quieted. And reality slammed him hard this time.

Images of her refusing to answer his questions,

threatening him with her gun, flooded back to him.
Beautiful woman be damned, he was pissed. She'd
kidnapped him. She'd stolen evidence in a homicide
case and, he suspected, fully intended to withhold
that evidence. She was only interested in getting her
damned laptop back. Not in stopping the killings by
the . . .

. . . *Tis Panagias ta matia!* By the eyes of the Holy
Virgin! What in hell *was* that thing in his backyard?
That overgrown *Kalikantzri* thing she called a zom-
bie?

A shudder radiated through him and he braced
himself in the chair. It ended as quickly as it had
started. He drew a deep breath, tried to marshal his
thoughts. He was a cop, God damn it. A trained police officer. He wasn't going to jump to conclusions,
act on incomplete information. He'd been in situations like this before.

Well, maybe not quite.

*Keep a lid on it, Petrakos, until you know what's
going on.*

He sucked in a second slow breath. She watched
him, head tilted slightly to one side. He studied her.
Her eyes were a golden yellow, like a cat's. Her skin
had a honeyed café-au-lait hue. Her hair had to be
ten different shades of gold, orange, and brown—
punk-streaked, he thought, but not as garish. It was
just short of shoulder length, more chin length in
front, with bangs that looked like she'd hacked at
them with a knife. She wasn't that gorgeous.

Oh, yeah, she is. And tough and capable. She'd
faced down that towering monster without flinching.
He wasn't used to being protected; he was the one

usually doing that job. So when someone else did it, and did it well, he recognized that. Appreciated it, as a cop. As much as he appreciated her face and form, as a man. *But ignore that, you can ignore that. It's just a case of temporary insanity. You'll get over it. Think of Camille. She's probably just like Camille.*

She held his gaze for a long moment, as if she knew he was studying her. Then she brought her fingers to rest in the middle of her chest. "Jorie. Mikkalah."

It must be identification time. Good. He needed facts. "Theo. Petrakos." He mimicked her movement.

"Peh-tra-kos."

"Yes. Ma-*cay*-la?"

"Yes."

"Where am I?" He turned one hand outward, motioned toward the room, toward the wide dark window. "Where's this?"

"Ship. Name is *Sakanah*."

He remembered asking her that before, remembered her answer. Ship. *This is not Carnival Cruise Lines*. "What kind of ship?"

"Kind?"

"Type."

"Ah." She nodded. "Red-Star Class Three intergalactic combat-and-recovery vessel."

At least, that's what he thought she said. She touched a small wedge-shaped panel set into the top of the table that he hadn't noticed until now. A semitransparent, green-glowing image sprang to life, hovering over the middle of the table. He flinched back in his chair. She touched another section of the wedge and the image rotated slowly. It looked like a cross between an incarnation of something from the latest episodes of *Battlestar Galactica* and a Klingon Bird of Prey: elliptical yet winged toward the stern.

"*Sakanah*," she repeated, pointing.

Ship. Combat-and-recovery vessel. A military ship. In space. In orbit around Earth, he assumed, though he couldn't see either Earth or the moon through the wide window. Every bit of common sense he owned told him this was nuts. Then another part of his mind—one that had performed dozens of police interrogations and discounted nothing as impossible, until proven—said: *Maybe. Maybe not. Listen. Learn. Gather facts.*

She moved her hand to an insignia in the center of her shirt. Three stars in a semicircle, one larger, two smaller. "Commander. Jorie. Mikkalah."

Commander? That would explain the weapons, her skills.

He reached in his back pocket for his wallet, flipped it open to show his Bahia Vista Police Department ID. He laid it on the table. "Sergeant. Theo. Petrakos."

Her eyes widened and then suddenly she laughed. Not cruelly, not like Camille, but a full, throaty, honest laugh. And he didn't think it was at all aimed at him but at herself.

"Bliss, bliss." She wiped at her eyes. "I should have known. Sergeant. You're very good."

"Good?"

She closed her fingers into the shape of a gun, extended her arm, pressed her thumb twice. "Zombie. Good aim. You know weapons."

Of course. She'd had no way of knowing he was trained as a police officer. He thought she had and that she'd followed him or sought him out because he had the laptop. Maybe that wasn't it at all. Maybe she was following the zombie.

"You speak English." He'd heard her speak it before, but then other times she didn't seem able to.

"Vekran. I speak Vekran. Like your..." and she said something he couldn't catch. "Words," she added. "Like your words, but different. Some things don't..." and another word he didn't understand.

"Translate?" he guessed.

"Trans-late?"

"Have the same meaning. Have the same correlation in my language and yours."

"Translate. Some things don't translate." She nodded.

He pointed to one of her holstered weapons. "Gun."

"Pistol."

"Okay. Pistol. We say that. But also gun."

She shook her head. "Never this gum."

"Gun."

"Gun."

He glanced around the room, spotted a wall sign with its ASCII letters. "Vekran?" he asked, pointing.

"Alarsh. My words. Words of everyone on this ship. Alarsh."

He finally understood. Vekran—English—wasn't her native language. He didn't know why that surprised him. He was bilingual, fluent in English and Greek. Tough to grow up in Maritana County's Greek community of Mangrove Springs and not be.

"Jorie Mikkalah," he said. "Home?"

"Home?"

He pointed to himself and then made a small circle with his hands. "Bahia Vista. Florida." He widened the circle. "United States of America." He put his hands together, forming a ball. "Earth."

She paused, then: "Pahn-Taris Station."

"Space station?"

"Like this ship. In space. No dirt."

"I know."

"Good. Pahn-Taris Station." She moved her hands in an elongated circle. "K'Dri Sector Seventeen." Widened again. "Chalvash System."

"How far away from here?"

She made that slight tilt of her head that infused him with a totally illogical desire to kiss her, smudgy face and all. "Four years' travel."

"You're on this ship four years?"

"Eight."

"Eight years? Why?"

She smiled, her gold eyes narrowing. But it wasn't a pleasant smile. "Hunting zombies."

With the language differences, Jorie still wasn't sure Theo Petrakos fully understood the gravity of the situation. His demeanor went from suspicion to curiosity, hovered almost to camaraderie, then firmly returned to suspicion again. She tried to make it very clear that the Guardians had no interest in his world other than to eradicate the zombies before the zombies eradicated them. He seemed, finally, to understand the threat the zombies posed but not the breadth or depth of it. He also didn't like the fact that the Guardians had no intention of contacting his governmental authorities.

He liked it less when she explained that the zombies were under the jurisdiction of the Guardians. Zombies were—and she admitted shame to that fact—a mech-organic entity produced by her own government to monitor commercial space traffic for contaminates, and to defend and repair the Hatches: portals that utilized the space–time curvature to link the spacelanes. They were designed to operate in small herds, all under the control of the largest zombie, designated the C-Prime.

Commands issued by her people to the C-Prime were then transmitted to the herd for action. If a herd member was destroyed, the C-Prime could replicate another. If a herd member malfunctioned, the C-Prime could repair it or terminate it.

Then something went radically wrong. The C-Primes stopped accepting commands from the Guardians and began making decisions on their own. It was a flaw, the result of a program upgrade intended to make the C-Primes more intuitive, more responsive. It ended up making them into monsters.

Her government, Jorie patiently explained, had created this problem two hundred years ago. They would fix it, even if it took them another two hundred years.

"We made a mistake," she said.

"That's one goddamned big mistake!" He leaned back in his chair, away from her, as he did every time he responded in anger.

"Agreed. Our mistake. Our solution."

"But it's killing my people!"

"Mine too."

"You can fight back. We can't."

She knew where he was going with this. Back to his "I have to warn my government" diatribe. But getting nil-techs involved not only wasted time, it cost lives. The Guardians had learned that two hundred years ago as well.

"Our solution," she repeated. "No choice."

He turned away from her, his hand fisted over his mouth as if he were trying to stop his words from escaping.

Through all this, Tam Herryck bustled in and out, bringing more data from Danjay's T-MOD, once again shielded and cooperating nicely. But Jorie didn't need more data. She needed a chunk of quiet time in order to compose a transmit to Galin about his friend's untimely but heroic death. Then she needed food and she needed sleep, and not necessarily in that order. She also needed a cleanser. Every time she wiped her hand over her face, it came back with more dirt on it. Petrakos looked rumpled and tired too, though probably not half as filthy as she did. He hadn't been crawling through the foliage then lying facedown in the dirt for the better part of several time-sweeps.

He wasn't dealing with the loss of an agent and a friend.

She sighed, rested her elbows on the tabletop and her forehead against her hands for a moment.

"You're tired." His voice softened.

She peeked up at him from over her hands. "Observant."

"That's why they pay me the big bucks."

"Hmm?"

"Nothing. I'm tired too. But people—*my* people—are dying. Being killed by *your* zombies. It's my job to . . . It doesn't seem right to go take a nap."

It took a moment for her to put his sentence together. She straightened. "Zombies nap."

"You mean they've stopped killing?"

"Temporarily. Their impetus," she wasn't sure he understood the word, but he nodded, and she continued, "their impetus was heightened by the frequencies of the unshielded T-MOD. We removed that unit to here. This ship." She tapped the table with her finger. "We have time before they start again. I know—*we* know—how. We know when. We study the data, the craving. Movement of the herd." She was losing him. She could tell by the slanting of dark brows over even darker eyes. "We have time for cleanser," she scrubbed at her face, "food," she touched her fingers to her mouth, "nap." She closed her eyes and tilted her head.

She heard him suck in a short breath. "Don't do that." His voice was low.

She opened her eyes. "What?"

"Nothing. So we have time to clean up, eat, sleep. Then what?"

"Then we go back down and we kill."

Herryck breezed through the sliding doorway again. "The captain says he's ready for you now, Commander."

Finally! She needed the old man's input on this, though she knew there was a good chance she'd catch hell's wrath over Petrakos. With that, however, she'd already formed some answers. "On my way," she told Herryck. The door closed behind the lieutenant. She rose. Petrakos's hand on her arm stopped her.

"Where are you going?"

Her conversation with Herryck had been in Alarsh. She summarized. "I must report to my captain."

He was silent for a moment, then he lifted his chin slightly. "Send me back down."

"Back...?"

"Home. Bahia Vista. My house. Structure," he added.

"No."

"I have a job. Duty."

Don't we all? She understood a little more about his job. It wasn't dissimilar to hers, though on a smaller scale. She very definitely understood duty. She was doing hers now. "No."

"If I don't show up at the department," he glanced at the metal band on his wrist, "by eleven-thirty, noon, people will be looking for me."

"Then they won't find you." She shook off his hand, stepped away.

He rose quickly, but she saw him coming, because she'd spent her life training for moves like that. She spun, bracing, pistol aimed at his chest. He stopped short, evidently not expecting that she'd see him. He was breathing hard.

He was a big man. She had to remember that, had to stop equating nil-tech with nil-abilities. His wide shoulders and muscular arms strained the fabric of his collarless gray shirt. But his wasn't stupid brawn.

He had training; he held the rank of sergeant in a dirtside security force. He'd taken out two orbitals on a zombie the first time he ever used a G-1. That kind of ability damned near matched her own.

She respected that, but there was simply no way she could oblige him.

"My sincere regrets to you," she told him. "But no."

"But when we go back down—"

"I go back down. My team. Not you."

"Why?"

She shook her head. Questions, questions. She'd already explained. "Our problem. Our solution."

"My planet!"

She nodded knowingly. "Regrets."

"Okay, okay." He held up both hands, backed up a step. "Your problem, your solution. I get it now. So put the gu—the pistol away."

She didn't, but she did lower it.

"After that. After you kill the zombies. Then I go home?"

Hell's wrath. She hated this part. It rarely went well with nils, who illogically tied their identities to an orbiting ball of dirt or, worse, to one locale on that same ball of dirt. Spacefaring cultures were so much easier to deal with. "Regrets."

It took a moment, then his face hardened. "Regrets? *Regrets?* What the fuck do you mean by 'regrets'?"

"Fuck?"

His hand fisted against his mouth again, and he abruptly shifted away from her. He was angry, very angry. But he was comporting himself rather well, considering the circumstances. She gave him credit for that. She'd dealt with far worse from nils.

He lowered his hand, turned back, and spoke with slow, controlled deliberation. "Am I to stay on this ship for the rest of my life?"

"No."

"No?" Surprise flitted over his features and, damn, there was a hopeful tone in his voice.

"Relocation." She hoped he understood that word. "New residence. New structure." It was inevitable that—in the hundreds of Guardian missions over hundreds of years—certain locals would become involved, as he had. In advanced societies that had space travel and an awareness of—if not relations with—other galactic cultures, the locals could return to their residences. That was never the case with nil-techs—a label Petrakos had bristled at when she'd explained it. But nils couldn't stay on board either. Yet they had to live somewhere. "Nice location. Paroo. Trees smell sweet."

Not surprisingly, the news didn't appear to infuse him with bliss.

"Paroo." He said the word as if it were the vilest of curses.

"Paroo."

"No. Bahia Vista. Florida. United States of America." His voice shook.

She sighed. There was something she hadn't considered or had overlooked because she was so flatline tired. He might be spoused. Have children. Sometimes . . . She could ask the captain. Sometimes they'd relocate the entire family unit.

She studied him briefly again. He was in his prime

as a male. Tall. Strong. And a good face. A very good face. Someone loved him, surely. And he loved her as well.

Lucky female.

That thought startled her. Sex was bliss, but being spoused didn't interest her. Especially after Lorik. She must be more tired than she thought. "You're spoused, aren't you?"

"Spoused?"

"Male. Female. Same residence. Have children. Have love."

Something she couldn't identify flickered across his face. His very good face. "I'm not married, no. No wife. No spouse. No children."

She almost asked if all the females he knew were blind and unsexed but thought better of it.

"Why would it matter if I were marr—spoused?"

"Because . . ." She hesitated, choosing simple Vekran words. "We have sincere regrets when we're required to send nils to Paroo. We try, we *very* much try, Petrakos, to make what is bad into bliss. We understand the family unit. If that was why you're angry, I would ask the captain to appropriate your family for you, send you all to Paroo. But family unit or not, that doesn't change what I must do. Or where you must go. You hear my words, Petrakos?"

He stared at her, his expression flat. Dead. His arms were taut by his sides. She watched his eyes, ready to raise her pistol again if she had to.

Finally he spoke, his voice bitter. "Kidnappers with a conscience. How nice. Go to hell, all of you."

She didn't fully understand the first part of his remark. But she clearly understood the last. She raised her chin and met his hard stare evenly. "Been there. Twice."

"Go report to your captain." His voice was a low soft growl.

She backed up to the door and exited without comment, locking the door behind her. Herryck waited for her in the corridor. "Get a security team to transfer him to secure quarters," she told the lieutenant as she holstered her pistol. "Stay here until they arrive."

"Problems, sir?"

"He's angry. And he's security-trained and very capable of doing something about it."

"If he tries, sir?"

She knew standard procedure as well as Herryck did. For all a battle cruiser's tech and weaponry, it was still a fragile environment. No place for a nil with a grudge who had the skills to fire a G-I or micro-rifle but not the understanding of what that could do to an exterior bulkhead in the vacuum of space. If he managed to obtain a weapon, there'd be no choice but one. She knew that choice. And she wasn't required to like it. "Hard-terminate, my authorization."

"Understood, sir."

Good. She was glad somebody did, because as she'd issued the command, it weighed on her heart. Heavily. She spun on her heels and headed for the captain's office.

4

"Good work, Commander Mikkalah. Regrettable loss of an agent, though." Captain Pietr leaned back in his office chair and laced his hands over his stomach. His swarthy face was lined, though his tightly curled silver hair was still thick. He'd been in command of one Guardian ship or another since before Jorie was born.

She had served under him her entire career with the Guardians. She respected him tremendously. On occasion, she even liked him. She wasn't yet sure if this was one of those occasions.

Petrakos probably thought of her as narrow, inflexible. Compared to Kort Pietr, she was wantonly lenient. The captain would never have risked losing the T-MOD to save one nil's life. Zombies didn't damage tech. She could have waited, let the zombie snack on Petrakos, then recovered the unit before the next zombie picked up its scent. What was one life when the data she brought back could save a million lives?

"Thank you, sir." She kept her shoulders back, her hands locked behind her waist, emotions tightly in check. "Agent Wain, like all of us, knew the risks. If shielding malfunctions and cannot be repaired, the T-MOD must be destroyed. Guardian Force Field Regulations, Section Twelve, Paragraph Three, Subsection A. Sir."

"Yet sometimes agents and trackers in the field ignore those very important regulations, Commander. They become enthralled with the hunt. They want to be the one to bag a powerful C-Prime. And they see an unshielded unit as bait." He rocked his chair slightly, his eyes half-hooded. "They reinterpret those regulations to suit their needs. They take unnecessary risks. Sometimes it works in their favor. In Wain's case, it didn't. A lesson for all of us, surely."

Jorie wasn't fooled for a moment, either by his posture or his words. Pietr was completely alert and by now had read everything she and her team had logged. He knew about Petrakos and might well consider her bringing the nil aboard unnecessary and in violation of not only field regulations but half a dozen Guardian Force general procedures as well. She chose, however, not to address that issue until he did. "An unshielded unit can spur a craving," she recited. "Actions of zombies caught in a premature craving can be unpredictable. I would never attempt such a maneuver, sir."

Pietr nodded. Silence filled his large office, broken only by the occasional change in pitch of the air-ventilation system or the muted click as his deskcomp downloaded incoming messages from his staff.

He arched his clasped hands, cracking his knuckles. "We have a nil on board, Commander."

"Yes, sir."

Those half-hooded eyes studied her. "Tell me about him."

She did, careful in her phrasing, careful to make it clear recovery of the T-MOD had been her priority.

"You could have terminated him."

"His presence, tied to the T-MOD at that point, was the zombie's focus." That wasn't totally truthful, but there was no way the captain could know that. "It permitted me to engage the zombie. Had he not been there, the zombie would have come after me and the unit might still be unrecovered."

Pietr arched one silver eyebrow. "More likely it would simply have taken you a little longer to terminate the zombie." He chuckled softly. "I don't believe there's a zombie out there that's a match for the intrepid Commander Jorie Mikkalah."

That was because in the field the intrepid Commander Jorie Mikkalah often broke more rules than she followed. She just made sure no one was around to record her transgressions when she did. "Thank you, sir. That's very kind of you. I can't operate under those assumptions, however."

"So now we have this Sergeant..."

"Petrakos, sir."

"...Petrakos on board. I'm sure you can arrange for his transport to Paroo at the proper time. Tell me, Mikkalah, are you going to attempt to connive me into sending his spouse and children with him as well?" His mouth curved into a wry grin.

"He's not spoused."

"That makes it clean and easy. I like that. I'm sure he'll find Paroo a blissful experience."

Jorie hesitated. She could still see the bleak desolation on Petrakos's very good face when she informed him he'd never return to his locale, his duty, that he was powerless over his life's path. Such impotence took a harder toll on those used to the freedom of command. It had almost destroyed her once. Maybe that's why his situation disconcerted her so much. "He's not quite accepted relocation, sir."

"Fighting you on it, is he?" He shook his head. "Nils and their love of their planets."

"I think it's his career as well, sir. He holds high rank in his locale's security forces. He feels a duty to continue to protect his people."

"A worthy attribute. We can recommend he be placed in a similar function on Paroo." That closed the matter. She could hear it in his voice. Relocation had been an effective Guardian policy for over two hundred years. Her job was not to question but to implement. Surely Petrakos would see that eventually.

"Now tell me about this unusual—and unexpected—herd." Pietr motioned to a chair in front of his desk. "And please sit down, Commander. I've reviewed your logs and Agent Wain's. This is not going to be a short conversation."

She rather suspected that. Then the captain ordered food and ice water brought in, and Jorie logged the meeting as one of the occasions where she liked him.

The bad news in Danjay's data—aside from the fact that the Guardians still had no idea why the zombies had targeted the planet—was in the size of the herd: three hundred eleven drones. The good news was that there was still only one C-Prime and none of the drones showed signs of mutating into a second. But the larger the herd grew, the more chance one would mutate. They had to strike now, before that happened, while the C-Prime was still overburdened and increasingly distracted with its herd duties.

One of the many questions Danjay's data didn't answer, however, was why the herd—which he'd dubbed a megaherd—had grown to such large proportions. The average zombie herd was fifty to seventy drones with one C-Prime. Up until now, the largest herd that had been recorded was one hundred seventy. Usually by that point, a second C-Prime mutated and the herd split, becoming adversaries and killing off the weaker drones, thereby reducing the herd.

Termination of a fifty-zombie herd was just another day's work for a Guardian team. Three hundred would take a little bit longer.

"Before we terminate them, we do need to know how they managed to populate so quickly and not split," Pietr said. "If this is a new mutation or resistance factor developing, it's imperative we be able to adjust for that, as it may hold the key to why they've chosen this locale—and why they will choose others."

"You think the C-Prime may have learned how to expand its capabilities?"

"I fear that, Commander. Our advantage has always been that, for all the zombie's offensive and defensive factors, it is innately a stupid creature, unable to learn. The code—regulating its mental and physical growth—guaranteed that. A C-Prime with over three hundred drones should be incapacitated. This one's not. It's slowed down, but it's functioning."

"I mentioned in my report on the Port Lraknal terminations that I observed what I thought to be intuitive behavior on the part of several zombies." But intuitive enough to consciously choose a location that showed none of the requisite tech frequency emissions? The question puzzled her, as she knew it puzzled Pietr. Her job, however, was strictly zombie termination, not psychology. She was a soldier, not a scientist.

Pietr was nodding. "That's why I'm giving you command of this mission. I believe we're at a critical juncture here."

He was giving her command? Jorie was one of the more experienced trackers on board, but still, Pietr's words surprised her. "Thank you, sir."

"You may well damn me before this is over, Mikkalah. This is not the ideal setup. It's a nil-tech world. We must operate completely covertly. Our agent, who could have provided us with not only a functional knowledge of the locale but a secure transport point for key personnel and tech, is dead. And we don't have another three months to waste infiltrating the populace, getting another agent in place."

That meant more dark, stinking, humid alleys. And, given the conditions, a damned tactical headache. "Understood, sir."

Pietr leaned forward. "Let me throw this into the equation. How old are you, Commander?"

Jorie tried not to frown. It never was a good idea to frown at one of Pietr's questions, no matter how digressive they seemed at the moment. "Thirty-nine, sir."

"Would you like to make the rank of captain before you turn forty?"

She sat very still. Would she like to make captain? Did a graknox like to roll in the mud? Did a fermarl like to copulate in *liaso* hedges?

"Yes, sir."

Pietr held up his index finger. "Find out how this herd managed to get so large without fracturing." He held up a second finger. "And then terminate it. Every one. And that captaincy will be yours."

So. All she had to do was ascertain why zombies were now capable of actions that were scientifically impossible and then conduct a ground war with small, less-than-optimally equipped teams in a nil-tech locale where the populace more than likely would consider those same Guardians their enemy. Definitely a tactical headache if she ever saw one.

But the bliss, oh, the bliss, if she pulled it off!

Theo sat on the edge of the bed, his elbows on his knees, his head in his hands. Anger, frustration, and exhaustion vied for control of his body. After twenty minutes of prying and poking into every corner of the cabin and moving what furniture wasn't bolted to the floor, he was unable to find any means of escape. Three armed guards and that curly-haired woman who seemed to be Mikkalah's subordinate had escorted him here, produced a tray of food from a dispenser set into the far wall, and left. He had no doubt that at least one of those guards was still outside his door. He could take one on, probably. Two would be difficult, but he was more than willing to make the effort, if he could just get the damned door open!

But he couldn't get the damned door open. And he couldn't find any other way out of the cabin. Which was, if he was in the mood to admit it, actually nicer than the room he'd stayed in at that new Holiday Inn Express in the Keys last year.

He rubbed his eyes. He had a raging headache. He was hungry. There was a tray and a pitcher of water waiting for him on the small table. He didn't know if those yellow apple-looking things really were apples. Or what the pale mushy stuff in the covered container was.

And he was too spent to cross the short distance to the table to find out. It was almost three in the morning, his body's time. So he sat, damning himself for walking out of his back door without his gun.

That would have changed things. He wasn't totally sure how or why, with his mind fuzzy and aching. He just knew it had been a stupid bonehead mistake a seasoned cop like himself should never have made.

Ta ekanes skata. In the back of his mind, he

could hear his Uncle Stavros telling him that he'd screwed up.

His second mistake was not using Mikkalah's own weapon on her, just before she'd sent them up to her ship. But he hadn't perceived her as the enemy then. He'd just wanted answers. He didn't want to hurt her, let alone kill her.

He wasn't even sure he could kill her now. He'd seen a zombie. He understood, with sickening clarity, what she had to do and why. But if the opportunity came . . . well, it would feel mighty good to give it a try. That he was physically capable of overpowering her he had no doubt. But he'd have to catch her off guard first, and that was no easy thing to accomplish. Her training was impressive. Maybe she had eyes in the back of her head. Hell, she was an alien. She probably did. She was probably as bad as those zombies she hunted. . . .

All women, he decided sagely as he rubbed at a knot between his brows, were zombies. Especially the beautiful ones. Like Camille. Like this Jorie Mikkalah. They show up in your life, bite your head, suck your brains out, and leave nothing behind but a withered corpse. Then your friends gather around and stare down at you and wonder why your eyeballs are so nice and moist.

Except his friends wouldn't have his corpse to stare at. They'd look and look and never know what had happened to him. It had to be a horrible feeling, that not knowing. He'd seen it destroy families in missing-persons cases.

Thank God his parents weren't alive. This would kill them. And he wouldn't even be dead with them so he could explain he was really on Paroo, eating brains with some zombies named—

"Petrakos."

Light shafted over his eyelids. Noise reached his ears. He blinked, realized he was flat on his back on a soft bed. He didn't recognize the matte-gray ceiling. He didn't recognize the sounds in the room, an intermittent muted clicking, a hushed rush of air. Where...?

"Petrakos." A woman's voice. *That* woman's voice. *That* he recognized.

Skata. Shit. He squeezed his eyes shut for a moment, ran through more curses in Greek that would have impressed even crusty Uncle Stavros, then levered himself up on his elbows. He must have passed out. His gorgeous alien commander stood poised in the open doorway. He could see two of the three guards behind her.

Her face was scrubbed clean, her hair brushed to a shine. The shorts and odd one-sleeved shirt had been replaced with a green-and-black jumpsuit. And only one gun now, hanging from a duty belt ringing her hips. She stepped in, but the door stayed open. He noted with some small satisfaction that she kept a hand on the gun. If she didn't fear him, she was at least cautious. *Good,* he decided as twinges of anger surfaced again. *Be cautious.*

"You didn't eat." She motioned to his untouched tray.

He let his gaze move around the room, touch on the overturned chairs at the small dining table, the sofa cushions in disarray, the storage doors hanging open. "I was busy."

"Foolish. You will stress yourself."

He snorted and sat up. "Being kidnapped isn't stress?"

She picked up a slice of the apple thing, bit into it. He heard the crunch. "Good. Try?"

"No." He glanced at his watch. Five-thirty. He'd been out cold for about two hours. He felt as if he could sleep two hundred more, but at least the headache was gone. Sleep deprivation had always been part of his job.

So were certain routines. He knew that around three in the afternoon, someone from the cyber squad would check the BVPD evidence room and find no laptop. People would start looking for him, a cop last seen at the site of a homicide. Now missing. He knew exactly what emergency measures would be taken to find him, and it pained him. Because unless they launched the space shuttle, they wouldn't work.

Unless he took measures of his own.

"I brought a thing for you to see." She took two steps toward him.

Adrenaline flashed through his body. Guards be damned, he could take her down. Right now. The hand on the gun had moved to a pouch on her belt. She was only a few feet in front of him, pushing the last of that apple thing into that beautiful mouth of hers.

One swift move would do it. Knock her to the floor, restrain her hands, grab her gun while the weight of his body pinned her underneath him. She'd fight, squirm, press up against him, her hips grinding against his...

"You want?" She tilted her head.

Panagia mou! Oh, Mother of God! Heat flooded him. His breath shuddered out. Yeah, he wanted, all right. But they were talking about two different things.

She had a square disk—about the size of his Palm Pilot—in her hand. He watched her squeeze its corners, and suddenly the flat disk became a cube. Colors, images, swirled on all four surfaces.

He should stand up, take it, but then she'd know what he wanted, and it wasn't whatever the damned cube was.

He braced one hand against his thigh, wiped his face with the other. *Christ, I'm losing my mind.* He had to keep emotions out of this. He had to think like a cop.

He blanked his expression, forced himself to look at the cube. "What is it?" Better to focus on that than on the delusional fantasies that sprang into his mind every time she came near him.

"Holographs. You know this word?"

"Photos. Images."

She nodded. "I thought perhaps if you see, you'll understand it isn't..." and then a word he didn't know.

"Isn't what?" How could two languages be so alike and so different? One more thing to tax his sanity.

"Not without a choice for you. Not all bad." She paused. "Believe me."

"What's not bad? Being a prisoner? That sucks." He knew she probably couldn't follow his speech. He wasn't sure he cared.

She turned abruptly and put the cube on the table-top. "Paroo." Her voice carried over her shoulder. "This will show you Paroo. A beautiful locale."

Did she know how vulnerable she was with her back to him? Or was that part of the plan? Two guards hovered near the doorway. He'd be dead before he ever made it halfway across the floor. He shot a glance in their direction, sizing them up. Two males, watching him watch her. Watching him notice how her uniform fit her rear end only too well. It occurred to him one of them might be her lover. Hell, for all he knew she was servicing the whole damned ship.

Camille would have.

Stop it, Petrakos!

He dropped his gaze to his hands clasped tightly between his knees. Counted to ten in Greek. When he looked back up, she'd turned.

"Paroo," he said. "You just don't get it, do you?"

"I don't acquire—"

"You don't understand." He stopped, feeling anger rise again. He waited until he had himself under better control. He wasn't usually like this. He was a cop, for God's sake. His personnel record lauded his calm demeanor under pressure, his ability to defuse potentially hostile situations. A hair-trigger temper wasn't remotely in his repertoire.

And he'd never lusted after a woman like some teenager whose hormones were raging out of control.

But he'd never been kidnapped by space aliens before either. That was no doubt a big part of the problem.

"It doesn't matter how beautiful the prison," he said finally. "It's still a prison."

When she didn't respond, he continued: "You understand that word? Prison?"

Her mouth thinned. It took a moment before she nodded. "Yes. Involuntary confinement. But you're still free to—"

"I'm not free."

"You are. Structure, friends, career. Anything you want—"

"I want my life on my terms."

"You make a new life on Paroo."

"Why should I?" He didn't care that he was pushing her. Even if it accomplished nothing, it felt better to vent his frustration.

She started to speak, stopped. He was definitely pushing her. "It's necessary—"

"Why?"

Golden eyes blazed. "You don't hear my words."

"I hear your words. I just don't like them."

"You will like Paroo!"

"A beautiful prison is still a prison," he repeated calmly, because he could tell by the rising tone of her voice that she wasn't calm.

She flung her hands out in a gesture of exasperation as a torrent of unintelligible words poured from her lips. None sounded like English or Vekran. All sounded angry. One of the guards cast an alarmed look in her direction. He realized she was probably swearing a blue streak at him in Alarsh. Then she stopped, her mouth a tight line. She was breathing hard.

He arched one eyebrow. "Now you know how I feel."

A chair lay on its side at her feet. With a rough movement, she reached down and righted it. She set one knee on its seat and leaned against its back, her arms crossed.

Classic defensive posture, he noted. Something he'd said rankled her. God, it felt good to analyze, to think like a cop again.

She glared at him. "I understand your situation, Petrakos. Much more than you can know. *You* don't understand mine."

"Sure I do. Beam down, shoot pistol, kill zombies. End of story."

"Nils." She almost spat out the unflattering term. "This is the prime reason we no longer involve nils. You have no..." and an unfamiliar word, maybe three, "planning and complexity. In a covert mission where we have no dirtside base of operations to facilitate..." More garbled words. But he began to catch some of them. It wasn't always the word. Sometimes it was her accent, her pronunciation.

He still couldn't figure out why it was so important to her that he accept being sent to Paroo, but he clearly heard her frustration in dealing with the zombies. No, not just with the zombies. With his world, low-tech by her standards. It was almost amusing, except he knew that he'd be at a similar disadvantage in Aristottle's day or, hell, even during the American Revolution. He could probably fire a musket, but riding a horse with any degree of competency was beyond him. People would peg him for a stranger, if not a total idiot, within ten minutes of talking to him.

He knew from friends who worked undercover how important it was to be able to blend into the setting. Officers lived under false identities for months—*years*—to become part of the drug culture or a terrorist's cadre.

And her people's sole operative on his world was a shrink-wrapped corpse with wet, bulging eyes.

An idea—small but maybe workable—formed in his mind. A bargaining chip. Why hadn't he seen this before?

"Wayne, your agent." He recalled what she told him in the ready room earlier. "He was key to stopping this zombie herd, wasn't he?"

She stopped mid-rant, studied him as if surprised he had the intelligence to ask the question. "I explained. The data in his T-MOD. This is of critical importance."

"But so was he, right? He lived in the apartment, what—three, four months? He spoke Engl— Vekran?"

"As well as he did Alarsh."

The idea grew. If it worked, he'd be back home restringing his guitar very shortly. But he needed more information first. "Why did he choose my city, my locale?"

"The zombies chose your locale. They like warm water, electromagnetic storm activity. Other reasons." She shrugged. "But those are two prime factors."

And the Tampa Bay region was famous for its warm beaches and violent thunderstorms. "So the

Guardians send Wayne, he learns the lay of the land and then provides you, the trackers, with a base of operations." He thought of the dead man's bungalow, heavily ringed by shrubbery. Very private. "Your people can beam in, work from there."

"Necessary. We can't utilize an air attack. Our craft aren't like yours. Your government would—"

"I understand. I know what covert is. I'm a cop. Security," he amended, remembering that was the term she'd used.

"A sergeant."

He nodded, only half-hearing her acknowledgment. He had his bargaining chip. And, if he played his cards exactly right, he'd also have his freedom. A shiver of excitement raced through him. *Don't get anxious. Set it up right so that she thinks it's her idea. Then she goes back to her mission commander and makes the offer.* "What happens now that Wayne's dead?"

She smiled grimly. "A big headache. For me."

"You?"

She nodded. "My mission."

"In charge of everything?" He made a circle with one hand. And if her answer was yes, he wasn't sure if that was good or bad news.

"I'm very good at my job, Petrakos."

He took that for a yes. "I know. I saw." He had to get her on his side. More than that, he had to convince her he was on hers. "But you don't have Wayne's apartment to use. You have his data but not his field expertise. You don't know shit from Shinola about daily life." He caught her frown. Good. He used the expression deliberately to remind her she didn't fully speak his language. "My squad, my security force, was investigating Wayne's death. You don't even know what we may already know about the Guardians."

That frown deepened. "Thank you for adding to my headache."

"Regrets." He used her expression of apology, inclining his head slightly as if he meant it. "We're in the same business. I understand what you face now. I guess maybe life on Paroo won't be that bad. New structure, new friends. No problems. Not like your situation." He prayed she didn't have some built-in alien telepathic lie detector.

Relief softened the tense line between her brows. "You understand."

"I know you have more-serious problems to deal with than whether or not I want to live on Paroo."

"Very serious. But it's also important to me—to us—that you know we're not without regrets. We wish you bliss."

"You're trying to save people's lives. I'm sor—regrets for causing you trouble." He forced his mouth into what he hoped was a sincere smile.

"It's normal. Change is difficult for many to accept."

Good, you're buying it. Hook, line, and here comes the sinker. "That's because people from my world haven't seen what you have. We don't have your experiences, your tech." *Now let's start to reel you in, slowly.* "You're very good at being a tracker. It's a shame you're starting with three strikes against you." The frown was back. An admission, again, that he knew the language and she didn't. "You have a disadvantage," he reiterated. Ah, she got that. "Of course, you could always delay the mission a few months. Live there yourself. Then start—"

"We don't have that kind of time. Unless you want to see more of your people dead?"

"I swore on my life to protect my people. But that's your job now. Too bad we can't switch places," he added in an offhand manner as he concentrated on keeping his words simple, understandable. It was critical she followed what he had to say next. "Just imagine: you could relax in Paroo, a place you know. I'd fight the zombies in a city that I know as well as you know this ship. It'd be very easy for me to have people come and go in my house. Big backyard. Thick bushes. Very private." He held his breath. *C'mon, c'mon, pretty lady. Connect the dots. Don't make me do it for you.*

She was very still, her face blank. Then slowly she eased down onto the seat of the chair. Her arms relaxed. She was thinking, hard. He could see it in the movement of those golden eyes, in the pursing of that lovely mouth.

Okay, one more thing. This would seal the deal or nothing would. He stood, casually strode the few steps to the table, picked up the cube. Images of white beaches ringed by lush green mountains flowed in his hand. It could have been Hawaii. Or Tahiti. "Looks nice."

She shot to her feet. "Petrakos." There was life in her face, her eyes all but dancing. "Don't go away. I'll be back."

She turned and, barking something out in Alarsh

to the guards, sprinted through the doorway. It closed behind her.

Theo sat on the edge of the bed, elbows on his knees, turning the cube over and over in his hands. He was always a pretty good poker player. But this was the first time he'd ever gambled for his life.

5

Pietr drummed his blunt fingers on his desktop. "I have no problem with your appropriating this nil's structure, Commander. However, I have serious reservations about having him participate in the mission."

"I fully understand. But his structure isn't a transient rental, as Agent Wain's was. That's the disadvantage. His neighbors know him. They'd question our presence unless he was there. On the positive side, his presence would remove a great deal of suspicion. And he is involved with the local security force, sir. He has access to information that could be vital to us." Jorie hesitated, well aware she was asking permission to do something that most likely had never been done before on a nil world. She couldn't begin to guess how many general-procedure regulations it violated. No, she could. Seven.

"He knows too much about us. How can we be

sure he won't relay that to his superiors in that same security force?"

"We can't. But as long as the zombies are a threat, I don't believe he will. He admits he needs us, sir. We leave and hundreds, *thousands* more will die."

The captain nodded slowly.

"He's not your average nil, sir. He has security training. He faced the zombie without panicking."

"I don't want him facing zombies, Commander. I want his structure and his knowledge of the locale."

"Yes, sir, I just meant—"

"I know what you meant. We don't know what he'll do after it's over, and that's my concern. Do we reward his assistance by a hard-termination? We're not the Tresh."

"He's accepted relocation to Paroo."

One silvered eyebrow arched. "Has he?"

"He indicated as much."

"And a man's never lied to you, Commander?"

Jorie's cheeks heated. *Hell and damn.* But it wasn't Lorik's lies Pietr was asking about. "That's always a risk."

"Yes." Those same fingers that had drummed the desktop now tapped against broad lips. "But less of one if we use a restrainer implant."

Jorie forced her face not to show the slightest sign of revulsion as an icy chill shot through her. Restrainer implants were used to control violent prisoners. The Guardian version wasn't the same as the one the Tresh Devastator operatives had used on her, but still, unease sprinted on spiked toes through her gut. Petrakos wasn't violent. He was willing. He wanted to help. He had a good face.

And now she had to tell that same good face that they not only wanted to inhabit his structure but invade his body as well.

Petrakos was seated at the table, eating the sweet-bulb slices, when she returned to his quarters. She sat across from him and slowly began to detail her plan: the use of his structure to facilitate equipment and personnel transport. The use of his knowledge of his locale to fill in the gaps in Danjay's data.

Would he be willing to deflect suspicion from them if his security force raised questions? He agreed, readily, enthusiastically. He'd seen a zombie. He'd seen Danjay's corpse. Two very compelling arguments.

"Captain Pietr and I express deep appreciation for your assistance." She'd poured herself a glass of water but couldn't drink it. She kept her hands folded on the table, afraid she'd make nervous movements that would betray her state of mind. She couldn't stop thinking about the implant. A fatal charge that could be detonated on a whim. At max level, instant death. But the Tresh had never been so kindly. No, the Devastator operatives had used low-level pulses on her. Wave after wave of incredible, unending pain while the Tresh commander, Davin Prow, stood there and smiled his angel's smile.

She shoved the memory away.

"It's the least I could do," he said. "You're the ones taking all the risks."

It took her a moment to fully translate his words. She was sadly out of practice with her Vekran. The more she spoke to him, the more she remembered. She just wished they were talking about something—*anything*—else. "Part of that risk is your knowledge of us. You understand, when this is finished, you still must go to Paroo."

He picked up his glass, took a sip of water. "It looks like a beautiful place."

He would like it there. He would find bliss. *Think of that,* she told herself. *Not what you have to do to get him to Paroo.*

"The captain . . . the captain requests one further effort from you, as to your intentions." Hell's wrath, she shouldn't have stumbled over her words. He put his glass down, his eyes narrowing slightly.

"He wants me to make a statement, an oath? I can do that." He paused. "You understand the word?"

"Oath. I understand. No, we have to . . ." Damn, damn, damn! It took all her concentration just to sit there. And her mouth seemed to have forgotten how to speak.

"You have to . . . ?" His voice was low.

She drew in a breath, let it out. "Put a security device on you."

His frown of suspicion turned to one of puzzlement. "An electronic monitoring bracelet?" He circled his wrist with his fingers. "Transmits a signal so you know where I am?" He shrugged. "That's fine."

"Yes. No. Not quite like that."

"Oh?" Suspicion returned. "And just what is it like?"

She barely registered her fingers splaying over the area beneath her shoulder next to her collarbone. Her thumb found the rough scar easily, even through

her uniform's fabric. "It goes here. Inside. Implant."
She glanced down at her fingers, then back up at his
face. It showed no expression whatsoever, and that
chilled her. "You understand this word?"

He nodded slowly. "And just what does this implant do?"

"It's a security device," she repeated. "Yes, it lo-
cates you. But it also...if you become a threat to
us—"

"It kills me."

Oh, if only he spoke Alarsh! Or her Vekran was
better. But that was the very reason they needed him.
"If you become a threat to us," she repeated, "it permits us to take appropriate action." She waited to
see if he questioned her words. He only stared at her.
She continued: "The device has different settings.
Hard-terminate is not the only one."

"What's the other?" There was a sudden bitter-
ness in his voice. "Slow, painful torture?"

She'd wondered if he understood her explanation.
He did, far too well. "We won't need to use it with
you. You want to help us destroy the zombies.
You're willing to relocate to Paroo. You're not a
threat. You come back to the ship. We remove it. It's
forgotten."

His hand clenched and unclenched on the tabletop. "If I refuse this security device?" He said the
words with obvious derision.

"The mission proceeds without you."

"Damn it!" He slammed both hands on the table,
then shoved himself out of the chair.

She shot to her feet, hand on her pistol, and questioned her decision to leave the guards outside, door

closed. But he was striding away from her, not toward her. He reached the far bulkhead, stopped, but didn't turn. She watched the angry rise and fall of his shoulders in silence.

He shoved one hand through his already spiky hair and then dropped his arm to his side. Finally, he faced her. "That's one hell of a way to treat a friend."

Her voice, when she found it, was not much above a whisper. "Regrets, Theo Petrakos." She meant it. The knowledge of what that implant could do—its searing, crippling pain—was still fresh, even after ten years. She didn't wish that experience on this man who was willing to help her, this man who, in his own world, was a protector of others. This man with a very good face who, under different circumstances, could well be a friend.

He came back to the table, his knuckles white as he clasped his hands over the back of the chair. She was still standing, right hand on her pistol. He stared down at her. "Who makes the decision if I live or die?"

"The captain. And the mission commander."

"That's you."

"Yes."

He asked another question, but the words were wrong.

"I don't understand."

"This decision. To kill me." His voice was harsh, raspy. "Two people say yes and I die? Or one person says yes and I die?"

"You're not going to die—"

"Two or one!"

"Two. Unless I die during the mission."

His mouth twisted into a pained smile. "Then I guess I better work real hard to keep you alive."

The entire procedure took less than ten minutes, disappointing Theo considerably. He'd wanted it to hurt. He needed the pain to remind him that just when he thought he'd figured everything out, he hadn't. He wanted Jorie Mikkalah to watch in awe as he gritted his teeth and took the pain like a man, without flinching.

Instead, an older woman with bright orange eyes, skin the color of a rich amber beer, and two long white braids trailing down her back held a small light over his bare shoulder for a few seconds as he sat on a padded table in what was obviously the ship's medical clinic. The light felt—illogically—cold, and by the time he realized his shoulder was numb, she'd pressed a wide metal disk just below his collarbone. He felt a slight thump, not much more than if someone bumped against him. There was no pain.

She took the light and the disk away, smiled at him, then said something in what he was coming to recognize as Alarsh. He caught Jorie's last name in the middle of it.

Commander Mikkalah was studying the data streaming over the clinic's wall. She hadn't even glanced his way during the entire procedure. Another disappointment. How could she watch him in awe if she wouldn't even face him? She turned, however, when the woman spoke. There was a tautness about her eyes and mouth.

Queasy over medical procedures? He hoped his having that implant shoved into him bothered the hell out of her. It more than bothered the hell out of him. But he had no choice. There was no other way they were going to let him return to Earth.

"It's finished," Jorie said. "You may place your shirt. Care with moving for a time. Soreness is expected."

Either she didn't want Doc White Braids to know she spoke his language better than that or she really was rattled. Or there was something about the implant she wasn't telling him.

He pushed himself off the padded table, accepted his shirt from the doc, then pulled it on. A little stiffness, yeah, as he pushed his right arm through the sleeve. But he'd played softball off and on for years, been hit by enough pitches, plowed into enough third basemen. Nothing he couldn't handle.

Except that this was an alien device that could kill him. He yanked his T-shirt down to his waist and watched Commander Mikkalah have a nice little chat with the doc as he tucked it into his jeans. Instructions on how to detonate the implant? He had to find out more about that thing in his shoulder. Which meant, as much as it grated on him, he had to keep his line of communication open with Jorie Mikkalah.

"We go now." She jerked her chin toward the door to the corridor.

He shoved his hands in his pockets, followed her out. The guards were gone. He noticed that immediately. Of course they were. She had the magic button, the one that could kill him.

She slowed her steps until they were side by side. He slanted a glance her way, tried to see if she had a new wristwatch or badge or something clipped to her belt that was labeled *Kill the Nil*. Nothing so obvious, unfortunately. And her face was still grim.

"Don't like doctors much, do you?" he asked, fighting the urge to grab her by the shoulders and back her up against the wall. Or grab her and shake her, scream at her for shoving a lethal device into his body. Theo Petrakos wanted to do that so badly, his throat burned. Sergeant Petrakos kept walking, making light conversation, knowing she had home-field advantage right now and he didn't.

But he would, soon. Patience was a virtue.

And revenge, when it came, would be sweet.

"Med-techs," she answered. "Vekran term is *med-techs*. And my opinion is that they're useful in many circumstances."

No, she definitely didn't like doctors. Good. If he got a chance, he'd introduce her to Suzanne Martinez. Preferably in Suzanne's clinic. With a little luck she wouldn't know what the word *veterinarian* meant.

He rotated his shoulder as they waited for the elevator, studied his surroundings as a way to keep his mind occupied, his emotions in check. The corridors here were busier than the one outside his cabin. They had passed ten, maybe fifteen crew on the way to sick bay, another dozen just now. Most could walk unnoticed on any Bahia Vista street, the orange or gold eye colors not immediately apparent. Hair colors, though, were brighter. He saw no soft shades. Blonds all seemed to be yellow-gold blond; black hair was shot through with blue. Reds were all orange tones. He saw only one other person—a younger guy—with Jorie's hair colors of orange, blond, and brown.

Races were tougher to define. And there seemed to be no correlation between skin tone and hair color that he could see. He'd pegged Jorie to be mixed race when he first saw her running toward him across his backyard. Later, in the conference room, he'd tried to pigeonhole her ethnicity based on his world's standards. Best he could come up with would be a combo of white, black, Polynesian, and Hispanic.

Her curly-haired sidekick, with her pale skin, could be redheaded Irish.

None of that applied now, of course, with the reality of where he was. But still, except for the mini-Wookiee person, any one of the crew he saw could stroll through his local Sweetbay supermarket and no one would think twice.

Makes it more difficult to identify the enemy, Theo Petrakos thought.

They're not the enemy right now, Sarge reminded. *We need them to exterminate the zombies.*

And after that?

Sarge was silent. Theo smiled inwardly.

The elevator doors opened. Jorie stepped into the empty cubicle; he followed. The doors closed. He glanced at his watch. Almost eight in the morning. Bahia Vista's morning. He still had several hours to get home before someone raised an alarm and started looking for him.

He loved the job. But—vacation be damned—he'd

never wanted to go to work so badly in his life. This was one whopper of a commute.

And he'd need one whopper of a story to cover what had happened to the laptop he was supposed to have logged in to evidence.

Damn. He'd been so caught up with getting back to Bahia Vista, he forgot about the laptop. He needed that back or there'd be questions he wasn't sure he knew how to answer. Being Baker-Acted out to a psych unit wasn't something he wanted to contemplate right now. He just wanted to get home, stop the zombies, and get back to work being a cop. He'd even forgo his scheduled vacation. The past several hours had been travel enough.

"The herd has shifted outer zones." She spoke suddenly, without any preliminaries. And without looking at him. She stared at the elevator's control pad.

"Is that good news or bad news?"

The doors opened. His corridor. At least, it looked like his corridor. He hadn't spent enough time in them to differentiate. And he couldn't read the damned wall signs.

"Not sure," she said, stepping out. "We have no T-MOD in," an odd-sounding word, "to relay accurate data."

T-MOD. The laptop.

"Then we're going home? Down," he corrected.

"Thirty minutes. Seeker 'droids must go first."

Thirty minutes! His heart jumped. They reached a cabin door. His, he assumed.

"Fine," he said. He had no idea what seeker

'droids were, but they'd just bought him thirty minutes in which to find that laptop.

She touched his door pad. "Eat. Nap." He stepped inside. She didn't. "Thirty minutes."

"Wait." His arm shot out, stopping the door from closing.

She tensed. He tried to relax his body so she wouldn't infer a threat. "I need...I need a favor."

She looked up at him, one eyebrow arched in question.

"The lap—the T-MOD. My department, my security people know it exists. It was photographed at the crime scene. I told you that we may already have information on the Guardians. If I don't return with that unit, there could be questions you're not going to like. Questions that aren't going to help you do what you need to do."

She regarded him, both brows now drawn down.

He pushed. "I agreed to let you put that implant in my shoulder. I don't want it, but I understand why you needed to do it. I need that T-MOD unit."

"Regrets. It's against regulations for our information to be presented to nil-worlders."

"It's evidence in a homicide case. If my lieutenant can't find it, he's going to restrict what I can do." He tried to keep his explanation as simple as he could. He needed her to understand and to *believe* that his participation was of critical importance. God help him if she found out he was clocked out for vacation and no one would miss him until after Christmas. "Then I can't help you as much as you need."

"I cannot—"

"I went through this," he touched his shoulder,

"to help you. A favor, Commander. I need you to help me."

Her lashes lowered briefly, then she looked up. "It's not that I don't wish to. It is, I cannot."

She turned, palming the door closed as she left.

Just on a long shot, he tried opening the door after it closed behind her. Still locked. Damn.

He ran one hand over his face. *Eat, nap,* she'd said. Forget that. He first had to look at what that med-tech had done to him.

He pulled his T-shirt over his head on his way to the cabin's narrow bathroom. The mirror over the sink area showed a reddened bruise on his shoulder, but that was all. It occurred to him that maybe nothing was actually implanted inside him. Maybe they just thumped him and were all having a good laugh right now.

But maybe not. And he couldn't take that chance.

It took him three tries to get the shower to operate, and then liquid—he wasn't completely sure it was water—shot out of a long thin slit in the wall. It had a slippery feel and was colder than he liked, but he needed his head clear and that would help. No towels, but an air dryer set into the same wall. He felt as if he were in a human car wash.

He pulled on his clothes, then noticed the image cube still on the bed where he'd left it. Evidence. Proof, in case he needed it. He might not have the laptop, but at least he'd have this. He positioned his fingers on the edges as Jorie had and squeezed. A slight vibration, then it flattened back into a square.

He pocketed it and was scratching at the stubble on his chin, trying to think of one last argument to gain that laptop, when his cabin door opened. He rose from the chair at the small dining table.

"We have a problem," she said, before he could ask for the laptop again.

He sat back down, his heart moving in a similar direction. "What kind of problem?"

She was clad in the same shorts—some kind of bizarre brown–orange camo pattern—she wore when he first saw her and the same one-armed shirt, funky boots. Two pistols, a short-barreled rifle draped over one shoulder, and God only knew what else hanging from her belt. A headset with microphone and eyepiece ringed her neck. This one-woman war machine punched at some touch pads bordering a screen on the wall behind him. He turned in his seat, watching her.

"Your structure had visitors. The seeker 'droid relayed this image."

Holy Mother of God. One of his neighbors must have called the police. The image on the screen showed a patrol car, a fire engine, and a bulky vehicle that had to be a utility truck from Progress Energy.

The devastation of his car, two palm trees, and a large section of his oleander hedge was obvious. The view was aerial, though, and he couldn't see if the back of his house was damaged. But he had to assume it was. Just as he had to assume—no, he *knew*—personnel on the scene were looking for him. Or his body. Because it looked like a small hurricane had ripped through his yard.

He had to get back there before his lieutenant made that phone call to the next of kin in his personnel file: Uncle Stavros and Aunt Tootie. They'd think the worst. No, Uncle Stavros would *know* the worst, because he was a retired street cop. Aunt Tootie would light enough candles in church to induce a bout of global warming.

"Okay." He rose again, hands splayed. "This is a problem, but not insurmountable. We can—"

He looked at her. Really looked at her, his mind already miles ahead on his plan to beam back down a few blocks away, then jog up with some excuse that he'd gone out to help anyone injured by the storm, act devastated by what had happened to his house.

Jog up with a one-woman war machine by his side.

Not a good idea.

"You have to change."

She did that damned head tilt, thick lashes shadowing her eyes, her lips slightly parted as if she were inviting a kiss. He fought the urge to lean into her. She was the enemy. She was an alien. She was not for him.

"Change?" she asked.

"Your outfit. Clothes." He made a short motion in the air with his hand and tried to direct his gaze anywhere but her cleavage or the curve of her hips. "I can handle my visitors. But not if you look like you're going to attack them."

She glanced down, then over her shoulder where the rifle peeked past. "Understand. But what is habitually worn?"

"The shorts," he pointed, "can stay. The top..." He shook his head. It was scoop-necked and cropped short, like those stretch sports tops women wore for exercise. And it showed off enough of her skin that he didn't want her wearing it. "A T-shirt would be better. This"—he motioned to her long sleeve studded with thin cables and what looked like computer serial ports—"has to go. And the guns. Pistols. The boots."

He could tell by the slanting of her brows she wasn't overjoyed with his suggestion. She flipped her hand toward the screen. "So I engage this situation in just my shorts, the rest of my body naked?"

Well, that would definitely deflect attention from the wreckage of the car and the trees. "Where's your cabin?"

"Why?"

"Show me your closet. I'll show you what to wear."

The elevator went sideways this time, or felt as if it did. Her cabin was almost identical to his, except it looked lived in and had computer equipment on just about every horizontal surface. In spite of his urgency to get home, he was admittedly curious; there was a shelf along one wall that appeared to hold personal items—another holo cube, a glittering crystal that reminded him of a geode on a stand, a long box that might be wooden, intricately carved. But apparently she was as aware of the time as he was. She shoved her closet doors sideways with undisguised impatience.

Four jumpsuit uniforms—three black-and-green, one a light gray—a long slinky pearlized green dress, two sweaterlike long tops, and a thick, deep blue robe were the choices that greeted him.

"That's it? Nothing like this?" He plucked at his T-shirt.

"For napping, yes." From a drawer set into the wall she withdrew a silky item. Short-sleeved, round-necked, like his T-shirt, though longer. But that's where the similarities ended. And his fantasies began. It was so sheer as to be almost see-through. Clingy, shimmering, soft. He'd love to see her with it on. He'd love even more to take it off.

Down, boy, down!

He went back to the closet, slipped one of the long-sleeved sweaters from its hanger. It would have to do. Something in the bottom of the closet caught his eye. A zippered duffel. He tossed the sweater on her bed, retrieved the duffel. "Rifle, pistols, any hardware you don't absolutely have to have in your hand, in here."

"Wear this?" She held up the sweater.

He nodded.

She unhooked the rifle and strap, shoved that into the duffel, then stopped, eyes narrowed. "Pistols are fine under this."

She was right. The long, unstructured sweater covered her double shoulder holster and weapons. As long as no one caught her in a bear hug, their existence would most likely go undetected.

"You have different shoes? Boots?" The combination of long sweater and nearly thigh-high boots were damned near erotic in tandem. All he needed was for Sophie Goldstein across the street to catch sight of that, and the whole neighborhood would buzz with the news that their nice Sergeant Petrakos was dating a hooker.

There wouldn't be a candle left in the whole state of Florida if Aunt Tootie got wind of that. And she would, just the way she knew everything else that went on in his life—from her daily phone chats with her longtime friend Mrs. Goldstein.

With a shake of his head, he turned back to Jorie's closet. His alien seductress's shoe selection was equally as limited as her wardrobe. No sneakers. Closest he could find looked like hiking boots. She fished out a pair of very normal-looking white socks, sat on the edge of the bed.

She had pretty feet. For an alien one-woman war machine.

Then she stood before him, hands on her hips. "Satisfactory?"

"Don't stand like that. I can see the outline of your weapons. Pistols."

Muttering something in Alarsh he was sure was nasty, she closed the duffel, then slung it over her shoulder. "Now we can go to the PMaT on Deck Fifteen, Sergeant Petrakos?"

He wanted to, badly. But he had to try, one more time. "The T-MOD."

"The data—"

"Strip out the data. I don't need that. I just need that unit with my evidence tag on it. If the state cyber guys can't make heads or tails of the rest of it, that's not my problem." He could tell by her frown she wasn't following his plea. He took a deep breath. "I just need the outside." He sketched the shape of the laptop with his hands. "Not the data. The outside, with the small paper on the corner." His evidence tag. "That will stop my security from asking questions."

She stared at him, eyes slightly narrowed. Thinking. She shifted her weight to her other foot. Still thinking.

He touched his shoulder. A reminder.

She looked away briefly, then back again. "Just the outside?"

"Just the unit. Broken. Malfunctioning." He thought of the wreckage in his backyard. It was conceivable the unit could have been crushed. He knew his sound system probably had been.

She nodded slowly, then flipped the thin microphone up to her mouth. There was a long series of strange-sounding words, then silence. More words. She took a few steps toward the door. He followed, apprehensive, hopeful.

"Now we go, Sergeant Petrakos," she said, after swinging the mike down. "My lieutenant will meet us on Deck Fifteen."

He took that to mean he was getting the T-MOD, albeit a bit altered. "Thank you." Now all he had to do was figure out how to get it into what was left of his car without the uniforms on scene noticing that.

6

It looked like another bright, beautiful day in paradise—once Theo's eyes focused and his stomach stopped doing nosedives. If he could only stop scratching at his arms, the back of his neck, his... For the first time in several hours, he saw a small smile curve across Jorie's mouth.

"What's so funny?" He didn't intend that to be the first thing he said when they materialized in a secluded section of the park two blocks from his house. He intended to give her a briefing of what to expect from the cops and emergency personnel at the scene. *Keep your mouth shut, keep a low profile, and follow my lead* was the gist of it. He would get to that in a minute. If he could only stop scratching. And she'd stop trying not to grin.

"Your stomach spins and a thousand flittercreepers dance on your skin, no?"

"Just a little itching," he lied. He had no idea

what flittercreepers were, but his body felt as if it had gone through the spin cycle on his washing machine. More than once. But he was not going to give her the satisfaction of knowing this nil couldn't handle it. Not after his embarrassing performance on her ship the first time. He urged her forward toward the short stretch of brick-paved street and glanced carefully down at his watch. His head did another looping spin, then settled. Ten after nine.

"Normal. The body reacquaints itself after a brief separation."

Neither he nor his roiling stomach wanted to think any further on that explanation. "Does it ever stop happening?"

"No. But eventually you ignore it. Don't worry. We use shuttles to Paroo."

He wasn't worried. He had no intention of going through that transporter gizmo again. And he sure as hell wasn't going to be on any shuttle to Paroo. "Okay, this is what's more than likely going to happen when we walk up. We need to have our stories straight. You say as little as possible, let me do the talking. Understand?"

She nodded. He described the different vehicles, their purpose, and their personnel as simplistically as possible, though he noted her English—or her understanding of his English—was improving. Once he showed his ID, he told her, the cops would know him and most likely accept his story that he was out checking for anyone needing help after the storm. He'd recognized Jorie as a neighbor and he was escorting her back home—careful of the tree limbs and downed power lines.

"They're not going to ask for names, specifics. I'm one of their own. I act concerned, you act concerned, we go inside and they leave. Easy. Simple. Understand?"

"When they ask which is my structure—"

"They won't. You're with me. But if they do, there's a mid-rise condo at the other end of my street just behind Cocoanut Grove Center. Grove Palms. Can you remember that?"

"Grove Palms," she repeated. "And a conto is...?"

"Condo. C-o-n-d-o. Tall structure, many levels, many small apartments. Residential. Like the ship, sort of."

"Ah. Conglom."

"Condo."

"Vekran, conglom. You, condo."

They left the park and walked down the shady side of the street, sometimes on the grass, sometimes, when the foliage grew wildly, on the street itself. There were no sidewalks. Late-morning noises surrounded them—the slamming of doors, the barking of a dog, a child's happy shout because it was Christmas break and schools were closed. Street traffic was light; only one car passed. It was after nine; most of his neighbors would already be at work.

Another minute and he could see the line of vehicles in front of his house.

For the third time during their trek, she pulled up one edge of her sweater, glanced at what looked to him like a longer, slightly wider PDA clipped to her belt. The magic button that would drop him, writhing, to the ground? He knew she'd stated that she and her captain would have to agree before she used it, but he wasn't fully sure he bought that. He doubted that if he were to suddenly grab her and go for her weapons, she'd politely hold up one hand and say, *Excuse me, I have to make a call.*

No, he was pretty sure she had full authority to end his life without a conference. All the more reason he had to appear completely cooperative until he knew exactly where that magic button was and its range.

She released the unit, pulled her sweater down.

"Messages?" he asked.

"This?" She tapped her side. "Scanner. *Right now* seeking energy changes that warn of a zombie."

"All quiet?"

"All quiet."

He nodded. *Right now,* she'd said. Right now that thing functioned as a scanner. It might have other functions as well. He wasn't going to cross it off his list yet.

The low rumble of car engines at idle reached his ears, topped by the grinding sound of the fire truck's diesel. The green-and-white patrol car sat at the curb in front of his house, one officer in a similarly colored uniform leaning against its trunk. Another uniform was probably around back or else behind the fire engine. Its large red bulk blocked his view of anything farther down the street. But the firemen were loading their gear, packing to leave. That was good. The less people who saw her, the better. He nudged Jorie forward, quickening his pace, falling into the role of Concerned Homeowner and Can You Believe What Happened?

Which was pretty much his opening line: "Hey, can you believe that storm?"

His shout made the uniform turn. He recognized the dark-haired woman as Carla Eddington, a patrol cop who knew him but not well enough to question his fabricated story or Jorie's presence. A real stroke of luck. She was only on the job about eight months, having moved down from Massachusetts. Sometimes it seemed everyone from up north sooner or later migrated to Florida.

Even space aliens and zombies.

"Sergeant Petrakos?" Her voice carried clearly over the engine noises. "Damn, are we glad to see you!" She jogged toward him, inclining her head to speak into the shoulder mike clipped to her white uniform shirt as she did, hopefully advising the others on scene that no body bags were needed. He watched her gaze dart to Jorie in her oversize sweater, shorts, and hiking boots, then back to him again. He was glad he'd altered Jorie's clothing. A woman—especially a woman cop—would have definitely noticed they were not the norm. "Where in hell have you been?"

"Out checking for injured. Helluva storm."

"Yeah, some kind of freak tornado. One of them microbursts, maybe. We thought it kidnapped you, Sarge. Couldn't find a body, but your yard, your car...Hey, that's what we have insurance for, right?"

"You sure it was a tornado?" He pasted a stricken look on his face.

Another glance at Jorie, then back to him again. "Must have been. We've got lines down all over the place. Progress has two trucks here, but power's still out on the street."

He shook his head, walking with her toward his house. "*That* I know. I went to check on the neighbors. Ran into Jorie." He jerked his thumb to his left, where Jorie kept pace silently. Thank God. "She lives down the block. I know her from the, uh, gym." Well, the duffel slung over her shoulder did look like a gym bag.

"C'mon," Eddington said to Theo as the fire truck gunned its engine loudly. "I'll take you 'round back."

He lightly grasped Jorie's elbow, bringing her with him.

The scene that met his eyes was worse than he remembered. The fallen palms, shredded hedges, and battered remains of his unmarked police sedan did indeed look as if a tornado had touched down. Maritana County was prone to such freak storms. He remembered when a small tornado tore the roof off one house in Treasure Island, touching nothing else on the street. He'd seen water spouts on the Gulf hop and skip over the barrier islands, then reappear again in the channel, heading for the elite Tierra Grande island community.

If he hadn't seen the zombie with his own eyes, he'd believe a tornado did this too. And he was not only a cop but a detective. Damn!

"Damn!" he swore out loud, his hands shoved in his back pockets as he walked around the twisted wreckage of his vehicle, Jorie at his side. He needed Eddington to go back to her patrol car so he could shove the stripped T-MOD into the trunk of his car.

"I must have been at the neighbor's when the twister did this. The lieutenant's not going to be happy. I'll call the wrecker—"

"The boss will just be damned glad you're alive, *amigo*," said a familiar male voice behind him.

Theo screwed his eyes shut. Shit! Zeke Martinez. Not him, not now, not with Jorie standing a hairbreadth from his side and Eddington yammering on about how this was one hell of a way to start his vacation.

He turned just in time to have Zeke clasp one arm over his shoulder. "Thought we'd lost you for good. I—well, hello there! Now I can see why you weren't answering your cell phone."

Zeke had noticed Jorie. Of course he had. Who could miss her? Though Theo obviously missed seeing Martinez's car. It must be behind the fire truck. "Jorie Mikkalah, Zeke Martinez." He stepped out of Zeke's embrace, realizing what it might look like. Did her galaxy have same-sex couples? "We, uh, work together in Homicide," he added hastily, praying Zeke didn't go all Latin and kiss him on the cheek.

"Jorie. A beautiful name for a beautiful lady." Zeke held out his hand.

Panagia mou! Did they shake hands in her galaxy? Or was it a rude gesture, some kind of major insult that would spawn an intergalactic war? He shot Jorie a tight smile, gave a quick, short nod of his head. *Take his hand, take his hand!*

"Thank you," she said, and—*thank you, God*—she reached out for Zeke.

He clasped her hand. "So, known this wayward bastard long?"

Theo saw her frown slightly, knew she had no idea what Zeke had asked. His mind blanked on any kind of amusing rejoinder to divert attention from her. And then something worse happened. Eddington answered for her.

"Sarge knows her from working out at the gym. He was checking on his neighbors and ran across her."

Zeke released her hand. A big grin crossed his face. "Is that so?"

Theo was in trouble now. Big trouble. He grabbed Jorie's arm, propelling her toward his back door. "I—we need to make sure all the appliances are turned off." Maybe then they'd leave and he could plant the T-MOD in the car.

"I'll help," Zeke said.

Shit!

"Might want to open your windows," Eddington called after them. "That cold front moved through and today's gonna be a hot one."

Things were hot already. He urged Jorie ahead of him, up the two steps, then stopped on the wide slab of his back porch. He plastered on his best good-buddy grin and faced Zeke. "Sorry to have worried you. Appreciate your coming over here. But, really, we can handle—"

"I'm sure you can." Zeke reached around him and opened the door. "Allow me, pretty lady."

Theo gave her a short nod when she glanced up at him. With a shrug, she stepped inside.

"Now, *that's* nice," Zeke said under his breath,

punctuating his words with a bad imitation of a jungle cat's growl.

Oh, Christ. He was in deep shit now.

He followed Jorie in. Cooler air met him immediately. That wouldn't last long, not with the air-conditioning and ceiling fans off. His appliances all stared blank faces at him as he pulled out plugs and flicked off switches. Jorie positioned herself on the far side of the kitchen table, duffel at her feet, hands behind her, her back straight, her shoulders stiff. He recognized the military posture: parade rest. He prayed Zeke didn't.

Then he realized her posture also showed—not clearly, but it showed—the outlines of her weapons. Zeke was just coming into the kitchen behind him. He'd notice. Zeke hadn't stopped staring at Jorie since he arrived.

Theo did the only thing he could. In two steps he was in front of her, one arm around her shoulder, the other around her waist in an intimate embrace. He leaned down, his face in her hair, his mouth against her ear, and pulled her against him. "Don't stand like that," he whispered. "Pistols. Relax!"

Her hands had snaked up to rest on his chest. She twisted slightly, looking up at him. Her lips parted as if she were puzzling out his words. And then she did that damned head-tilt thing.

She was too close. She was too warm. She smelled fresh and soft and sweet, and though his arms were very aware of her laser pistols, his chest was equally aware of her breasts brushing against him.

Theo lost it. His head lowered. A short kiss, that's all. Something brief, intense, just to get it out of his system. Damn her, she *owed* him that much, for what she'd put him through. He brushed his lips against hers, then, caution be damned, he forced his mouth down hard. He expected her to jerk away. But her mouth opened, and his opened more. Tongues touched, teased. Plunged.

The feel of her, the taste of her, exploded through his senses. Heat surged through his body. The groan he was holding back threatened to strangle him. With a gasp, he released her mouth, then clutched her tightly against him, hand on the back of her head so she wouldn't look up at him, tilt her head again. "Sorry," he rasped into her ear. "Regrets."

Behind him, Zeke applauded loudly. "I'll start with the windows in the living room. Might help cool things off. Though I doubt it." He slapped Theo on the back as he walked past, snickering.

Theo waited until he heard the first screech of a casement window being forced open. He stepped back, putting Jorie at arm's length.

Wide-eyed, she looked genuinely startled.

He shot a glance toward the living room. "Regrets," he said again, quietly. "He needs to believe...Did you understand words out there?" He motioned to the backyard.

"Evidently not." She spoke slowly.

He couldn't tell if she was angry or in shock. Maybe she'd never been kissed before. Nah. That mouth, that tongue knew exactly what it was doing. So maybe it was that she'd never before kissed a nil. She—

Good Lord. He'd just kissed a woman from another planet. Another galaxy.

Screech, slam! went a window.

Zeke. He had to explain about Zeke. "He knows me. Very well. I lied to the officer. The security woman. Gym. Gymnasium." Her frown prompted another word. "Exercise." He pumped his right arm as if he were lifting a hand weight.

"Yes?"

"I said we met in an exercise place—"

"And?"

"Detective Martinez knows I don't go to an exercise place. I have some equipment here. At home. At structure. *In* my structure." He stumbled over the words.

"You kissed me to apologize for lies?"

"He could see your weapons. I had to cover your body."

She nodded. "Commendable sacrifice, Sergeant."

Commendable sacrifice? The only thing he was going to sacrifice here was his sanity. "But now," he continued, "if he asks, he needs to believe we . . . that is, that you and I are . . ." He pointed to her, to himself, then to her again.

"Lovers?" she said. "You understand this word?"

He did. So did his body. He swallowed hard. "Lovers. Yes." Oh, sweet Jesus, Mary, and Joseph. What was he getting himself into?

Nothing. A charade for the next ten, twenty minutes. Zeke would leave and they'd go back to being Nil and Commander on a covert operation to exterminate zombies. He'd catch some razzing from Zeke later, but he could handle that.

He was about to ask Jorie to give him the T-MOD

when Zeke stuck his head through the open kitchen doorway. "You two cooling off yet?"

Theo stepped away from Jorie. "Very funny."

With a snort, Zeke disappeared.

Theo's kitchen had two windows, one over the sink and one to the left of the door to the backyard. He leaned over the sink, pulled on the cord to raise the slatted blinds, and opened that one. Jorie was staring at the other. He walked over and, making sure she was watching, duplicated his movements. Then he flipped the small latch on the frame of the bottom window, braced his palms under the frame, and shoved.

Screech!

Life in air-conditioned Florida. People rarely opened windows. "Got it now?" he asked her.

"I have acquired knowledge, yes." Jorie snagged the duffel as he headed for the living room.

"Always admired your decorating," Zeke said. "Glad to see everything finally matches."

Camille had taken a lot of the living-room furniture when she left, except for his television, leather recliner, and two end tables. Theo had finally bought a leather two-cushion love seat last month at a Rooms-to-Go clearance sale and dragged the floral-print sofa bed Aunt Tootie had given him—Zeke called it his "daisies on drugs" couch—into his spare room. Zeke had been to his house enough times that he knew that. The comment had to be for Jorie's sake.

"Don't have a lot to clean that way," Theo quipped back. Thank you, God, his brain had finally kicked back into gear. All he had to do was act normal, talk normal, let the banter flow like it always did. This was no big deal. So Zeke thought he had a girlfriend. There was no way he'd know she was a space alien.

Jorie dropped the duffel onto his recliner, took the few steps into his dining room—also empty, thanks to Camille—and opened her first casement window like a pro. A breeze clattered through the blinds as she lowered them. *Good girl.*

"You here to help or stare?" he asked Zeke.

"Didn't do the bedroom yet. Thought you two might want to, uh, tackle that."

"I'll take the spare room." Theo headed down the short hall. The room had two large windows. He had to angle around his weight rack and padded flat weight bench piled with gun and car magazines to get to one window and kneel on his small sofa bed to open the other. When he finished, Zeke was leaning against the doorjamb, arms crossed loosely over his embroidered tan guayabera.

"You sneaky son of a bitch! Going home to restring your guitar, eh? How long has this been going on?"

"You know I don't discuss my private life."

"Theophilus, this is Zeke you're talking to."

Theo hooked his thumbs in the waistband of his jeans and stared at the floor for a moment, his mind working a million miles a minute. Should he—could he tell Zeke the truth about outer-space aliens here on a mission against those things called zombies? Would Zeke even believe what Theo said? He had that Paroo cube in his pocket. Proof. Except that someone like Zeke wouldn't know it was an alien object just by looking at it.

And Jorie and her magic *Kill the Nil* button were in the next room. Theo didn't know what she'd do if she saw Zeke inspecting the cube.

It would be better to wait, play the game the way Jorie said he should, for now. "I didn't want to say anything about her until I was sure," he said, looking up. That sounded good and fit what Zeke knew of him.

"And are you sure?"

"I've never met anyone like her in my life," he admitted honestly.

Zeke stepped to the weight rack, picked up a twenty-five-pound weight, hefted it. "She even old enough to drink?"

Theo pursed his lips, frowning. "Of course." He had no idea how old Jorie was. He had no idea if space aliens even drank liquor. All he knew for sure was they drank water and had apples that tasted like watermelons.

"Where does she work?"

"What is this, an interrogation?"

Zeke grinned, then put the weight back on the rack.

Theo used the few seconds to hammer his brain for an occupation for his one-woman war machine, with her gizmos and gadgets and... "She's a computer programmer for TECO." He named the large electric utility company on the other side of the bay. No way Zeke should know anyone there.

Jorie appeared in the doorway at that moment. Theo realized that if he'd given Zeke the alien cube, they would have been caught red-handed. "Task completed," she said. "Anything else required?"

He watched as Zeke turned toward her and knew Zeke heard it—that odd lilt of an accent. The oddly formal choice of words. This was not the time to raise questions. Not until he was sure he'd be believed and people—his people—were in a position to act.

"You're not a local gal, are you?" Zeke was asking.

"Locale? Good one, very pretty."

Shut up, Jorie! Theo crossed the room in two seconds, cupped his hand on her head, and ruffled her funky, streaked hair in an affectionate gesture. In reality he was trying to shake some sense into her brain. "She's, uh, only been here a few months. Her English," he stressed the word, "isn't that good. Isn't that right, sweetheart?"

She glanced up at him, eyes narrowing for a moment. "English isn't optimal."

"*¿Habla español?*" Zeke tried.

"She's Canadian," Theo blurted out, his mind grabbing the images of the Canadian license plates he saw every winter. "From Quebec." There, that would explain how she knew English but not well.

"Ah, *français!*" The minute Zeke said it Theo's stomach dropped to his feet. Shit, shit, shit! How could he forget? Suzanne Martinez spoke French.

"My wife's parents are from Montreal," Zeke said. "Bring Jorie to the house. She and Suzanne will have a great time together."

Like hell he would. "Sure. After the holidays." He dropped his arm to Jorie's shoulder, hugged her hard against him, trying to signal to her to let him do all the talking. "We're kind of busy until then."

"*L'amour toujours!*" Zeke winked.

His back door slammed. "Sarge, you in here?"

Eddington. "Yeah," he called in reply. Keeping Jorie tightly to his side, he pushed past Zeke and headed for the kitchen. God help him if he left her alone with his partner. There was no telling what their miscommunications might reveal. "What's up?"

The dark-haired woman stood in the open doorway. "We're leaving. Wrecker can't get here until after eleven. The guys from Progress are still out front, working on the downed power lines. Seems they got a substation problem too."

"Thanks for your help. Sorry to worry you." He meant that. He knew the heartbreak that ran through a department when one of their own was lost. It had been one of the reasons he'd had to come back.

"Thank you," Jorie chimed in.

"One more thing," Eddington said as Zeke sat down at the kitchen table, making himself far too much at home. "We recovered a stolen car down the street. A-One Rentals downtown reported it missing. Looks like your tornado scared off the joyriders." She shrugged. "Well, take it easy."

Theo waited until the screen door closed behind Eddington's retreating figure. One down, one to go. "Oh, jeez. Look at the time." He glanced at his watch. Quarter to ten. He needed to put the Paroo cube in a secure place and then get that laptop where it belonged. "Let me straighten up a few things here, then I'll meet you back at the station, okay?"

"You walking there?" Zeke jerked his thumb in the direction of the backyard.

Theo didn't have a car. His Jeep Wrangler—his personal car—was in the shop with a burned-out clutch, and his department sedan was a twisted wreck. Jorie, she...Christ. The stolen rental. He'd never asked her how she got from Wayne's apartment to here. Now he could guess. He was harboring not only an outer-space alien one-woman war machine but a car thief. What next?

As if in answer, a pinging noise sounded from underneath Jorie's sweater. He felt her flinch. Her hand slapped her side, brought up the palm-size scanner gizmo with its yellow-green lights flashing. Her zombie detector.

Adrenaline slammed through Theo's body. *Oh, God. Not now.*

Jorie jerked out of his grasp and bolted into the living room.

Theo was on her heels, heart in his throat, praying he could get to a weapon in time. *Not now, not now!*

7

"Where? When?" Theo shouted at Jorie. She was bent over his recliner, pawing frantically through the duffel bag. The memory of the slash of bright light and that glowing hole in the sky filled his mind. Adrenaline spiked. He shouldered next to her, intent on grabbing one of her laser pistols.

She slapped his hands away from the top of the duffel, then yanked a metal circlet through the opening, snapped it over her hair, and twirled the mouth mike into place. A torrent of unintelligible words flowed from her lips.

She pushed him away again, more forcibly this time.

He took the hint and stepped back. Zeke tapped his shoulder.

"What's the matter?"

Theo had no idea. But she wasn't digging into the duffle for anything further. No laser pistols filled her hands. No green glow emerged through his cream-colored living-room wall. The whole problem seemed to be whatever the conversation was. She was no doubt talking to her ship, to the captain—

Fuck. His hand rose involuntarily to the sore spot on his shoulder.

"Theo?"

He turned and wondered just how much he'd be able to tell Zeke before someone pushed that magic button and he dropped dead at his detective's feet.

"Umm," he said. Behind him, Jorie's clipped staccato softened. No zombies, then. And no instant death. He was still breathing.

"Cell phone," he offered lamely, with a shrug. "Must be some kind of emergency at her office. Maybe they had a storm there too. Probably a server down. Or something."

Zeke was frowning, looking past him. "Doesn't sound like French."

His mind whirled, grabbed another lie. They'd be the death of him yet, if Jorie's magic button didn't kill him first. "Eskimo." He *had* said she was Canadian.

"Inuktitut?"

"Huh?"

"She speaks Inuktitut?"

Oh, hell. Was that what the language was called? Trust Zeke to know.

"Yeah, sure," Theo answered, praying the man wasn't fluent in it as well.

"Didn't know TECO was hiring Eskimos." Another frown.

"Cultural-exchange program or something." Time to end this conversation. He grabbed Zeke's arm, nudging him back to the kitchen. Away from Jorie. He had to keep Zeke as far away from Jorie as he could. The last few minutes showed him just how easily his lies could unravel.

"I will need a ride," he said as Zeke leaned one hip against the kitchen counter. "Pick me up at eleven-thirty, after the wrecker gets here?"

"You might need some help with the mess in the yard. And the lock on the casement window in your master bath is stripped out."

"That's okay. I've got a week's vacation to fix things. Plus, Jorie's here." And there was no way he could sneak the laptop into the car while Zeke was around.

A slow, knowing smile played across Zeke's mouth. "She sure is." He cuffed Theo on the arm. "Eleven-thirty. And the full story on the drive in. You sly bastard, you."

"Who, me?" Theo splayed his hands and pasted a look of mock innocence on his face, keeping it there until his back door closed behind Zeke and he heard the man's footsteps fade. Then he sagged against the kitchen wall and ran one hand wearily over his face.

Sweet Mother of God. Things were happening faster than he could counter them. This might be Jorie's mission, but, damn it all, it was *his* house. *His* planet. Time to make some rules.

He shoved himself away from the wall and headed back to the living room.

Jorie heard the back door slam. She yanked one arm out of her sweater and tapped furiously at the resynchronization keys on her technosleeve. Damned nil! She should never have utilized his suggestion to strip out of her gear. Two of her team were set to transport to Petrakos's structure. Fortunately, Herryck had sent the advisory of the impending PMaT action to her scanner as well, or else their covert operation—as Petrakos liked to call it— would have become distinctly *not* covert.

Nils. Nils everywhere. Inside the structure. Outside the structure. Coming and going without the requisite petition for permission. A nil kissing her . . .

She stopped that thought, not wanting to follow it, not wanting to remember the hot jolt of desire that flooded her when Petrakos's lips parted her own.

It was all a ruse. He, surely, felt nothing. His only concern was to keep his nil associate, Zeekmarteenez, from seeing her weapons. So now, when Zeekmarteenez was around, they had to play at being lovers.

Thanks to Lorik, she knew that game well.

"What in hell made that thing go off?" Petrakos, striding in from the structure's galley, pointed to her scanner.

She looked up from her calibrations, aware of the sweater bunched awkwardly around her neck, and met him glare for glare. "My team preparing to arrive. Which I knew nothing of because my tech"—she jerked her chin in the direction of the open duffle— "was in that. Fortunately, Lieutenant Herryck sent a duplicate alert to my scanner. Or you would be kissing three trackers so that Zeekmarteenez wouldn't ask what we all are doing here."

An odd expression crossed his face, his eyes widening ever so slightly, one corner of his mouth quirking, as if something she said surprised then embarrassed him. Maybe he didn't like being reminded that he'd kissed her. Or maybe he just didn't understand what she'd said. She'd spoken rapidly, not caring to choose words she was sure he'd understand. She was angry at him and with herself. Her team arriving at an unsecured structure could have created serious problems. And the blame would have rightly fallen on her. She dropped her gaze back down to her technosleeve, resumed her calibrations. Her captaincy was at stake. And Danjay's death would go unavenged.

"Zeke. Martinez," he said, pausing between the two words. "Zeke's his first name."

She caught that she'd erred in her pronunciation. A small matter. If his planet had been civilized enough to speak Alarsh or even decent Vekran, none of this would even be a problem.

"I must have a secure structure for this mission." She shoved her arm back through the sweater's sleeve, pulled the sweater down over her hips, then adjusted her headset. "Zeke Martinez and the ones out there working from the large land vehicles. If they have unquestioned access, it will be counterproductive."

"Zeke would be the only one. But if he thinks we're living together..." He paused, lips pursing, brows slanting down slightly.

She didn't understand his hesitation. Language again? "I comprehend living together. Like spoused but without contractual agreement for children."

"Right," he said, but his frown stayed in place. Then he shook his head. "We need a cover story. A reason why you're in my house. If Zeke believes we're living together, that would accomplish that."

She didn't see a problem. "Let him believe I live here, then. We forget conglom as my structure."

The frown lessened, but he still regarded her oddly. "Sure. Great."

There was a flaw in the plan and he wasn't sharing it with her. She saw that in his face, heard it in his voice. And it wasn't just her military experience that taught her to read those signs. Lorik had lied to her too. She sighed. "Petrakos. You dislike this ... cover story." She used his term. "If we are to work together, complete communication is essential. Why is this option not satisfactory?"

"It's fine." He pointed to the duffel bag. "I have to get the lap—the T-MOD into my car before the wrecker comes."

She grabbed the stripped unit and handed it to him, wordlessly. She'd had to pull in more than a few large favors to get that for him—every time he reminded her of the implant in his shoulder, her heart constricted. That's why she'd gone against the captain's orders. Guardian tech was never to be left in the hands of a nil. *This is only a shell,* she'd convinced herself. *And some broken data-mech.* It didn't really violate general-procedure regulations.

She followed him to the galley but not out into the yard. It took several minutes before he pried open the twisted rear hatch of his land vehicle and shoved the T-MOD inside. She waited by the open window, the breeze warmer now and more humid. Sounds reached her ears—land vehicles, she guessed. But there were other sounds—mechanical ones—she couldn't place. A droning buzz nearby. A low rumble.

She watched Petrakos turn the T-MOD at various angles. His gray shirt had wet streaks down the back, and when he bent over to adjust the unit again, she decided he had an extremely attractive posterior. For a nil.

He strode toward the house but stopped at a small shed attached to an exterior wall and withdrew a flat shovel. When he slammed the edge into the T-MOD, she realized two things: he was making the damage to the unit correspond to the vehicle, and there was no chance—given that same damage—that the unit would ever be recognized as Guardian tech.

A weight lifted slightly from her shoulders, and by the time he trudged up the back steps, she'd figured out how to work the water dispenser, located his drinking glasses, and had a chilled glass of water waiting when he opened the door.

He took it with a nod. "Usually not this hot this time of year," he said before he downed the contents.

"Zombies," she told him, and, at the slanting of his brows, sought a simple explanation without revealing that the Guardians were still in the process of trying to understand what was happening on his planet. "The herd is uncharacteristically large. To generate their portals, they utilize fluctuations in electrical-magnetic currents in the atmosphere. It affects weather patterns."

He put the empty glass in the basin, then glanced

over his shoulder at her. "I think it's time you gave me a complete education on these—"

"Yoo-hoo! Theophilus?" A high-pitched voice echoed through the structure, followed by an insistent rapping noise. "Yoo-hoo!"

"Shit." Petrakos's voice was low, harsh. "My neighbor Sophie Goldstein," he said, before Jorie could ask. "Stay here."

Another unauthorized intruder, and one—if *neighbor* had the same meaning in Petrakos's language as it did in Vekran—more than familiar with the immediate locale. Her perfect plan, Jorie realized as Petrakos strode swiftly from the galley, was gaining considerable imperfections. It must be that the zombie attack generated an unusual state of confusion surrounding his structure. She could tell from Petrakos's reactions that these visitations were not the norm.

Stop looking for problems where there are none, Galin often chided her.

The thought of her brother momentarily distracted her from the voices in the next room. She'd crafted her transmit to him on Danjay's death as gently as she could. She didn't know if he'd watched it yet. But she already knew what his pain would feel like.

With no little impatience, she waited for Petrakos to dispense with this latest—and she hoped last—intruder.

"Don't worry, Mrs. Goldstein. Everything's fine," Theo called as he crossed the living room toward the squat image of his gray-haired neighbor. Mrs.

Goldstein jiggled the handle on his screen door. It took a certain—deliberate—combination of pressure and twisting to open it. One of many little idiosyncrasies he'd added to his house as a means to protect his privacy, in addition to the usual burglar alarm.

And of course, the Glock in his nightstand.

"Of course I was worried." Sophie Goldstein had the screen door open and was three steps into his living room when he came up to her. She was in a bright lime-green tracksuit that matched the polka-dot scarf wrapped like a headband around her frizzy hair. "That's what women do. Worry."

So much for his privacy protection. And his privacy. What Mrs. Goldstein knew, his aunt Tootie would know. Which meant he had to keep Jorie away from—

"I was frantic, what with the police car and fire truck and everything. Something serious happened, I told Tootie."

Theo winced. He should have assumed Mrs. Goldstein would be on the cell phone to his aunt, first thing. She disseminated information faster than a police APB.

"Then I saw you and that young gal walking down the street," she continued, craning her neck, trying to peer around Theo's broad form. "She's still here, yes? Just wanted to make sure you're both okay. Terrible storm."

Theo moved right as she sidled left. "Just some tree-limb damage. I'll call Aunt Tootie—"

"Known that young gal long?" Mrs. Goldstein edged right, forcing Theo to take another step back as he countered. "I described her to Tootie, but she said you've never dated a redhead. Though her hair's really more of a gold and chestnut, isn't it?"

They were almost to the kitchen doorway. Theo heard a soft *clank* and *thunk* behind him. His back porch door closing. Someone else arriving or Jorie exiting? He prayed it was the latter, because there was no polite way he was going to keep Mrs. Goldstein out of his kitchen—or from getting a closer look at Jorie so she could report back to his aunt. That, he surmised, was her current mission.

When no voices hailed him from behind, he half-turned and leaned back against the doorjamb. Out of the corner of his eye he saw movement in his yard: Jorie, head bowed over her scanner, marching around in widening circles.

"My car was totaled," he told Mrs. Goldstein as she squeezed by him. "Jorie's out there recording the damage now. She's a big help."

"Jorie?"

"She's a computer programmer. We have to get back to work shortly." Theo spoke to the back of Mrs. Goldstein's head. She'd glued her face to his kitchen window and was intently watching Jorie pace the length of his oleander hedge. "One of my detectives is coming by to give me a ride in so I can pick up a new car."

"Jorie."

"Known her for a couple weeks. We're, uh, friends."

That earned him a glance from Mrs. Goldstein, over her shoulder.

Friends, he'd said. Friends, because that would keep Aunt Tootie from jumping to conclusions. But, damn, part of his cover story with Zeke was that Jorie was living with him. Sophie Goldstein was far more likely to witness any comings or goings from his house than Zeke was. *Friends* was not going to cut it with sharp-eyed Sophie.

Theo shoved his hands into his pockets and tried to re-create the sheepish look he'd bestowed earlier on Zeke. "Actually, she's become very important to me. But I didn't want to get Aunt Tootie all excited.... Well, you know how it is." He shrugged and gave her an embarrassed smile.

Mrs. Goldstein turned completely around. "So, you've been seeing her for a couple weeks?"

"Two, three months. We met working on a case," he said, and the last part wasn't a lie. "She does some consulting work."

"She ever been married? Any kids?"

Spoused. He could hear Jorie saying her term. He wondered if she was or ever had been. "No. But," he added, thinking of her teammates who would be using his house, "she comes from a large family. They're from Canada. *Northern* Canada. Lots of cousins. Very friendly family." He smiled.

Mrs. Goldstein smiled back. "Oh, how nice."

He could almost hear her and his aunt already planning the wedding with its large guest list. "Once we get this all cleaned up, get settled, we'll, uh, ask you over for coffee sometime. Next week or so. Okay?"

"Tonight—"

"My vacation starts today. We already have plans." He ushered her out of his kitchen and back toward the front door. "Some of Jorie's cousins are coming by."

Mrs. Goldstein patted his cheek as he held the screen door open for her. "Make sure she knows how lucky she is to have you, Theophilus. Not like that Cam—"

"Yes, ma'am," he cut in quickly. He didn't want to talk about Camille. He shoved thoughts of his ex-wife away, along with his unease at sharing his personal space with a woman again. But Jorie wasn't just a woman. She was an alien one-woman war machine, and her presence was part of her job. That was all. It wasn't like he had to carry on conversations with her, care about what she did or where she went.

He shut the screen door and jiggled the lock into place as Sophie Goldstein hurried across the street. Probably couldn't wait to tell Tootie all she'd seen and heard. The cell-phone towers would melt from the heat of the two women's rapid exchanges.

Which meant his aunt would be calling him shortly thereafter. He hoped she'd call on his cell phone. He'd warn Jorie not to answer his house phone if it rang. And he had to remember—maybe he should really write down—just what he was telling Zeke and Sophie about Jorie.

With a frustrated shrug, he returned to the kitchen, yanked open his porch door, then trotted down his back steps to catch up with Jorie. The breeze had picked up slightly but it was getting hotter, Florida's humidity lying against his skin like a damp cotton cloak.

The tips of Jorie's multicolored hair were stuck to her face. Her eyes narrowed as he approached, but she wasn't looking at him. Green lines slithered across the screen in her hand. He wondered if one of those represented the deadly tracking device in his shoulder.

"Mrs. Goldstein's gone," he said when she didn't look up. "But we may have to deal with her—talk to her," he corrected, not sure if she understood the expression, "at a later date. Unfortunately, she's friends with my—what's the problem?"

Red and blue lines suddenly crisscrossed the screen.

"Zombies start to wake. Again." Jorie tapped at the screen with quick, deft motions. Colors shifted, changed. She frowned.

Shit. Monster naptime was over. "Coming here?"

"Insufficient data at this juncture. But this, see?" She pointed to a pulsing red line. "Energy surge. An awareness coupling floats in its wake. This," she said, shifting her finger to a blue triangular pulse, "is their C-Prime. He is past marginal elevation on his output. He should not even be able to output! Yet clearly—"

"Marginal elevation?" This wasn't clear at all, but he guessed it was some kind of overload situation. Like when his computer told him *insufficient available memory to perform the requested operation.*

Jorie looked up at him, lips tightening, then she murmured a few soft foreign words that sounded like some kind of plea. "My Vekran is insufficient for detailed explanations, Petrakos. And there is no time—"

"Okay, just tell me, how long before a zombie shows up in my backyard again?" He had a sudden visual of a battle between the tow truck—due to arrive shortly—and the razor-clawed zombie. He wasn't sure who would win.

"Four to five sweeps."

"Sweeps?"

She was shaking her head again. "Increment of time. How do you measure it?"

Theo thought of the minute hand sweeping a clock face, then remembered she had used *minutes* before. "Seconds. Minutes. Hours. Sixty minutes in each hour."

"And your standard day? Sunwake to sunset?"

Sunwake. She must mean sunrise. "Twelve hours, sunrise—*sunwake*—to sunset. Twelve hours, sunset to sunrise. Twenty-four hours total. That makes one day."

"Hours," she repeated, though with her accent it sounded like *ow-wears*. "Vekran, sweeps. Four to five sweeps, your hours, zombies come back."

Four to five hours? *Cristos!* It would be mid-afternoon. Normally not a busy time, but this was Christmas week. Kids were home from school. Families were running to the mall, buying presents. Dozens of people might not only see those things but get hurt. Or killed. "Can you get a bigger team here?" Theo's mind shifted into plan-and-attack mode as he envisioned some kind of galactic SWAT team moving into place. "We could kill the zombies when they show up."

"This is the problem, Petrakos. It is not only time. I know the zombies will arrive, I cannot yet tell where their location will be."

"You mean they might not show up here in Bahia

Vista?" That could be good news. Maybe they'd ooze out of their glowing green hole in the middle of the Sahara Desert. Or on an iceberg somewhere. "They could go to another part of this planet?"

Jorie was shaking her head. "Unlikely. Your locale, this Florida state. It has electromagnetic storms, precipitation rate, humidity. I have explained this."

There were other hot and humid tropical locations, and he said so.

"Their C-Prime established . . . No. That is not the word. Their C-Prime claimed—*marked*—this hot and humid locale with its scent trail. So this is now their primary region. Not just Florida state. But this," and she swept her hand and the scanner out toward his yard. "Your city-region."

"So they *are* coming back here?"

"To your residence? Unlikely. But here," and her hand moved out again, "yes. Somewhere in your city-region, they will come." She pinned him with a hard stare as her words chilled him. Unknown killers were about to strike in his city, and no one knew where. "I have called my team," she continued. "In one sweep, two, we will have more data. We need that so we can arrive at the portal site before the zombies."

We. He heard the *we* and knew it included himself. He was their cover, their transportation. Their only hope of getting to the zombies without causing more terror.

Except he had no car. Zeke was due here in forty-five minutes—and he'd find a house full of outer-space aliens girding for war. Still, Theo knew that if he tried to explain what had happened—the

Guardians, the zombies—Zeke wouldn't take him back to the department for a replacement vehicle. He'd take Theo to Bayfront Medical to lock him in the psych ward.

Because unless Jorie beamed down that Wookiee-looking one, none of the outer-space aliens looked outer-spacey enough to raise an alarm.

For a moment he considered asking Jorie to beam Zeke up to her ship. Let the detective experience what Theo had. But then Zeke Martinez would be another nil with too much knowledge about the secretive Guardians. Jorie's captain would order an implant inserted in Zeke's shoulder. And Theo might be the cause of Suzanne becoming a widow.

Because there was no way in hell Zeke would go to Paroo and leave his wife behind. Suzanne was as much a part of Zeke as his Glock and his badge. His friend would fight to stay here on Earth, and the Guardians would either kidnap him or kill him.

Theo couldn't live with that. He couldn't risk his closest friend's life.

Nor could he risk the citizens of Bahia Vista having their brains sucked out by worm-covered intergalactic zombies.

He was, he realized grimly, his planet's lone soldier.

And this was turning out to be one helluva start to his long-overdue vacation.

8

Theo leaned one hip on the edge of his kitchen table and tried to look nonchalant as Zeke strode up his back porch steps. It wasn't easy. He was far too aware that Jorie and three of her outer-space commandos were hunkered down in his spare bedroom, with all sorts of blinking and glowing computer-type equipment nestled in between his weight rack and sofa bed. He recognized the curly-haired redhead from the ship. The other two—both guys he caught only a glimpse of—he didn't remember seeing. One looked to be mid-twenties, Caucasian, fair hair shaved close. The other was older—mid-thirties— and could have been the heartthrob hero in a pirate movie, right down to his long black ponytail, tanned complexion, and silver hoop earring. All that was missing was a parrot.

Fortunately, his power had come back on ten minutes ago, so he'd tuned his kitchen CD-radio to a

Tampa sports-talk station to drown out the sounds of their voices. He also had the shower running in his second bath—something that caused his alien one-woman war machine to launch into a half-Alarsh, half-English tirade about wastefulness. He gave Jorie permission to turn it off once he and Zeke left.

Cover story.

"Wrecker's not here yet?" Zeke asked, pulling open the screen door.

The devastation that had been Theo's car still sat at the end of the driveway.

"It's Christmas week. Nothing runs on time," Theo answered.

"True, very true. Where's your little friend?" Zeke's grin had a distinctive devilish curve.

"Getting cleaned up." Theo pushed away the brief fantasy that sprung into his mind of a wet and naked Jorie in his shower. "I told her I'd take her out for a bite to eat when I come back." He knew Zeke wanted to see Jorie again. There was no way Theo was going to allow that. And he didn't want Zeke wandering through his house and stumbling over the space commandos, even if they looked not the least bit spacey clad in T-shirts and sweatpants plucked from his closet.

Zeke would hate being on Paroo, away from Suzanne.

Theo pulled a slender digital camera from his pants pocket and waved it in the direction of his battered car. "I have photos of the damage for the lieutenant. But the trunk's jammed. The laptop we found at the scene is still in there." As was his sound system—or what was left of it. That was really going to put a damper on the lieutenant's holiday party.

"Ouch." Zeke winced as he shot a glance over his shoulder. "So much for preserving the evidence."

Theo shoved himself away from the table. "Yeah, I'm going to catch some shit from Stevens on that." The lieutenant didn't like to hear excuses. Colton Stevens kept a miniature skateboard on his desk that he used as a bullshit gauge. A detective knew he was in trouble when Stevens would pick up the toy and start spinning the wheels—a not-so-subtle hint the lieutenant felt *you* were spinning your wheels, and wasting his time. "Help me with that trunk, will you? The wrecker should be here any minute."

"Sure, boss." Grinning, Zeke followed Theo out the door.

Theo propped the lid of the trunk up enough so that Zeke could snake his arm inside and grab the laptop.

"Not good," Zeke said, passing the dented unit to Theo as the sound of a rumbling engine—the tow truck, probably—grew louder.

"The geek squad might be able to do something with it. I've heard of worse cases." But Theo doubted any of them had originated in another galaxy.

The increasing noise was the tow truck—a flatbed, actually. Theo greeted the driver with a wave and endured the man's ribbing about the condition of his car. Fifteen minutes later his car was secured and on its way back to the garage.

Theo jerked his chin at Zeke's silver four-door department-issue sedan parked on the street. "Let's get going so I can get back here. I *am* supposed to be on vacation."

Zeke dug in his pants pocket for his keys. "Your friend in the shower—what did you say her name was?"

"Jorie," Theo supplied as they headed down his driveway.

"And Jorie's part of your vacation plans, I take it?"

Theo only grinned and ducked into the passenger seat. The less said, the better. That way he wouldn't have to remember any more lies.

Though Zeke, being Zeke, wasn't about to let the matter drop without one more try. On the ten-minute ride to the department's two-story brick building on Central, Theo stuck to his story, adding only the few additional items he'd mentioned to Sophie Goldstein: he'd met Jorie about three months ago, they'd hit it off, and things were now moving to a more serious stage. She was going to spend the next week or so with him, see how things went.

Then Theo deftly switched to the topic of the Tampa Bay Lightning's recent winning streak and listened—with relief—as Zeke debated the strengths and weaknesses of the team's current goalie.

"I think last year's knee surgery has made him too cautious. Yeah, nothing gets through his five-hole, but if someone roofs one . . ."

Theo propped his arm against the passenger-side window and—letting Zeke ramble on—glanced casually at his watch. Four to five hours before the zombies returned and began sucking the brains out of Bahia Vista's citizens, leaving behind only bulging wet eyeballs.

It would probably take him thirty to forty minutes to secure a new ride, another thirty to let Lieutenant Stevens chew him out over the condition of the laptop, and another ten after that—traffic permitting— to get back. It felt like time wasted, even though Jorie had assured him that there was little he could do until they had a definite entry point for the zombies. After that . . . he had no idea. He had a huge information gap as far as these zombies were concerned. Partly, he knew, it was the language differences between Jorie and himself. But partly he suspected there were things she simply didn't want him to know.

One more thing to worry about.

He massaged the ache in his shoulder as Zeke turned on to Central Avenue. It would be so good to have an ally in this. The desire to blurt out the truth was almost choking him. Besides Zeke, there was David Gray, a former Maritana County deputy, now a top agent with FDLE's Tampa office. Damned good man, damned fine shot. The three of them could—

No, they couldn't. Theo rubbed his shoulder again. He didn't want Zeke or David to meet Doc White Braids.

Plus he'd left the Paroo cube—purposely—in his nightstand drawer. No temptation to present it as evidence and risk others getting sent to the nil retirement home in another galaxy.

"Sure, I'll ask Jorie if she wants to go to the Lightning game next week," Theo said, dropping back into Zeke's monologue on ice hockey. "But her family has some kind of big party coming up. Not sure when."

"You pull something?" Zeke pointed to Theo's hand pressing against his shoulder.

With a slight self-conscious flinch, Theo jerked his fingers back from the small area where his live-or-die locator was embedded. "Must have, when I tried to get the trunk open earlier."

"There's this great herbal goo for sprains, has emu oil and other good stuff," Zeke said as he pulled the car into an empty space in the department's parking lot. "Stop at the health-food store on Ninth on your way home, pick some up. It'll work wonders. Then you can..."

Theo pushed open the door as Zeke's herbal-remedy recommendations droned on. "Drop the laptop off over at evidence, will you? I gotta go see Stevens. Then I have to see what Gretchen has available. I don't know how long the paperwork for the new wheels is going to take."

"Sure, boss. Just make sure they don't give you Ackerson's old car. He has the big dog that gets carsick all the time. I hear they still can't get the smell out. I told them to try that holistic citrus-enzyme stuff. I even got Suzy using it at the clinic. But do they listen to me? No."

Theo glanced again at his watch as Zeke strode away. Three hours thirty-five minutes until the zombies arrived. Stale dog puke and citrus enzymes were the least of his worries.

The first bright spot in an otherwise baffling, nerve-racking day, Theo thought, flipping the keys to his replacement vehicle around in his hand. Well, maybe two days. He'd somewhat lost track of time since outer-space aliens had kidnapped him. No, it was only one day. It had been about one in the morning when that glowing green hole erupted in his back-yard. It was now almost two in the afternoon of the same day.

Are we having fun yet? echoed sarcastically in his mind as he approached the five-year-old white Ford Expedition parked along the chain-link fence. Theo's ears were still ringing from his lieutenant's terse rep-rimand over the condition of the laptop. His day's bright spot now centered on his acquisition of a de-cent vehicle. He would have been satisfied with a clean four-door sedan. But when Gretchen offered him the option of the SUV—high mileage, dents, and all—he'd jumped on it.

For one thing, cramming three space commandos into the backseat of a Crown Vic wouldn't be the best idea. Second, the extra height and interior room of the SUV would work to their advantage. He hoped.

Theo wasn't really sure what would give them an advantage over towering zombies that had arms like razor-sharp wrecking balls. But a four-wheel-drive SUV had to be a better deal than a four-door sedan.

He turned the ignition and the engine churned, rattling the SUV with a shudder that probably ap-proached 6.5 on the Richter scale. Great. But it, like most pool cars, was a high-mileage vehicle. He had to expect some wear and tear.

He tapped the gas pedal, hoping a little more juice would settle the engine down, aware that what he'd thought was his day's bright spot was considerably dimmer. He cranked the AC to the highest setting. Hot air rushed against the side of his face. The driver's side vent was missing completely. He scanned the dashboard. Two more vents were broken, and the passenger one was gone as well.

Oh, joy.

Everything else appeared roughly the same as in his now-totaled Crown Vic. A blue light was tucked behind the rearview mirror. Connections for a city-issued computer protruded from an obtrusive, swivel-arm stand that hovered over the trunk-mount radio, conveniently blocking access to the most essential piece of equipment: the dual cup holder. Theo bowed his head briefly, wondered, *What next,* then flicked the strobes on, faintly catching the blue light's reflection on the dash due to the sun's glare. At least *that* worked. He tested the PA and siren, shutting the blaring high-low pitches off once satisfied they functioned.

His cell phone trilled while he adjusted the rearview mirror. He quickly checked the caller ID. *Right on time.*

"*Yassou, Thia* Tootie," he greeted her in Greek. "How are you?" He put the SUV in reverse—praying the back bumper wouldn't fall off when he did so—and swung out of the space.

The AC chose that moment to kick on and—miracle of miracles—stayed on even after he took the vehicle out of reverse.

He was heading north on Eighth Street, past the old oak-shaded rooming houses mixed in with those converted to office buildings, by the time Aunt Tootie finished grilling him about the "storm" and started her inquisition on the subject of Jorie. The young woman was from Canada, Sophie had told her.

"Northern Canada. She's thirty...uh, thirty-two," he said, figuring that sounded about right. "Works for TECO, doing technical stuff." The more vague, the better. Plus his aunt had more than a passing knowledge of that "technical stuff"—at seventy-three, she blogged, Web-surfed, had her own page on MyWeb, and belonged to at least a half-dozen Poggle groups where she and hundreds of her closest cyber-friends chatted about the latest romance, sci-fi, and mystery novels.

His uncle Stavros controlled the TV remote.

It was a very happy marriage.

"And you'll bring her over to meet us after Christmas?" his aunt was asking. "You *are* having Christmas dinner with your uncle and me, aren't you, Theophilus?"

Skata. He'd forgotten all about that. Christmas dinner had always been at Uncle Stavros's house, even before his father's job with Southwest Sea Freight kept him away from home more and more, even before his mother decided her heart belonged to Las Vegas, even before his parents divorced. It was, plain and simple, Aunt Tootie's cooking. No one made *souflima,* that wonderful pork dish, like Aunt Tootie did. Then there was always the *avgolemono,* a savory chicken and lemon soup. And plenty of *Christopsomo*—sweet Greek bread—feta cheese, olives. After that would come the *kourabiethes* and syrup-soaked *melomakarana,* and, of course, *baklava* in all its glorious feather-light layers. And the coffee. Thick, sweet, pungent...

Theo's stomach rumbled. When had he last eaten? Did that even matter? If Jorie and her commandos couldn't stop the zombies, there'd be no one left in Maritana County to worry about a holiday dinner or syrup-soaked *melomakarana*.

"I hope to be there for Christmas dinner," he told her, running a traffic light as it flashed from yellow to red. He had to get home, had to find out if Jorie had any more information on the zombies. Plans had begun to form in the back of his mind. "But one of my detectives caught a case last night. I might be working."

"Your vacation—"

"Part of the job. You went through that with Uncle Stavros." His uncle had been a street cop his entire career with BVPD. Theo still went to the burly old man for advice from time to time. In fact, he could—

Nah. Doc White Braids's image surfaced again.

His aunt sighed and murmured a protective prayer in Greek.

"I'm always careful," he told her. "If not Christmas, then New Year's, okay?"

"*S'agapo,* Theophilus."

"Love you too, Aunt Tootie." He meant it. Tootie and Stavros had been the sole stable influence in his life. "Hug Uncle Stavros for me. I'll talk to you in a couple days." He closed the cell phone with a snap and—fingers tapping impatiently on the steering wheel—found himself stopped behind a line of traffic slowing to turn into the Sweetbay grocery store parking lot.

The questions in his mind, however, just kept on coming.

Jorie sat cross-legged on the carpeted floor of the small room, her gaze flicking from the data scrolling across her T-MOD to her team. To her left, Herryck and Trenat were dissecting the latest information on the herd's movement. Their voices rose and fell, halting only when Rordan—Commander Kip Rordan, on her right—swung away from his T-MOD to interject something.

Immediately, Tamlynne Herryck's expression would change from studious concentration to unabashed bliss. Her wide mouth would soften, and her light eyes would unfocus slightly.

Not that Tamlynne had any particular interest in Rordan. But there wasn't a female on board who minded looking at Kip Rordan, Jorie included. A few had even done more than look at the tall, well-muscled commander who kept his shoulder-length shiny black hair neatly pulled back and clipped in a tail. Jorie didn't think Tamlynne was in that group, but it didn't matter. Rordan might be blessed with an extremely good face—she thought him almost pretty in spite of his strong mouth and straight nose—but he was also a good tracker, and he was even better at analyzing and synthesizing herd data from a T-MOD. Handicapped by Danjay Wain's death, Jorie needed a team that could obtain information quickly and respond even faster.

So when Captain Pietr had recommended Rordan's inclusion in her team at the last moment, she'd agreed. Even though Kip Rordan was equal to her in rank and head of his own tracker team. And even though Kip Rordan was Lorik Alclar's close friend.

But that could be a benefit. Jorie was determined to gain the captaincy Pietr dangled before her. Let Rordan be witness to her team's success and report it, firsthand, to Lorik.

A success that could well start with their first chance to challenge the zombies. Data on the herd was coming in more quickly now as the juveniles—always on the outer edges—were thrumming in anticipation of creating scent trails from their kills.

"They're weaker," Tamlynne Herryck said, pointing to the oscillating lines on her T-MOD that represented the younger zombies.

"But there are more of them," Jorie answered just as Rordan did, her words running over his.

"Look at their numbers."

She glanced at Rordan, nodding. "Exactly."

"Ten," Trenat offered.

Ten juveniles at the front of a craving. There were rarely more than six.

"Should be interesting," Jorie quipped, then: "We have two sweeps, seven minutes before primary emergence. We—" And she halted, hearing a rumbling mechanical noise outside the structure. Most likely that was Petrakos returning. One of the lines of data on her T-MOD represented his location, and last she checked, he was less than a mark from his structure.

But he could also be with that shorter man, that Zeke Martinez. Petrakos had said it was normal for Martinez to come by. Though Jorie's pretense of being Petrakos's lover was supposed to put a halt to that.

Unless their pretense hadn't been convincing—something Lorik would probably find amusing if that information got back to him. From Rordan. He stood as she did. She waved him back down as she tugged her headset through her hair and let the metal circlet drape around her neck. "If he's with one of his coworkers, they expect me to be here. Run one more deep scan on those juveniles, confirm their R-Five levels again. I'll be right back."

Jorie sidled through the half-closed doorway and headed for the galley. *Kitchen,* she corrected herself, as a boxy white land vehicle lumbered into view. She could see Petrakos at the helm. No one else seemed to be with him, and no other vehicle followed. A curious sense of relief—and validation that she'd judged him correctly—flooded through her as he guided the vehicle to a halt. He thrust both hands through his short, spiky hair and, for a moment, held that position. Then with a movement that hinted at restrained anger, he shoved open the vehicle's door and stepped out.

She opened the kitchen's solid door, then the mesh one leading outside—a rush of warm, moist air hitting her instantly—and watched him approach.

He'd come back alone. Jorie hadn't been sure... Clearly, this wasn't a blissful experience for him. But she knew that he understood the potential of the restrainer implant: he could be located and terminated without warning. More than that, she knew he understood the threat the zombies posed. Had Theo Petrakos returned with a contingent of his own to force the Guardians to expose their existence, had he added more weapons to the nil-tech projectile one that was clipped to his belt—or if he'd not returned at all—she wouldn't have been completely surprised. As Captain Pietr was fond pointing out, nils, so egocentrically tied to their own small ball of dirt, believing the universe started and stopped at their front door, were prone to do those kinds of things.

Theo Petrakos hadn't. She couldn't afford to discount that he might have plans in direct opposition to her own. But for now he was cooperating.

This was the first test she'd put him through—and he'd passed. His eventual reward would be banishment from everything he held dear. That fact put a damper on the small surge of bliss she'd experienced upon his return.

"Any news?" he asked as he mounted the wide steps. His gaze had been on her the entire trek from his vehicle. He was still focused on her now.

Jorie raised her face as he came up to her, tried to read past the expected concern and fading tinge of anger there, and failed. "There is movement on the outer edges of the herd. No portals yet. But we expect formation in less than two sweeps."

As always, she hesitated, waiting for him to question the meanings of her words. Their language incompatibilities—while decreasing hourly—were still an impediment. But he was nodding.

"Where?"

"Come. I'll show you."

Jorie heard Trenat and Rordan arguing over the potential strength of the three lead juveniles as she returned to the small room, Petrakos on her heels. She listened for a moment, mentally filing away the data as she hunkered down in front of her T-MOD and then motioned for Petrakos to do the same.

Herryck scooted sideways, making room.

"Thank you," Petrakos said with a nod to Jorie's lieutenant.

"You are . . . well go," Herryck replied haltingly.

Petrakos frowned, then a small smile played across his mouth, erasing some of the worry Jorie had seen on his face—his very good face—since he'd returned. "Welcome," he said. "You're welcome."

"Well come," Herryck repeated.

Petrakos nodded. "You don't speak . . ."

"Vekran," Jorie supplied as he crouched down next to her. "Herryck is learning."

"Herryck?"

She hadn't introduced him to her team. There'd been little time to do so; plus, there wasn't a need. Petrakos would be in their lives for only the few days it would take to deal with the zombies. When the mission was finished, he'd return to the ship with them, of course. But he'd be isolated. The less he knew about the Guardians, the better.

Or so regulations stated.

Still, that didn't mean he couldn't learn her team's names. Conversing with Petrakos would give Herryck much-needed practice in a language similar to Vekran. Though the lieutenant didn't need to learn the variations that turned Vekran into English.

Once this mission was complete, Jorie doubted they'd visit this nil world again.

"Tamlynne. Herryck," Jorie said, with a small gesture at Tam. She pointed to Trenat. "Jacare. Trenat."

"Kip Rordan," the commander said before Jorie could, irritating her slightly. She'd never had any problems with Rordan before. But she hadn't worked with him since she'd ended her relationship with Lorik.

Now she had seniority over him. Or did she?

The thought struck her—had Captain Pietr offered a promotion, a captaincy, to Rordan as well? It was no secret that she and Rordan had different command methodologies. She doubted he'd ever asked Pietr to relocate a nil's family. But she'd *earned* the right for special concessions—her success rate was one of the highest in Guardian records. Higher than Rordan's, in fact.

Could that too be an issue?

She shook off her disquiet and watched Petrakos nod at the introductions.

"Theo Petrakos," he said, hand on his chest in much the same manner as when he'd named himself on board the *Sakanah* hours earlier. "Theo."

Theo. No, the use of his first name was too personal for her. He was a nil with a restrainer implant, and he would be sent to Paroo.

"Petrakos," she said, and brought his attention back to her T-MOD. "We have several unusual things." She stabbed one finger at the cluster of small icons representing the juveniles at the herd's edges. "The juveniles"—when he nodded his comprehension of the term, she continued—"are usually at the leading edge of a craving. Four, six of them most often. This time, we have ten."

"Ten?" he echoed.

"The entire herd is much larger. It is singular to our experience."

"So many juveniles or the large herd?"

"Both."

"The herd is—" And he continued with words she didn't understand.

He must have caught her puzzlement, because he started over. "The herd acts as if with one thought, all together? Or each zombie in the herd acts on its own?"

"The C-Prime controls all." She remembered telling him much of this on the ship. But he'd just been through his first PMaT, and his brain, understandably, might not have been functioning at optimum. "But the C-Prime can code instructions into one or a smaller group, send them on a mission. They perform this, they return, they reintegrate. You understand?"

"So this C-Prime sends ten juvenile zombies—"

"Yes and no." Jorie bit back a sigh. It wasn't only the language difficulties. The Guardians had studied the zombies for over two hundred years. To impart that information in a few minutes was difficult, even if she didn't have to rethink each word she used. "It is somewhat inherency. Juveniles perform a function in a craving that goes back to the original zombie program of protecting stations, worlds, from unknown infectious agents. The craving—the seeking out of potential viruses on ships and passengers—is their motivation. The C-Prime...it need not say yes or no."

"You're saying it's instinct."

"Instinct?" She wasn't familiar with the word.

"It's inherent—instinct for the juveniles to move at the start of a craving."

"It is their inherency, yes. The C-Prime, it can guide. But the inherency, the need to define and eradicate the threat, is already there."

He was nodding. "And where is the C-Prime guiding them to?"

Jorie glanced at Herryck, received her nod, and then turned back to her T-MOD and Petrakos. "Here." She tapped at the screen, bringing up a regional map created by her ship's seeker 'droids.

Petrakos sat back on his heels. "Fuck."

She'd heard him utter that word before, didn't know its meaning, but he was clearly never blissful when he uttered it. "We have one and a half sweeps before the first portal, Petrakos. I need everything you know about this place. These buildings—"

"It's a shopping center," he told her, and she could hear the tension in his voice. "We call it a mall. Everything under one roof—stores, restaurants, all inside."

"I understand. An enclosed plaza with many establishments offering items for purchase."

"Good. Across the street, there's a movie theater and another shopping plaza. All together, hundreds, thousands of people."

"It will be near sunset," she told him, because the dismay she heard in his voice unsettled her. "The people will return to their structures to celebrate the evening meal—"

"You don't understand." He suddenly leaned forward, hands fisted. "This is the biggest shopping time of the year. Everyone will be there. Not only the store workers but families, children. There is no way you're going to be able to keep the zombies' existence *or* the Guardians' existence a secret." He uncurled his fingers and pointed to her screen. "Not there. You're going to have to deal with the zombies openly."

Herryck, Trenat, and Rordan had all turned from their duties and were watching her. She knew Trenat understood none of Petrakos's words, but Herryck had a working knowledge of Vekran, and Rordan spoke even more. But even if they hadn't, they couldn't miss the anguish in Petrakos's voice.

She translated into Alarsh a summary of what Petrakos had told her. "If this wasn't a nil world, we could bring down two gravrippers. For their speed, if nothing else." A cloaking device for the craft would be ideal, though the Guardians had yet to perfect one.

"We'd still have to jam this planet's sensors," Trenat pointed out. "They're just advanced enough to track us on descent. We can't permit that."

No, they couldn't. Above all else, their presence here must remain undetected.

"Then we wait," Rordan said.

Herryck's face jerked toward Kip Rordan. "Wait?" she asked, before Jorie could.

"Wait," Rordan repeated. "These are only juveniles. They'll most likely cease after fifty, one hundred kills. We go to the portal site, put a full sensor sweep out on them, pull all the data we can, but don't try to stop them. Their scent trails when they return to the C-Prime will be strong. That will heighten the craving, force the C-Prime out in the open more quickly. Then," and Rordan smiled harshly, "then we move."

Trenat bobbed his head in agreement. "I reviewed Dr. Alclar's case studies on juveniles before this mission. He states that R-Five levels on juveniles in megaherds are too weak for us to learn anything overly useful from their capture."

Trenat was reading Lorik Alclar's research? "The R-Five levels aren't the only thing we're looking at here," Jorie put in firmly.

Petrakos touched her arm, frowning. She shook her head in response. She wasn't about to explain something she knew he definitely wouldn't want to hear.

"Killing those juveniles is a waste of our resources and we risk exposure," Rordan said. "General Procedure Six permits—"

"I'm familiar with Gen Pro Six," Jorie snapped. "But letting ten juveniles feed on dozens of locals—"

"Nils," Rordan said.

"—is not acceptable."

"Exposure of our mission here is a violation of our orders." Rordan's voice was hard.

"Our orders," Jorie countered, "are to stop the zombies."

"Our orders are also to determine how this herd managed to get so large without fracturing," Rordan said, and Jorie clearly heard echoes of Captain Pietr in his words. "You know Lorik's research shows that we need to let the juveniles feed to do that."

Yes, she did, but no, they didn't. There were other ways to obtain that data, but those were ways that also violated several orders and more than a handful of gen-pro regulations. She'd never discussed those particular methods with Lorik, and, hell's wrath, she wasn't about to reveal them to Rordan.

She rose. "I will consider your suggestions, Commander."

"There's nothing to consider, Jorie. Lorik's data clearly indicates that two or three of the weaker juveniles should die off in the first throes of the feeding, giving their scent trails to the remaining ones. This will increase their R-Five levels, giving us a stronger lock on their C-Prime. We bag their C-Prime and we save this wretched planet. Plus we can analyze the mutations in the C-Prime's codes. Surely that's worth a hundred or so dead nils?" His eyes narrowed. "Captain Pietr thinks it is."

Captain Kort Pietr. She was no longer sure she liked him. Because he'd done more than just offer her refreshments and a chance at a captaincy. She was sure—very sure—he'd made the same offer to Rordan as well.

Rordan's placement on her team was no chance suggestion. Now she not only had to fight the zombies but she had to contend with Kip Rordan.

But Kip Rordan also had to contend with her.

"Work out the specifics for a scent-trail grid," she told Trenat, ignoring the flash of alarm in Herryck's eyes at her stated capitulation to Rordan's plans. "I need to get familiar with the land vehicle Sergeant Petrakos brought us."

At the sound of his name, Petrakos looked up at her, suspicion playing over his very good face. She switched to Vekran. "We go outside. Now."

"And your team?" he asked, rising.

"Yet has work to do. Come." She turned brusquely away from him and headed for the door, her mind already sorting through a dozen scenarios and rejecting two dozen more.

Sergeant Theo Petrakos was *not* going to like what she had to tell him.

But Commander Jorie Mikkalah—who fully intended to make captain—wasn't going to give him any choice.

She just hoped she wasn't making a mistake in trusting him.

9

"We cannot go to your shopping plaza." Jorie faced Theo Petrakos on the wide back porch just as the mesh door clanked closed behind him.

"What do you mean?" There was a tightness in his voice and a corresponding tension in his face. His dark brows were drawn down, his eyes narrowed.

"I mean," she said, motioning him toward the land vehicle, wanting to put more space between their conversation and Kip Rordan's eyes and ears, "what I said. We cannot risk exposure among your people. It is an edict we cannot ever violate."

"Did it ever occur to you," he asked, his words clipped and terse, "that my people will be paying more attention to the zombies than to you?"

She walked the few steps to the front of the land vehicle and stopped. He was still on the porch, arms rigid at his side. There was so much he didn't understand. He knew it. She knew it. But this was not the place or time. "Petrakos," she said. "Come." She met his narrow-eyed gaze with one of her own. "Please," she added, barely under her breath.

He walked slowly down the steps, her command clearly not infusing him with bliss, even with her soft addendum.

Jorie caught a flicker of something in one of his structure's aft viewports. Rordan? Trenat? Rordan, she decided. The shadow was too tall for Trenat.

"Workable size," she said, running one hand over the vehicle's front cowling. "Take the helm, activate the engine so I can assess its power."

He stopped in front of her, his body mere min-meters from hers. The line of his lips was tight; the set of his shoulders stiff. "Don't bail on me now, damn you. I will not have thousands of innocent people die just because some bullshit regulation states you can't be seen here."

She understood his tone more than his words. She raised one hand, pushing her hair back from her face as if she were irritated. "Covert," she said quietly, when the angle of her arm blocked her face from whoever was looking out his structure's viewport. "Vehicle. Now."

His shoulders relaxed only slightly, then, with a shake of his head, he turned and stalked toward the pilot's door. She opened the copilot's door and pulled herself in. Warm air, almost stuffy, enveloped her. No automatic enviro. In spite of that lack, she liked the vehicle's added height and interior expanse immediately.

Petrakos slammed his door shut and looked at her expectantly, brows still down.

"Activate the engine," she told him.

He grasped the helm and twisted a knobbed protrusion. A rumbling growl sounded from under the cowling. A puff, then a stream of air, slightly cooler, brushed over her face from rough-looking holes flanking the control panel.

She leaned one elbow on the console, angling her body toward him, her back almost to the structure. "This vehicle has many added functions, yes? Act as if you were demonstrating them for me."

He flicked at a lever. "Windshield wipers."

Two thin rods moved rapidly back and forth over the viewport. Petrakos touched something else and water sprayed. The rods made a squeaking sound against the glass as the water evaporated. Odd that nils would waste something so precious on a vehicle. She nodded. "Very good."

He pushed against the middle of the helm and a claxon blared. "Horn," he said, watching her closely now.

"Excellent. And these?" A wide console full of switches, buttons, and what she guessed to be power ports ran between the two front seats.

"Siren, lights, PA system—loudspeaker. Laptop, like your T-MOD, goes here," he said, pointing to an elevated stand. Then he closed his fingers into a fist. "Explain covert and the shopping mall."

She played with the empty swivel stand between them, as if that were her sole concern and not the additional work it would take to circumvent Rordan's presence. She damned the fact that she still needed his expertise. "We are forbidden to disclose our presence to your people."

"I *know* that."

"So does Commander Rordan." She fought the urge to turn and see if they were still being watched. But that would reveal that she knew. Rordan had to believe she didn't. "Therefore, if I order my team to your shopping plaza, Rordan will act to prevent that."

"But you're the mission commander."

"I am—unless Rordan finds reason to take that from me. Violation of the general procedures' primary edict would guarantee him that chance."

"Fine." The anger was back in his tone and his face. "Then give me a couple of your rifles, those Hazards—"

"Hazers," she corrected him as she pulled out her scanner—holding it out of sight below the console— and accessed the data from her T-MOD, still running and recording inside the structure.

"—and I'll go myself."

"Not required." She tapped three key codes into her scanner, watched the new data crawl across the screen, then turned the unit toward him. "Because the zombies will not be at your shopping plaza when you get there."

"Where—"

"That large vacant region." She changed the screen to the map image supplied by the seeker 'droids. "Vegetation. No structures. Just these two open areas. You know them?"

He studied it in silence, then: "That's a baseball field. The other is the tennis courts."

"Structures?" His last word puzzled her. She knew

what a court was but had no knowledge of a *tennis* as part of a legal system.

"No. A place for outdoor games, exercise."

She shrugged off yet another misinterpretation. "Probable population at risk?"

He was quiet for a moment, frowning again, but the tension had left his shoulders. "A lot less. There's a school across the street, but it's closed for the holidays."

"How many people might be there for outdoor games?"

"No way to know for sure, but we can assume ten, twenty. Most out walking for exercise."

She nodded. "You're security in your locale. You have the authority to make them leave. They won't question. Correct?"

Petrakos started to answer her, lips parting, then he stopped. "Possibly."

"Possibly?"

"If I could involve others in my security force, it would be more effective. But I can't—*won't*—have them face this." He touched his shoulder where the restrainer implant had been inserted.

The restrainer implant wasn't the impediment. Involving more nils was. She'd already pushed several regulations to the limit with Petrakos. She wasn't going to push even more—especially not with Rordan on the scene. But she couldn't tell Petrakos any more about Rordan and Guardian regs and Captain Pietr's possible machinations than she already had. She'd reached the boundary of her trust with him for now. She had a feeling that if he sensed a weak link in the Guardians, he'd try to exploit it.

If their positions were reversed, she would.

So she nodded. "Then we must be satisfied with what you can accomplish."

A sigh of frustration blew through Petrakos's lips as he leaned back in the seat. The vehicle's engine chose that moment to give an odd little shudder, and the cooler air that had brushed against her face turned hot and stale-smelling. With a harsh, murmured word she didn't understand, he twisted the knob on the helm and disengaged the engine. "All right," he said finally. "I'll clear the park. But we're going to have to get there at least forty minutes beforehand for me to do that."

Forty minutes before the scheduled time she and her team would normally arrive to counter a zombie portal would work out like blissful perfection. "Understood. Now we go back to your structure so Commander Rordan can show me how wrong my data was and that his new and better data shows that the zombies will not be visiting your shopping plaza after all. They are going to the tennis law."

She reached for the door lever, but his hand on her arm stopped her.

"Tennis court." The small, odd smile that played over his lips faded. "And you did something to the zombies, didn't you?"

There was nothing threatening about the large fingers draped over her wrist, but the warmth of their skin-to-skin contact unsettled her. Perhaps because there *was* nothing threatening. She knew he was still angry, yet his touch was one of unexpected gentleness.

"Tampering with MOD-tech to affect a craving is

not only dangerous, it's against Guardian regulations, Petrakos." She met his questioning gaze levelly, pulling her thoughts back to the situation. The zombies. Rordan. Not Sergeant Theo Petrakos with his very good face and his very real concerns.

Yes, she'd taken a risk, a calculated risk, but she didn't want his questions and she didn't want his gratitude. She was just doing her job—a job she was very good at. One that could lead her to a captaincy.

Moreover, Rordan and Lorik Alclar were wrong. Based on research the Interplanetary Marines were doing—research Danjay Wain had been aware of—there was every reason to believe that low R-5 levels limited only the information that could be gained on the C-Prime. It didn't affect what Jorie might be able to learn about the zombies themselves—and their increasingly disturbing abilities.

Granted, bagging a juvenile—alive—was risky. But no one on the *Sakanah* had captured a juvenile in the past ten missions or more. A juvenile taken from this rapidly mutating herd could be compared to older captured zombies. Any changes found would be apparent and significant.

It was a risk, but it was a valid one.

So she didn't need Petrakos's thanks. She wasn't doing it for him or his nils, or because his unwavering concern for his people touched something inside her, she assured herself. She pushed open the land vehicle's door, then stepped out. She was doing it because of her oath as a Guardian and to make sure Danjay's death hadn't been in vain. She was doing it for her chance at a captaincy.

She was doing it because she knew she could.

And if it proved Rordan—and Lorik—were wrong, she'd blissfully pour herself an extra glass of ice water just to celebrate.

She might even be persuaded to pour one for Petrakos too.

Theo had spent the last several years of his BVPD career interrogating people who lied—either by accident or design, out of fear, greed, or stupidity. It was one of the first rules he'd learned as a rookie: *Out here, everybody lies.* Yet Theo wasn't ready to brand Jorie Mikkalah a liar. At least, not quite.

She just wasn't telling him the complete truth. Which fit in exactly with the corollary from Rookie Rule Number 1: *Always know that you are never, ever being told the whole story.*

He wasn't. Not about the implant in his shoulder, not about the zombies, and not about her plans. And especially not about whatever was going on with her team of space commandos.

He thought of that as he drove west on Twenty-second Avenue toward the mall. Jorie, still clad in her oversize sweater, was perched in the front passenger seat.

It was almost three forty-five in the afternoon. The ETA for the zombies was now less than an hour. A surge of adrenaline shot through him every time he thought about that. He tamped it down. *Be calm. Think.* He'd handled a zombie before, with far less preparation. He could do it again. His Glock was secured on his right hip, his zip-front sweatshirt keeping it and his gun belt with extra ammo hidden from sight. He'd also donned his black tac vest, very aware that something that could so easily trash a car wouldn't be hampered by it. But he had to wear it—and his smaller Glock in the ankle holster. For extra protection, his assault rifle was racked in its usual place.

By comparison, the weapons the space commandos wore seemed strangely small and light. Jorie was decked out in much the same manner as when he first saw her: headset with its eyepiece (swiveled down for the moment), dual laser pistols, and various gizmos attached to a belt (all hidden by the sweater). Her high-tech rifle rested on the floor.

Oddly, it wasn't their weaponry that was foremost in his mind at the moment. Their camaraderie—or lack of it—was.

He glanced at the passengers in his backseat through the SUV's rearview mirror. There was a power struggle under way. He'd been with BVPD too long not to recognize one. But this one centered on him and the lives of everyone he knew.

A detective's sixth sense told him he'd been off the mark in his initial appraisal of Commander Mikkalah. She was responsible for his kidnapping and that damned thing in his shoulder, but, despite that, he began to see that Jorie did take people's lives into consideration. That same sixth sense told him Rordan didn't.

And that, he suspected, was where the lines were drawn. The players had chosen their sides.

On Jorie's was Tamlynne Herryck, now wearing his old black-and white Tampa Bay Lightning T-shirt over her sleeveless uniform top. Tammy, he'd dubbed her. But Jacare Trenat—Jack, wearing one of Theo's Old Navy T-shirts—had sided with Kip Rordan. Theo didn't speak a word of Alarsh, but he knew if he dubbed Rordan Pompous Asshole he wouldn't be too far off the mark—though Uncle Stavros would probably call Rordan a *malaka*. Too bad he'd loaned Rordan his Bucs jersey. He hoped like hell he'd get that back.

Jack, it seemed, was doing all he could to get his nose far up Rordan's butt. Though to be fair, Jack was young. Just a rookie. He had that bright, shiny look in his eyes that was a combination of a desire to please and a belief that he could save the world.

And Rordan, with his swagger, was just the kind of *malaka* a rook like Jack would admire.

Of course, saving the world—Theo's world—*was* Jack's job. If it hadn't been his own world at stake, Theo might have found the entire situation amusing: intergalactic space commandos falling prey to petty office politics. He only hoped Jorie Mikkalah was up to the task of not only the zombies but whatever Rordan was planning as well.

He stopped for a red light. Jorie had been focused on her scanner gizmo since they'd left his house, but she looked up at him now.

"Ten minutes," he said, anticipating her question.

She nodded. "I need to position Rordan and Trenat first before we remove your people."

"And Tammy?"

"Tammy?"

He inclined his head toward the Tampa Bay Lightning fan seated behind her.

"Lieutenant Herryck and I will take the opposite

position. You can return to your structure. We'll meet you back there in about one sweep."

"Whoa, wait a minute." The light turned green. He stepped on the gas. The SUV stuttered, then surged forward. "I'm part of this mission, remember? And it's a long walk—"

"We'll use the PMaT to transport back to the ship when the juveniles have been dealt with."

Peemat? Oh, that damned thing that spins your guts out through your eyeballs, then puts you back together again as you go from Point A to Point B. A thought struck him. "Why do you need me to drive you to the park if you have that transporter?" It was certainly quicker and more efficient, though nauseating.

"Zombies track PMaT," came Rordan's answer from behind Theo. Another glance in the rearview showed a slight smirk on the man's face.

Yeah, okay, so I'm a stupid nil. Theo returned Rordan's reflected smirk with one of his own. *"Skata na fas, malaka,"* he said under his breath. Eat shit, asshole.

"Because all PMaT transits are unshielded," Jorie said, as if Rordan hadn't commented. "Zombies have what we call a sensenet. Through that, they're aware of surges created by unshielded tech. And they react."

"But you said you're going to transport back—"

"The zombies will be neutralized at that point," she continued. "But to engage the PMaT in the proximity of a forming portal holds danger."

Rordan said something in Alarsh, short and quick.

Theo saw Jorie shrug. Her answer was equally short and sounded—though he had no idea of the content of the exchange—casual, almost offhand. But her fingers were tight around her scanner.

He didn't like not understanding their language. He liked it even less that Rordan understood his. He hoped this was just petty office politics and that they were all on the same side when it came to the zombies.

But he couldn't be sure and he couldn't ask. He could only remember what she'd told him earlier, denying—lying about—tampering with her tech to change what the zombies did. He gleaned from their conversations on her ship that's what had turned Wayne, her agent, into a parchment Mr. Crunchy with moist eyeballs.

And here she was doing the same thing because Rordan—and intergalactic office politics—prevented her from saving lives at a crowded mall during Christmas week.

So Theo decided to do the only thing he could: tilt the balance in Jorie's favor. He made his decision as he dropped Rordan and Jack at the far end of the park by the tennis courts, then Jorie and Tammy at the other, next to the baseball field. A quick trip around the perimeter announcing—via his PA system, with blue strobe going—the possible sighting of a rabid raccoon cleared away the few remaining joggers.

Theo pushed the traffic gates shut, then set the *Park Closed* sign in place. Jorie had told him to go home once the park was clear. But he was not going home until this batch of zombies was dead and that

PMaT thing was spewing Rordan's unworthy molecules all the way back up to the ship.

He turned the lumbering vehicle back toward the ball field, parked it just behind the row of low bleachers, and got out. Jorie trotted toward him, frowning. He leaned on the front of his SUV, arms folded across his tac vest.

"I'm staying."

She glared at him. He glared back. When she flung her arms wide in exasperation and let out a now familiar-sounding string of Alarsh curses, he knew he'd succeeded. A mixture of elation and relief washed over him.

Which ended a split second later when a discordant wail erupted from the scanner in Jorie's hand—and echoed out of one dangling off Tammy Herryck's hip.

Jorie favored him with one last hard glare—partially obscured by her eyepiece—as if to let Theo know he was now edging his way to the top of her shit list. Then she thrust one of her small laser pistols into his outstretched hand.

"Opticals, remember?" she asked, teeth gritted. She swung her rifle around. "And legs. Stay with me."

Opticals. Eyes. And legs. And writhing energy-worms and long, flailing, razor-sharp extenders. He sprinted after her to where red-haired Tammy stood, rifle in one hand, scanner in the other, then stopped. Both women's heads were bent over their scanners but, damn it, no one was *looking* around. Someone should be. He remembered the green glowing circle, the thing oozing out—impossibly—from its center.

He turned, squinting through his sunglasses into the late-afternoon light.

Something slammed him from behind, crushing him to the ground. Grass, dirt, and gravel were pushed into his face, and he heard his sunglasses crack. Then, with sickening clarity, Theo realized he could no longer breathe.

10

Theo rolled onto his back, gasping, choking, eyes streaming. Pain radiated through his face and chest, but he kept both hands firmly on the laser pistol. Two words blared in his mind from years of training: *failure drill!*

He lifted his shoulders off the ground, arms outstretched, and squeezed off three blasts in under two seconds: two to center mass, one to the head of the monster looming over him. The zombie shuddered for one, two heartbeats, then lashed out with a long, tentaclelike arm, razor claws flexing.

Damn, not head. Eyes! He fired again, aiming for the thing's eyes, aware there was no time to roll out of the way of the claws swinging toward him. But he hit something—one eye, definitely. There was a *pow! pang!* A flash of light like a huge handful of crazed sparklers streaked overhead, dissolving against the field's backstop. Then a hard rush of air scraped across his face and scalp, something metallic glinting only inches from his nose. A high whine filled his ears, and his sunglasses were ripped from his face.

From out of the corner of his eye he saw the second claw coming. No time to scramble to his feet, nowhere to go. He squeezed off two more shots to the thing's head, praying he hit the other eyes, then merged himself with the dirt beneath his back, his teeth clenching so hard his jaw ached. The sharp claw, descending, suddenly arched up, moving to his left, moving away . . .

"Theo!" Jorie cried.

He watched the zombie topple backward and land on the field with a muted thud.

He took his focus off the monster just long enough to glance to his right and see her outstretched hand. And, behind her, a small sickly green oval wavering into solidity out of nowhere, about where the shortstop ought to be.

He grabbed her hand, pulled himself to one knee, and fired past her.

She spun as he rose, the stream of laser fire from her rifle invisible except where it laced the edge of the glowing hole. He shot another burst at the opposite edge. The portal waved, fizzled, then faded with an eerie whoosh of air.

Damn.

Watch your six. Another rule ran through his mind, and Theo glanced over his shoulder—as sweat trickled down into his eyes and blood pounded in his ears—to assure himself the first zombie wasn't moving. It lay in a grotesque, twisted heap. He remembered the one in his backyard exploding into nothingness. Why this one hadn't, he didn't know. And there was no time to ask.

Tammy was jogging toward them, shouting something. Jorie nodded, then grabbed his arm, dragging him backward.

"Double!" she shouted. "Twins!"

Twins?

Two circles, almost a figure eight, solidifying in the air in front of the pitcher's mound, maybe twenty-five feet to his right.

Twins. And not the Doublemint kind either.

Shit.

Jorie and Tammy sprinted apart, blasting the figure eight in measured increments. Theo backed up, pistol still out, watching his and their six o'clock position, searching the area for more glowing circles while at the same time keeping part of his attention on the women working efficiently as a team. He felt more than a little stupid and out of synch. He'd think later about how close he'd come to getting himself killed.

The figure eight collapsed with an odd *fooshing* noise and—this time—a small flare of sparks.

Then there was silence, broken only by the women's harsh breathing and the sound of his own heart thudding in his ears.

His gaze caught Jorie's. She was sweat-streaked, with a few twigs caught in her hair, making him wonder if she too had been knocked to the ground. Her lips were slightly parted, her cheeks flushed. *Cristos,* she was gorgeous. And he knew he had to be totally insane for even thinking of that at the moment.

She'd also saved his life. He didn't want to think on that at all.

"How many dead?" he asked. He had no idea how much ammo their weapons held or what lay ahead of them. In the distance, he heard the first rumble of thunder. A late-afternoon storm was on its way.

"Four." She said something to Tammy, then added, "Rordan reports two."

That meant six down, four to go, if her estimates were correct. He shot another look at the dead one behind him as thunder rumbled again. The worms had stopped undulating and now lay like smudgy ciphers on the thing's skin. Even in death, it was butt ugly. "Including this one?"

She was nodding when he turned back. "This one we keep."

That prompted more unintelligible exchanges between Jorie and Tammy, uninterrupted by any squeals from her scanner, so Theo used the moment to inspect the dead zombie again. It was smaller than the one he'd seen in his backyard. It lay twisted, but he guessed that up straight it would be maybe four or so inches taller than his own six foot three.

Then one of its four upper limbs twitched. Twice.

"Jorie!" He said her name quickly, harshly, keeping his laser pistol trained on the thing's head. "It's moving."

She stepped over to him. "Stasis." She pulled out her scanner and showed him a screen full of triangles and lines that meant nothing to him.

Then, as he watched, the zombie disappeared into thin air. "Where—"

"Ship." She jerked her chin upward, and he caught the small smile on her lips. "First one in some bit of time, yes? Risk to transport, but—"

Two scanners screeched out a warning. Another green oval glowed faintly in the air. He raised his laser pistol, but Jorie held up one hand, stopping him.

Beyond the oval's haze he could see two figures sprinting quickly in his direction through the outfield: Old Navy Jack and Rordan Pompous Asshole, wearing Theo's Bucs jersey that—shit—now had a rip down one sleeve.

Jorie twisted a thin tube—mouth microphone, Theo guessed—up to her face and spoke rapidly into it. Tammy sidled next to him as Jorie suddenly jogged off toward the two men.

"Here. Do as me." Tammy fired at the zombie portal in several short bursts.

He did as her, the thin glow of laser fire peppering the oval barely visible in the late-afternoon light.

"Up small space more," she said, and he moved his line of fire above hers.

But this time the portal didn't implode. It grew, becoming more solid by the moment in spite of his and Tammy's barrage. He had no idea if he was doing something wrong, because he had no idea what he was doing. Other than firing an alien laser at something that had no business being on his planet.

Rordan's voice reached his ears, sounding excited over the low hum of their laser pistols, but Theo didn't know if it was a good excited or bad excited.

"Good? Bad?" he asked Tammy without taking his eyes off the portal, knowing her language skills were limited. But Theo needed to know what was going on. He fired off a few more charges.

"Good. Bad. Yes," Tammy answered, telling him nothing. She let loose with a rapid series of charges, then murmured something under her breath that sounded nasty.

"Petrakos." Jorie had returned and grabbed his elbow. "With me. Here."

He moved sideways as Rordan came up next to Tammy, holding a weapon Theo hadn't seen before: short and double-barreled but with thin blue lines pulsing up and down the stock. Rordan fired off three shots at the portal, which wavered, losing some of its solidity.

Then a loud screech behind Theo shot a jolt of adrenaline up his spine.

Jack's scanner wailed in his hands, almost drowning the younger man's short, hard words.

Rordan nodded quickly. Jorie dragged Theo even farther away.

Protecting him because he was a nil and didn't know what to do. His own gun was still holstered, his assault rifle still in its rack. All he had was a weapon he didn't fully understand against an enemy he understood even less. It was like being a rookie again, but a hundred times worse because this was *his* city, *his* planet. And the one thing that Theo Petrakos did not handle well was being helpless on his own turf.

When Jorie reached for the pistol in his hand, he couldn't stop the bitter anger welling up inside him. "Damn it, just give me a chance—"

"Feeding frenzy is building." She spoke as if he

hadn't. "You understand?" She turned his laser pistol over and tapped at the small indentations above the trigger.

To his surprise, she handed the weapon back to him. "Feeding frenzy? Yeah." He nodded. "Uncontrolled. Crazy."

"Very crazy." She pointed to his pistol. "Now the G-One is set for herd-terminate. Now we finish what we came to do here. Yes?"

It took a few seconds for her words to sink it. His weapon hadn't been set to kill. It had been set to... He had no idea what it had been set to, only that what he'd been firing hadn't been at full power. *That* would explain his ineffectiveness. He suddenly felt immeasurably better and very pissed off. Did she think he would shoot himself in the foot or her in the back?

"You finally trust me with this?" He didn't bother to keep the anger out of his voice.

She started to walk away, stopped, and turned back to him. "Trust?"

He strode up to her. "You set it to low power."

She kept walking away from where Rordan, Tammy, and Jack stood. Things were quiet, but Jorie seemed sure a zombie feeding frenzy was about to start. Which meant it was the wrong time for him to be asking questions. He couldn't help it, though, so he followed her, staying at her heels. "You should have told me that up front. I can handle—"

"Killing zombies? Yes." She glanced up at him just as lightning flashed in the distance. A split second later, thunder cracked. "You and Rordan. Everything is kill. Understand me, Petrakos. Kill doesn't give us answers. For answers, it's capture. Not kill."

Understanding dawned, and his anger, fading, shamed him. "I thought—"

"No, you didn't think." She stopped and faced him, waving one hand as she spoke. "You. Rordan. Hell and damn! I need answers. Not corpses."

And dead zombies tell no tales. He looked at the pistol in his hand. The small lights that had been yellow now glowed bright blue. Full power. "And now?"

"A feeding frenzy." She pulled her scanner away from her hip, eyes narrowing. "Count to ten, Petrakos. You're about to join me"—her scanner screeched out a warning as another clap of thunder echoed over the trees—"in hell."

Two green portals—no, three—popped into existence. The portals were small, but their color was stronger and their appearance more solid.

They fired in a pattern of short bursts, rising up one side of the oval first, then the other. It was the same pattern Tammy had showed him. He peppered the middle portal, switched to the one on the right, then back to the middle again. Jorie did the same, concentrating on the one on the left, then firing at the middle when he didn't.

The middle portal fizzled within moments, but the other two—stubborn bastards—resisted.

A flutter of movement to Theo's right made him dart a glance in that direction—Tammy, Rordan, and Jack. Green ovals had popped out there too, like some kind of airborne measles. But far more deadly.

And silent. Other than the sizzle of the laser fire against the portals—and the increasing rumble of thunder—their battle was waged in relative silence.

Until Jorie's scanner gizmo squealed again. And so did she.

"Theo, down!"

He dropped, rolled, keeping his pistol firmly in his grip as a rush of air passed over his scalp. He came up on one knee, not thinking, just reacting, sensing, and there it was, maybe ten, fifteen feet away, opticals pulsing with a red glow. A long clawed arm shot toward him.

He targeted the eyes, fired. The zombie jerked as one eye flared out.

Theo hit the dirt again, the second claw missing him by inches.

Once more on his knee—standing up would be not only stupid but fatal this close—he pulled off two more shots. Another eye sparked, then flared out.

A keening rumble howled out of the zombie's jaws. Theo's skin crawled at the sound.

It staggered slightly. He was focused on the remaining eye when a flash of white under its grinding jaws caught his attention. It looked...alive. Vulnerable.

Theo jerked his aim down slightly, pulled off three quick bursts right under the thing's jaw.

And was rewarded with a huge ball of green gas mushrooming outward, then imploding back in on itself. The zombie was gone.

"Bliss!" Jorie's voice and undisguised glee sounded off to his right.

He shot to his feet, turning toward her, his heart pounding, his mouth dry. She grinned at him. That started his heart pounding even harder. Another green oval, no—two. Twins. Just to Jorie's left.

Shit.

"There!" He fired off two short bursts, hitting the larger oval's right side. It surprised him by *fooshing* into nothingness. The other one, farther away, did the same under Jorie's barrage.

Foosh!

Foosh!

The air around him was filled with *fooshes.* Then a flash of lightning split the sky, followed immediately by a double crack of thunder. The skies opened up. Rain came down in thick sheets, blinding him.

Theo spun, pistol out, searching for green ovals, but he could see nothing. Nothing but the rain and white flashes of lightning stabbing toward the ground.

"Jorie?"

His heart constricted, but he pushed the emotion away and focused. He turned again, water stinging his face and eyes. But there was no Jorie. No zombies either. And no Rordan, Jack, or Tammy.

"Jorie!"

Nothing. He paced off the area in the driving rain, calling her name, looking for her. She was gone. They were gone. Through the downpour he could barely make out the outlines of his white SUV. A flash of lightning arced toward a palm tree, and the hair on the back of his neck tingled ominously. He bolted for his vehicle, the loud clap of thunder drowning out his litany of curses in Greek.

Once her stomach stopped heaving and her brain ceased trying to flow out of her ears, Jorie shoved one hand through her wet hair, pushing her dripping bangs out of her eyes with undisguised ire. "Which one of you damned fools initiated an emergency transport?" She glared at the occupants of the *Sakanah*'s PMaT transport platform.

Trenat, on her left, was kneeling on the platform, retching. She discounted him, as she did Herryck, who looked no less green but was, at least, standing. And would never authorize an emergency transport without first alerting Commander Mikkalah.

Jorie turned to Rordan, on her right, and took no little satisfaction in the sallow color of his still-handsome face or the way he leaned against the platform's curved wall.

As if he could feel her gaze on him, he straightened, or evidently thought he did. One hand clutched his stomach as he wavered, a little left, a little right. But his eyes, when he raised his chin, glinted. "General procedures—"

"*Don't* quote gen pro to me, Commander." She wanted to take the four steps to put him within reach of her fist but knew if she moved her feet right now she'd fall flat on her face. "And we left Th—Petrakos back there."

"The nil can take care of himself."

Theo Petrakos—a nil—had actually hit a zombie's

white heart. So, yes, he could. But that wasn't the issue.

"Ronna," she called to the PMaT chief. "Get a med-tech up here to help him." She pointed to Jacare Trenat.

"Aye, sir."

"Trenat, hang in there. It'll be better shortly. Herryck, you okay?"

"Almost, sir." The rain had turned Herryck's red curls into dark streaks, and water dripped from the bottom of the shirt Theo had loaned her.

A second wave of disorientation hit Jorie. She'd tried to do too much too soon. She bent over at the waist, her palms on her thighs, and sucked in a few long breaths. The spinning in her head slowed and her stomach crawled back to its rightful place in her body. She straightened and looked over at Rordan again.

He'd straightened as well and stopped wavering. "You and I need to talk, Commander."

Yes, they damned well did. "My office, now," she snapped, and strode off the platform, her soaked sweater as uncomfortable and heavy as her heart.

11

What did he expect? *Thank you? Nice shooting? Glad you were there to help?*

Theo charged out into the rain to shove the park's traffic gate closed, then sloshed back to the SUV. He pulled himself into the driver's seat. The seat was soaked; he was soaked.

He slammed the door shut.

How about *good-bye*? At least something to let him know Jorie was going back to her ship, so he wouldn't be left standing in the rain, heart pounding, breath coming in short gasps as he wondered if she was lying on the ground somewhere, injured. Or dead.

He threw the vehicle in gear and headed toward Twenty-second Avenue, windshield wipers barely able to keep up with the pummeling rain. Drains were backing up, streets flooding. Cars exiting the mall slowed as they edged cautiously around larger puddles. Sheets of water sprayed out from tires in arcing fans. Another typical Florida deluge.

For a moment he superimposed the green portals, the razor-clawed zombies, onto the parking lot on his left. It wouldn't yet be raining, and people—families—would be strolling leisurely, arms full of packages, small children in tow. The portals would have confused them, maybe even drawing one or two of the curious dangerously close.

The zombies would have terrified them.

Innocents would have died, caught in the invisible laser crossfire, if a zombie didn't get them first.

Because one of the things he'd learned as he worked with Jorie's team to stop the zombies: they could appear without warning. Guardian scanners didn't always work. That could be the only answer for his getting nailed from behind. And for the few portals that popped into existence while the scanners were silent.

Which meant that there was no way Jorie's team could counter them all—even if they were willing to expose themselves to the local populace.

Thank you, Petrakos. You helped save a hundred or so lives today.

You're welcome.

His portable police radio chattered with the usual fender benders and advisories on flooded intersections—and nothing, thank God, about any unusual noises in the park just past the mall. It was still raining when he pulled down his driveway and around to the back of his house. Theo's sole thoughts now were on stripping out of his gear, then a hot shower, a hot meal, and his recliner, in exactly that order. Then bed and sleep. He didn't even have enough energy to drag out his guitar.

Commander Jorie Mikkalah—he was sure—was probably already snug and dry and dining on apple mush that tasted like watermelons.

At least he hoped like hell she was.

Damn her.

Commander Jorie Mikkalah stopped in front of her desk, yanked the wet sweater over her head, and threw it on the small couch that ran the length of her even smaller office. The sweater landed on top of her Hazer micro-rifle and MOD-tech gear, leaving room for little else. It didn't matter. She wasn't about to ask Kip Rordan to sit.

Rivulets of water ran down her back as she turned and faced him. He was as wet and disheveled as she was, only—she hazarded—he probably looked one hell of a lot better. Kip Rordan at his worst was still passably gorgeous.

Unbidden, an image of Theo Petrakos slipped into her mind. His strong, angular face, his spiky hair. Not at all smooth like Rordan. But a female would be lucky to—

She pushed the thought away. "The feeding frenzy had ceased," she said without any preliminaries. "Your emergency was...?"

"Possible MOD-tech leakage."

His reply came so quickly, it was as if he couldn't wait one minsecond longer to hurl the accusation at her.

"I heard no warning from my scanner. Or yours. Or Herryck's or Trenat's."

He stared at her a long moment before answering. "Scanners don't register leakages on the zurad frequencies."

"Because a zurad-frequency leakage has a seventy-two percent error rate."

"Which is why you use them."

Jorie kept herself very still. "Are you accusing me of tampering with tech, Commander?"

He shifted position, slightly widening his stance as if he expected that fist she'd so wanted to smash into his jaw earlier to come flying now. That thought would have amused her but for the seriousness of his accusation. If Rordan could prove that, Pietr could strip her of her rank.

If Pietr found out what she'd done to Theo's restrainer implant, he'd probably space her out the air lock.

But she knew damned well Rordan couldn't prove she'd tampered with the MOD-tech. His suspicions, though, could hamper her mission and play against her bid for a captaincy. The same captaincy she was sure Rordan was after.

His eyes narrowed, then he shook his head slightly. "You're very good at what you do, Commander." He hesitated. "Lorik didn't deserve you."

His added comment and the sudden softening in his tone took her by surprise. He'd already turned and stepped for the door by the time she found her voice.

"Lorik has nothing to do—"

"Lorik's a fermarl's ass, Jorie," he said, turning back to her after he punched the door's sensor panel. "I'm just trying to keep you alive long enough for you to realize that."

Kip Rordan stepped swiftly into the corridor, the door closing behind him before Jorie could even think of a reply.

The captured juvenile zombie, however, was not so silent. A harsh, keening cry rose and fell from between its serrated jaws as it lay immobilized on the stasis table in the ship's xeno-mech-biology lab on Deck 19. It was blinded, thanks to Petrako's excellent aim. It was also separate from its herd for the first time in its existence.

No one knew if zombies felt fear. But if they did, this one probably felt it now.

Jorie shifted her attention between the zombie and the data scrolling down several of the lab's analytical screens. She didn't look at the lanky form of Dr. Lorik Alclar, his chin-length white hair tucked neatly behind his ears. She didn't look at Commander Kip Rordan in his clean, dry uniform. Quite frankly, she didn't want to see either of them right now.

She liked what she saw on the analytics even less.

Lorik walked to her side while she studied the data. He twisted his lightpen in his long fingers, then used it to point at a box on the right corner of the screen. "It appears, if this youngster is not an aberration, that their command centers have expanded."

Their command centers. Their brains. Zombies

were increasing their capabilities to learn. Exactly what Captain Pietr feared.

"Natural mutation?" She couldn't imagine who could get close enough to a rogue C-Prime to tinker with its mech-biotronics and live. No, she could, though she almost didn't want to think about it.

The Tresh.

"Let's hope it's natural," Lorik answered. "I don't even want to consider that we could be up against someone who found the code."

Not just someone. More likely several someones in the Tresh's Devastator ranks. They were the only ones who'd have the knowledge and the cunning to use it. Like Commander Davin Prow.

The scar on her shoulder chose that moment to itch. Autosuggestion, she knew, but fought to keep her fingers from rising to the area under her—nice, dry—uniform.

"Either way," Lorik said, as if reading her mind, "it's bad news."

"If it's only this herd, this C-Prime, it's solvable by their full termination." Maybe the intuitive behavior she thought she'd witnessed by the zombies at Port Lraknal was just an aberration caused by other factors.

Like the Tresh. Her mind kept coming back to that. But if the Tresh had found the code to alter the zombies—*these* zombies on this nil world—then that brought forth an even deeper problem.

What else were the Tresh doing here? She had to be wrong.

"Their full termination is required, regardless," Lorik answered. Stating the obvious, Jorie felt. But

he always said it with such authority that it sounded
as if it were some glorious pronouncement that only
the magnificent brain of Dr. Lorik Alclar could devise.

"When will you have more-conclusive data?" she
asked. Data. Not answers. Asking Lorik for answers
elicited a lecture on the structure of scientific theory.

"Twenty, thirty sweeps." He glanced over his
shoulder, then back to the screens. Jorie could almost
feel Rordan's gaze on her and Lorik. Or maybe she
was just imagining things. She was tired. She was
hungry. Maybe Rordan's earlier comment about
keeping her alive was simply one of teammate to
teammate.

It had to be. She was misconstruing. He'd been
Lorik's closest friend for years, the two together so
often that Jorie's friends had teased that she had two
lovers for the price of one....

Hell and damn.

Lorik droned on about the delicacy of the work
required and how one sample couldn't be taken as
conclusive and one hundred percent accurate.

"Then we'll bring you another one."

Rordan's voice, damned near in her ear, almost
made her jump out of her skin.

"A mature one, Kip, not another juvenile." Lorik
spoke to Rordan as if he, not Jorie, were in charge of
the mission. "Try not to damage to the opticals this
time. The command processor took some overburn."

"The nil took out the opticals," Rordan said.

"Well, that explains it. Sloppy. Didn't think it
looked like your handiwork."

"Or Jorie's," Rordan put in easily.

Jorie stepped away from the two men. She did not want to be so close to either of them, and she did not want to be part of this conversation. And she didn't know Rordan had followed her out into the corridor until he called her name.

"Share last meal with me," he said when he caught up to her.

"I'm late for a briefing with Herryck," she lied.

"That shouldn't take long. I'll wait." He gave her a small, charming smile. Herryck would be melting in her boots about now.

Jorie thought of another smile—a delicious, somewhat feral grin. "Thanks, but I have to monitor the nil."

"Let me do that while you brief Herryck. You've been on this nonstop for over twenty sweeps. You need a break."

"I appreciate that," she said formally, "but I need your expertise on the herd data. The loss of those juveniles will create changes. Get that thing's R-Five levels from Lorik. I need to know what I'll be up against at the next spur."

"We," he said. "Whatever it is we'll be up against, Jorie, we'll be up against it together." He held her gaze for a long moment, then, with a curt nod, turned back to the labs.

Jorie headed for the lifts. Rordan was right. She was tired. She was hungry. She'd managed a quick cleanser and change of uniform before going to see Lorik, but that had altered only her outsides. Not her insides.

But she was afraid that if she stayed on board, Kip Rordan would track her down.

She stopped at her cabin just long enough to talk briefly with Tam on intraship, then she grabbed her scanner, weapons, and a dry sweater and headed for Deck 15.

With the MOD-tech her team had left in place in Petrakos's structure, getting a lock and clear transport was an almost effortless experience. The way things should be, would have been had Danjay Wain lived.

One thing she'd never taught Danjay was how to use zurad frequencies, how to artificially stimulate portal formation. She wondered now, as the blinking equipment she'd left in Petrakos's structure solidified into view, if someone had. That might explain—

"That wasn't the problem." A female's voice, strident, pleading, reached Jorie's ears, along with the light tinkling of music. She froze, her hand on the half-open door. Hell's wrath! Was Petrakos's neighbor visiting again?

Then a man's voice, gruff and angry: "No, you married me readily enough."

"Because I loved you!" The female again, sounding angry as well. Angry, it seemed, because having children meant the loss of her career on the starport. . . .

Love? Children? *Starport?* Jorie didn't recognize the voices but felt sure this wasn't Petrakos's elderly neighbor. Suddenly she remembered his odd evasiveness when she'd agreed to pretend to live with him as his lover in his structure. He'd said he wasn't spoused. But what if he'd lied?

That would very much be Theo Petrakos, Jorie realized, ignoring an odd tightness in her chest. He would do anything in his power to protect someone he loved.

Jorie hovered at the edge of the doorway in the small room, completely unsure of what to do. Intrude on this highly emotional moment? Another nil would then know she and the Guardians existed. Another nil would be sent to Paroo...

...and Petrakos would have bliss. This must be the reason he'd clung so fiercely to his home world. There was a female he loved here.

She carefully dropped her rifle and her sweater to the floor, then, head high, she strode quickly toward the sound of the music—and stopped. She expected to find Petrakos and a female standing, arguing. But Petrakos wasn't standing.

He was lying in a chair with an elevated footrest, a blanket draped loosely over his baggy gray pants. White socks covered his feet. His eyes were closed, his bare chest rising and falling evenly.

The music faded.

"You're being archaic," a man's voice said.

Jorie whipped her gaze to her left. A large screen—a vid! The female, the man, the argument were all a vid! Relief washed over her. Petrakos didn't love the beautiful red-haired female who now paced what appeared to be the bridge of a small scoutship on the screen.

A very nice scoutship. And since when did these nils have tech like that?

But her concerns were interrupted by the sound of a low sigh and slight cough. Real sounds. Not vid entertainment.

Petrakos shifted in his sleep, his hands fisting, the blanket sliding off his legs to the floor.

Jorie picked it up and studied him for a moment. His short hair was still damp. He was probably chilled, with no shirt on. She could see the slight redness on his shoulder from the implant. And the hard curve of muscles on his arms and chest, both sprinkled with dark curling hair.

But it was his face that drew her gaze again. She couldn't say exactly why she found it pleasing. Other than it was an intelligent face, a hardworking face—a face that had laughed and a face that had wept.

The man and the female on the vid resumed arguing, but she ignored them and leaned over Petrakos, fluffing the soft blanket over his chest.

Strong hands slammed against her shoulders. Jorie flew backward, landing on her rump with a yelp of surprise. Her elbows hit the floor, pain shooting into her arms as she went flat on her back, one large hand on her throat. Hard thighs locked her legs to the floor.

Then dangerously narrowed dark eyes widened and Theo Petrakos gave his head a small shake. "Ah, *Cristos*. Jorie." He removed his hand carefully from her throat and sat back on his haunches. "I'm—regrets. You okay?"

She unfolded her fingers from around the G-1 on her utility belt with no memory of how her fingers had gotten there. But then, from the look on Petrakos's face, his reaction was the same. He hadn't intended to hurt her.

She could have killed him.

She relaxed her body. "Optimal," she said. "But

better if I'm not on the floor." She levered up as he grabbed her arm, pulling her toward him. Her face ended up brushing against his neck. He smelled warm and male and slightly soapy. More than slightly blissful.

And it was insane, crazy for her to even think this way. She scooted back and was pushing herself to her feet when he cupped her elbows, drawing her up against his so warm, so very bare chest.

She knew if she found her face in his neck again, she would be sorely tempted to take a taste of him. So she looked up instead and found in his dark gaze an unexpected confusion. Did he know she had this overwhelming, frightening desire to nibble her way down his half-naked body?

"Theo," she said, wanting it to sound like a reprimand but, hell and damn, it came out sounding more like a plea.

Noise boomed out from the vidscreen. She twisted out of his grasp, aware of his gaze following her before he shook his head slightly. He snatched a small rectangular box studded with buttons from the seat of his chair. He pushed one and the voices stopped, the image going black.

He stared at the blank vidscreen for a moment, then ran one hand over his hair. He faced her. "I think it's time you told me what's really going on."

"I have told you—"

"Bits and pieces. Then you disappear back to your ship and leave me standing in the rain."

She could tell by the sharpness in his voice that that had bothered him. "I know it makes no difference, but that wasn't my decision."

"Let me guess. Rordan."

She sucked in a slow breath. "Commander Rordan did what he thought was right."

"Right for the mission or for himself?"

She hadn't quite figured that out yet. "He maintains there was the danger of MOD-tech leakage."

"So he doesn't know what you do, or does he?"

Hell and damn, this was not where she wanted the conversation to go. She only returned to assure herself of his well-being and to check current data on the tech running in his structure. Not to stare at his bare chest and indulge in foolish fantasies. And not to argue about what had to be done. "I do what I think is right for the mission and all involved, Sergeant Petrakos."

"A minute ago I was Theo. I pissed you off, didn't I?" He hooked his thumbs in the waistband of his gray pants and rocked back on his heels.

She was at a loss with that last comment, but his body language spoke to her loud and clear. "I don't know what this 'pissed you' is. But if you would prefer to argue over words rather than cooperate with me, then so be it. I still have a job to do." She spun away from him. She'd go back to studying the data on her MOD-tech in his small room. Nice, cooperative data that always spoke to her in a language she understood. Not an argumentative nil who didn't know how to follow orders, who questioned her decisions in matters he knew nothing about.

And that, she knew, was one of the key problems. Petrakos was not a man to blindly follow orders. He refused to act like a nil. He wanted full information on what was going on.

Jorie was a commander who was used to working with team members who already had the information—or had faith that Commander Mikkalah did.

Petrakos took nothing on faith.

And—even if doing so didn't violate ten different gen-pro regs—Jorie had no time to fill in the gaps in his knowledge.

If only he were a Guardian tracker... For a moment she let that fantasy blossom, seeing him—with his talents—as her teammate, her partner. He was a bit more conservative, where she was impetuous. But he was also more proactive, where she had a tendency to be too analytical. With a start she realized they'd probably work extremely well together, balancing each other's shortcomings. And they might even possibly—

No. Of all the things she had no time for, she had no time to be distracted by the heat generated by his touch.

She'd settled cross-legged on the floor, keyed in her first request, and was studying the pattern when he padded in. He folded himself down on the floor and held a tall glass out to her.

"Truce."

She looked at the glass—water?—and then at him. In spite of her mental chastisements, her annoyance at him faded. If he really wanted to make amends, she noted wryly, he'd put on that shirt he'd draped around his neck. But she couldn't tell him that, couldn't risk his laughter if he figured out how increasingly disconcerted she was by him. Handsome Kip Rordan's smiles left her cold. But this nil's feral grin tempted her beyond reason.

It must be that she was tired, hungry, and thirsty. She took the glass with a nod and sipped at it. Water. Ice cold. She knew this planet-bound nil had no idea how precious a commodity ice water was on a ship. She closed her eyes a moment in appreciation.

When she opened them, he'd pulled his knees up and rested his arms on them. "What happens next with the zombies?"

"That depends on what Lorik—Dr. Alclar finds with the one we captured." She nodded her head upward as if the ship was directly above them, which, for all she knew, it was. "The herd is in a rest period again. The feeding frenzy—"

"That wasn't supposed to happen."

She looked back at the screen. "That may have been my fault."

"Because you tampered with the tech stuff."

"Theo." She let out a short sigh. "It's best that you forget I ever mentioned that. If you were to say it, even in accident—"

"When Rordan's around."

"—it could have negative consequences." She turned back to him.

"I can keep a secret." He grinned. "So what happened?"

"I don't know." She flicked her fingers at the screen. "Nothing indicated a frenzy would result. I'm . . . better than that. And now everything is as it should be. The zombies are in a state of negative activity. But . . ."

"But?"

"But if the zombies have developed the ability to think, to *plan*, then that would explain their unexpected reaction. The frenzy. It might also mean that everything we've known about them to this point may no longer apply."

He was quiet for a long moment. "How would they learn to plan?"

"Only two possible ways. One, a highly unlikely but natural mutation. Or two, an unnatural tampering. A reprogramming."

"You think someone reprogrammed them, don't you?"

This time she was silent, wrestling with what gen-pro regs said she could and could not reveal. What Pietr would do if he knew she'd disclosed certain aspects of Guardian history and procedures to a nil. Yet ignorance could kill him. "It's not supposed to be possible. Someone would have to gain access to the C-Prime without killing it or getting killed. The only way would be through the Mastermind Code."

"And that's not possible because . . . ?"

She slanted him a glance. "The only person who knew the code died over two hundred galactic years ago. No one has been able to re-create it since. We've tried. Believe me, we've tried. Our best scientists, mathematicians, and no one has been able to obtain it."

"Until now."

She nodded slowly. "Until now."

"And whoever has this code controls the zombies?"

"No. Whoever has this code, Theo, controls the universe."

12

Life, Theo Petrakos decided, was not cooperating with him at all. It ruined his vacation, trashed his car, dumped unwanted houseguests into his accustomed solitude, threatened his planet, and made him start to care—far too much—about a woman he had no business caring about.

All in about twenty-four hours.

He couldn't wait to see what the next twenty-four hours would bring.

Invasion and subjugation by something called the Tresh, according to Jorie. Though probably not in the next twenty-four hours. That would take a little longer, she assured him. Like a week. Just when he'd be back on the job.

Oh, joy.

It was almost midnight. Tomorrow, he realized with surprise, was Christmas Eve. Aunt Tootie and Uncle Stavros would be sitting at their kitchen table sharing *vasilopita,* the traditional Christmas cake with the lucky florin inside. And he was sitting across his kitchen table from the woman he had no business caring about, watching her devour her second first-ever peanut butter and jelly on white bread sandwich with an expression so rapturous it was damned near erotic.

When she lovingly licked stray morsels of peanut butter off her fingers, Theo shoved himself out of his chair and headed for the refrigerator. He needed a glass of something cold. He really needed to pour it over his body, but drinking it would have to do. He reached for a beer but changed his mind and pulled out a can of orange soda instead. He might not be formally on duty, but he needed his mind clear.

"These Tresh tried to take over your government ten years ago?" He thought of all the wars that had erupted on Earth over the centuries. Most inevitably boiled down to *you have something and we want to control it,* even if that something, like with the terrorists, was the way you thought and believed.

"The Border Wars started eighteen years ago, ending about ten years past. But we—the Interplanetary Concord—have had issues with the Tresh since before I was born." She broke off the corner of her sandwich and chewed thoughtfully. "You have wars on your world, yes?"

He nodded. "Lots."

"Then you know. It's never clearly only one issue. It's always part economics. With us, the concord regulates the spacelanes, regulates trade for the seven systems and thirty-four sectors within its jurisdiction. Over two hundred fifty years ago, the Tresh broke all agreements, pulling out. They tried block-ades. We tried sanctions." She shrugged. "I'm not a politician."

"Two hundred fifty years is a long time to fight."

"Not when the people you are fighting have no words in their language for compromise or negotia-tion."

Point well taken. "So the concord invented the zombies to keep the Tresh from using your space-lanes to trade?"

"Initially, zombies were used to monitor the Hatches and detect possible contamination from vis-iting ships and crew. Infections. Viruses."

Like the CDC. Or perhaps more like the way shut-tle astronauts were quarantined upon return. He nodded.

"When the Tresh became a threat, the functions of the herds were augmented to be proactively defen-sive. But," she continued, "as I told you when we were on the ship, that failed. The zombies themselves became a problem. The Guardian Force then had to take over security of the Hatches and, with the tracker division, eliminate the zombie threat. Most of the zombies were successfully terminated when the concord realized the malfunction. But a few rogue herds escaped. Those are what Guardian trackers have been hunting ever since."

"So when will this Lorik guy have an answer on the zombie's brain?" He leaned against the front of the refrigerator, regretting for a moment that he'd pulled a T-shirt on. The cold metal against his skin would help. Jorie had dipped her spoon into the peanut butter jar and was now sucking on it with that beautiful mouth of hers as if it were a peanut butter lollipop.

Lord, give him strength.

"Twenty sweeps, most likely."

Twenty hours before Jorie would have to present her captain with two options: Plan A—continue to destroy the zombies, or Plan B—prepare for an attack and invasion.

On Christmas Eve.

"But Lorik will not accept that as final proof," Jorie continued. The tip of her tongue traced the edge of the spoon. Theo took a long swig of ice-cold soda from his can.

"He's already indicated we need to bring him another zombie. Alive. Not a juvenile this time. He needs to see how far this mutation has progressed." She hesitated. "You understand my words?"

He nodded. He did, more and more, now that his ear had become accustomed to her accent and now that her English—or Vekran, or whatever it was—had improved. "So that means you're going to have to do funny stuff with your computer again to capture one."

She shot him a look that clearly said he wasn't supposed to mention her funny stuff. "Essentially, yes."

"When and where?" He intended to be there.

She examined her empty spoon, seemed to consider dipping it in the peanut butter again, but after a moment placed it on her plate. "Thank you. That was most excellent."

She pushed her chair back and stood.

"When and where, Jorie?"

She was heading out of the kitchen. In two strides he was right behind her.

"Jorie."

No answer.

"*When* and *where,* Jorie?"

"I don't know yet," she told him when they reached the middle of his living room. She turned left into the hall.

Evasiveness, thy name is Jorie Mikkalah.

He followed. "When will you know?"

"Not in the next few sweeps." She stopped in front of her blinking computer equipment and rubbed one eye with the heel of her hand. "I need a three-sweep nap, minimum. Five would be bliss."

She'd turned away from him, and something told him she was ... prevaricating. Not lying, not quite. She was tired. Hell, he was tired. But there was another layer to whatever was going on here.

He stepped around until he could see her face. She had a smudge of peanut butter on one cheekbone. Probably had it on her fingers and it came off when she rubbed her eyes. In spite of the situation, that made him smile.

"Hey," he said softly. "You missed some." He swiped at the peanut butter with his index finger and held it out for her inspection.

"Ah, treasure!" She grasped his hand, brought his finger to her mouth, and licked.

Heat rocketed through his body. That was followed by a sudden cold draft on the back of his neck, an icy chill, as if someone had opened a door to the North Pole. He watched Jorie's eyes—which moments before had fairly sparkled—narrow.

"Commander," she said, releasing Theo's hand.

She wasn't talking to him, he knew that. Not just because that wasn't his rank—she wasn't looking at him. And he had a feeling he knew who she was looking at. His initials would be P.A. Uncle Stavros would call him a *malaka*.

Theo angled around. Yep. Pompous Asshole Rordan had joined them. And, from the expression on his face, was none too happy.

Rordan stepped toward them. Six-one, two-ten, Theo judged. Even in his stocking feet, Theo was taller, though not by much. Pretty ponytail aside, a lot of Rordan was muscle. Theo judged that too. He wouldn't look forward to going hand-to-hand with the guy. But he could take him down if he had to. He'd taken down bigger ones.

"Jorie," Rordan said, then a long sentence in their alien language. It left Theo feeling at a disadvantage again, though he'd begun to catch a few familiar words. Like *nil*. But the rest was still unintelligible. He didn't like that, so he used the time to watch the man's expressions and movements as Jorie replied with a short series of more unknown words.

What he'd initially thought was anger on Rordan's face shifted to something else. Disapproval? Maybe. But why?

Because you're a nil, Petrakos, that's why. And she's here talking to you.

"Problems?" Theo asked Jorie, keeping his own expression neutral.

Jorie opened her mouth to answer, then stopped. Theo realized he needed to teach her to speak Greek, a language he hoped Rordan wouldn't know. Fair's fair.

"Commander Rordan was concerned because I wasn't on board the ship," she said after a moment.

Is he your keeper? Theo wondered, then gave Rordan an understanding nod. They were, after all, supposed to be on the same side. "She's safe here."

Rordan ignored him and spoke to Jorie again.

"Sergeant Petrakos is also part of our team, Commander," Jorie said evenly. "A team that will work much better if we all speak the same language."

Theo watched Rordan closely. The man did not want Theo party to what was said. So he was surprised when, seconds later, Rordan lowered his gaze for half a heartbeat, then shrugged.

"My Vekran," Rordan said slowly, "need have practice. But," and he faced Theo, "when things have importance, I speak such. Since is impossible that nil speak Alarsh."

Nice little put-down. The nil could never learn Alarsh. Wanna bet?

"So I say again," Rordan continued. "You are over your time to work here. Nothing has critical. Five, six sweeps, you have nap."

"I'm not sure we have five sweeps." Jorie crossed her arms over her chest. "The zombies have changed. We can't trust old data to be accurate any longer."

"And you are not accurate with no nap. Is that not truth, Petrakos?" Rordan glanced at Theo.

So we're buddies now? Theo wanted to argue with the man, but there was no sense in it. Jorie had to be as exhausted as he was. "Go nap. I need some downtime—to nap too." Sleep would definitely help. Maybe it would clear his mind and stop his heart—and his hormones—from doing double time whenever she came close to him.

She glanced at him with that slight tilt of her head. The words were out of his mouth before he could stop them. "You could nap here." *With me.*

"I stay here to monitor tech," Rordan said. And Theo poured cold water on his fantasy of Jorie in his bed—even if he played the gentleman and slept in his recliner.

"And guard the nil," Rordan added. He held out one hand. "The G-One. The one Commander Mikkalah provided. Return, please."

The Guardian weapon was in his nightstand. But Theo had no intention of returning it—at least, not until the zombie problem was solved. He didn't discount that Rordan would feed him to the creatures if he could. "I—"

"I have it already, Commander." Jorie's voice rode over his. "Your diligence is appreciated but not necessary."

She could be flawless when she wanted to be, Theo realized. There wasn't a trace of deception on Jorie's face. No fluttering hand movements, no little side glances, nothing to give away that his alien one-woman war machine was lying through her teeth.

Yet he'd been so sure he could tell when she was lying—well, prevaricating—before. Or maybe she'd been flawless then too.

But she was letting him keep the laser pistol. Was that her way of telling him she trusted him more than she trusted Rordan? Or were she and Rordan playing a game? Why should he think that good cop–bad cop was confined to his planet?

So he watched to see if Jorie passed her scanner— or any magic *Kill the Nil* button—to Rordan before she left. Nothing changed hands. And then it was just him and Rordan as Jorie disappeared into a cold rush of air.

Rordan turned his back on Theo and—without a word—lowered himself to the floor next to the pulsing screen.

Was that trust, stupidity, or a dare? Theo had no valid reason to harm the man, but he could still hear his field-training officer telling the rookie cop Theo Petrakos, *Be professional and courteous, but never forget that the next person you meet you may have to kill.* Rordan, he suspected, never learned the professional-and-courteous part. So Theo locked his bedroom door, shoved a full clip in the gun he kept in his nightstand, and put it under his pillow. He put his service weapon on the floor under the edge of his bed. The Guardian laser pistol he tucked into the box spring through a tear in the fabric. He worked on the assumption that if someone or something came through his door, the floor—with his antique wrought-iron bed between him and whoever— would be the safest place to be. From there, it would be clear access to his bathroom and out the casement window with its now-unlockable lock.

Something else he should be concerned about. But that was also what the gun under his pillow was for.

He settled back on the lumpy pillow and stared at the ceiling in the dark, less worried about intruders outside than those making inroads from within.

He'd started to trust—*wanted* to trust—Jorie Mikkalah. But that, he knew now, could be a huge mistake on his part.

He was probably correct in his earlier assessment: all women were zombies. Especially the beautiful ones like Jorie Mikkalah. They show up in your life, bite your head, suck your brains out, and leave you on your lumpy pillow to die.

Jorie contacted Captain Pietr's office when she woke from her nap, but his message 'bot informed her the captain was in conference. Just as well. She had a number of things to do before she returned to the surface, not the least of which was indulge in a hot shower. Several issues plagued her. The shower was her favorite place to plan.

Forty minutes later—some plans already in motion—she caught up with Captain Pietr in the corridor leading to the ready room.

"Did you get sufficient rest, Commander?" he asked her.

"About five sweeps, sir. My team is still on the scene. Lieutenant Herryck—"

Pietr's raised hand stopped her words. "You needed rest, Mikkalah. Your tendency to work yourself into exhaustion is no secret. And, yes, I've seen Dr. Alclar's preliminary report. I assume that's why you skipped first meal and tracked me down?"

Was there nothing this man didn't know? It seemed impossible that Pietr could keep an eye on the over four hundred fifty on board the *Sakanah*, but somehow he did. More than one crewmember had remarked how little got by the Old Man.

"Sergeant Petrakos keeps a stocked galley, sir." And something so delightful that it should have a far more magnificent name than *peanut butter*. "I'll have first meal there when I brief him. But I wanted to go over the report with you first."

The captain tapped the palm pad at the ready-room door. She followed him inside.

"*Brief* the nil?" he asked her as he settled into the chair at the head of the table.

"Only about necessities, sir," she replied calmly, knowing damned well that good Guardian agents following regulations didn't brief nils. "Petrakos's presence insures that my team's arrivals and departures aren't a source of speculation in his neighborhood."

"Of course. Sit, Commander. Tell me what troubles you about Alclar's report."

Jorie sat, reluctantly. She'd have preferred to stand. She really wanted to pace, but that would be an obvious sign to Pietr that she was not in control at the moment. And she was. She had to be.

"I'll try not to take up too much of your time, sir." She wanted to get back to Theo's structure. Herryck had relieved Rordan on watch two sweeps ago, and the brief conversation Jorie had had with her showed the zombie herd still in a negative energy state. That was good and bad. Good that there was no immediate threat. Bad because the herd should be showing some movement, and it wasn't. "I know there's yet work to be done. But I'm concerned that Dr. Alclar is not pursuing the option that the zombies' increased

learning capabilities might not be a natural mutation. I think we can't yet rule out that someone might
have uncovered the code. Sir."

There. She'd said it. And Pietr hadn't thrown back
his head, snorting with laughter at her pronouncement. Or busted her down to ensign for being a fool.

Yet.

His eyes did narrow, however. Then he sighed. "If
someone—and I assume you have a certain group in
mind—did uncover the code and now controls the
zombies, don't you think they'd be doing more than
playing with a herd on this remote world?"

So. Captain Pietr had not only read Lorik's preliminary report, he'd spoken to him too. That was almost word for word how Lorik had ended their
conversation not ten minutes before.

"I know Dr. Alclar believes that the Tresh would
have moved on the Hatches immediately, yes," Jorie
told him. Lorik's pronouncement was no surprise; he
echoed the same belief that the Guardian Grand
Council had held for over a hundred years. "But
what if they weren't sure the code would work?
Maybe they're testing it, testing some changes, both
here and at Lraknal."

"Then they'd know we'd found them and uncovered their secret." Pietr leaned back in his chair.
"Commander, the Tresh—and I think you know this
better than most—are far more devious than that.
Aside from the fact that we have no evidence of the
Tresh in this system, on the highly remote chance
they obtained the code before we did, they'd not be
so ineffectual as to let us get access to any altered
zombies. And I think, in your heart of hearts, you

know that. You need to look beyond your personal issues with Lorik Alclar. He's one of the best. He knows what he's doing."

Personal issues. Jorie sat very still and kept all emotion off her face. "I have the highest respect for Dr. Alclar's work. I have no personal issues with him, Captain."

"I told him I was sure that was the case. Just as I assured him your previous captivity with the Tresh—and those nightmares he says you still occasionally suffer from—in no way affect your perception of this mission."

She would kill Lorik Alclar. First chance she got. No. Better. A quick fist to his far-too-pretty jaw, bind his hands and feet, drag his body to the PMaT, and send him on at least a dozen emergency transports to the surface and back. When he was weak, retching, dizzy, and shivering, his head on the verge of exploding, she'd do it again. Make him beg, whine, *scream* for mercy.

Then she'd strap a leaking T-MOD to his ass and leave him for the zombies to chew on. The same ones he believed were undergoing a natural mutation.

She stood. "Thank you for your faith in me, sir. I won't let you down."

"Good. Concentrate on getting Dr. Alclar the specimens he needs, then terminate the herd. Then we have matters in the Gendarfus sector the council wants me to look into." He sighed. "Trouble never rests, does it, Commander Mikkalah?"

"No, sir. It doesn't."

She saluted smartly, tapped open the doors, then headed down the corridor, every inch of her furious.

And afraid. To ignore that the Tresh might be behind this, to ignore that someone might have uncovered the code, was not only foolish, it could damned well be fatal.

It was time to take a chance—a big one. One she wouldn't take if she felt there were any other options. She saw none. She saw only what she had to do with the one person she could honestly trust.

And that revelation scared her almost as much as breaking gen-pro regs did.

It took her a sweep to dig out what she needed, which required pulling in more than a few favors. And there would still be a lot of work to do before anything would actually be functional once she transported it to Theo's structure.

On top of that, she had to do it all before the next craving spur hit the zombies *and* without Rordan finding out.

Pietr was right. Trouble never rests.

Theo plodded out of his bathroom the same way he did most mornings: naked, his hair still damp from the shower, a towel draped across his shoulders. Except this morning Jorie stood in the middle of his bedroom, hands on her hips, one eyebrow arched.

He yelped and whipped the towel from around his neck. Fumbling and cursing, he wrapped it around his waist.

"Don't you believe in knocking?" he asked more harshly than he'd intended to, but his heart still pounded. And though Sergeant Petrakos would never admit to blushing, he could feel a definite heat on his face.

"Knocking?" She did that head-tilt kiss-me-now thing that made him want to turn around and head back to his shower. A cold shower.

"The door." He pointed. The towel slipped. He grabbed it. "Before you come into someone's room. Someone's private bedroom."

"I didn't use the door."

Then he noticed the square black containers stacked between his dresser and his guitar case. "Okay." He took a breath. "Maybe I didn't explain myself sufficiently yesterday. You can use the spare bedroom, the hallway if you need to. But my bedroom is off-limits. Got it?" God *damn* it, a man had to have some privacy, somewhere.

"I've acquired knowledge, yes, as to our permissible areas. But, regrets," and she hesitated, an uncertainty playing over her features. "Theo, I need your help. This," she thrust one hand toward the containers behind her, "is not permissible."

He tucked in the edge of the towel tighter as he stepped toward her. It slipped again. He gave up and hung on to it. "What do you mean by 'not permissible'?"

"It's a lot—a very *big* lot—of . . . funny stuff. If Rordan finds out—if my captain finds out—it would be serious in a most negative manner." She raised her arms slightly, then let them fall to her sides in exasperation, words spilling from her, quick and nervous. "They think the mutation is natural. They're not willing to consider the Tresh might be involved. I . . .

I don't know what else to do. This has never happened before."

"Your captain's always agreed to every suggestion you made?" *Great place to work, if true,* he thought wryly.

"Of course not. But there are other things in this situation now. Things that..." She pursed her lips and shook her head. "I am so stupid."

No, she wasn't stupid. Theo could hear that clearly in the desperate, almost downtrodden tone of her voice. And he could see it clearly in the tightness of her mouth. He regretted his flippant comment of moments before. She wasn't stupid at all. She knew exactly what was going on. And she was hurt. And afraid.

He had a sudden urge to put his arms around her, hold her, tell her things would be okay, except he had no idea if that was true. And worse, to do that, he'd have to let go of the towel. Not good.

"Let me put some clothes on," he jerked his thumb toward his closet, "then you can fill me in on the situation."

She nodded, then sat on the edge of his unmade bed, looking at him as if she expected him to drop his towel then and there.

Are the Guardians nudists?

He refused to let his mind follow that admittedly enticing thought. He grabbed clean boxers from his dresser, a pair of faded jeans and his favorite black Tommy Bahama T-shirt from his closet, and headed back into his bathroom.

Something was very wrong, he told himself as he quickly pulled on his clothes. Admittedly, he'd only known Jorie Mikkalah for about a day—*Sweet Jesus, was that all it had been?*—but he'd yet to see her exude anything but confidence.

Okay, so it had only been a day. But his job required him to be able to size up people quickly and accurately. Commander Jorie Mikkalah was no wilting wallflower. Hell, she could probably kick the shit out of BVPD's SWAT team.

He opened the bathroom door. She was still on the edge of the bed and turned toward him as he walked up to her.

"Start at the beginning." He sat on her right—an instinctual move guaranteeing he'd be between her and anything that tried to come through his bedroom door.

She drew a deep breath, then launched into a detailed explanation of how Guardian trackers worked on a mission. How the mission commander structured the plan, how her team followed it. How divisions on the ship acted in support with tracking 'droids and weaponry and scientific analysis.

It was the latter where things had gone wrong.

"So Lorik—this Dr. Alclar—he's a scientist who works with zombies? And he's the one who won't listen to the possibility that the Tresh are involved?"

"And convinced the captain of this, yes."

"How?"

"Lorik...revealed information that made the captain believe I discounted his conclusions for personal reasons. That I'm reacting emotionally and not logically."

"Is it true?"

She slanted him a quick glance, a light sparking

dangerously in her eyes. "The fact that I would will-ingly feed Lorik Alclar to a herd of frenzied zombies has nothing to do with my capabilities as mission leader."

"Whoa, whoa!" He held up his hands. That was the first surge of energy he'd seen from her in the past fifteen minutes. It fairly sizzled. He didn't know what poor Lorik had done to deserve her ire, but he wouldn't want to leave the two of them alone in a room.

She shoved herself off the bed and paced several steps. "What happened between Lorik and myself has nothing to do with this mission."

Her choice of phrase registered. And he didn't think it was a dispute over who got the desk by the window. It was personal. Emotional. And judging from the defiant lift of her chin, it hadn't been one bit pleasant for Jorie.

Bastard. Theo didn't even know who Lorik was, but he didn't like him. Because whatever that per-sonal emotional thing was, Lorik had run tattling to the captain, making Jorie look bad in the process. He didn't have to be a detective to figure that out, but being a detective helped him put those pieces to-gether that much more quickly. And helped him frame a response that would pull the rest of the in-formation from her—information he knew she didn't want to admit. "So Lorik used you and is now using that against you."

Some of the anger bled from her, her shoulders dipping slightly. She stopped pacing and nodded.

"You were..." It took a moment for him to re-member her term. "Spoused?"

"We had a concord. It's not quite the same as being spoused. You understand?"

"You were serious about each other. Maybe get married someday, have kids."

"Yes, we were serious. But children aren't possible without a contract and removal of..." and she touched her side briefly and said an unfamiliar term. Built-in permanent contraception, he gathered.

So a concord was like an engagement? The term didn't matter. The hurt he saw in her eyes did. "What did the bastard do?"

She sat back down on the bed, folding her hands for a moment before continuing. "Over three galactic years now, we've been lovers. But four months ago, that changed."

Three years should have been the start of a decent relationship. Jorie and Lorik had a bit more longevity than he and Camille. "So Lorik ended the, uh, concord?"

"I ended it. He violated the concord by taking other females as lovers. I confronted him. He professed regrets, but I couldn't stay with him. Not after that." She looked away from him now, her voice dropping. The memory hurt her.

He understood. His memory of Camille's infidelity hurt him too.

Funny that he and Jorie were galaxies apart, and yet they had this one deep ache in common.

She shrugged. "I don't know if on your world it's important to be faithful—"

"It is. At least, it is to me."

"It is to me too." Another shrug. "But Lorik, I don't understand him anymore. He's always listened to the information I've brought him on the zombies because he knows I'm in the field, that I see things he cannot. Every mission is a cooperation between the tracker dirtside and the science officers on the ship. But now . . ." She shook her head. "Now Lorik's data is infallible. And my observation, my experience, is worthless."

"Because you left him."

"That makes no sense! Lorik is a professional. Why can't he act like one?"

"Because you left him," Theo repeated, and realized he was damned glad she had. "You made the decision to leave. You took that control away from him."

Jorie looked at him for a long moment, and he was aware—very aware—of the bed they sat on and the softness of her mouth, and of a shared pain. It would be so very easy to kiss her again, to touch her, to numb that pain—his and hers—for a little while.

But the space commandos were in his spare bedroom, and the zombies were theoretically just outside his door.

And Jorie Mikkalah was not the type for a quickie.

Neither, he noted with a self-effacing mental nod, was he. Maritana County had no lack of badge bunnies. Not one had made it to his bed.

"So how do we prove that Lorik's wrong?" he asked.

"We don't know he's wrong. I only know that we cannot afford to ignore the possibility of the Tresh being here. My only option"—she drew a deep breath—"is to establish a second mission. Very covert. One only you and I know about."

A second mission? He was flattered, but: "I know Rordan's a pain and Jack's not sure who's in charge, but I thought Tammy was your friend."

"She is. But I won't risk her career on an illegal mission."

He understood that. "What do you want me to do?"

"I have to set these up first." She motioned to the crates. "Then, Sergeant Petrakos, we should go to your security department."

"We go *where*?"

"Where you are a sergeant."

"It's restricted. I can't—" *Walk in there with an alien one-woman war machine.* She had no ID. There was no way he could get her a visitor's badge. Though if he walked in with her by his side, she might not need one. But Jorie would definitely be noticed in her shorts and long sweater. At the very least, he had to find her something else to wear. Unless... "You want me to show you the building where I work?" Maybe she only wanted to gauge the size of the department, in case they needed backup.

She was shaking her head. "It would help to see all incidents of zombie attacks that happened before I arrived. Information my ship doesn't know because we couldn't recover everything from our agent's tech."

As far as Theo knew, there had been no other zombie attacks. At least, not in Bahia Vista. And since neighboring police departments didn't routinely send lists of their homicides—or any other crimes—to his, the only way to get that kind of information was through a search of the data on VICAP and FCIC. Zeke had probably already put in requests for all cases of spontaneous mummification both locally and statewide. But a positive hit wasn't the same as having a case file. Answers could take days, even weeks, especially during the holidays. Granted, Theo as a sergeant might be able to escalate a request. But he was on vacation. Poking his nose into Martinez's and Holloway's case was bound to raise questions.

Questions that could easily result in an implant and a trip to Paroo for Zeke or Amy. Yet by protecting his friends, he could well be risking the lives of everyone in Bahia Vista. Everyone in Maritana County.

Theo leaned his elbows on his knees and dropped his head into his hands for a moment, wishing he could suddenly wake up from this nightmare. Then he straightened.

Everything had changed and he hadn't even seen it happen. What did he have to do, walk around with his gun clipped to his belt, his damned badge on a damned chain around his neck, just to remind him to think like a cop?

His sole reason for not getting someone like Zeke Martinez or David Gray involved had just disappeared. This was an illegal mission, Jorie had said. One outside the boundaries of the Guardians' knowledge. Therefore, revealing Jorie's presence—and purpose—here to Zeke or, hell, to the entire BVPD wouldn't result in a trip to her ship or ultimately to Paroo for anyone involved. Because her captain would be the one to order that, and there was no way Jorie could afford to let her captain know about this second mission—or those participating in it.

But would Commander Mikkalah be willing to break a regulation, an oath, that he suspected she held inviolable?

There was only one way to find out.

13

"It is the oldest of Guardian regulations. It was in force for centuries before I was even born. Petrakos, you have no idea what you're asking of me." Jorie pinned him with a hard stare, then turned back to the futuristic gizmos she was assembling in the middle of his bedroom floor.

She was calling him Petrakos again. "But—"

"No."

"Jorie, there's no other way." He squatted next to her. "Lorik and your captain have you backed up against a wall, don't you see that? You need our help."

"No."

"You said it yourself: this is an unofficial mission. No one will know—"

"That I betrayed the Guardians' existence to a nil world? That I violated the most sacred of my oaths? Even assuming your people were capable of being trusted with that information, *I* would know." She shot him another hard glance. "I would know."

"And this funny stuff you do with your computers," he waved his hand at the assortment of parts in front of her, "this violates nothing?"

"That's not the same."

"It is. It's for a greater purpose, a greater good." A phrase echoed suddenly in his mind, and he spoke before he realized what he was saying: "The needs of the many outweigh the needs of the one." Christ, he was quoting *Star Trek* to her now, but for the life of him he couldn't remember if it was Spock or Kirk who said the line.

Surprise flickered across her features, her lips parting slightly. Then her eyes narrowed. "It's *the needs of the many outweigh the needs of the few*. If you insist on citing Vekran sacred text, at least cite it correctly." She inserted a thin metal card into a small box she'd been working on for the past few minutes, then snapped the cap on.

This time he stared at her. *Sacred—No. Don't ask. You don't want to know.*

She shoved herself to her feet. "I have to speak with Lieutenant Herryck. She's due to return to the ship shortly. Ensign Trenat will transport down."

Which meant, as Jorie had explained to him earlier, that she couldn't spend so much uninterrupted time working on her secret project in Theo's bedroom. Tammy, a longtime friend and colleague, accepted Jorie's occasional absences during a mission.

Jack was another matter.

Theo watched the bedroom door close behind her, then got to his feet, retrieved his worn pair of

Top-Siders from his closet, and slipped them on. He stuck his head in the spare bedroom just long enough to see her talking quietly to Tammy. It was almost ten o'clock and he hadn't had a cup of coffee yet. No wonder he wasn't thinking clearly. Given the lack of caffeine in his system, he was surprised he was still alive.

He tried not to think about how tenuous an existence he might have—coffee or no coffee—and instead concentrated on spooning in enough grounds for six cups. He poked the switch, and his coffeemaker responded with its familiar gurgle and hiss.

Now that he'd found a way to circumvent the usual Paroo trip for any newcomers, he still had to convince her to let him tell Zeke what was going on. Zeke, Amy Holloway, maybe David from FDLE. Barrington over at the sheriff's office. Other names, faces, ran through his mind.

She'd managed to secure his laser pistol without Rordan catching on. She'd managed to beam down boxes of tech. Getting a few more weapons shouldn't be a problem.

They'd need them. He'd already seen one zombie feeding frenzy, and those were juveniles. There was no way, if he and Jorie had to handle an adult frenzy, they could do so with only the two of them. He could still hear the *foosh! foosh! foosh!* of the green circles in the air. It made the hair on the back of his neck stand up.

No, they'd need help.

He was leaning against his kitchen counter, halfway through his first cup of coffee, when she walked in.

"I don't like the data I'm seeing," she said. She was frowning and, even though she was speaking to him, Theo had the feeling that the majority of her brain was focused miles away.

"The zombies are moving?"

"They should be. They're not." She walked past him, stopping at his kitchen window. She rested one hand on the marble sill, her fingers tapping lightly in some silent refrain. "Lorik calls it bliss luck. He feels the C-Prime's weakening."

"And you don't."

She stared out the window, her face in profile. Her fingers stopped tapping. "I need your land vehicle. Something is happening. Bring that G-One I gave you. We're going to find out just what it is."

Jorie so very much missed a decent four-seater gravripper with a locator system. Left, right, left, right in this large land vehicle was incredibly inaccurate. And a waste of time when they had no time to waste. Something was wrong with the way the zombies were acting. Or not acting, in this case.

She didn't know what bothered her more: the fact that she couldn't pinpoint the problem or the fact that she almost could.

It was as if the answer was just out of reach, hovering at the edges of her mind. But she couldn't come up with it. Even running theories past Tamlynne hadn't helped. And Theo—*Petrakos,* she reminded herself. Petrakos was like a one-note symphony: *my people can help. My people can help.*

He started again while they were momentarily

stopped at the intersection of two streets, waiting for the approval of the dangling colored lights before they could proceed. "But you must have worked with some local police—security agencies—when you've tracked these things before."

"We no longer do so on nil worlds," she told him, studying a large expanse of green on her right while the scanner was integrating the next data update. The green space was very much like a park, except for the nils navigating it in small, square, open-air vehicles. Others walked, stopping only to swing long sticks in the air. But she could see nothing there to strike. Very odd.

"Why?"

"It caused *wars*. Cities against cities, nations against nations. They want our tech. Then they want participation and representation in our council. But they're not yet at the point where they can comprehend what that entails." She glanced at her scanner, then over at Petrakos, as his vehicle glided forward. "Turn left, next chance, please. Did your security chief simply hand you weapons with no training?"

He slowed the vehicle as they came to another set of colored lights over the traffic way. "I had to go through the police academy. I was trained to handle weapons. It wouldn't take all that much for the Guardians to train us."

For the Guardians to train nils? Jorie doubted this entire planet was comprised of people who could handle weapons in the way Petrakos could. But that wasn't the core problem. "It would take a special edict passed by the council. Then it would take an allocation of funds and of personnel. Things that are currently needed in other areas."

"A temporary expenditure. Once we're trained, we're an asset."

"One of limited use. It was a touch of bliss luck one of our scouts picked up zombie emissions in your remote sector. Captain Pietr almost decided against investigating. Do you hear my words? Your world has no purpose for us other than to terminate the zombie herd. Your world has nothing to offer the Guardians, nothing to offer the council."

"We have peanut butter," he said as he made the turn.

A small smile found its way to her lips in spite of her current apprehension. "So misnamed. They should call it glorious butter." Jorie sighed and watched the power grid pulse weakly—and illogically—on her scanner. "Continue straight on, as much as possible. I'm not a senior council member. I'm not even a junior council member. I can't change what has been in force for hundreds of years."

"What if we alerted only a few of the people I know we can trust? No city leaders. Just a few more eyes and ears out here. We tell them what to look for—"

"They'd see nothing without this." She raised her scanner.

"But the herd—"

"Is difficult to detect until they activate a portal. I thought you acquired knowledge on that."

"I've been trying hard to acquire knowledge, Jorie." Theo pinned her with a hard stare. "But you have a tendency to keep me in the dark."

She didn't completely understand. He was lapsing into his locale's phrases again. "There's insufficient light in this vehicle?"

"What I mean is, what are we looking for, driving around?"

"Scent trails. We need to turn left again, when possible. Do you remember what I said last night about scent trails?"

"That zombies leave behind trails that you track on your scanner? Yeah."

"Zombies *navigate* by scent trails. The data from the scent trails is like a personal letter from them to me. You understand?"

"These scent trails tell you what they're going to do next?"

"What they likely will do, yes. There's always a chance of error."

"Turn left here?"

She checked the readout again. The power-grid figures were still so weak. Hell and damn. "A bit farther."

Data fluctuated, flattened. A slight rise in energy, then an almost simultaneous drop. It made no sense. They should—

Hell. And. Damn!

"Right! Now. Turn right!" She barked out the order and was about to give an exact heading, but—damn, damn!—they weren't in a gravripper.

"I can't now," Petrakos shot back.

A quick glance away from the scanner's damning data to the landscape outside showed Jorie that *turn now* would put them into the center of a three-story building.

"What's going on?" he continued, with a flick of his hand at her scanner.

What was going on was that she hoped, she *prayed* she was wrong. But until she got closer, until she could get a definite clear reading...Another ghost of data flickered across her screen. Her heart thumped—hard—in her chest.

"Theo, it is essential we travel to the right." She heard the tension in her voice and knew—by his frown—that he did too.

"I will at the next intersection, just a few more feet. *What* is going on?"

"Trouble. Very big trouble." Hell's wrath, sometimes she hated when she was right. Or about to be right. But she wouldn't contact the ship until she had confirmation. Nothing like Commander Mikkalah reporting one of her nightmares to Captain Pietr to hasten her ride into career oblivion—if she was wrong.

Theo slowed the vehicle, a low clicking sound starting as it always did when the vehicle changed direction. "What kind of trouble?"

"Preliminary data appears to indicate the possible presence of an additional entity with the capabilities of altering PMaT emissions," she said, as carefully as if she were sitting in Captain Pietr's office. But this wasn't the captain beside her. This was Theo Petrakos. He didn't know about her nightmares. She dropped the formal edge from her tone. "This could be why nothing seems logical. It's not the zombies alone causing the problem. It has to be an outside source. The Tresh."

"The—Why would they do that?"

The data on Jorie's screen came more quickly now that she knew what she was looking for, and she made a few key adjustments to the scanner.

"Essentially," she told him, "because we defeated them during the Border Wars. If they can control the zombies, they could control the—Can this vehicle not increase speed?"

"Not here. Sorry."

She glanced at the small residential structures fronted by thick trees, then back to her scanner. She bit back a sigh of frustration as the data scrolled down her screen and she saw energy patterns she hadn't seen in ten years. Masked Tresh transport trails. Tresh fuel signatures were unlike the Kedrian fleet or Guardian ships. For decades they'd perfected masking them. But flying combat in the Border Wars had taught Jorie how to look for what wasn't there.

Which was almost exactly what she was seeing now. Almost. She had to be sure.

"What's in the direction we're heading?" Water, there had to be water.

"Gulfview. A small town center. A few bars, restaurants, some little shops—"

"Water?"

"The bay, yes. Why? Jorie, why would the Tresh be in Gulfview?"

Ah. A bay. Small body of water. She risked a moment to change screens, bring up the map downloaded from seeker 'droids' data, and integrate that with the current data. She saw the water and where they were in relation to it. Then she flipped immediately back to her tracker screen. She couldn't afford to lose this trail, couldn't afford to make a mistake. Not if the Tresh were here.

"The water," she said, her voice taut but professional. She was back in combat mode. "Direct me to the water, and I should be able to answer your question."

She threw an extra scrambling filter over her scanner. If the Tresh were dirtside, she didn't want their tech picking up hers. Though they'd have to have seen the *Sakanah,* she realized with chilling clarity. But her ship would have seen theirs, and alarms would have immediately been sent to her scanner, her team....

And she'd received nothing.

So were the Tresh here, or was the information scrolling down her screen some aberration—hell's wrath, she hated nil-tech environments—caused by Petrakos's world?

A small trickle of apprehension slithered again up her spine. She flipped her mouth mike down, about to open contact with the *Sakanah,* then stopped, fear of looking like a fool holding her back once more. If she was wrong, the mission would end for her now.

Equally, if she was right, contacting the *Sakanah* could lead the Tresh directly to her and Petrakos.

Wait. Assess. Then act. It was only a little farther.

"This is as far as I can go."

She jerked her head up. A short grassy area and a wooden walkway met her gaze. Then a small sandy beach and, beyond that, a short expanse of dark-blue water. She could see the spiky outlines of buildings on a distant opposite shore.

She needed to be over that water, hovering,

picking up scent trails and PMaT trails captured in the rising water vapors...but this was as far as Petrakos could go.

She saw the confusion and frustration on his face. Her own frustration and helplessness roiled like an angry storm inside her. She snatched the Hazer from the floor behind her seat, then shoved open the vehicle's door.

"Jorie, wait!" Theo's cry ended abruptly as she slammed the door behind her.

She couldn't wait. If the Tresh were here, every second's delay meant they were all that much closer to death.

No, not death. A slow, painful, torturous descent into a hell she was far too familiar with. One she could not, would not, face again.

God damn *her!* Theo bolted after Jorie, hitting the remote lock on the key chain as he ran. His one-woman war machine was heading like a bat out of hell for the bayfront beach, an obvious weapon in one hand and—if her long sweater hiked up any more—two more obvious weapons on her hip.

"Jorie!" Damn, she could run. Thank God it was Christmas Eve and only a few people were in the park. And none close enough to see the weapon she carried or the Glock on his hip under his T-shirt. Still, if one of the fishermen on the pier turned...

He gave an extra push and—lungs burning—came up inches behind her. He grabbed the rifle's strap. "Jorie!" Her name came out as a harsh rasp.

She tried to wrench away from him, but he locked

his hand on her arm. "Damn it, stop! You can't . . . have weapons . . . here." He was sucking in air. She twisted again. "Stop it," he hissed. "You want every police—security department here asking questions?"

She faced him, eyes wide, face flushed, mouth slightly parted as if both questions and answers were finally coming to her now.

So was unwanted attention. Running after her and shouting had not been the best idea, but he'd had no choice. Now two men in baseballs caps and dark T-shirts with faded logos watched him turn Jorie in a slow, dancelike movement as he tried to get control of this situation—and her—and hide her weapons. He yanked her arm and the rifle between them, and knew the only way he could legitimize their stance would be to be extremely stupid and kiss her again.

They had to look like lovers, perhaps lovers having a fight. He had to divert suspicion.

Their kiss was brief, intense, and far too pleasurable. Even the small taste of her made him want more. Which was very stupid. Useless. Downright dangerous. Some kind of outer-space bad guys had evidently arrived, and all Theo could think about were all the other places on her body he wanted to put his mouth. He was definitely, as Zeke was prone to say, thinking with his little head and not his big one.

He rested his face against hers, the hard length of her rifle between them. "Listen to me," he whispered, his fingers threading their way into the softness of her hair. "You can't walk around with pistols here. People over there," and he raised his face and jerked his chin to his right, "are watching you, watching *us*.

I don't know what's wrong, but you have to go back to my car now or we're going to have a lot more trouble than just these Thresh things. Understand?"

"Tresh," she corrected, her voice soft against his neck, her rapid breathing starting to slow. "Regrets, The—Petrakos. I have to—"

Theo saw the taller of the two men put down his fishing pole and stride off the pier just as—judging from her halted explanation—Jorie did. The man headed directly for them, his intention to find out what was going on clear from the frown on his face.

"Hell's wrath," Jorie said harshly. Then she kissed him. She *kissed* him, arms going around his neck, pulling his face down to hers, bodies merging, rifle pressing painfully into his chest. Jorie had more padding in that area, padding he was very acutely aware of as her tongue toyed with his and her hands stroked his shoulders.

Theo broke the kiss with undisguised reluctance and peered over the top of her head to see the fisherman slow, then, with an amused shrug, turn. The fisherman no doubt inferred from Jorie's actions that she was a willing participant in kiss-and-make-up. His role as rescuer wasn't required.

"Regrets," Jorie said again, turning her face as Theo did to watch the man clamber back onto the fishing pier. "But I must get to the water to take a sample. I didn't think—I forgot the rules on your world."

He shoved away thoughts of how pleasant her body felt against his—rifle and all. "Are we in any immediate danger from these Tresh things?"

A quick glance down at the gizmo in her hand. "Immediate?"

"Are they attacking us?"

"At this point, no. But until I take readings from the water vapor, I can't tell anything more."

Water vapor. Well, Native Americans had used smoke to send signals. He guessed the Guardians or maybe the Tresh could use water vapor.

He shifted her rifle between them and, holding her close against his side, urged her back to the SUV. "There's an old boatyard a block or so from here. We can go out on the dock, but, for Christ's sake, don't take that rifle out where people can see it."

Theo unlocked the doors with the remote. When he cranked the engine, the two fishermen didn't even turn to watch. Good. He cut through one of the back alleys that crisscrossed the small town, then turned down the short, rutted road that led to the ramshackle marina. The newer waterfront condos, complete with private boat slips, had put a hurt on the small boatyard business in the area. This one had closed a few months back, the large yellow-and-white signs nailed to the fence proclaiming its transformation into an *enclave of luxury waterfront town houses* next year.

Jorie was quiet but clearly tense as he drove past the fence, her concentration on her scanner, the seat belt he insisted she wear pulled taut as she leaned forward. She was going to bolt again as soon as he stopped the car.

He exited as she did, hit the remote lock, and sprinted around the front of the SUV to catch up to her. He grabbed her arm. It was time to push for more information. "What are you looking for in the water?"

"Proof that someone is using zombie scent-trail energies to mask his PMaTs," she said, striding forward in spite of his hold on her, the parking-lot gravel crunching under her boots. The marina might be abandoned, but the smells of paint, pitch, and varnish still lingered, mixing with the slight fishy tang of salt in the air.

It took him a moment to remember that *peemat* was actually an acronym for her ship's transporter. "These Tresh don't want you to know they're here?"

"That is my estimation, yes."

"Are they like the zombies or are they human?" Only after he asked did he wonder if Jorie was human or even used that term. "Like you, me, Tammy, and Rordan?"

"They're soft-fleshed, bipedal sentients," she said, mounting the steps to the wooden dock. He released his hold on her elbow but stayed close to her side. "In physical appearance, I could be one and you'd not know. But they're not like us." She glanced up at him, golden eyes narrowing. "They're not like us at all."

Something in the tone of her voice made his skin crawl. And Sergeant Theo Petrakos didn't spook easily.

"What happens if you find proof they're here?" he asked.

"It will change this whole mission," she said, the dock creaking as she picked up her pace. "It may well change your whole world."

A warm breeze buffeted his skin as they neared

the end of the long dock. Sunlight dappled the water in silver-blue patches that reflected a bright blue sky and white cottony clouds. Had Theo not spent almost two decades as a cop, the threat implied in Jorie's words could seem almost out of place on this picture-perfect Florida day. But evil was often the very definition of equal opportunity.

The cop with almost two decades' experience felt hampered by the fact he still knew very little about the zombies and nothing of this evil called the Tresh. "Jorie—"

She held up her free hand, halting his words. In the other hand she waved her scanner in a slow, wide arc. Water slapped softly against the dock's piling. Her scanner was humming, pinging, beeping.

She was frowning. Then she stopped, frozen in place like a statute for two, three heartbeats before she spun quickly toward him. "Here." Her voice was a harsh rasp. "They're here."

"Who?"

She flipped the curved mouth mike up, her foreign-sounding Alarsh words short and intense. Then she stopped, looked at her scanner, and tapped at it.

"What's going on?" Theo could almost sense her adrenaline racing. His had started to, and he didn't even know what in hell was going on.

She ignored him, flipped up her mike again. More words. Another pause. Then she smacked her scanner against her thigh, her eyes sparking in anger. "Dead zone! You understand these words?" She was marching down the dock, back toward his SUV.

He trotted hurriedly after her. "You can't transmit, can't receive."

"It happened before. At the residence where Danjay was killed. I discounted it then. Stupid! It's not a dead zone."

"Then what is it?"

"I'll know more when I find it." She stopped at the top of the dock stairs and made a small half circle with her scanner. "The Tresh have appropriated a structure somewhere near here, just as I use yours. It's . . . good. There." She shoved the scanner back under her sweater and bounded back to the SUV.

Theo was on her heels.

"I need the Hazer," she called out over her shoulder.

"Jorie—"

"Petrakos, now!" She'd reached the vehicle and yanked on the passenger-door handle.

He palmed the remote but didn't unlock it. "You can't go charging around with a rifle in plain sight. Tell me what needs to be done. I'll find a way to do it."

She faced him, eyes narrowed. A gust of wind from the bay blew strands of her hair across her face. "I need the Hazer."

"Not until you—"

A series of chimes he'd not heard before sounded from under her sweater. She spat out a short harsh word, shoved him aside, and took off at a dead run for the street. Again.

"Fuck." The woman was a goddamned gazelle. Theo hit the unlock button, grabbed her Hazer, and pounded after her.

14

Theo caught up with her in one of the unpaved narrow alleys that ran behind most houses in Gulfview, only too aware that a Bahia Vista cop had no jurisdiction in this town and no business running around it with a rifle in his hand. If the local cops didn't shoot him, the residents might. Florida was a gun-friendly state.

Jorie slowed just as they came to a ramshackle-looking detached garage with some kind of flowering vine growing in wild abandon over one side. Theo was sucking air in great gulps but had enough energy to grab her arm and jerk her back against him. Not for the first time, he thought of taking her down to the ground, knee in her back, hands locked behind her, until she told him exactly what the hell was going on here. He was getting goddamned tired of this, in more ways than one, and told her so.

"You run from me one more time like that and I'm

cuffing you to the fucking car." Which probably would have sounded a lot more threatening had he not still been wheezing as he said it.

She shot a dismissive look at his hand clamped around her upper arm. "This way." Her voice was hushed. She lifted her chin in the direction of a house barely visible beyond the garage. "Where's your G-One?"

It took him a moment to remember she meant the laser pistol. "I have it." He kept his voice low as well. "But we just can't go running into a house shooting—"

"Agreed." She grabbed the Hazer from him, looped the strap over her shoulder, then pulled the scanner out again. He watched her gaze dart back and forth from it to the thick foliage in the backyard ahead of them. The screen appeared mostly blank to him, save for a few squiggles. She'd said there was some kind of dead zone.

"How do you know who's in there if you can't get a reading on that?" He pointed to the scanner.

"Because I can't get a reading on that, that's why," she answered softly.

"You could also have an equipment malfunction."

"I had a memory malfunction. I forgot the last time I saw something like this. But I remember now."

She tugged him toward the side of the garage. "Quiet. Covert, yes?"

Covert, yeah. And if this turned out to be some kind of computer glitch, he swore he would throw her over his shoulder, take her back to his house, and handcuff her, once and for all, to his bed.

Could be fun...

Shit, Petrakos, pay attention.

He sidled along the garage with her, praying the gray clapboard house with the rusted metal awnings was vacant of innocent civilians, which at this point included kids smoking dope or some drunk sleeping off the morning's binge. Zombies he could handle. But she said these Tresh looked like people. They—

A loud hum flashed by his ear just as Jorie's boot kicked his leg. His vision hazed blue-white, and the next thing he knew he was facedown in the grass and gravel, an answering hum sounding over his head.

"Theo!" Jorie's voice was strained.

He came up on his hands. She was kneeling next to him, her Hazer against her shoulder, her left hand blindly grabbing the back of his shirt.

"I'm okay," he said as she fired the rifle again.

Small starbursts erupted at them from a broken picture window.

She was swearing, scrambling backward. Light flashed overhead.

He levered up, fired his laser pistol where he'd seen the last flash, then punched off a few more shots to the right of that, assuming whoever, whatever, was in there was moving.

A barrage of starbursts exploded in answer, showering him and Jorie with chunks of leafy branches and palm fronds from the trees above them.

All this was happening with nothing more than a barely audible hum and hiss. He could be sitting in the yard next door and think nothing more was going on than a couple of birds fluttering and fighting in the trees.

One thing he knew for sure: whoever, whatever,

was in there was no Florida resident he'd sworn to protect and to serve. He had a feeling he'd just met the Tresh. He also wished he'd brought his tac vest.

There was a tug on his waistband.

"This way!" Jorie rasped.

She was backing up again.

Nothing wrong with fighting in the opposite direction, he could hear Uncle Stavros say. He scurried back, staying low, trying to watch his six and her.

They rounded the garage and came into the alley again. He squatted down next to her, his back against the wooden garage door. He hoped those starburst weapons couldn't cut through the garage. If they could, he hoped the garage was full of enough junk to stop them. "Tresh?" he breathed.

"Tresh." She nodded. "Three. I want to try going down this side." She motioned behind her to her left. "Find a doorway in. There are some small structures we could use as cover."

He'd noticed the shed and the stack of old siding about four feet high.

"Risky. They could come up on either side of us."

She glanced at him. "No." She angled the barrel of her rifle up. "Sunlight. They're deep-space adapted. They can see in direct light for only a minute or so and can't tolerate the sun's rays on their skin unless they use special apparatus and a protective suit. But after moonrise..." She nodded. "Trouble."

Cristos. First zombies. Now vampires. He was about to ask her if they sucked blood too, when her scanner chimed out in warning.

She swore, shoving herself to her feet. He rose at

the same time. She was tapping furiously at her scanner, squiggles racing across the screen. Then the screen went blank.

She let out a strangled cry of frustration, spun, and kicked the garage door. It rattled, creaking.

He guessed. "They're gone."

"I jammed them!" She shook the scanner in his face. "Exactly what they did to my tech, I did to theirs. But they—" And she let out a string of Alarsh curse words.

He made a mental note to have her teach him some, if and when their lives ever calmed down. They sounded as good as the ones he knew in Greek.

He motioned back toward the house. "Maybe they left something behind. We can—"

An explosion burst through the air behind them, shaking the garage and the alley under his boots. Theo shoved Jorie to the ground, covering her body with his. Dust and debris flew past them, and he could hear things—big things—bouncing off the garage's roof.

"The only things the Tresh like to leave behind," Jorie said harshly as he pulled her to her feet, "are death traps."

A siren wailed in the distance. He tucked the rifle between them and, arm over her shoulders, held her against his side. Neighbors would be pouring out into the alley at any moment. They needed to get out of there quickly and without raising suspicion.

"Walk, don't run. Yet," he told her. And when a bare-chested balding man in cutoff blue jeans almost bumped into them at the back of a house two doors down, Theo grabbed the man's arm, bringing his attention to himself, not Jorie. And not the barely visible rifle.

"Could be a gas leak, man. Get back! Keep away!"

"Shit!" The man's eyes went wide, then he whipped around. "Serena! Don't light that grill!"

Keying the remote, Theo popped the rear hatch as they reached the SUV in the marina parking lot, then quickly took the rifle from Jorie. He stowed it in the cargo compartment beneath the floor. "In case we get stopped and questioned," he told her. "Pistols. G-One," he said, remembering the term and listening to the sirens grow closer. She handed them to him without question.

First time. Amazing. If they weren't so obviously where they shouldn't be, he would have kissed her, just to say thank you for finally listening to him.

It wasn't until they were on the road, heading away from the sirens, that he asked her what had happened. How did she know the Tresh were in the house, but more important, how did the Tresh know Jorie and Theo were there?

She held one hand up. Her headset ringed her hair again, the mike over her lips. She hadn't said anything but had been tapping at her scanner since, he realized now, they'd pulled out of the parking lot.

"*Sakanah*," she said hurriedly. "*Sakanah*." Then a few short Alarsh words, her name, and more Alarsh words. Short. Tense.

When she repeated the name of her ship again,

more insistently, Theo knew something was wrong. Very wrong.

He glanced at her. "What's the matter?"

"I cannot contact my team." Her voice was a harsh rasp.

"Another dead zone."

"No." She held the scanner up. He glanced away from the line of traffic and saw lots of squiggles, which he assumed meant it was working.

"Maybe they're busy talking to your ship."

"You don't understand. I cannot contact my team *or* my ship. I cannot warn them about the Tresh. The transcomm streams are all dead." She clasped his arm. "We must get back to your residence. The Tresh may have found my team!"

Her panic flowed into him. Her team. Who were in his house, protected from sunlight. But not from an attack.

Theo went Code 3 and, with strobe flashing and siren screaming, headed down Twenty-second South Avenue, out of Gulfview. Watching cars—and for anything else that didn't—move out of his way. Listening to the chatter on his police radio for any problems occurring not from the explosion behind them but in his neighborhood. He crossed the intersections with extra care and tried like hell not to let the panic in Jorie's voice affect the driving skills he'd learned years ago on patrol.

"We have six normal communication streams for surface to ship—three emergency and two other high-priority command private. Our transcomms, what I use to contact my team, can synchronize through any of them," she explained in between her continued attempts to reach her ship. "None is responding."

"You're sure it's not a hardware malfunction on your end?"

"I have triple-checked that. Plus my scanner functions as a backup transcomm. It's sensing the ship, but it's showing no Guardian communication traffic of any kind."

"When's the last time you talked to someone back at my house?"

"I sent the preliminary data on the possible Tresh emissions to Tam," she glanced at her scanner, "thirty-seven minutes ago. She confirmed receipt."

That had to be while they were at the beach park and not in the firefight with the Tresh.

"I thought she was going back up to the ship."

Jorie shook her head. "She agreed with my theory on the Tresh and opted to take Trenat's shift."

Because Tammy had to know Jorie trusted her more than she trusted Jack.

"So she doesn't know what happened at that house?"

Jorie was shaking her head. "It was another dead zone. The dock. The residence. That whole area. I started transmitting to her as soon as we cleared its perimeter. No response."

"But you took readings of the Tresh in the house. You jammed their signal."

"Readings, barely. And only because I knew how to counterprogram for a short-range scan. But scans, readings, aren't transmissions." She shook her head.

"I can't explain our tech now." She was clearly frustrated. And for the first time, she sounded frightened. "You simply have to accept I know what I'm talking about. We have a problem."

Theo pulled out his cell phone and flipped it open. He punched in his home number. He doubted Tammy would answer—she'd been specifically told not to. But if his answering machine picked up, that at least meant the Tresh hadn't beamed a dozen zombies into his living room and trashed his house. "Who else should be at my house?"

"Kip Rordan. Trenat comes on duty in four sweeps. But only Kip would have a Hazer," she added, as if reading his mind and his concerns. "Tam just has her pistols. Under nil-world regulations, all other weapons must stay on the ship until we see another craving spike forming."

The phone rang in his ear, then his answering machine kicked on, and he listened to his own not-home-leave-a-message. "Remember the telephone I showed you in my kitchen? The one I told you never to touch?"

She nodded. He held the cell phone out toward her. "I'm calling, *contacting,* my house. My answering machine picked up, which means there's a good chance there's no major damage there."

"The Tresh will not destroy your residence without provocation. When I jammed their tech back there, they knew someone had found them. With the dead zone they created, I needed to force them to reveal themselves. But at your residence, if they can attack my team successfully, they will do so and leave. Quietly."

He noticed her hand move up to touch her collar, something he'd seen before when she mentioned the Tresh. That made him curious, but this wasn't the time to ask.

"But thank you for attempting contact," she added.

He flipped his cell phone closed and used it to point to his radio. "That's my security force's central communication. If there was any disturbance at my address, we'd hear about it." For a moment he considered calling Sophie Goldstein but quickly opted not to. If there was some kind of problem at his house, he didn't want Sophie to go charging into the middle of it. "Any more weaponry in all the extra equipment in my bedroom?"

She huffed out a short sigh. "Two standard Hazers and the double-stack," she motioned to the cargo hatch, "which is my personal rifle. But I didn't tell Tam I transported the Hazers or the MOD-tech down."

Because Jorie wouldn't risk her friend's career. Unfortunately, it didn't escape her that she might have risked her friend's life, and she was probably berating herself about it. "The minute I suspected the Tresh were here, I should have had Tam lock down all the tech in your structure on heavy scramble. We automatically shield against zombie detection. But after the war we ceased to consider the Tresh a major threat. Plus we had no reason to believe they'd be interested in a system as remote as yours."

Scenes from movies like *Independence Day* and *War of the Worlds* filled Theo's mind, with ovoid ships and helmeted outer-space aliens decimating what was left of his oleanders and scaring the hell out of Sophie Goldstein.

He crossed U.S. 19, siren wailing, and headed for the northbound ramp of the interstate. He'd seen zombies. He was very sure that these Tresh could do a hell of a lot more than just scare people. "You could have ignored the whole Tresh angle, like your captain and that other guy wanted you to. You didn't. You told your theories to Tammy. You beamed down that extra stuff. You're still ahead of the game." He glanced at her. "Rordan's a big boy. Tammy's no slouch." Then, because he knew she knew that—even if she didn't quite understand his expressions—he added what he knew she really wanted to hear: "We'll get there in time."

She nodded, then went back to tapping commands into the screen on her scanner, her voice tight with tension as she repeated the ship's name into her mouth mike. In front of him, a knot of cars refused to move, ignoring his lights and siren. He was forced to pull to the right, squeezing the SUV past on the shoulder and clipping the curb more than once on his way to the ramp.

Traffic on the interstate was blessedly light. He cut the siren but kept the lights flashing. Fifteen minutes, max, and they'd be home.

They'd just passed the baseball dome and the second downtown exit when she pulled her mouth mike down. She closed her eyes briefly, and when she opened them, her expression was grim.

"What is it?" he asked, not liking at all what he saw on her face.

She didn't answer for a moment, and when she

did, he could hear a slight tremor in her voice. "My ship is gone."

"What do you mean, gone?" He stopped himself from asking if it had been destroyed. This was a ship she'd said she'd spent years on. He was sure she had friends, and, experienced zombie hunter or not, contemplating the destruction of everyone she'd known for the past several years had to be horrifying. "Maybe it's in a different orbit?" he added lamely.

There was a bleakness in her eyes when she faced him. "My tech no longer picks up evidence of its existence in any orbit around your world. If they had to flash out, I'd have received an emergency notification, even with the transcomm inoperative. We have seeker 'droids for that purpose. You don't abandon a team—regulations define our emergency procedures." She held up her scanner. "The only thing I show now is this." She touched a pulsing teardrop shape on her screen. "It's a Tresh—a *possible* Tresh—resonance within range of where my ship was. Until I synchronize with the MOD-tech back at your structure, I won't know more."

Two more exits and they'd be almost home. A dozen insistent thoughts whirled through Theo's mind as he pushed the SUV's speed up over eighty, not the least of which was the possibility that Jorie Mikkalah might be spending the rest of her life on his planet. In Bahia Vista, Florida. As much as that oddly pleased him—logistical problems of her lack of verifiable citizenship aside—it had to terrify her.

The fact that his planet might now have little in

the way of defenses against not only the zombies but the Tresh came pretty close to terrifying him.

"It's time you told me everything, Jorie. And I mean everything." He shot her a determined glance as, slowing, he flicked on the SUV's turn signal. The Thirty-eighth Avenue North ramp was up ahead. "We have to work on the assumption your people can't help you at this point. Not with the zombies. Not with the Tresh. But my people can. You're going to have to ditch regulations, change the structure of this mission, and make us all part of your team."

Or all of us, Theo feared, reading all too well the expression on her face, *are going to die.*

"There is nothing your governments can do," she said, after a long moment of silence. "If the Tresh want to take your world, your cities, you don't have the weaponry to stop them. Regrets. I know that's not what you want me to say, but it's fact. We—the Chalvash Interplanetary Concord—were barely able to defeat them ten years ago. If they start a war against you, you will lose."

Theo hit the siren again as they came to the end of the ramp, anger supplanting the fear he'd felt moments before. Traffic moved out of his way as if it sensed the coming explosion. "God damn it, I refuse to give up and do nothing!"

"The Tresh hold no belief in deities. And I'm not advocating surrender. I do, however, want you to fully understand the situation. I'm the only one with any direct experience with the Tresh. I spent six years flying combat during the Border Wars. Both Kip Rordan and Tam are career Guardians. They know a lot about zombies, but they've never fought the Tresh."

Any more bad news? Theo turned onto his street and was slightly relieved by the lack of emergency vehicles. He had feared another scene like the one they'd left behind in Gulfview. "But they know how to shoot. I know how to shoot. And I can get you a lot more people who are trained, who know how to shoot."

"Petrakos, you do *not* hear my words! If Tresh ships are here and the *Sakanah* is gone, we cannot stop them by shooting handfuls of their people here and there. The only way we can stop them is by *thinking*. We must be smarter than they are. We must be more devious—you understand *devious*?"

"Completely. We have to find out their plans and use that against them." Finding out the Tresh's plans was something he believed Jorie could handle. Using everything his world had to offer to stop the Tresh was his area of expertise. Galactic baddies or not, starburst weapons or not, they were on his turf now.

His mind played with a few scenarios: Jorie locating Tresh hideouts like she'd done in Gulfview, Theo sending a SWAT team armed with Hazers in after them. More jamming scanners so they couldn't beam up and escape. Of course, Jorie would have to be the one to explain how to do that. But, hell, there had to be some special ops geek at MacDill AFB who could duplicate her scanner gizmo.

And what a coup Guardian tech would be for his country! Maybe he and Jorie would even get an invitation to the White House....

But there was a downside to his daydream. He sensed that but couldn't quite grasp what it was, and then they were approaching his house. He shifted his mind back to real time, daydreams and downsides forgotten.

He slowed. All appeared normal, but then, he honestly didn't know what to look for: an X-wing fighter parked on his front lawn? No starbursts appeared in his windows.

"Continue on," Jorie told him. "We—"

"Can't risk that the Tresh are inside and see us coming. We'll leave the car at the park and double back."

He backed the SUV into a parking space under a large oak tree, turned off the ignition, then hit the remote to open the rear door. Shaded from view by the tree and adjacent shrubbery, he retrieved her rifle and the G-Is from the cargo hatch, handing her weapons to her.

Jorie plucked his G-1 from his hand and touched two buttons on the side. "Now it's set back to stun," she said. "If the Tresh are there, we try to take them alive. We need to know what they know. But if there are serious problems," she pointed to the power buttons, "change settings to hard-terminate by pressing both."

He tapped his index finger on the buttons above the trigger and watched the power lights go from yellow to blue. It was an easy move. "Got it."

She held his gaze for a long moment. "You're very good at what you do, Sergeant Theo Petrakos. There may have been things I've said to make you feel I don't value you. That I don't respect your experience.

I want you to know that's not the truth. I value you more than you realize. And I am honored to have you not only on my team but," and she hesitated slightly, "I hope, as a friend."

Something in his chest tightened at her words and the emotion he heard underlying them. He pulled the rear hatch shut, then, before she could step away, reached over and cupped his hand around the side of her face. "I'm the one who's honored," he said, and didn't even try to hide the emotion in his voice. Then something about the way they were standing facing each other—facing danger, facing death—made him think of a line from a movie, even though this was a shady park in Bahia Vista and not the smoky interior of a bar in Casablanca. "Of all the crime scenes in all the towns in all the world, you had to walk into mine."

"Crime scenes?"

He sighed and patted her cheek gently. "Give me the rifle. My neighbors won't question my carrying it."

She hesitated for a moment, then, with a nod, handed it to him.

He locked the SUV and guided her on the grassy area along the curb and onto the brick-paved street. A little more than a day ago they'd walked this same path: he, fresh from his meeting with Doc White Braids, and she, having pulled some trickery to get him his laptop with the evidence tag.

It startled him to realize how much his life had changed in that short period of time. And how much a total stranger—an alien one-woman war machine—had come to mean to him.

She was, for all intents and purposes, alone on his world. Even if Tammy and Rordan were alive—and Theo had to work on the premise they might not be—Jorie could give the order to abandon the mission. There was no ship to report to, no captain to question her decision. He suspected—because they had set up Wayne in the rental—that they had some resources here. She could walk away and leave Theo and his world to fend for themselves.

Yet he knew in his gut she wouldn't. Even if she was the sole Guardian on his world, she would never stop fighting to protect his people. The very essence of Commander Jorie Mikkalah was a sense of honor and duty.

When everyone else would be running away from a crazed, worm-covered, razor-armed zombie, Theo knew Jorie would be running toward it.

Theo also knew he'd be at her side.

The brick-paved street that circled the park ended after half a block.

"We'll cut through my neighbors' yard, stay hidden by the bushes," he told her as they walked at a brisk clip. "Greg and Stacey are up north visiting relatives this week. Then we approach my house from the west, use that big tree"—*the one that the zombie shaved a fair chunk out of*—"as cover. If we come through the back door, the kitchen window is our only problem. But we can duck under that." Plus, his front screen door—his homemade intruder alarm—squealed like a cage full of screaming monkeys. But then, he never thought he'd be breaking into his own house.

For a moment he thought of the broken lock on his

bathroom window. But that would mean the two of them climbing through one by one. It would restrict access to their weapons if they needed them quickly. Not the best idea.

"Can you tell if the Tresh are already there?" he asked as Jorie hiked up the edge of her sweater and darted a glance at her scanner screen again. He thought for a moment about the implant in his shoulder. He suspected her gizmo controlled that too. But he no longer viewed her or that device as a threat, and not just because her ship was gone.

"If you hear the hum of laser fire, then they're there," she said grimly. "But at this distance, unless they're running a dead zone or some tech I can positively identify as Tresh, I can't. That's what I'm watching for, what I saw earlier—something that shouldn't be there. But they wouldn't be here to appropriate your residence. They'd kill or kidnap my team, take the data from my MOD-tech, and leave."

It had been at least forty minutes since Jorie had last heard from Tammy. Chances were good they were either going to walk into the middle of a fire-fight or a morgue. Great.

A blue Chevy minivan loaded with kids in the back and two women in the front seat breezed by. Theo recognized the driver as he casually put his arm around Jorie, shielding their weapons: a young legal secretary who lived with her schoolteacher husband and their twin boys a block away. He'd seen them many times rollerblading together. Now the mom and boys were out with a friend and her kids, proba-bly heading for the mall to see Santa. The normality of their activity made his own seem that much more bizarre.

Dear Santa, All I want for Christmas is a container of double-stack Hazer rifles so I can kill all the zombies, and a couple of intergalactic starships to blow holes in the Tresh fleet.

It wasn't a fleet they'd face in his house, though, but a Tresh team who looked human, according to what Jorie had told him. And if her ship had realized the Tresh were here, they might have sent down reinforcements. He hoped. "If we come into the middle of a fight, how will I know a Tresh from one of your people?" he asked, stepping back from her again as the minivan passed. "I couldn't see them at that house. Do they wear specific uniforms?" *Or have fangs like vampires?* He remembered her remark about their sensitivity to light.

"If they're operating covertly in a nil environment, no. They'd adopt your mode of dress, as my agent did."

"Dan Wayne." He almost said Mr. Crunchy but caught himself in time. "So how will I know?"

She slanted him a glance, then pointed to her eye with her index finger. "The color of their eyes shimmers. Iridescent? You know this word?"

"Like a rainbow," he said, taking her arm and pulling her into Greg's empty driveway, catching a glimpse of the front of his house as he did so. All still appeared normal. Quiet. He hoped it wasn't the quiet of death. "Blue, green, purple, yellow—"

"To me, sunbow. But Tresh eyes aren't so bright. The colors are more muted, and they shift and change. It's also why they cannot see in planetary daylight."

"And that's it? Nothing else?"

A slight shrug. "Only their beauty."

He turned the corner and stopped at Greg's back steps. "Beauty?" After seeing the zombies, her comment was unexpected.

"Beauty. They're incredibly, flawlessly beautiful." She tilted her face and looked up at him. "Does your world believe in angelic beings, Theo?"

"Angels? Yeah." He'd been shooting at angels in Gulfview?

"The Tresh are a visual heaven. But in truth, they're the living embodiment of hell."

He headed for the tall oleander hedge that separated Greg's property from his. It seemed illogical that an entire race or breed or whatever the Tresh were could be uniformly beautiful. But a lot of what Theo had long accepted as fact—or as impossible—had been blown out of the water when he'd stepped off that transporter platform and followed his one-woman war machine into that ready room with its view of the star-studded galaxy.

"I know they have weapons, lasers. But are they trained in hand-to-hand combat?" he asked, handing the double-barreled rifle back to her when they reached the wall of shrubbery. Maybe they had other handicaps besides limited day vision.

She glanced at the Hazer's yellow lights, then looped the strap over her head. "They're masters in the art of pain."

And Jorie wanted to take them alive. Oh, Christ. For the second time in one hour, he wished he had his tac vest. He thrust the laser pistol into the waistband of his jeans and double-checked the Glock in his hip holster. That had only one setting, but he'd try real hard not to kill any Tresh unless he had to. Unless one threatened Jorie. Then all bets—and promises to try to capture one alive—would be off.

15

The street cop called Theo Petrakos wanted to be first through his kitchen door, gun out, clearing each room for Jorie. But Detective Sergeant Petrakos knew Jorie had a much better chance of recognizing her own people and assessing any potential Tresh threat than he did. So—with great reluctance—he shoved his ego into his back pocket, kept his Glock holstered, and agreed to let her take point. He'd follow and cover her with the laser pistol on stun.

They reached the corner of his house and stopped. She pulled her scanner out.

"Dead zone?" he whispered, not sure if a yes was good or bad news.

She shook her head. "Only my MOD-tech. Nothing from the ship. No response from my team's transcomms."

"And people?"

"Incomplete data." She frowned, tapping the

screen, then: "Tamlynne." There was hope in her voice. "I'm reading Tamlynne!"

Tammy was in there but not answering. If she was singing in the shower and unaware anyone was trying to reach her, he'd gladly help Jorie bust her lieutenant down to ensign.

"Okay," he said. "Let's go."

They flanked his back door for a moment, listening. No cursing, no crashing of furniture. But that was the way fights happened in his world, not hers. He remembered the soft, eerie hum of the laser fire as it split the air in Gulfview. It gave a whole new meaning to the term *deathly quiet*.

At her nod he yanked the screen door open, then, as it bumped against his shoulder, twisted the doorknob and shoved. She inched in quickly, crouching, pistol out, eyes narrowed, focused.

He muffled the sound of the door closing with his foot and then was right behind her, swinging his laser pistol opposite to hers, looking left when she looked right. His kitchen was empty, a half-filled glass of water sitting on the drainboard by the sink. He saw her eyes widen as she stared at it. He didn't know why, but it was important. And it troubled her.

She squatted down quickly on the right side of the doorway to his living room, motioning for him to follow suit.

He dropped down, one shoulder against the refrigerator, adrenaline surging.

And then he realized what else was wrong. It was too quiet. Every other time the space commandos had been in his back bedroom, he'd had to keep the kitchen radio on to mask their conversation.

There was no sound in his house. None at all. Not even the shower running.

With a sinking feeling Theo realized they had come back too late. He was about to walk in on his second homicide crime scene in two days. But the killers would never be brought to justice.

Jorie switched her pistol to her left hand and brought the scanner up in her right. She balanced it on her thigh and tapped furiously at it, frowning, glancing up in the direction of his living room, then frowning again.

Finally she stopped and brought her hand and the pistol to her lips in a clumsy signal for silence. At least, that's what he hoped she was signaling.

He nodded.

She tapped the scanner one more time, then let it fall back to her side. Quickly she switched her pistol to her right hand, raising her left, five fingers splayed. Then four, three, two . . . one.

A high-pitched squeal reverberated through his house, damned near—he was sure—cracking his windows. It hurt his ears like hell, but she was rising and so was he. Diversion tactics, he guessed. She swept into his living room, hugging the walls. Theo was on her heels, swinging around, pistol out, double-checking for anything in the shadows. For once, he was glad there was very little furniture for anyone to hide behind.

She flattened herself against the wall by the entrance to his short hallway. He sidled up next to her just as the squealing abruptly ceased. Just as something or someone moved like a blur past them into the living room.

Without hesitation, Jorie fired. The woman—Theo saw now that it was a woman—spun, twisting, raising a square black pistol in her hand. Theo pulled off two shots, center mass. The woman's arm jerked up as she fell, gun tumbling from her fingers, platinum shoulder-length curls flaring out around one of the most incredibly beautiful faces Theo had ever seen.

This was a Tresh?

"Watch her!" Jorie's voice was a low rasp. She snatched the small black pistol from the floor, then hitched up her sweater and pushed it into her belt.

Theo stared at the Tresh woman lying motionless in front of his television. But breathing: he could see the rise and fall of her chest under her pink *Life's a Beach* T-shirt. She looked like a Victoria's Secret model lying there. No, she looked better than any Victoria's Secret model he'd ever seen. Perfectly sculpted, classical features. Long legs encased in white jeans, slender waist, and one helluva rack.

Damn.

Then a noise in his hallway had him and Jorie flattening themselves against the wall again.

Next victim, he thought, wondering how many more cover-model types were in his bedrooms. He and Jorie could simply stand here and pick them off one by one as they came out of the hallway.

But, of course, the Tresh had to realize that too. Then it would turn into a standoff until he and Jorie could force them out of the rooms. A smoke bomb or tear gas would come in real handy then. Or maybe a row of high-intensity UV lights. Unfortunately, he had none of those.

But this blonde had been stupid enough to come out. Maybe the others would too. Jorie had said they couldn't beat the Tresh by outshooting them but rather by outthinking them. If this was any indication of Tresh thought processes, this wasn't going to be difficult at all. All they had to do was wait.

Unless—*shit for brains*—they climbed out the windows, like the one in his bathroom, and came in through the front or back door. Jorie had said they could withstand sunlight for a minute or two. And that's about all it would take.

Watch your six.

He spun back, heart pounding, pistol aimed at the kitchen doorway just as Jorie's scanner emitted two short screeches from under her sweater.

She holstered her pistol and brought her rifle up in a smooth, practiced move.

But it was too late.

The Tresh didn't need to use the windows.

A tanned, pale-haired man shimmered into existence in the far corner of Theo's living room, just to the right of his leather sofa, looking like he stepped off the cover of *GQ* magazine. The man jerked his short rifle up, and a bright starburst flared from the muzzle.

Theo hit the floor, firing, as behind him a woman screamed in pain.

The first of Jorie's shots missed as she dropped to the floor, partly shielded by Theo's chair. Laser fire slashed overhead. But the second from her specially modified double-stack Hazer punched through the

shields—L-1s, according to her rifle's readouts—
around the Tresh Devastator. A Devastator! She
should have guessed that elite squad would be involved. In the back of her mind, she thought she recognized the male as he staggered, but it had been ten
years. There wasn't time to dig out a name or rank.
Theo was on the floor off to her right, firing, and
somewhere else in the structure a female was screaming.

Hell's wrath. Tam.

Jorie thumbed the Hazer to hard-terminate as she
came up on her knees next to the chair. She had one
live Tresh—the unknown female. This one could be
permitted to die. The male, stunned but still standing, swung around toward Theo. "Terminate!" she
shouted, and put two blasts at his back, decimating
his shield completely. Theo's laser flared blue—and
fatal—against the Tresh's chest.

The male bucked, writhing. Jorie sprang to her
feet, but Theo was faster, knocking the rifle from the
male's grip and pointing his laser at his head.

Only as the male lay sprawled—unmoving—on
the floor did his name come to her: Cordo Sem. A
Tresh Devastator she'd sworn she'd kill if she ever
saw him again.

She'd just gotten her wish. But if Sem was here,
that meant...

She bolted into the hallway, heart in her throat.
She knew who had Tam.

The back bedroom was empty, her MOD-tech
shattered in pieces. She swiveled around, searching
for clues. She didn't know who'd destroyed the equipment: Kip and Tam, picking up the Tresh emissions

and not wanting to lead them to the *Sakanah* and Jorie; or the Tresh, spiteful and angry. It didn't matter. The deed was done.

The *Sakanah* was no longer there to render aid, anyway.

So that left only Theo's personal bedroom. They wouldn't have transported Tam or Kip back to their ship. She realized something she should have already figured out, something that hit her the moment she recognized Cordo Sem. Old scores had not been settled. They'd tracked her down. They wanted revenge.

Another scream.

Hell's fire. These monsters stopped at nothing.

Jorie stepped quickly but cautiously into the hallway just as Theo did. Sem's rifle strap was draped over Theo's shoulder, his laser pistol at the ready, chest heaving. She held up one hand.

"My game." She wasn't sure he understood.

"Jorie—"

Stars, the worry on his face pulled at her heart. "Mine," she repeated, her voice shaking. "They have Tam." She hoped to find Kip Rordan in the room too. Hoped her scanner was malfunctioning and just not picking up his readings. "They want me. This is mine to do. Watch the Tresh female. Stun her again if necessary." She moved toward his bedroom door, knowing full well what lay behind it.

It was time. In fact, it was ten years overdue.

"Jorie—"

"No," she said firmly, pointing to the female on the floor. "Watch her. We need her alive." Then she kicked in the door to Theo's bedroom, her double-stack raised and ready.

Devastator Senior Agent Davin Prow filled her sights, his angelic smile beaming from where he stood over Tamlynne Herryck, a restrainer field pinning her to the floor. Another shield glistened around him. The readout on her Hazer's tiny screen showed it to be a Level-2 Defensive, stronger than the one around Sem. Gritting her teeth, she checked fire—he was too close to Tam, the two fields intertwining. A familiar Devastator maneuver, where an attack on the Tresh agent kills the hostage.

"Lieutenant—no, forgive me, *Commander* Mikkalah." Davin Prow gave a slight nod of his darkly handsome, square-jawed face. "A pleasure to see you again."

Jorie took her eyes off Prow—and the small laser pistol in his hand—only to glance down for a few seconds. Tam was alive. Bruised but alive. There was no sign of Rordan or Trenat. She couldn't think about them now. She had to concentrate on getting Tam out of here without getting them both killed by Prow.

She'd done it before.

Though where'd they go—*no, don't think about that. Don't think about the ship. Just get Tam and get out alive.*

"What do you want?" she asked him, her finger lightly on the trigger button of her rifle. Prow was a top agent, but she doubted he could tell by looking at her Hazer that it had been modified and could punch holes in damned near any shielding he erected—even an L-2, though it would take several shots. But until he moved away from Tam, she was forced to hold back. "I'd say I'm flattered you came all this way, after all this time, just because of me. But I very much doubt that's why you're here."

"Judging from the tech you've transported down to this structure, I'd guess you know very well why we're here. Your being here, however, is the added honeyfroth on the pudding. It makes my mission that much sweeter."

She watched him, assessing him while he spoke. She'd always been fast with her pistol. So had he. It had been ten years, but she was willing to bet his reflexes hadn't slowed any more than hers had.

So why hadn't he fired on her when she kicked in the door? She was unshielded. Then she saw why. His pistol—a newer configuration of the powerful Slayer 6-1—would create too much backwash if fired through a Level-2 personal defensive shield. He'd have to drop the L-2 to fire.

So he wasn't here as an assassin, like Cordo Sem. He hadn't drawn her in here to kill her. Yet.

Interesting.

"What do you want?" she repeated, only then realizing they'd been conversing entirely in Vekran—a language the Tresh were rarely integrated for.

That told her something else. Prow and the Tresh had been on this planet for at least as long as the Guardians had, if not longer.

"You're alone on this nil world. I'm sure that fact has come to your attention."

Did you destroy my ship? The question was on the tip of her tongue, but she held back. Prow would lie, or, rather, he'd tell her whatever would make her easier to manipulate. Which was, yes, that the *Sakanah* was gone.

"I've worked solo or with a small team before."

"They're not coming back for you, Mikkalah."

Because they flashed out or because you destroyed them? She shrugged. "Someone will. I can wait. I've waited in worse places." *Like your prison compound.*

"Waiting is a waste of your time and considerable talents. Talents we recognize and could use." He smiled at her, and killfrost spun its way up the crevices of her spine. "I have an offer."

"I'm not interested."

"You haven't heard it."

"I don't have to."

He stepped to his left, his L-2 undulating as he moved. Jorie could hear Tam's harsh, strained breathing. *Hang on, Tam.* All Jorie needed was for him to take two more steps. One might even do. Her modified Hazer packed one hell's wrath of a punch he wouldn't expect. Hopefully it would get to him before he had time to respond.

She could also use Theo's bed between them for cover and, if Prow was still standing, her Hazer could keep him away from Tam while she set off another earsplitter—all that Tresh beauty came with a price—from the MOD-tech behind him. Tech he hadn't destroyed because he hadn't had time? Or because he knew what she knew about the zombies? And he needed it like she did?

"Respectfully, I disagree," he was saying. "You do need to listen."

Respectfully? Jorie would have laughed out loud,

but that would require her closing her eyes, however briefly. She couldn't do that.

"Your charm overwhelms me. Release my lieutenant. That might put me in a more blissful frame of mind."

"I fear it's a bit too late for that. And her."

No, don't look down. He wants you distracted.

She saw him tap a small band on his wrist. And she heard a corresponding thin, keening wail from Tam, followed by a harsh panting. Then a short, very soft two-tone chime.

Bile rose in her stomach. She knew that sound. A Devastator restrainer implant recycling up to the next power level. If her hands had been free, Jorie knew one would already be clasping the scar near her neck.

"Kill her and you'll have nothing to bargain with," she said harshly.

"Isn't that like *negotiate*? Sorry, not in my vocabulary." Prow touched his wrist.

Tam screamed.

"Stop it, Prow!"

"The memory never fades, does it? You know exactly what she's going through." He moved his fingers to his wrist again as he stepped toward her. Away from Tam. "Are you ready to listen to me now?"

It was the only chance she had. She had to let him touch the implant signal. She had to pray that, in that microsecond, he'd be focused on the implant, and his reflexes with his pistol would be just that much slower than hers.

Head shot. The rifle would lose a little after breaking through the shielding, but a head shot was her best chance. She watched his fingers. *Forgive me, Tamlynne. But it's going to hurt for a little longer.*

"Go to hell," she told him through gritted teeth.

Prow's shield suddenly flared bright red and he staggered back, body twisting at the waist, iridescent eyes wide in surprise.

Out of the corner of her eye Jorie recognized Theo, his large projectile weapon clutched in both hands. Theo moving steadily toward her out of his bathroom doorway.

Prow stumbled, one hand now clutching his shoulder. Blood gushed between his fingers as if he'd been stabbed. No, not stabbed—shot by Theo's niltech pistol. How and why that was, she had no time to consider. Prow raised his weapon.

Jorie darted sideways and fired, Hazer energy boring a yellow ringed hole in the already disintegrating L-2 shield. Prow ducked, twisting again. Another loud crack from her left. Another red flare.

Prow screamed something into his transcomm, and before she could get him in her sights again, he was gone.

The restrainer field around Tamlynne Herryck evaporated with his departure.

"Tam!" Jorie dropped to her knees, pressing her hand against her lieutenant's pale, damp face. The woman shivered, convulsions starting. There was no time to deal with them. The Tresh could be back at any moment. She had to secure the structure.

"Theo—"

But he was already there beside her, on his knees.

"She's going to convulse," she told him quickly.

"Keep her stable. Don't let her hurt herself. I have to set shields around your structure. Then I can help."

She sprang to her feet, lunging for the row of tech along the wall. She pushed her mouth mike into place, and with three words she segued her scanner to the larger tech units and continued to work voice commands while her fingers keyed in overrides.

Theo's structure wasn't large. She could lock it down for now. The Tresh might eventually unscramble her shielding, but it would buy her time. Time to get help for Tam. Time to search for Rordan.

"Grid One in place. Grid Two." She spoke out loud, hoping Tam could hear her and would know what her commander was doing, why she wasn't at her side. "Grid Three. Holding, locking. Grid Four. Almost there. Locking now. Grid Five. Synchronizing. Holding. Locking." She took one last look at the security pattern, checking for breaches. "We're secure."

She sucked in a long breath and pulled her hand away from the screen. It was shaking.

She turned around. Theo had wrapped a blanket around Tamlynne and was holding her head back, keeping her airway clear. He glanced at her.

"The Tresh can't beam back in?"

"Not now," Jorie said, crouching down beside them, scanner out. She picked up the resonance of the unit Prow had injected in Tam almost immediately. "He put an implant in her," she told Theo as the scanner searched through hundreds of combinations to find the right code to neutralize the implant. "Like yours. Except—"

"Much worse."

"Much." A series of numbers fell into line, then vanished. No. Close, but not the code. Vomit-brained whore spawns!

"You had an implant," Theo said. "A Tresh one—not one like mine."

She pulled her attention from the screen and looked at him. He must have heard her conversation with Prow while he was in his bathroom. How had he gotten in there? And how had he destroyed an L-2 shield? Questions she needed answered—later. "I was taken prisoner by the Tresh during the war. They put an implant in me, yes."

He just nodded, his eyes darkening with emotion.

She went back to her screen. She didn't want his pity.

More numbers lined up. She held her breath. Could it be . . . ? Yes. Yes. The implant's power field dropped down three levels. Tam's shuddering halted, and her cries of anguish were replaced by soft moans. Jorie couldn't shut down the Tresh restrainer completely. But she could at least make the pain somewhat bearable, until a med-tech . . .

"Will she be okay?" Theo touched Jorie's arm.

"I . . . For now." There were no Guardian med-techs here. And, depending on what kind of signal she could rig from whatever tech remained, it could be months, even a year, before a Guardian ship could find them. *Damn you, Prow!*

"What's wrong?" Theo asked softly.

Damn you, Petrakos, she wanted to say. *Sometimes I swear you read my mind.*

"Can you put her on the bed? If she's warm and she sleeps, it will be better."

Theo lifted Tam gently, Jorie unwrapping the blanket as he did so. Then she tucked it around Tam again as Theo pushed a pillow under the lieutenant's curls. Tam whimpered, but exhaustion and pain took its toll. Her eyes fluttered closed.

Jorie ran through the codes two more times but found nothing better. She put her scanner on the bedside table. Its signal would block the implant as best it could until she could rig a dedicated unit out of what was left of the tech in the spare room.

"It's still hurting her." It wasn't a question. Theo seemed to know Jorie couldn't shut down the implant.

"That's not the only problem." She ran both hands through her hair, her muscles suddenly taught with anger. "It will kill her. Two, three days. If we don't disengage it, it will kill her. And the ship, my med-techs, aren't here to help. Damn it!" She spun away from him, from Tam lying helpless in the wide bed, and headed for the hall, chest tight, eyes blurring.

Theo caught up with her at the doorway, one arm circling her waist, the other around her back, gathering her and her rifle against him, hard. For a moment she stiffened, wanting to pull away, but she didn't. She couldn't. Theo's face—that very good face—was in her hair. He whispered her name, telling her, "Hush, it will be all right."

It would not be all right. Her ship was gone. The Tresh were here. The zombies were in Tresh control. She was stuck on a nil world. Her top lieutenant and close friend was dying. And she had no idea if Kip and Jacare were even alive.

So she clung to Theo, her good friend Theo, just for a moment. Clung to his reassuring warmth and hard-muscled strength and closed her eyes, tucking her face against his neck.

It would not be all right. But at least for the next few moments, she was not alone.

"Hush, Jorie."

She raised her face. "I have more problems. And work to do."

He brought his hands to rest on her shoulders. "We have work to do. And we'll solve these problems together. But first," and he grinned sheepishly, "I have to rescue my laser pistol. It, uh, got wedged behind the toilet when I climbed through the bathroom window to try to sneak up on Prow."

"You climbed through . . . ?" Jorie shook her head distractedly at his embarrassment and at the mental picture of Theo's large form squeezing through the small opening. "Why didn't you use the Tresh rifle?" It was still draped across his chest.

"I've never shot it."

She'd forgotten, again, that he was a nil. "I'll show you later," she said, and stepped into the hallway, her mind already sorting through plans, options. A bit of bliss luck: they'd acquired two more weapons. But their locale was her immediate concern. Theo's residence was small enough; she might be able to set the shields in a randomizer pattern that would baffle the Tresh for a good long while. That would provide her with a secure base of operations but would also limit her movements.

A lot also depended on how large a base the Tresh had here. They must have more than that house she'd found. Obviously the Guardians had underestimated them. Interrogating the Tresh female could—

She stopped in the main room. The female wasn't on the floor. Hell's wrath! She flipped the Hazer back to stun, turning quickly. "Petrakos!"

Quick footsteps from the hall behind her. "Here. What—"

Jorie glanced over her shoulder at him. "Where is she?"

"She?" He had his G-1 out now. "Fuck."

Jorie understood the emotion behind the word if not the meaning.

Theo crossed the room and stopped at the galley doorway, his weapon angled against his chest. Jorie sprinted behind him, listening for the same thing he was: a Tresh female, waiting for them.

She heard nothing. She checked the readout on her Hazer, looking for the possible resonance of an L-1 or L-2 shield—the best she could hope for without her weapon pointed at a target. Nothing again. She signaled her lack of information to Theo with a shake of her head and a slight shrug, then flipped her oc-set into place.

"On three." His voice was barely above a whisper. "One. Two—"

He swept into the galley, moving right. She followed, going left. The galley was empty. They both spun slowly around one more time, then lowered their weapons.

"Shit," Theo said through tight lips. Jorie held back from pointing out that while a spoor trail would certainly be helpful in finding the female, the Tresh didn't routinely leave behind excrement in their wakes. She'd begun to figure out that references to deities, excrement, and certain other bodily functions, when uttered in anger, were a sign of intense displeasure on this world.

"Let's recheck the house." Theo pushed past her, out of the galley. Jorie hurried after him. Five minutes later they were in the galley again.

Theo leaned against the counter next to the water dispenser and shook his head. "My fault. I take responsibility. She was out cold. I even cuffed her." His eyes narrowed. "Bitch has my best cuffs. Unless..."

He was reaching for the door to go outside when Jorie grabbed his arm.

"Don't! Your structure's shielded."

He shot her a puzzled look, brow furrowing slightly. She stepped in front of him and pulled at the door. "Here." She took his wrist and brushed the back of his hand against the faint haze visible through the ocular over her right eye.

He jerked back with a short yelp. An alarm wailed briefly from the bedroom, then silenced. "That could be a problem if one of my neighbors comes over unexpectedly. Is there any way we could set it to only zap the Tresh?"

"No, but I can reset the security perimeter to within your structure's wall. Or only around specific rooms," Jorie told him, again damning the fact she had to operate in a nil environment and not a military one. "But then you'll have to be more careful." He didn't have an ocular and couldn't see the shield as she could.

Theo gingerly pushed the door closed. "I can deal with that better than I can deal with an innocent neighbor getting fried. Besides, if that Tresh woman does come back in, she's not going to be much of a threat with her hands cuffed behind her back."

Jorie sagged back against the galley table, perching one hip on its edge. "I don't think she's out there. Sem's body is gone. The Tresh must have transported them while I was confronting Prow." And before she'd locked the structure down in a grid shield. Damn! Hell and damn. Eight years of hunting zombies with the Guardians and she'd gone soft on tactics against the Tresh.

Theo had been staring out the door's viewport. He turned to her. "Tell me about Prow and the other two Tresh."

"They're Tresh Devastators. An elite force. You understand—"

"Elite. Yes. Just go on. If I don't understand something, I'll ask."

Both their language skills had improved. One less thing to have to compensate for.

"I only recognized the two males: Cordo Sem, the one we terminated in the main room. And Prow. Davin Prow. He's Sem's superior, or was. I have no reason to think that's changed. Their presence tells me this is a very serious operation. It also tells me they're close to completion or the Devastators wouldn't be here. They're not an advance team. You noticed Prow spoke Vekran?"

"I heard him speak English, yeah. No offense, but he has no accent. I understood him better than I do you."

"He's integrated—the Devastators can do that."

"Integrated?"

Yes, of course, was on the tip of her tongue, but she stopped. The way Theo moved, the way he handled weapons, the way he almost unconsciously seemed to pick up on what needed to be done kept lulling her into a false sense of who and what he was. A male from a nil planet who knew nothing of the past several hundred years in the Chalvash System, who'd never heard of the council or the Tresh Border Wars.

She sought the words she needed in Vekran, then simplified them as best she could. "It's like another kind of implant, but one that enhances his brain's natural abilities. A Tresh agent qualifies for this implant when he reaches Devastator status."

"A built-in translator?"

"Yes. Among other functions."

"Like?" he prompted.

She shrugged. The variations were so vast. "It depends on the parameters of the original bioprofile."

A slight drawing down of dark brows. "You're telling me the Tresh are biologically engineered?"

Ah! "You have that technology here, then?" There'd been nothing on that in Danjay's reports. But perhaps Theo's security status afforded him access to that information.

"Rudimentary. Cloning of farm animals, that kind of thing. But it's not common. And it's never used with people. Humans."

"It's very common in most technologically advanced systems. To the Tresh it's—how is it said on Vekris?—the highest art."

Theo nodded slowly. "They're all perfect. By deliberate design."

"Devastators most of all. If there's a lack—as in linguistic abilities—it's augmented biomechanically." She watched his face. He was still nodding.

"Got it," he said after a moment. "So these Devastators came here already programmed to speak my language."

No, he hadn't quite acquired knowledge, and she told him so. "Programmed to learn your culture and your language—which is very similar to Vekran, as you know—at a faster rate. From his fluency I'd say he's been here longer than Danjay was. Which now also makes me question the zombie attack that killed him." Something hovered at the edges of her mind again. She tried to focus and articulate it. "It didn't seem right somehow. Danjay wasn't stupid. We flew together. He was my gunner and—"

And Prow knew that as well. Prow had had the files on her entire squadron and had taken great pride in showing them to her. And had no doubt integrated them into his memory.

"And?" Theo prompted.

"And Prow knew that if I was on the *Sakanah,* Danjay's death would bring me dirtside." She'd been so blind, so very blind. Like everyone else, she viewed the Tresh problem as solved. What else had she missed?

"You mean you specifically? Or the Guardians?"

"We've been here for almost four of your months. The Tresh could have called their ships in to confront us at any point." And they hadn't. Another puzzle. "But Danjay's death..." She shook her head, her mind still sorting through everything. "I think that was aimed at me specifically." She looked up at him, wondering how he'd perceive her when she told him why. Yes, he was in his planet's security force. But he'd explained that his duties were protection. She'd been an assassin. "I killed Prow's brother."

"Because of your war—"

"Nikah Prow wasn't a Devastator. He was a medtech who designed the restrainer implants the Tresh use. It was happenstance my team came across him during a raid on a Tresh station. We were after their data. We had no indication he would be in the lab complex. I made the decision to take him with us. That was my error. It cost us time to subdue him. The Devastator team almost caught us. So I needed a diversion and decided he was it. I put him—bound—into an airlock and rigged a small explosive to the outer hatch. I knew his brother would stop to rescue him. They were"—Jorie put her index fingers side by side—"twins."

"Go on."

"I knew his brother would try to rescue him. I knew about how long it would take for them to open the door we'd jammed. At six seconds to go, I blew the outer hatch and spaced him." She watched Theo's face and then, when she saw little change, remembered where she was. His people might have more technological experience than she'd first surmised, but Theo most likely had no direct experience with what happens to a live body when it's sucked into the vacuum of deep space.

"It is," she continued, "a very horrible way to die. A horrible thing to witness. I'm not proud of what I did. But it bought us time. And..." She closed her eyes briefly. "And I kept thinking of all my people who'd been tortured by the device he'd perfected. I was angry. I wanted him to suffer. I wanted his brother to suffer."

"That saved the lives of your team, allowed you to escape."

"We would have escaped anyway. Using Nikah Prow as a diversion gave us the time we needed. I had no reason to space him other than"—she drew a short breath—"other than I wanted to."

"Was this before or after his brother took you prisoner?"

"Before."

"And he didn't try to kill you for that?"

A faint smile twisted her lips. "Personally, Davin hates me for killing Nikah. But he's a Tresh Devastator. Professionally, he appreciates a job well done."

Theo was silent for a long moment. "And now he wants you to work with him."

"Believe nothing a Tresh says, unless it's 'I'm going to kill you.'" She shoved herself away from the table. The condemnation she'd halfway expected to hear from Theo over her actions hadn't materialized. That made her feel marginally better, but she still wasn't sure he fully understood what she'd done. Though he seemed to grasp why. "I have to check on Tamlynne."

"Jorie." His voice stopped her in the doorway. She turned, expecting a question about Nikah Prow's death. "Your ship's gone. All we have is you and Tammy. If you accept his offer, will that protect my city, my world?"

His words jolted her. She stared at him hard, part

of her recognizing it was merely a question. He was a nil. Security trained or not, he didn't know. But another part of her wanted to lunge at him and plant her fist in his face.

She could face his condemnation for being an assassin. She could not live with being a traitor.

She flexed her right hand. "I have to check on Tamlynne. And reset the shields." She spun away from him and this time ignored the sound of her name—and the pain in her heart.

16

The shields were easy to reset within the structure's walls, taking less than five minutes of her time. But the scanner hadn't been able to devise a better combination, even after twenty minutes of intense concentration on Jorie's part. The implant in Tamlynne's shoulder still pulsed pain—with spikes of death—into her system.

Tamlynne's eyelids fluttered briefly, then closed again, when Jorie lay her hand on Tam's forehead. Sleep was a good escape. But eventually even sleep would fail to provide respite.

Jorie sat on the edge of the bed, fighting waves of exhaustion and frustration. Right now she'd gladly trade all her weapons for a med-tech's JS-6-4. Then she'd have a chance of removing the unit. She was wondering if she could somehow modify her scanner into even a basic JS-6-1, when Theo appeared in the doorway.

"I had to ask about Prow's offer," he said, coming to stand beside her. "I have to explore all options."

Jorie adjusted the blanket around Tamlynne without looking at him. She didn't know what she'd see on his face—suspicion? Dismay? Or perhaps neither, just a basic devotion to duty, something she was supposed to understand. Most times she did, except when it came to Theo Petrakos. Being with him set off a chain of unsettling emotions she did not want to—*could not*—deal with at the moment. "I cannot make decisions for you or your people, Petrakos. Perhaps that best be said now. But the Tresh are not and will never be an option for me or any Guardian."

Tam uttered a soft moan, then shivered. Jorie's throat tightened. She'd lost team members before. She didn't know a Guardian—or a marine—who hadn't. But there was something different about dying in the heat of battle, leaving this existence kicking and screaming, and succumbing slowly, helplessly, to pulses of unending pain.

And something was even worse about losing Tam after just losing Danjay. She was still trying to process his death, going over and over in her mind if she'd done something wrong. Or if she hadn't done something that might have kept him alive.

And then there was Kip Rordan. What limited scans she could perform gave no hints of his whereabouts or his fate.

"What are the Tresh doing here?" Theo's question brought her out of her dark ruminations.

"Prow didn't share that information with me. I can only guess."

"Then *guess*." Theo's voice was insistent. "It's crunch time, Jorie. Do or die."

She did look at him this time and saw the intensity in his dark eyes, the taut line of his mouth. "I need data in order to formulate my guesses."

She stepped away from Tam's still form on the bed, then hunkered down in front of her array of MOD-tech on the floor. She pulled up her mouth mike and spoke soft commands in Alarsh. Data rose and merged, scenarios and probabilities appeared. Her tech continued to pick up energy streams even after the Tresh had destroyed the main units in the other room. Why Prow had left these untouched...

It may have been simply that their return interrupted his plans. Or it might be something else.

She went back to her data, peripherally aware of Theo prowling about his structure—but evidently remembering her warning about the structure's shielding, because she heard no curse-filled yelps or jangling alarms. Which was just as well. She didn't want to think about Sergeant Theo Petrakos, because when she thought about him, she felt things. And she couldn't afford that luxury now. Her worries about her ship, about Tam, Kip, and Jacare could overwhelm her if she let them. Her disappointment in Theo Petrakos—*If you accept his offer, will that protect my city, my world?*—threatened to choke her.

For no reason! He was a nil, a damned nil. Nothing more.

Except...

A soft nudge against her arm. Th—Petrakos with a glass of ice water. "You want something to eat? It's almost seven. Dinnertime."

She accepted the water and sipped at it.

Then her scanner emitted three strident tones.

She dropped the water glass, aware of its thud against the floor, aware of the slosh of the precious, invaluable liquid against her skin. She didn't care. The harsh tones signaled a medical emergency.

Tamlynne Herryck had stopped breathing.

Jorie shot to her feet, heart pounding, and was at Tam's side in three long steps. She grabbed her scanner, saw the ineffectual codes, and damned the fact she had no functional med-kit in the structure. Her skin chilled in spite of the anger welling up inside her as she worked frantically to reset the codes and block the implant.

"What's the matter?" Theo clasped her shoulder.

"Respiratory failure! And this unit won't—"

Theo shoved her aside and grasped Tamlynne's face, one hand over her lieutenant's nose, his mouth covering hers, forcing his breath. . . .

Manual resuscitation. It was such an antiquated method that it took Jorie a few shocked seconds to process what she was seeing. She'd seen teachtapes of the method but never used it. With med-'droids or med-techs everywhere—even during the war—there'd been no need.

Until now.

She prayed it worked. She tore her gaze away from Theo breathing life into Tamlynne and concentrated again on the scanner. She had to weaken the implant, decrease its output. The jamming codes the scanner had produced weren't sufficient. She needed a damned JS-unit. Unless she could somehow bypass the units codes altogether and—

"Keep her alive!" she rasped at Theo, and lunged back at her tech stacked along the wall. There had to be something in the emergency datafiles, even though this was all Guardian tech—Guardians who were concerned only with destroying the zombies. Not with confronting the Tresh. If she could access the ship . . .

But she couldn't. She barked search terms into her mouth mike, barely waiting for the results of one query to appear before demanding the next. Ten, twelve years ago she'd have had this information at her fingertips. But she was no longer in the marines, with intelligence data on the Tresh coming in daily.

If she didn't find those Tresh overrides, Tamlynne would die.

"She's breathing on her own." Theo sounded hoarse but elated.

Jorie glanced at him over her shoulder, relief rising, then waning. "It won't last. This is the first of many attacks. It just happened sooner than I expected."

Theo dropped down on the edge of the bed, hands against his thighs, head slightly bowed. His shoulders sagged, then he turned and seemed to study Tam's still form. Jorie shared his frustration. The anger—and helplessness—inside her seethed so virulently, she felt that if a zombie were to appear in the room right now, she was perfectly capable of tearing the thing apart with her bare hands.

But that wouldn't help Tamlynne.

"I thought that buffered the pain," he said, turning back and pointing to her scanner on the bedside table.

"Only temporarily. I told you—"

"Yeah. It will kill her." He wiped one hand over his face. "So what do we do?"

"I'm trying to find override codes. The Guardians were never involved in the war with the Tresh. They don't archive data on them like the Kedrian Marines do. If the ship were here, I could access its library or link to the military libraries at Central Command. But—"

"Can we remove the implant?"

"Remove?"

"Your med-tech put one inside me. How does it come out?"

"With a JS-Six-Four," and as she said it she knew that meant nothing to him. "It's essentially a miniature PMaT. I don't have one."

"How about surgically?" Theo made a cutting motion with his hand down his shoulder.

"The JS-Six-Four is used in surgery."

"No. With a knife. Or your laser on low power."

Jorie stared at him, grotesque barbaric visions of sliced flesh oozing blood coming to her mind. "We haven't used those methods in hundreds of years. I wouldn't even know how—"

"I know someone who does. It's the way things are done here all the time. She's a doctor. And an EMT—an emergency medical technician. The wife— she's spoused to Zeke Martinez."

"A nil?"

"A *doctor*."

"Theo, to involve a nil med-tech would reveal our presence—"

"Damn it, Jorie!" He shot to his feet, hands fisted

at his sides. "If you don't get that thing out of Tammy's shoulder, she's going to die. Is that what you want?"

A soft, pained whimper came from the bed behind Theo.

Jorie closed her eyes for a moment, her training and all the platitudes about a Guardian's duty warring inside her, battling against what she knew she had to do.

"No." Jorie rose and faced Theo. Captain Pietr and the entire council could strip her of her rank one hundred times over for violating gen-pro regulations if they wanted to. If it came to that, she would face them. She would accept their punishment, their censure.

She'd already lost Danjay. But she was not going to let her lieutenant die.

Theo punched in Zeke Martinez's cell-phone number as he trotted down the street toward the park where he and Jorie had left his SUV. Twilight was edging into night, the air cooling but still warm for late December in Florida. He tried to remember if Zeke and Suzanne went to her sister's for Christmas Eve dinner. Maybe it was New Year's. All he did know was this was a bad time to call and ask for a favor.

He had no choice. And it wasn't just Tammy's condition that forced him to take action. It was that Jorie was alone on this mission. He wasn't going to have her lose her life too, for his world.

Not if there were options. He felt there were.

He put the cell phone to his ear and waited for Zeke to answer.

It didn't take long—third ring. With caller ID, Zeke already knew who was calling.

"*Yassou, amigo*. What you got?" Zeke asked, mixing the Greek word for *hello* with Spanish.

"Unofficial business. You and Suzanne with family or something?"

"Business? Man, it's Christmas Eve. You're supposed to be on vacation."

"*Un*official, Zeke. And it's actually Suzanne I need." Theo could hear voices, laughter, and the clatter of dishes in the background. "You at her sister's?"

"The neighbors'. You were invited, if you remember."

He did now. Zeke had mentioned it last week. Before Liza Walters offered her cousin Bonnie to him. Before his one-woman war machine came into his life and turned everything upside down.

"So what do you got, a sick cat? You don't even own a cat, Theo."

Suzanne's voice was faint but audible: "People don't own cats, cats own people."

"Suzanne says—"

"Yeah, I heard her. Listen, when will you two be freed up? You know I wouldn't ask unless it was important."

"We haven't even had dessert yet—ow!"

Theo could envision Suzanne smacking Zeke on the arm. He'd seen her do it enough times. Especially when he heard, "Zeke, ask Theo what he needs."

"I need Suzanne to meet me at her clinic as soon

as she can," Theo said, before Zeke could repeat his wife's instructions. And because Jorie couldn't unequivocally discount that the Tresh might track—and respond to—the implant's removal: "I need you to bring your Glock and rifle, and it's probably not a bad idea to wear your vest."

"My—what do you got, some kind of wild dog? Sure you shouldn't be calling animal control?"

"No wild dogs. No cats either." Theo searched for the right words to at least alert Suzanne she'd be dealing with a human, utilizing her EMT skills as well as her veterinary ones. "I've got an illegal military operative with a time bomb in her shoulder."

"A spook?" Zeke dropped his voice to a harsh rasp. "CIA?"

"Something like that." He'd reached his car, blessedly still where they'd left it. It beeped twice as he unlocked it with the remote. "I need to keep this totally below the radar. When can you break free?"

"Sure you're sober?"

"Completely." Though when this was all over, a three-day binge might be a great idea. If he had any vacation time left.

"Hang on."

Theo slid in and started the engine, then backed out of the tree-shaded space.

He shifted to drive and Zeke came back on. "Forty-five minutes okay for you? Quarter to eight?"

"Quarter to eight is great. And thanks, Zeke. I really mean this. I didn't want to get you two involved, but our backs are against the wall here."

"Our? Wait. This operative. Is that the gal I met? Jorie?"

Theo hesitated. "She's one of them," he admitted as he pulled down his driveway. "But not the one who's injured."

"There are more?"

"I'll explain when I see you." He flipped the cell phone closed, climbed out of the SUV, and locked it. Jorie nudged open the back door—she must have turned off those sizzle shields. When he pulled the door shut behind him, she was busy making peanut butter and grape jelly sandwiches. She stopped just long enough to tap at her scanner. Shields back on, he assumed, as he grabbed a can of orange soda from the fridge. Jorie had her usual glass of water. Helluva Christmas Eve dinner. No *vasilopita,* no lucky coin. But they had to eat something. He couldn't remember the last time he had a real meal. He didn't know when they'd get the next chance to eat one.

"We leave in fifteen minutes," he told her, snagging half a sandwich from the plate as they stood together at the kitchen counter near the sink. That gave them plenty of time. It would take, max, twenty minutes to get to Suzanne's veterinary clinic. Less if he ran Code 3.

"You remember what you thought when you were on the *Sakanah?* When you understood exactly who the Guardians were, why we were here?"

He bit into the sandwich, nodded, swallowed. "Yeah, I know—"

"Revealing our existence never goes well with nils. I accept this is necessary to save Tam's life. I'm grateful. But you need to be prepared. This will not be a blissful experience, Theo."

That, he mused, finishing off the rest of the PB&J,

was probably the understatement of the century. But at least she was calling him Theo again. He took another swig of soda, then reached for his second sandwich half. "Zeke and I go back a long time. He trusts me. I trust him." He wondered for a moment how Jorie would react when she found out Suzanne was primarily an animal doctor, not a people one, her years as an EMT notwithstanding. He shrugged it off as the least of his worries.

Right now it was more important that he and Jorie start working as a true team. "Tell me what guesses you've been able to come up with about the Tresh's presence here."

She stared past him for a moment, and he was aware of the shadows under her eyes. And he was aware, once again, of what Commander Jorie Mikkalah had to be feeling, facing. When that Tresh agent, Prow, had pointed out how alone she was, she'd said—with a chin-raised confidence Theo tagged as pure Jorie—that someone would be back for her.

But pure Jorie, Theo had learned, didn't always tell the truth. And he doubted she'd tell a Tresh how frightened she was.

He didn't know if the Guardians would come back for Jorie. He didn't think Jorie knew that answer either.

She turned to him. "Once I factored in the Tresh presence here and factored in what I know they're capable of, it all became clear. Or more clear." She shook her head slightly. "One never completely knows with the Tresh. But my best guess, and I think you can take that as almost a certainty, is that they've been using your world as a breeding ground for an altered zombie. A more perfect one."

"Like the Tresh themselves," he put in. And then, because he'd been a cop too long and making light of a serious situation was second nature to him, he added, "Are they at least going to make them prettier?"

She shot him a narrow-eyed look, mouth pursed.

He held up both hands, one of which contained his half-eaten sandwich. "Guilty as charged. Go on."

"I originally thought they might have acquired the code. Now I think they've programmed *around* it. Bypassed it somehow. My tech"—she waved one hand toward his bedroom, where Tammy lay asleep—"picked up duplicates of everything Lorik transmitted while we were out. It didn't appear he knew what he was looking at but sent it for my input because he recognized—finally!—that he might have been wrong in his primary assessment. His report didn't state the Tresh were involved. But he did agree that someone was tampering with the zombies. He delineated some tests to run on the next zombie we encountered. Lorik always has to be more than one hundred percent sure on everything," she added, almost as much to herself as to him.

Theo pushed away his unease at the fact that Lorik no longer appeared to be on Jorie's shit list. "Why do the Tresh need a more perfect zombie?"

"Not perfect so much as obedient only to them. And this *is* a guess. But it's one I'm fairly certain of, one I've told you before: to control the Hatches—our ships' gateways through space."

He remembered that. The zombies had been built to maintain and guard the Hatches and check incoming ships for potentially deadly infections. Then something had gone terribly wrong, turning them rogue, wreaking havoc on various planets. It all had meant little to him the first time she'd explained it—was it only yesterday? Now it was all too real. And personal. The Tresh were using his world. And they would, if they could, kill his Jorie in order to keep on doing so.

"How do we stop them?" He put the empty plate in the dishwasher. It was almost time to bundle up Tammy and put her in the SUV's backseat, along with whatever other gizmos Jorie decided they'd need.

"We can't stop the Tresh. Even with your friend Zeke Martinez... even with your full security force." She let out a short breath, then raked one hand through her hair. "Our only choice is to stop the zombies. Destroy any chance the Tresh have of altering them for their use."

"All of them?" Last he asked her, she said there were over three hundred. Theo didn't know how many more parks he could close under the guise of a wandering rabid raccoon just so they could turn the zombies into *fooshing* green circles.

"That's what the Tresh would expect a Guardian to do: terminate the herd, starting with the juveniles. It's standard Guardian procedure. And that's exactly why we won't do that."

"Then what—"

"We must locate and terminate the C-Prime—who will be heavily guarded by the juveniles and the mature drones." Jorie shoved herself away from the counter. "If Lorik's last summations are correct, we only have one replication cycle—roughly six of your days—in order to do so. Or else the mutation the Tresh have programmed will progress to the next generation. Six days after that, the next. Once the hatchlings are out, nothing short of a full Guardian attack force will be able to stop them. And that's something we no longer have."

He followed her back to his bedroom in silence, his mind working over the import of her words. Then, while she gently woke Tammy and prepped her for the ride to the clinic, he grabbed his tac vest, heavy-duty boots, sweatshirt, and his ankle-holstered backup gun, and ducked into his bathroom to change.

Theo waited for something to go radically wrong— in keeping with everything else that had happened so far—on the drive to Suzanne Martinez's veterinary clinic, with Tammy lying on the backseat and Jorie talking softly to her in her own language. But other than his aunt Tootie calling on his cell phone, sounding forlorn that he was working and might not make Christmas dinner tomorrow, the twenty-minute drive was uneventful. No Tresh zoomed by in X-wing fighters, firing starburst lasers at them. No zombies materialized in the intersection, slashing at the overhead traffic lights.

Traffic was sparse. He didn't have to hit his lights or siren once.

That gave him too much time to think and only

made his nerves worse when he pulled around the back of the L-shaped white stucco clinic and saw Zeke's unmarked Crown Vic in the parking spot marked DOCTOR S. MARTINEZ. Lights shining through the low palm trees shading the clinic's rear windows told him his friends were inside and waiting.

Well, here we go.

He had no idea how Zeke would react to the news that outer-space aliens resided in Bahia Vista. No, he did. Every cop on patrol had had more than his or her share of Signal 20s who claimed to be the galactic emperor from Alpha Centauri or who believed that FBI agents lived in his refrigerator and Martians were camped out in his attic—which was the reason for lining his baseball cap and his underwear with aluminum foil.

And shooting BB pellets at the neighbors.

All Theo had were Jorie, her gizmos, and his Paroo cube. The latter of which, he realized as he put the SUV into park, wasn't all that much unlike one of those high-tech toys found in a Sharper Image catalog. Or on eBay.

But helping Tammy was his main priority right now. Let Suzanne get that damned thing out of Tammy's shoulder—he'd talk to her later about the one in his. Let Tammy be, if not overly mobile, at least able to work with Jorie on the zombie problem verbally.

Maybe that would take some of the pinched look out of Jorie's golden-hued eyes. God knew she had enough to worry about.

So did he. Zeke was going to Baker-Act him for sure.

"How's she doing?" he asked over his shoulder as he turned off the engine. Jorie had spent the entire trip on the floor wedged between the front and rear seats, her scanner gizmo doing whatever her scanner gizmo did to keep Tammy alive and as pain-free as possible.

"I be...okay." Tammy's voice was strained, weak.

He looked at Jorie. She was shaking her head. "No change."

"Wait until I come around to help you with her."

The back door of the clinic swung open when Theo's boots hit the ground, the muffled sounds of dogs barking flowing out. The separate kennel wing—rebuilt to hurricane-proof specifications two years ago—was off to the right but attached to the main clinic a few feet from the back door. Zeke appeared in the doorway, silhouetted by the light behind him, rifle in one hand.

"Does Suzanne have a stretcher, a gurney?" Theo called out.

Zeke ducked back inside and reappeared moments later, pushing a gurney.

Tammy tried to sit up. Jorie moved up on the seat behind her and held her upright until Theo could slip his arms under her legs and around her back. He placed her carefully on the gurney.

"*Ay, madre mia,* so young," Zeke said as he secured the straps around Tammy's body. She tried to smile, but then her eyes fluttered closed.

Theo had no idea how old Tammy was. He had no

idea how old Jorie was. So he only nodded and stepped back, letting Jorie go ahead of him inside.

The barking became louder, a cat meowed, the sounds filtering through the metal crash-barred door that led to the kennel wing.

"Theo!" Suzanne Martinez, in powder-blue scrubs dotted with frolicking kittens and puppies, hurried to his side and brushed a quick kiss across his cheek. She was a stocky—pleasingly plump, Aunt Tootie often said—brunette with a heart-shaped face and upturned nose. Her long hair was pulled back into a ponytail and tied with a gold bow—incongruous with her outfit and obviously a remnant of their aborted evening plans. Theo again felt a pang of regret for taking them away from their party—and quite possibly risking their lives. But not only had he not known what else to do, he truly felt this was the *best* thing to do.

He heard Zeke lock the door behind them.

Suzanne was already stroking the hair out of Tammy's face. "Hi. I'm Suzanne Martinez." She looked back up at Theo. "Zeke said she has something in her shoulder? Shrapnel?"

"A small device. Like a microchip, I think. Jorie can—Jorie." He touched Jorie's arm, taking her attention from Tammy. She'd been hovering over her lieutenant like a nervous mother hen ever since they'd arrived. He'd probably be the same way if he was in a hospital with Zeke on the gurney. "You remember Zeke Martinez? This is Suzanne, his wife. *Doctor* Suzanne Martinez."

Suzanne nodded. "I hope Theo told you—"

Theo held up one hand, halting Suzanne's words

and explanation, he believed, of her status as a veterinarian. "Suzanne, this is Commander Jorie Mikkalah."

"Commander?" That from Zeke, now standing next to his wife.

"And this young lady?" Suzanne asked, looking back down at Tammy.

"Lieutenant Tamlynne Herryck," Jorie supplied.

"I be ... okay," Tammy said softly.

Jorie patted her hand, said something Theo couldn't understand. Tammy closed her eyes again.

"Is she in immediate danger?" Suzanne asked.

"She had a small seizure about an hour ago, but she's stable right now," Theo said.

Suzanne looked troubled. "I assume there's a valid reason you brought her here instead of to a regular hospital. And requested that my kennel staff be kept out of this. After all my years being a cop's wife, I'm used to not asking. Or rather, not getting answers when I ask. But I want you to very clearly understand the difference in my skills here." She glanced at Jorie. "He did tell you that I'm a veterinarian?"

"No," Theo said, before Jorie could answer. "English isn't her native language."

"Inuktitut," Zeke told his wife.

"Eskimo?" Suzanne's eyes widened.

"No!" Theo said again, forcefully enough that both Zeke and Suzanne turned abruptly to him. "Zeke, I'll ... I'll explain in a bit. But first let's get that thing out of her, okay?"

A parrot—at least, Theo assumed it was a

parrot—chose that moment to let out a raucous shriek. A cat meowed loudly in answer.

"You have companions here?" Jorie asked.

"Companions?" Theo and Suzanne said at the same time.

Jorie spread her hands, delineating something small, then something larger. "Creatures of feather and fur for emotional comfort and guidance. You use them to heal your patients?"

Suzanne eyed Jorie quizzically. "No—that is, yes. I'm a veterinarian. A...companion doctor."

Jorie nodded solemnly and Theo saw relief spread over her face, her shoulders relaxing. "That's the first blissful news I've had since—well, thank you." She turned to Theo and laid her fingers on his hand. "Accept my regrets for doubting you."

"Doubting me about what?"

"When you said this female was a med-tech. I was afraid the skill level...Regrets." Jorie nodded to Suzanne again. "I was afraid she'd not have the skills because of the low level of technology on your world. But a med-tech who heals companions is the most skilled of all. Thank you."

The blatantly puzzled expressions on Suzanne's and Zeke's faces would have been funny if the situation weren't so serious.

Suzanne was the first, however, to catch on. "On *our* world?"

Theo was saved from answering by a soft whimper of pain from Tammy. Jorie immediately had her scanner out. Suzanne stared over Jorie's shoulder, eyes wide.

"The implant." Jorie pointed to an image on the screen.

"Is that a . . . handheld MRI?"

"It does a lot of things," Theo told her. "Jorie will explain as much as she can later. But right now can you remove that thing?"

Suzanne reached for the scanner. "May I?"

Jorie handed it to her, and for the next few moments, the blue-walled back room of the clinic was filled with the soft sounds of the two women's voices, the staccato barking of a dog, and the occasional shriek of a feathered companion.

Theo leaned against a grooming table, feeling useless.

"Theophilus." Zeke flanked Theo's right side. "What in hell is going on?"

"I could tell you, Ezequiel, but you won't believe me."

Suzanne raised one hand, catching Theo's attention. "I'm going to take her into surgery. We'll call you boys if we need anything."

"How long?" Theo asked.

Suzanne exchanged glances with Jorie. "I want to run some tests first. That shouldn't be more than fifteen minutes. Then, if we don't encounter any complications, half an hour to forty-five minutes. That . . . thing is fairly close to the surface. But I'll want to monitor her in recovery for at least two hours after that. I suggest you two find the coffeemaker in the staff room and get it brewing."

With that she turned and, with Jorie on one side, wheeled Tammy down the short hall.

Theo watched them go. He could feel Zeke staring at him the entire time.

"You won't believe me," he said before Zeke could repeat the question.

Zeke rocked back on his heels. "Try me."

"Make some coffee. I refuse to be Baker-Acted without sufficient caffeine in my veins."

17

It took Theo over half an hour to explain—or try to explain—about Jorie and the zombies and the Tresh. Then he sat in silence, sipping a cup of Zeke's wonderful black-as-mud coffee, as his friend and former partner examined the Guardian laser pistol, Hazer micro-rifle, and, lastly, the cube showing holographs of Paroo.

"Looks like Tahiti," Zeke said.

Theo leaned forward and pressed an icon on the side of the top screen. He'd figured out the zoom feature yesterday after returning from the confrontation with the zombies in the park.

"Tahiti with the cast from *Star Wars*," Zeke amended. "Means nothing." He handed the cube back to Theo, who pressed two sides to flatten it, then shoved it back in his pocket.

"I know. But that and the weapons are all I have right now."

"If it was anyone but you—"

"I know."

Zeke picked up the rifle again, hefting it. Theo glanced at his watch. Almost nine o'clock. And this wasn't a residential neighborhood. "Okay," he said, knowing what Zeke wanted and might finally take as proof. "One shot. Outside in the parking lot. But I'm going to turn on my strobe so we don't get any funny calls from any passersby or Suzanne's kennel staff reporting a strange blue flash."

"I'll call Nina on the kennel intercom and tell her not to worry about the strobe." Zeke was grinning, clearly excited about seeing the rifle in action.

The air outside was still warm, muggy. Zeke propped open the clinic's rear door with a folding chair while Theo unlocked the SUV and hit the switch for the blue strobe behind his rearview.

"Two settings," he said, angling the Hazer so that Zeke could see the small buttons. "Stun." A yellow light pulsed down the side of the rifle. "And dead." The light turned blue. "You got something you don't need?"

"Suzanne remodeled the nurses' station last week. There are two old metal desks behind the Dumpster. They're heavy bastards. I'll give you a hand."

Theo looped the rifle's strap over his shoulder, then pushed while Zeke pulled. Theo turned the desk so the file drawers faced Zeke and were in line with the Dumpster. If the charge kept going, the Dumpster should stop it.

Then he trotted to the far end of the parking lot, Zeke by his side. "Ready?"

"Fire at will."

"Poor Will." Theo shouldered the rifle and took aim. "He's always getting shot at." He punched the trigger button.

Blue light bored through one side of the desk with nothing more than a low hum, then flared brightly against the front of the Dumpster.

"Damn!" Zeke broke into a trot, heavy-duty flashlight in one hand, and stopped to kneel in front of the smoldering three-inch hole in the desk. "It went completely through both file pedestals. Hot damn."

Theo shut off the strobe, then walked over to the blistered, buckled section of the Dumpster. "If Suzanne catches any shit about this, let me know. I'll kick in some bucks for a new one." He looked at Zeke.

His friend sighed and shut off the flashlight. "Okay, so you've got some really sweet weapons there. But we've got lasers. That doesn't prove she's an outer-space alien."

"I told you." Theo grabbed the edge of the battered desk and pulled it toward the Dumpster. "I've been on their ship."

"Beamed up, yeah." Zeke pushed, grunting. "You've seen *The Wizard of Oz*. Little girl gets smacked by a tornado and dreams all kinds of things. You say you were out in the yard when the tornado hit—"

"Zombie," Theo corrected.

"Tornado. Microburst," Zeke countered. Together they shoved the desk back up against the Dumpster. "The whole thing is just a hallucination."

"Jorie's real. This rifle's real."

"She could be some kind of terrorist. Or super-spy."

"Who just happened to be in my backyard at the exact moment this supposed microburst clocked me?" Theo kicked at a stone and sent it skittering across the asphalt as he walked back toward the clinic's open door. "And who then set up an elaborate video display of fifteen-foot-tall monsters, not only in my backyard but in the park by the mall? And, oh, the ones in my house where people beam in and out like a scene from *Star Trek*? Why, Zeke, why?" They'd reached the doorway. Theo crossed his arms over his chest. "If these are high-tech terrorists from some third-world country—who couldn't afford this kind of technology to begin with—why me? Why a Homicide cop in a small Florida city? Why not a police chief in Miami? Or an FDLE lieutenant who would have access to far-more-sensitive information than I do? Why go to all this trouble for me?"

"Did you run NCIC on her?"

"I didn't think NCIC included starship pilots' licenses."

Zeke stepped inside. "Fingerprints."

Theo followed and closed the door. "You're not going to find Jorie or Tammy in our databases."

"Outer-space aliens don't have names like Tammy."

"Tamlynne," Jorie's voice said behind him. "Her name's Tamlynne."

Theo turned, quickly reading her face. No tears. No sadness. Hope rose that Jorie would at least be spared this heartache.

"She's in recovery." Suzanne was walking toward them, surgical mask loose around her neck. "She's doing very well."

Theo reached for Jorie. "You got it out? She's okay?"

She took his hand. "Yes and yes. And it's fully disabled. The Tresh have no way of tracking it." Finally, a small smile. "Dr. Suzanne is excellently skilled. Companion med-techs always are."

He stood staring at her, aware of the warmth of her hand in his, aware that Zeke had come to stand beside him. He didn't care. He gave her hand a small squeeze.

"Contact lenses," Zeke said.

"Zeke, what are you babbling about?" Suzanne sounded annoyed.

"Her." Zeke gestured at Jorie. "She has Theo believing she's from some other planet. The hair, the gold eyes. Has to be contacts."

Jorie glanced at Theo. "Nils," she said quietly, pulling her hand out of his. "I warned you."

"Zeke," Suzanne said, but Zeke had flicked on his flashlight and aimed it at Jorie's face.

"But you can always see the lenses in an oblique light."

"Zeke." Suzanne, again.

Jorie blinked.

"Look that way." Zeke pointed to the wall.

Jorie shrugged and turned in profile to him.

"Zeke!" Suzanne had lost patience. Theo heard that clearly. He wondered what had happened in surgery, what Jorie had told or shown her. Something, obviously. Because Suzanne didn't seem the least bit disturbed by Zeke's mention of "another planet."

Suzanne—in a very familiar move—smacked Zeke on the arm. He stopped squinting at Jorie's eyes. "Suzy—"

"I believe Jorie is who she says she is."

"What?" Zeke straightened.

"So is Tamlynne," Suzanne continued. "Though whether they're actually from this Chalv, Cal . . ."

"Chalvash," Jorie said.

"Thank you. Chalvash System—that, I don't know. But I do know that small scanner of hers is far beyond any kind of medical equipment we have. Nothing I've seen even comes close."

Zeke looked at his wife. "You can't really think that—"

"I do. I watched Jorie sonically seal my incision. I do know what I'm talking about, Zeke. Nothing we have here—nothing—can do that."

Zeke switched a look from his wife to Jorie and back to his wife again. "So she's not wearing contacts?"

Suzanne angled her face around toward Jorie's. "Nope. Interesting eye color, almost feline. Do you know if it's a dominant or recessive gene?" she asked Jorie.

"It's what my parents chose," Jorie said.

It took a moment for Theo to realize what she said, and then it startled him. Evidently the Tresh weren't the only ones who played with biological engineering.

Zeke shoved the flashlight back in his duty belt, disbelief playing across his features. "This is crazy."

"I *so* know that feeling," Theo intoned wryly. He clapped Zeke on the back. "Now that we have that settled, let me give you the bad news: Jorie and her people aren't the only outer-space aliens here. And the zombies aren't the only issue. We've got problems, big problems, *amigo*. Go fire up that coffeepot. We need to tell you about the Tresh."

Zeke was skeptical. No, more than skeptical. He could not, did not want to believe Jorie was a Guardian who'd come to Florida via a spaceship right out of *Star Trek*. Theo could see it in the way the detective leaned back in the chair in the staff room, arms across his chest, eyes narrowed.

"C'mon, Theo," Zeke said, when Jorie paused in her recounting of the Tresh Devastators showing up in Theo's house. "Don't you think NASA or NORAD or one of those agencies would notice a bunch of space cruisers hanging out up there?" He waved his hand in a circle over his head.

Theo rested his elbows on his knees and scrubbed his hands over his face. It was almost eleven o'clock. The end—or what should be the end—of another grueling, confusing day.

Another hour and it was Christmas.

Christ.

"We take considerable efforts not to be noticed by nil-techs," Jorie said. She too had her arms crossed over her chest and leaned back in her chair across the small staff room from Zeke.

This was not going well.

"I know it's hard to believe," Theo said finally.

"I'm still having a difficult time processing what I've seen. But I can't change the facts: these zombie things are here, the Tresh are here, and Jorie's ship and crew are gone. We need help. But if you don't want to get involved, I understand. Suzanne's removing that implant from Tammy is above and beyond the call. We really have no right to ask for anything more." His own implant could wait. He shoved himself to his feet. "If Suzanne says it's okay, we'll take Tammy back home now."

Zeke grimaced, his mouth twisting slightly. "You really believe all this shit, don't you?"

"I wish I didn't," Theo answered honestly.

"Let me print her," Zeke said. "Her and her friend. I want name, DOB, everything. Run them through NCIC."

"You're not going to find anything."

"Then what are you worried about?" Zeke replied smoothly.

Shit. Standard interrogation setup, and he'd walked right into it. He would have laughed out loud, but he was too tired. "You got a kit in your car? Go get it."

Zeke strolled out and Theo explained the procedure to a frowning Jorie.

"Why would there be a record of my biological signature in your criminal files?" she asked.

"There won't be. That's why I'm saying it's no big deal. Not important," he amended. "But he's a friend. And friends double-check each other sometimes."

"He thinks I'm deceiving you."

"He thinks it's a possibility, because he hasn't seen

what I have. So he has to gather his own information, to be sure."

"Nils," Jorie said softly as Zeke returned, but a corner of her mouth quirked up in a grin and she let Zeke take her prints. She had no idea what a Social Security number was. Her response to his request for date of birth was equally perplexing.

"Esare three nine seven Tal one Nifarris," she told him, and even obliged by writing it down.

"Which makes you how old?" Zeke asked.

"My age on my world? Thirty-nine."

He'd thought she was younger, but then, he didn't know if his years were the same as Chalvash System years, or wherever in hell she was from. She could be thirty-nine or nineteen or seventy-nine. He had no way to know.

"And you have no driver's license, no identification?" Zeke was asking.

Jorie pulled her scanner out from under her long sweater and flicked through several screens. "This."

Theo stepped forward, craning his neck, and saw a small head-shot image of a very serious Jorie with shorter hair, and then lines of squiggly or angular characters to the left of the image. Characters like the ones that had scrolled down the screen of Mr. Crunchy's laptop and had graced the corridor walls of her ship.

"Can you translate that to Vekran?" he asked.

"Trans . . . ah!" She tapped the screen a few times. The angular letters shifted until Theo saw a somewhat recognizable alphabet.

Not totally English. But, damn, he could almost read it.

Commander Jorie Mikkalah, Guardian Force
Hunter Status C7-1.

He saw the word *Sakanah* and recognized it as the
name of her ship. Then there were lots of numbers
that meant nothing and a couple of symbols that
meant even less.

Zeke made some more notations on his pad, then
left to find out if Suzanne was ready to give Tammy
medical clearance.

"You see why we don't work with nil-techs?"
Jorie asked as Zeke's footsteps faded.

"You worked with me."

"You're..." And she closed her eyes briefly.
"Different. Special."

He almost asked her to define *special* but didn't
want to get his hopes up that she meant something
personal. It was safer to respond as a cop. "And
that's why you came looking for me?"

She sighed. "Unlike what Zeke Martinez believes,
I did not come looking for you. I wanted my agent's
T-MOD, which you had. Had you relinquished it
when you should have, we would not now be having
this conversation."

Okay, score one for Jorie Mikkalah. Yes, he had
hoped to catch her off guard and get her to admit
she'd targeted him. Listening to Zeke had opened
that small, worrisome doubt. Illogical because he'd
seen the zombies, the Tresh, her ship.

But he also saw himself starting to care very much
about what happened to her, and not just because
heat roared through his body when she did that
head-tilt thing. It had moved beyond that—he didn't

know quite when and where, because the past two days were now becoming a serious blur.

Like all cops, he was trained to never become emotionally involved with an investigation—especially not with the subject of an investigation.

With Jorie Mikkalah, he'd broken that rule, bigtime. And that scared him almost as much as being Baker-Acted to the psych ward.

It would be so much easier if Zeke was right and Jorie Mikkalah was some kind of foreign superspy with James Bond–like toys. He could arrest her, turn her over to FDLE, which would in turn send her off to the FBI. He could forget her. And they could deport her back to...the Chalvash System.

Except that not the FBI, the CIA, hell, not even NASA would know how to send her there.

Which was just as well. He didn't want her to leave. He wanted her here, with him.

And that scared the hell out of Theo Petrakos even more.

Tamlynne should, *would* be fine. Jorie let that one worry drift away from her as Theo guided the white land vehicle—the Essuvee, she corrected herself—back to his structure. Her fears for her ship, for Captain Pietr, for Rordan, Trenat, Lorik, and everyone else plagued her. Maybe she should have asked Prow if the *Sakanah* had been destroyed. Not that she believed he'd have told her the truth, but perhaps she could have inferred something from his tone, the shift of his eyes. Then, at least, she'd know.

Not knowing was eating her up inside.

Once Tamlynne regained full consciousness—Jorie checked on her lieutenant with another glance over her shoulder at the rear seat—she might have some answers to a few of those questions. But up to this point, with the pain from the implant lacing through her body, Lieutenant Tamlynne Herryck had been able to provide little coherent information about the Tresh attack in Theo's structure.

Jorie didn't discount that the Tresh might have interfered with Tamlynne's memory of their arrival and subsequent actions. She doubted Dr. Suzanne Martinez—as skilled as she was—would have any way of restoring that. Her tech, like most everything else on this ball of dirt, was rudimentary.

Peculiar world, this planet named for dirt. So many large gaps in technology. Yet some of the nils—the inhabitants—she'd met were so . . . special. Extraordinary.

She turned back to find Theo watching her, though in the vehicle's dark interior she felt his gaze more than saw it. The vehicle was stopped, idling, because of the colored-light edict. Foolish and unnecessary, as there were no other vehicles in the immediate vicinity. She shifted in her seat, but Theo didn't move his gaze. She couldn't read his expression, but, oddly, what she felt more than saw pulled at her. Heat blossomed on her cheeks, and she was suddenly very aware of his presence mere minmeters from her. His strength. His warmth.

"Theo?" she asked softly, not wanting to wake Tamlynne. Suzanne Martinez had given her a medication to encourage a healing rest.

He said nothing for a moment, then shook his

head and turned away. The vehicle moved forward again.

She shook off the sensation. She was stressed and tired. That was all.

When Theo pulled behind his structure, she already had her scanner out, verifying shield integrity before she temporarily disengaged it. No breaches. Whether any had been attempted she wouldn't know until she went inside and checked her tech.

"I'll take her," Theo said, after Jorie had hopped out of her seat and was opening the rear door. He pushed that metal ring he always carried into her hand, then picked out a short object from the bunch. "To open the kitchen door.

"It's a key," he said, when she held it up in his back porch light to examine it.

"Ah." She nodded.

"Key to my heart." His tone was light, but his voice was soft.

Heart? She knew he referred to his structure as a *house.* She shot him a puzzled glance and was about to ask for an explanation when he shrugged.

"Never mind. It's . . . it's just a joke." He gathered Tamlynne's limp form into his arms.

They'd reached Theo's bedroom door when a possible problem occurred to Jorie. "I'll need to work in there. And she needs someplace quiet to rest. Best I move my tech—"

"It would be better to open the sofa bed in the spare room. Let her stay there. That way I don't have to bother her to access my stuff."

"Sofa bed?"

Theo set Tamlynne down on his bed. "I'll leave her here for now. Come with me."

The sofa bed turned out to be a colorful couch with a bed folded within. Not unlike the recessed bunks on Kedrian troop ships but much nicer. Jorie ran her hand over the mattress, then helped Theo secure the sheets and blanket he'd pulled from a corridor closet.

She moved the broken remnants of the Guardian MOD-tech to the corner behind his exercise machine. Theo brought Tamlynne in.

"Nice, so nice," her lieutenant murmured in Alarsh as she snuggled against the blanket. Jorie pulled off Tamlynne's boots and loosened the top of her uniform. They would need clothes, clean clothes, soon. There was nowhere to get supplies. The ship...

She pushed it away.

"So nice," Tamlynne whispered again.

Jorie sat on the edge of the mattress and brushed the curls off Tamlynne's forehead. "Nap, Tam." Whatever medicine Suzanne gave Tamlynne must be working. Her skin was less clammy.

Tamlynne sighed, her eyes slitting open for a moment. "Theo is...so nice."

Theo? Yes, Theo. Even Tamlynne wasn't immune to his very good face or his delicious grin, it seemed. Though it had been a while since Jorie'd seen the latter. "Yes, he is, Tam. Now nap. I'll be in the next room, working."

"You work too much. Sir." Tamlynne smiled dreamily. "Theo likes you."

"And you're hallucinating." Jorie smiled back.

"Do you . . . like him?"

Did she like Theo Petrakos? Her body heated in answer. "Of course."

"A lot?"

"Yes, a lot," she admitted, surprised by her own truthfulness. But less surprised at the reasons why she felt that way. Images of Theo handling her weapons with ease, firing on the zombies, escorting her all over his city without question, breathing life into a failing Tamlynne filled her mind. Yes, he had the Guardian implant in his shoulder, but she knew that wasn't what motivated him. It wasn't why he brought her glasses of precious water or showed her how to make peanut butter and bread meals. It wasn't why he pushed himself as hard as she did.

There was an uncommon courage and dedication in him. It made her feel stronger just being with him.

"Good," Tamlynne whispered. "I think you two—"

"Close your eyes and your mouth." She tapped Tamlynne teasingly on the nose. "That's an order, Lieutenant."

"Sir. Yes . . . sir." The last word was muffled as Tamlynne turned her face into the pillow.

Jorie smoothed the blanket around Tam, then got slowly to her feet. Tamlynne would be more herself by sunwake. And if the Tresh hadn't tampered with her memories, she'd be able to provide answers as to Rordan and the *Sakanah*. She'd be functional, coherent, not babbling silliness about—

Theo. Standing just behind her, leaning against the edge of the doorway. He'd removed his security vest. His tight-fitting black shirt clung only too well to his

broad shoulders and defined, only too well, the outlines of the muscles on his chest and arms.

Her breath caught, embarrassingly so. He was
looking at her. She could see an intensity in his eyes
that she'd only felt before in the darkened vehicle.

Had he heard...? But no, she and Tam had spoken only in Alarsh.

Hadn't they?

"Everything okay?" His voice was a deep rumble.

"A good nap will help," she said, moving away
from the sofa bed. "I need to..." and she waved one
hand in the direction of his structure where her tech
still gathered data. But she couldn't think of what he
called that room or even how to describe what she
needed to do. Because the way he was looking at her
incinerated every sensible thought in her head.

Theo curled his fingers around her wrist and
pulled her toward him. She went without resistance,
as if she were a ship caught in a tow field. He stepped
back into the corridor and she followed, his gentle
pressure on her arm guiding her closer. Then he
reached behind her and shut the door.

"Jorie." His arm slid around her waist. The fingers holding her wrist raised her hand to his mouth.
He brushed a lingering kiss across her palm. The in-
cinerator in her brain unleashed a flash of heat that
rushed down her body and flared between her thighs.

Trembling, she uncurled her fingers. She traced
the rough line of his jaw, then her thumb found the
softness of his lower lip.

He pulled her more tightly against him. He lowered his face but she was already raising hers, her
mouth seeking his, not with the hard, desperate in-

tensity of their earlier feigned kisses but more gently. Carefully. Something was happening, changing between them. It made no rational sense. She knew with the same, unerring clairvoyance that had kept her alive all these years that what she was doing was dangerous. Theo Petrakos was dangerous.

She didn't care. But she would be careful.

His mouth brushed hers, the warmth of his breath flowing across her face. She answered with the smallest of kisses, the slightest meeting of tongues. She dropped her hand from his face and splayed her fingers against his chest. She could feel his heart beating rapidly.

It matched her own.

He rubbed his face against hers, his mouth touching her cheekbone, her jaw, and, as she angled her head, trailing down her neck. A soft heat, gentle and searing at the same time.

He took another step back, bringing her with him as he leaned against the wall. She went willingly. His hand at her waist pressed her to him, clothes and weapons—bulky—merging.

His light kisses were sheer torture, but she didn't push, didn't ask for more, because his restraint was as much of an aphrodisiac as his touch. A powerful man controlling his power.

A passionate man willing to take his time.

Her own desire teetered on the edge of exploding. It would be so easy to tear Theo's clothes off and blank her mind, lose her worries in a hard, driving sexual encounter with this man whose body trembled under her fingers.

But that wasn't what he was asking for. And it wasn't what she wanted.

She was very aware that what he wanted and what she wanted might never come to pass. There were the Tresh and the zombies. There was a city about to be under siege. There was the very real problem of survival.

And if—*when*—the *Sakanah* returned, she would leave. It was her duty. Just as it was his duty to protect his city.

A low chuckle rumbled in his chest as he ran his hands up the length of her back, as if he too suddenly realized this was a desperate foolishness. His voice was a husky whisper in her ear. "You make me crazy, *agapi mou*."

Jorie understood *crazy*—especially as it related to Theo Petrakos—only too well, though his other phrase was lost on her. She turned her face, brushing his mouth with hers, then moved away. His arms loosened around her, but he didn't let go.

She sighed with more forcefulness than she wanted to and, when she looked at him, saw a sadness in his smile that echoed her own.

She touched his mouth with her fingers one more time. "We have work to do," she told him.

He nodded, then draped one arm over her shoulders. She wrapped her arm around his waist and headed for his bedroom, where her blinking array of MOD-tech was now their only lifeline, their only hope.

18

Agapi mou. My darling. My love. Theo knew the phrase because he'd been raised speaking Greek, but he'd never before said it to any woman out loud. Not through his high-school years, not through college or the police academy. He'd never said it to Camille.

To speak those words in the language he'd heard from infancy was too intimate. It exposed his heart.

Yet he didn't give a damn that it had been only two days. He'd touched Jorie, kissed Jorie, argued with Jorie, and fought by her side. There was no doubt. *Agapi mou.*

It was just another bit of damned irony that this was the worst possible time for him to feel that way.

He sat on the edge of his bed and watched her tap requests into the yellow-green screen, listened to her utter soft commands in Alarsh. It was almost one-thirty in the morning, officially Christmas. Children everywhere were snug in their beds, dreaming of

Santa Claus and sugarplums or however the old poem went. Yet zombies and the Tresh were more likely to land on their roofs than eight tiny reindeer.

Helluva Christmas present.

Jorie stopped tapping at the screen and rubbed tiredly at her face.

"Anything I can help with?" he asked, because he felt so useless and because he wanted her to know she didn't have to carry the burden alone.

She looked over her shoulder. "No, but thank you." She went back to her computer with a soft sigh.

He stood, restless energy unsettling him. He wanted to stay awake in case she needed something, but to just sit there and listen to his mind think—and his heart break—was driving him crazy. Hurry up and wait had never been his strong point, which was why he liked detective work. He could always find something to do.

But here, too much had happened, and so much of it had been out of his control. He needed to refocus . . . yes. He grabbed his guitar case. Duty belt and weapons were carefully placed on his nightstand. Boots came off. He propped his pillow against the wrought-iron headboard and brought his guitar into his lap. The well-worn Brazilian rosewood was smooth and cool under his fingers—and very familiar. He dug out his slide, then picked aimlessly at a few strings until a blues refrain he'd been toying with came to mind. Zeke had been busting his butt for over a year now about his reclusive ways since his divorce. *You still singing* The Down Home Divorced Guy Blues? was Zeke's constant taunt.

So Theo actually started writing the song. He closed his eyes and let himself sink into the sassy notes of the music, keeping time with one foot against the blanket. He hummed the melody softly—he was still working on the lyrics.

The tension leached from his neck and shoulders. He went through the refrain twice, then something made him open his eyes. He realized the room had grown quiet. He no longer heard Jorie's voice or her tapping on the screen just on the edge of his hearing. That's because she'd turned, her eyes wide in question.

Skata. He should have asked if playing his guitar would bother her.

"Sorry. I'll stop." He shifted forward to put the guitar back in its case.

"No. That's blissful." A small smile played across her lips.

"I don't want to disturb what you're doing."

"I've done all I can for now," she said, and rubbed her hand over her face again. "Until the zombies take a new action, I can only watch and wait."

"And the Tresh?"

"I'm no threat to them until the zombies wake again," she continued. "And since they know more than I do about the *Sakanah,* they may not consider me a threat at all."

Theo could hear the strain in her voice at the mention of her ship. He wished he had answers for her, but that too was out of his control.

She motioned to his guitar. "Please. It sounds so nice. And I need something else to think about for a little while."

Was that why she let him kiss her? Was that part of the playacting they'd started—*he'd* started—earlier? And he had started it, he admitted ruefully.

But somehow, no, he didn't think she was toying with him. And he hoped it wasn't only his male ego making that claim.

He glanced at his watch: two-ten. He pulled another pillow against the headboard, then patted the mattress. "Come, sit with me."

It would be temptation, Jorie next to him on his bed. But playing his guitar would keep his hands occupied. Because after what had happened in the hallway, he knew if he touched her again, he wouldn't be able to stop.

She pulled off her boots, then climbed across his bed on all fours, looking almost childlike, an impish smile on her face. She settled next to him and drew her knees up, wrapping her arms around them.

He found himself playing Traveling Ed Teja's "Blue Light," because it was soft but upbeat at the same time. Somewhere in the middle of the song, Jorie's head came to rest on his shoulder. He smiled to himself and kept playing, going through the song a second time, then segued into Teja's "Blue Dime."

He plucked the last few notes softly. She'd curled up against him, her knees resting against his thigh.

He put his guitar and case carefully on the floor, tucked the G-1 under his pillow, then turned off his bedside lamp and drew her into his arms. She murmured something unintelligible. He smoothed her hair back from her face and she settled into slumber again.

Theo listened to her breathing, the muted clicking

of her computer, and the rustle of the night breeze through the fronds of the palm trees outside.

It was Christmas, and somewhere, sweet voices were singing, *Silent night, holy night . . .*

While all of unholy hell waited just beyond his door.

Jorie woke to a dim, shadowed room and a man's arm draped over her waist. She recognized the intermittent *click-whir* of her tech and saw the green glow of a nil-tech timekeeper on the wrist lying across her forearm.

Theo. His breath ruffled her hair. Everything he was tugged at her heart.

She glanced at his wrist again—she knew how to interpret the symbols to this locale—and then at the pale light filtering through the covered viewports. It was just before sunwake. She—they—had been asleep for a little more than four sweeps. Hours, she corrected.

With no emergencies, no Tresh transporting in, no zombies crashing past—bliss, that.

She slipped out from under his arm.

"Jorie?" His voice was thick with sleep.

She thought of the last few times she'd slipped out of a man's embrace in bed. She hadn't heard her name whispered, but another female's. She touched her finger to his lips. "I'll look in on Tam and be back."

She would. She desperately needed rest, and if the zombies were in an inactive phase—she checked her readouts as she padded by, and they were—then she wouldn't look a gift fermarl in the ears. She needed all her strength for when the next spur hit.

Her scanner showed Tamlynne to be resting comfortably, her shoulder healing with only a little swelling. But some of the clamminess had returned to her skin. Jorie remembered that well. The nightmares she knew so intimately weren't over for her lieutenant yet. The implant's removal only halted further damage. Suzanne Martinez had no way to correct what had already been done.

The med-techs on the *Sakanah* could help, she thought, as she slipped back into Theo's bedroom. But her ship wasn't here.

She sat slowly down on the edge of the bed, not wanting to wake him. She was fully capable, as her brother often reminded her, of worrying enough for the both of them.

Galin. How long before a Guardian officer delivered the news of the destruction of the *Sakanah* and the death of his sister? Just after he'd learned of the loss of his longtime friend? It wasn't that Galin wasn't strong—he was. It pained her that she would be the cause of such suffering....

"Hey."

Theo's arms went around her and Theo's warmth encompassed her as he sat behind her on the bed. And only then did Jorie realize she was shivering, her breath coming out in small hiccuping gasps. Hell's wrath. Would the damage the implant caused never grant her peace? Or had seeing Prow and Sem reawakened old horrors?

"Hey," he said again, his voice a low rumble. He drew her back against him. "Come here."

She turned in his embrace and let him lower her to the bed, fitting herself tightly against him. She couldn't stop shaking.

"Is Tammy okay?"

She nodded under his chin. "Fine."

"What is it, *agapi mou*?"

"Nothing." She buried her face into his shirt and bit her lip to try to refocus her body's reaction. It didn't work. "It'll pass."

Strong hands massaged their way up her spine and down again.

"You've had a very stressful few days," he said.

"Yes." But she'd had worse. She should be able to handle this. That too made her weary.

He worked the muscles on the back of her shoulders with a gentle pressure. She sucked in a series of long breaths, tried to focus on the sound of Theo's heartbeat. Focus on the fact that Cordo Sem was dead. Davin Prow, she thought, might have been wounded. There was something about that encounter she felt she was missing, but she couldn't bring it to mind now. The last thing she wanted to see in her head was Prow.

Slowly, the knife-edged insanity that wore a Tresh Devastator's face slipped back into the depths of her mind where it belonged. Thankfully she'd only gotten the shakes and not awakened screaming from a nightmare. She felt limp, a little boneless. Theo's fingers slowed.

"Better?"

"Thank you." She pulled her face off his chest with a sigh, then rolled away from him, onto her back.

He leaned over her, his lips touching hers with a light kiss, then pulled back. "You're welcome."

He propped himself up on one elbow and watched her. "You want to tell me now what happened?" he asked after a long moment of silence, during which she was far too aware of the heat of him next to her.

She laid her fingers on the edge of her sweater near her collarbone. "Bad memories."

"The implant the Tresh put in you."

"Yes. Ten years past."

He folded his hand over hers. "How long before it was removed?"

"Forty-four of your days."

He uttered an unfamiliar series of harsh words. "But you still remember the pain."

"It has nothing to do with remembering. The Tresh device is insidious," she continued. "You know that word?"

"It causes collateral damage."

"Even Tamlynne, with the few sweeps it was in her body, will have resultant issues. It's good, then," and Jorie realized it was, "that I'm here. She may have small episodes, and I can help her work them through."

He was nodding but frowning slightly. She thought she knew why. "Guardian restrainer implants are noninvasive. Not like the Tresh one. There's no neural interface."

One corner of his mouth lifted. "So mine just gives me a zap if I piss you off."

She owed him the truth. "Yours does nothing. I neutralized it."

His eyes widened. "When?"

"When I did my funny stuff." She gave him a small smile. She liked that phrase he used. It was so very much Theo. "Before we went to capture the juvenile zombie at your park. Kip Rordan..." She forced from her mind the question of whether he was dead or alive. "I was worried he had some issues with you."

"You mean an intense mutual dislike?"

"He had the command codes when I wasn't here. And his understanding of the mission, his goals, were different than mine." She sighed, her mind coming back to the one fact she couldn't push away. "If they'd only listened—"

"Hey." He kissed her lightly. "You can't change the past. Let it go, Jorie. All you can do is what's here and now."

"But—"

"I know. Believe me, I *know*. When you beamed me up to your ship, I thought I'd lost everything, everyone. I reacted stupidly, getting angry, going over all the mistakes I'd made that brought me there instead of thinking and looking at what I had where I was. What I could work with. What I could do."

She remembered his bursts of temper and his subsequent, not always successful, attempts at self-control.

"And last year when Camille and I split up—"

"Camille?"

His mouth pursed wryly. "I was married. Spoused."

"Oh." There was a female he loved. Jorie's heart wilted.

"Was," he repeated. "I fell into the same stupid

trap. Remember you told me about the guy who cheated on you? Loren?"

"Lorik."

"I went through the same thing."

"She had you and chose someone else?"

"That was only one of the wonderful things she did, yeah."

"Vomit-brained slut bucket."

Theo barked out a laugh. "What?"

"It's an expression. Sadly, it doesn't render well in Vekran."

Still chuckling, he dotted her jaw with kisses.

She turned her face and found his mouth. His mirth abated and he sighed against her lips.

"We should get some sleep," he said.

"Yes."

But he didn't move and she didn't move.

His mouth brushed hers again. "You should have kept that zapper implant in me working," he said, his voice rough. "Keep me under control. Make me leave you alone."

"I don't want you to leave me alone."

His breath fanned her cheek. "Last chance. Say, 'Go away, Petrakos.' "

She ran her hand up the side of his face, then through his short hair. "No."

He closed his eyes, leaning into her touch, his capitulation sending a wave of desire through her. She knew he was aware of how dangerous this was. It could only cause them both heartache.

But she might not live so long. All she had was now. Wasn't that what he said? Here and now. And right here and now, she wanted Theo Petrakos very, very much.

She wrapped her arms around his neck and brought his face back down to hers, letting him lead with kisses and answering with caresses of her own. His body was taut muscle that yielded to her fingers. She arched up into him and he groaned.

"You're making me crazy, babe."

"I think that's good."

"Do you?" He watched her through hooded eyes dark with passion.

"Yes." Her fingers found the waistband at the back of his pants and pulled his shirt away. She needed the heat of his skin under her hands.

"Oh, babe." He kissed her hard, then pulled back. "You'd better be very sure what you want—"

"I want," she told him, more than a little breathless because her fingers weren't the only ones now doing the exploring. His hand had slipped under her sweater and sleeveless tracker shirt to cup her breast and tease her nipple. "Theo, I want you."

She felt his body throb in response even as he said her name, his kiss deep and desperate. He tugged at her sweater, and she pulled away from him just long enough to sit up and yank it and then her shirt over her head. Bliss, when she rolled back to him, his own chest was bare and they were heated skin to heated skin.

Her shorts came off next, his pants, their socks, clothes flying into the dim corners of the room. Then hands were replaced by mouths, kissing and nibbling and leaving hot, wet trails. His touch left her panting, damned near delirious with pleasure. She murmured to him in Alarsh because her brain couldn't find any Vekran words.

He moved up her body to claim her mouth again. "Tell me what you're saying is good," he rasped against her lips, the touch of his hands and the feel of his body throbbing against hers intoxicating.

"Very good. Oh—"

He thrust inside her, hot and hard.

"—yes!" she gasped, heat and tingles of ecstasy spiraling through her as she moved in rhythm with him.

His kisses deepened as he took her over the edge with him. Sparks of pleasure raced again through her veins as he groaned her name, shuddering into her. Then, even spent, his fingers threaded into her hair and he nibbled on her ear, her neck, and back up to her mouth.

Their bodies were hot, sweat-slickened. He turned on his side, gathering her up against him, curving his body around hers as he drew the sheet and blanket over them. He murmured something exotic-sounding in her ear. It wasn't Vekran or his English.

"Hmm?" she asked, his warmth lulling her into sleep.

He kissed her shoulder. "I'll tell you in a few hours. Sleep."

"Is it good?"

Laughter rumbled in his chest. "It's good, *agapi mou*."

"What does that—"

"I'll explain that too. Hush now. Naptime."

Jorie didn't remember falling asleep. But waking up again was a blissful experience, with Theo trailing kisses down her neck. She didn't know the time, but the room was brighter. "I should look in on Tam."

"Just did." A strong hand slid slowly down her hip, pleasure radiating in its wake. "Brought her some water." He nipped her ear. "She's a little weak, but I think she'll be okay."

Decadent. Wanton. Jorie dutifully chastised herself as Theo shifted his body on top of hers, his hands and his mouth working magic. She surrendered willingly, let herself stay in the here and now just for a little while. She'd have the rest of the day to ruminate about her problems.

And there might not be a tomorrow.

She returned his magic with some of her own, mesmerized by the heat in his dark eyes and by that delicious, feral grin that had captured her from the moment she first saw it. He was a man who loved life. He was a man who was not afraid of duty—or death. She felt as if she'd known him forever. And knew that no matter how long she would know him, it would never be long enough.

She explored him more boldly as the morning's soft light intensified, inexplicably pleased by the way her touch made his breath hitch. But when his teeth nipped the soft flesh of her inner thigh and his tongue traced every intimate corner of her body, she was the one twisting the bedsheets between her fingers, coherency once again fleeing.

"We're good together," he whispered huskily, when heartbeats finally slowed and she was cradled in his arms.

Yes, they were.

Later, while Theo was in the—wasteful!—

freshwater shower, Jorie borrowed his soft blue robe and, scanner in hand, slipped into Tam's room to take the next set of medical readings. Her lieutenant was sitting up, but her gaze and her concentration wandered if the conversation went on for more than three or four sentences.

And the only answer Tam could provide about the ship or the crew's whereabouts was that Commander Rordan was in Theo's galley, getting a glass of water. Wasn't he?

It was as if time had stopped for Tamlynne Herryck.

Suppressing a shiver, Jorie remembered seeing the half-empty glass on the galley counter when she and Theo had returned.

When she walked back into the bedroom, Theo was dressed in faded blue pants and a dark-green shirt.

Being decadent and wanton, she indulged in a wasteful freshwater shower—the water felt so blissfully better than the ship's recycled synthetic liquid—and once again sorted out problems and priorities in her mind.

It all came back to one thing: she had to terminate the C-Prime. It wouldn't stop the Tresh. But it would stop the Tresh from using the zombies to destroy this world's inhabitants and—ultimately—control the Hatches.

She didn't discount that the Tresh could move their entire experiment to another remote nil-tech world. But at least this one—with Theo Petrakos on it—would survive.

19

Theo was standing in his living room, taking the first few sips of coffee and flipping through channels to find the news, when he saw the bright purple horror heading at a determined clip straight for his front door.

"Shit!" He hurriedly put the remote and his cup on the end table, sloshing hot coffee over his hand, then bolted into the bedroom. He prayed Jorie was out of the shower. He had no idea how to work her scanner gizmo, and frying Sophie Goldstein would not win him any brownie points with Aunt Tootie.

Jorie was standing naked near the end of his bed, small drops of water still beading on her tawny skin. She turned, head tilted, and eyed him quizzically.

In spite of impending doom, Theo stopped dead in his tracks, his breath hitching as his body heated. Sweet Jesus and Mother Mary. She was...

incredible. And unless he'd missed something important in the past few hours, she was his.

Sweet Jesus. And Merry Christmas.

"We have company. My neighbor," he stammered out. "The house shields?"

She leaned over to retrieve her scanner from the nightstand.

Nice ass.

God, he was hopeless.

"Disengaged," she told him.

"Thanks." He stared at her a few more long, worthy seconds. "You might want to get dressed. Mrs. Goldstein's"—his doorbell rang—"here."

When he opened the front door, Sophie was already shoving a plastic food container past the screen door that was propped against her shoulder. She had on a purple tunic-type blouse with silver embroidery on the round neckline, purple pants, and— Theo noticed with a quick glance down—purple flip-flop sandals.

"Working during the holidays! Tootie is upset. I told her I'd bring you some butter cookies and fried honey puffs. I've been making them since Hanukkah. It was no trouble to do up another batch."

He leaned against the doorjamb, blocking any attempts by the purple horror to enter his home. "Thanks—"

"So you got some kind of big case? You want some latkes or brisket? I can make that too. You can't fight crime on an empty stomach."

It wasn't quite ten in the morning yet, but Theo's mouth watered at the mention of Sophie's brisket. The honey puffs, little bits of fried dough drenched in honey and flavored with orange and cinnamon, were a nice treat too. And potato latkes—no. He had to keep Mrs. Goldstein—he had to keep everybody—away from his house.

"I really appreciate this. But, yeah, I'm working, and I have no idea if I'll be home later or not. But thanks. I mean that." He nodded and smiled down at her.

She nodded and smiled up at him. And made no move to leave his front porch.

"Thanks," he said again. "Uh, happy holidays."

"You should really at least try to see Tootie and Stavros. Not that I'm trying to tell you how to run your life, Theophilus. But your uncle always managed to spend some part of Christmas with you and Tootie, even if he had to sit in his patrol car in the driveway." She pinned him with a hard stare. "They were always there for you, especially after your *meshuga* mother decided her life's calling was to be a craps dealer in Vegas."

Well, yes. The four months he'd spent living in Sin City were certainly memorable ones for a twelve-year-old boy. Then his father and Uncle Stavros showed up with a court order. And the jingling sounds of slot machines and "Place your bets! Ante up!" were replaced by the familiar cries of the seagulls down at the sponge docks and Aunt Tootie singing Greek hymns very off-key in church every Sunday.

Life was—if not as interesting—better.

"I'll try to cut some time out and see them," he told Sophie. So what if the fate of his planet teetered on the brink? The zombies were in nap phase again, according to Jorie.

But the truth was, he didn't want to leave Jorie alone. Not that she wasn't capable of kicking serious ass. The last time they left the house, however, the Tresh showed up and Rordan went missing. Two events that Theo wasn't sure weren't somehow connected.

And then there was Tammy. Not rowing with both oars in the water yet. Which only made him wonder even more what Jorie had gone through as a prisoner of war with the Tresh. And made him admire even more her sheer determination to survive.

"I'll call Tootie and tell her to expect you." Sophie Goldstein reached up and patted him on the cheek. "Merry Christmas."

There was a little spring in her step as she returned to her house. Sophie Goldstein, Problem Solver and Amateur Ann Landers, had made everything right again.

If only everything else was so easy.

Theo locked the front door, then, container of sweets under one arm, stuck his head through his bedroom doorway. No Jorie. He found her dressed in her sleeveless top and funky shorts, sitting on the bed with Tammy, scanner beeping softly as colors swirled over the screen. He pried open the container's lid and plucked out a sticky honey puff. They were still warm. "Take a bite. You'll like this."

She did. He waited. A rapturous expression crossed her face. He grinned and handed one to Tammy, whose coloring was still too pale. She chewed, then leaned back against her pillows with an appreciative sigh.

Both women were licking their fingers when Theo's cell phone trilled. He handed the container to Jorie and dug the phone out of his pocket.

Zeke. He flipped it open. "*Amigo*. What's up?"

"You home?"

"Yeah. Why?"

"I'm five minutes out. Don't go anywhere. I have to talk to you. Now."

Theo watched Zeke roll up around back, nosing his sedan just behind the white SUV. House shields were off. When Theo saw Zeke tuck a manila case folder under one arm as he shut the car door, Theo's personal shields went up.

Zeke had found something in FCIC or NCIC on Jorie. Even though he knew, logically, there was no way that was possible, that's the first thing that jumped into his mind. Jorie was not who she said she was. Their growing closeness, their growing intimacy, was a sham. It was Camille all over again.

He was cursed, just like his old man.

Stop it, Petrakos!

Zeke climbed the short steps to the porch, his short-sleeved button-down shirt tucked into dark slacks, his detective's shield and gun clearly visible on his belt. This was no social call. Theo shoved the kitchen door open before Zeke could reach for it.

"Jorie here?" Zeke asked. No greeting. No perfunctory off-color joke. Not even "Merry Christmas," and, Christ, it was.

Fuck. "Yeah."

"Go get her."

Theo stepped back, then something warred within him. He had to know the truth before he faced her. "Tell me why."

Zeke tossed the folder on the kitchen table and flipped it open.

Hands clenched at his side, Theo stared at the photographs on the table. Relief and fear tumbled through him. Three parchment-wrapped, wet-eyeball mummies stared back. He grabbed the photos. "I'll get her."

Jorie stood at the galley table, Theo's hand lightly on her shoulder, Zeke Martinez's flat photographs at her fingertips. She would have preferred holographs, where she could examine the bodies in more detail. But this nil world made that impossible.

This nil world also affected her MOD-tech. Zombies had fed and she hadn't known about it. When Theo brought the photos into the bedroom, she'd immediately run a scan and a backup data grab. There was no trace of any craving spur in her data, which still assured her the zombies were in a negative phase. Napping.

Obviously they weren't.

"Tell me again why you think zombies did this." Martinez leaned both hands on the back of a chair.

He still wasn't convinced that what she and Theo had told him at Suzanne's med facility was true. She could hear that in his voice, see it clearly in his stance. But he had come here asking for her input. That seemed to matter to Theo.

She outlined as simply as she could how the zombies used the portals, how, in their now-perverted quest for viral infections, they were drawn to the warm, humid environment, the high rate of electromagnetism, and, under the right stimuli, the life force of soft-fleshed sentients. How his world, his city, provided them the perfect haven, enhanced by the fact that it was so far off the usual spacelanes that no civilized fleet would think to come here. Except the Tresh.

But whether or not they were civilized was debatable.

Martinez puffed out his lips and blew a sigh of exasperation. Frustration. Disbelief. Then he shook his head and raked one hand through his dark curly hair.

"The lieutenant's going to Baker-Act us both," he said to Theo.

A cryptic comment. She'd ask Theo later what the act of making bread had to do with the zombies. She also wanted to ask him what he'd said in those odd, softly lyrical phrases when they were in the heat of passion. But that definitely would have to wait.

She went back to the photographs. "This happened yesterday. You're sure?" she asked Martinez.

"The bodies were *discovered* yesterday by the SO—the Sheriff's Office. Two down at the east beach on Fort Hernando. One by the Gandy Bridge."

The locales meant nothing to her. "All by water?"

Martinez nodded. "We won't know time or date of death until we get the ME's report."

"Medical examiner," Theo added when she

looked over her shoulder at him. "Med-tech who investigates dead bodies."

Then it could have occurred the day before, when she'd captured the juvenile in the park. Or it could have been ... anytime. It was one of a tracker's worst nightmares: insufficient data due to tech failure.

"Let me run the data one more time." She headed for the bedroom, Theo and Martinez on her heels. She folded herself down on the floor and slipped her headset over her hair. "Voice system activate, confirm ident," she said, and then stopped, realizing she'd spoken in Vekran. She repeated the command in Alarsh and ignored the impulse to smack herself.

But there was nothing in the data. She even recalibrated search parameters to double their usual grab rate. Nothing. It had to be the lack of input from the ship's seeker 'droids that was hampering her. When the *Sakanah* disappeared, so did the 'droids. It was like working with one eye blinded.

Maybe that's why Prow didn't destroy these units. He knew they were ineffective. He—

Prow. Prow had been in here with Tamlynne. And she didn't know for how long and doing what. A chill clamped around her heart like a graknox's jaws on its luckless prey's head.

Theo hunkered down by her side. "What did you find?"

"It's what I didn't find. And what I, stupidly, didn't even consider. Prow was in this room with my T-MOD." She initiated a diagnostic but was fully aware that Prow might have assumed she'd do so and taken countermeasures. She would have.

"Ass-faced demon's spawn!" She shoved herself to

her feet. Theo moved up with her but stepped back as if he knew she had an overwhelming urge to hit something, hard.

She spun away from him and Martinez and strode into the spare room, which now functioned as Tamlynne's bedroom. Her lieutenant was sitting in the middle of the foldout bed, rocking back and forth.

"You work too hard, sir." Her voice was dreamy.

Jorie's anger spiked, then dissipated. *Oh, Tamlynne.* "Merely the usual problems, Lieutenant. It will be okay," she told her in Alarsh.

"Theo likes you."

"I know, Tam." *Sometimes a flower grows in hell.* It was an old, overused Kedrian saying, but the truth of it hit Jorie as it came into her mind. In this hell, she'd found Theo. The only positive thing in the midst of all this. Even Tam, as disordered as she was by the effects of the Tresh implant, recognized that.

With a sigh, Jorie squatted down and sorted through the broken remains of the MOD-tech. It was time to get creative.

She brought what she deemed salvageable back to Theo's bedroom. Theo and Martinez's voices filtered in from the structure's main room.

"I agree with you, Zeke, but I don't think we have the luxury of time here," Theo was saying. "The brass will want to set up committees, research teams. They're not going to just take Jorie's word for this. I still don't think *you* believe her."

Jorie tuned them out as she stripped out the components from the secondary T-MOD and inserted the salvaged ones. All house shields were disengaged, except for the roof. PMaT transports were primarily vertical. If the Tresh transported into the backyard and came through the door, rifles flaring, she'd have a battle on her hands.

But her two MOD units couldn't maintain the shields, continue to scan, send out a scrambled seeker signal, and continue to interpolate data while she swapped out components. It was as if she were working under battlefield conditions again. Except this was Guardian MOD-tech, not Interplanetary Marines. And, yes, that meant there were crucial differences, including the lack of necessary redundancy and a reliance on a correlative data source—the ship, now unavailable.

She resealed the units and restarted the tech programs, holding her breath for the ubiquitous program-failure warning screen. The blue screen from hell. When none appeared after five minutes, she relaxed somewhat. First hurdle cleared.

But it would be another ten minutes for the units to completely synchronize and another ten for the diagnostic to initialize and complete.

She pushed herself to her feet. She was thirsty. And perhaps a spoonful or more of that glorious peanut butter. And a honey puff if Theo and Martinez hadn't eaten them all.

She clipped her scanner to her utility belt. It erupted with a screech, sending her pulse racing. She jerked it up, noted coordinates, then spun and grabbed her Hazer from the bed, damning herself for dropping the shields.

Theo heard the familiar screech, dropped the plastic container of honey puffs on the kitchen counter, then pulled his gun out of the hip holster under his shirt. Only as he lurched toward the living room did he re-alize it was his Glock. Not the laser pistol. Too late. Something was already oozing out of the green glow on his living-room wall.

"What the fuck?" Zeke rasped from behind him.

Theo knew Jorie had to be on the way in here, but he couldn't take a chance. He fired rapidly three times, center mass.

The zombie screamed, its cry grating on his ears. A juvenile, he realized. Razor-clawed appendages thrashed, neck twisted—damn! His new leather couch!

He saw the pinpoint of white and fired once more.

The head jerked back. Four arms flailed outward. The creature slammed against the wall and, with a violent shudder, crumpled to the floor.

A stream of Alarsh curses reached his ears. He shot a glance to his left. Jorie, double-stack rifle in her hands.

"Is it . . . ?" he asked her.

She angled the rifle down, then whipped up her scanner. She nodded. "Dead." She turned to him, eyes widening. She stared at the Glock in his hand. "You terminated it with . . . that?"

He looked down at his gun. "Yeah. But it didn't disappear."

She trotted over to where the zombie lay, serrated jaws agape, some kind of yellow liquid spilling onto the floor. The worms writhing on its surface were slowing, spasming. She squatted down, ran the scan-ner over the hideous length of the thing, then rose.

"Hell's wrath," she whispered, and raised her gaze

as he stepped next to her. "We just might have a chance."

A gagging sound behind Theo made him turn. Zeke, hand over his mouth, looking decidedly green. The detective's eyes were wide as he bolted for the kitchen doorway and then—judging from the sound—proceeded to lose his honey puffs in the sink.

Theo had never liked the yellow curtains in his spare bedroom, anyway. Camille had picked them out. He yanked them down and handed them to Tammy, who carried them without comment or question to the living room. Jorie was explaining the different functions of the zombie's appendages to a thoroughly embarrassed Zeke Martinez as they awaited Suzanne's arrival. If they had to move the zombie—and Theo suspected Suzanne might want to take it back to her clinic—the curtains would come in handy. If they didn't move it, they would still come in handy. Just because he didn't puke his guts out like Zeke did when he first saw one didn't mean he enjoyed looking at that thing on his living-room floor.

"Why didn't the shields stop it?" he asked. Tammy was on his leather couch next to the pile of curtains. She gave him a smile as he walked toward Jorie.

"I disengaged the shields when Martinez arrived," Jorie said, and Theo nodded, remembering now. "All but the overhead. I couldn't reactivate them and repair my tech, so they stayed off. But I forgot that I'd reduced their dimensions to fit within this structure's walls. Because of her." She pointed toward the front window and, ultimately, Mrs. Goldstein's house. "That left a gap. A slight one, but enough that a vertical insertion could occur."

"You're saying the Tresh sent the zombie?"

"The Guardians have worked with the fact that the zombies' appearances were at random locales even when spurred by a craving. That no longer appears to be true. The Tresh now can control them. It's almost as if they've returned to their original programming."

"You sound pleased about that."

"I am. Anything that can be programmed can be reprogrammed. Our problem has been that the zombies defied programming for all these years. But there's something that pleases me even more." She glanced up at him, head tilted, mouth slightly parted.

Oh, hell, yeah. He knew what pleased her more. Same thing that pleased him, and they'd done it twice since early this morning. But he had a feeling that wasn't at all what she was talking about.

Down, boy. Heel.

"Don't keep me in suspense."

"The Tresh sent this zombie in shielded. Another reason I know the Tresh now control them. I told you about the shields the Devastators used here, the L-One and L-Twos."

He nodded, grateful for all those years watching *Deep Space Nine* and *Next Generation*. He wouldn't even begin to guess what she was talking about if he hadn't.

"This," she pulled at the rifle strap slung over her shoulder, "is the only thing I have that can penetrate those shields. Devastator shield technology utilizes extremely complex phase patterns."

"But you modified that Hazer, right? We don't have any more of those."

"We don't need them. We have that." And she pointed to his hip and his gun's holster peeking out from under the edge of his T-shirt.

He pulled out his gun and held it in his palm. "This?"

"Very basically, the shields are high-level energy fields used to counter high-level energy weapons. Not a nil-tech projectile weapon that no one has seen, let alone used, in hundreds of years."

He slid the gun back into his holster. "But the house shields reacted to my hand."

"Because they're patterned to counter denser, physical intrusions. A body. An asteroid. They also require a larger generator and a much larger energy source. Ships and structures can maintain them. A single individual's personal *portable* shield generator cannot. It would be"—Jorie lifted her scanner—"at least five times this size. It takes both my MOD-tech units in your bedroom to generate a basic shield around this structure, and that's working them at capacity."

Theo stared at her, trying to grasp all she said. It sounded like good news, though he wasn't totally sure why.

"How does this help us defeat the Tresh?" he asked as he heard the sound of a car pulling down his driveway. The edge of a red roof moving past his side window told him it was Suzanne's Jeep Cherokee.

"It doesn't, not exactly," Jorie said. "What it does

tell me is that I can get to the C-Prime with far less problems than I anticipated. The drones and juveniles guarding it will all be L-One or L-Two shielded. With only one modified Hazer, there was no way I could defend myself on all sides. Even the Hazer takes several concentrated shots to dissolve a shield. But if we have help," Jorie glanced at Zeke sitting on the arm of the recliner, listening, "and sufficient projectile weapons, we have a damned good chance."

That sounded encouraging. "But why is its body still here?"

"First guess, without studying data? Same thing. Your projectile weapon simply punctures, thereby ceasing the zombie's functions. But it doesn't utilize energy as an implosion catalyst the way a G-One would."

His porch door clanked closed and then there were quick steps across his tile kitchen floor. Suzanne arrived in blue jeans and a red T-shirt bearing the image of a scowling orange tabby cat wearing fake fuzzy antlers on its head. *Paw-Humbug!* was in white lettering across the top.

"What do we have—" Suzanne stopped and stared down at the dead zombie lying against the wall. Then she put her hands on her hips and, with a shake of her head, turned to Theo. "That's the most butt-ugly thing I've ever seen in my life."

As Suzanne Martinez examined the zombie, Jorie checked on both MOD-tech units and, satisfied they were functioning, reinstated the house shields. Then she keyed in another diagnostic, looking for anything Prow might have left behind. The program would run slowly due to the power drain from maintaining the shields. But now that she had a possible solution close at hand, she was willing to wait for the results.

She returned to the main room and touched Theo on the arm. "House shields are activated." She looked at Martinez, then at his spouse. "You understand? Don't exit, don't open a window, without telling me first."

"No more zombies, no Tresh?" Theo asked.

"In this room, no."

"How'd they know we were here?" Martinez asked.

"They're not sensing us." Jorie gestured to Martinez, then to Tamlynne. "They're sensing the resonance of Guardian equipment. They may have been monitoring the shields, looking for changes. Or they may have simply been taking a routine sweep of the area, knowing we've been here in the past. Either way, when I changed shield patterns, they knew."

That was why repairing tech in the field was so risky. She'd thought she'd secured the locale—it was secured by Guardian standards. But not by marine field-combat standards. She had to work that way in the future or it could cost lives.

Damning herself, she walked over to Tam on the couch and repeated her instructions about the shields in Alarsh. Tam nodded. "Understand, sir."

"I'll keep an eye on her," Martinez offered, evidently figuring out what she'd said to Tamlynne. He looked a little less pale, but Jorie noticed he was keeping his distance from the zombie. "How is she?"

"There's some memory loss, some disorientation," Jorie told him, moved by his concern. "I've seen it before. If we weren't in this situation, it wouldn't be an issue."

"You really are from outer space."

Jorie grinned wryly, in spite of her consternation. Martinez's earnest amazement was almost endearing. "It's not outer space to me. The Chalvash System, the worlds of the Interplanetary Concord, and the spacelanes that connect them. That's home to me. To us." She nodded at Tamlynne.

"What are you going to do if you can't get back?"

Jorie opened her mouth, then hesitated. It was the one thing never out of her mind, and yet she had no answer. Then she felt Theo's hand brush her shoulder and come to rest against the back of her neck.

"She'll be fine," Theo said.

"Sorry." Martinez splayed one hand outward in apology. "I shouldn't have asked that."

"The Guardians never abandon a team member," she said finally. But they couldn't rescue her and Tam if they didn't know they were alive.

Yet if they did, that would mean she'd never see Theo again. She wouldn't let them send him to Paroo. She'd tell whatever lie she had to in order to prevent that. His life was here: his friends, his neighbor, his duty, his aunt and uncle he spoke so fondly of. She could never ask him to make that sacrifice. No, the pain would be hers alone.

She pulled away from the warmth of Theo's fingers—and the growing ache in her heart—and knelt down next to Suzanne. "There are some components I need extracted from its chest. It will have to be invasive." Next nil world she visited, she would make sure a JS-6-4 was standard equipment in all field packs. "There may be fail-safes, autodestructs. The Tresh are famous for that. Can you do an extraction here, or should we take this to your clinic?"

"The clinic. I have access to all my equipment there. Nina's on duty again, but she won't come in from the kennel wing unless I ask her to, and I won't. Plus, I don't think it's a good idea to leave this in Theo's living room. The neighbors might object when putrefaction sets in and it begins to smell."

"God, Suzy, please!" Martinez looked pained.

"Ezequiel, my love, I'm still baffled how you ended up in Homicide."

Martinez waved dismissively at Theo. "His fault."

"I'll drop the rear structure shields," Jorie said as Theo, behind her, tried unsuccessfully not to laugh. "Which vehicle?"

"Mine's larger," Theo said. "I'll fold down the backseats. Zeke can ride with me—"

"I'll ride with Suzy, thank you," Martinez said quickly.

That feral grin Jorie loved so much played over Theo's lips. "Okay, Jorie rides with me and the zombie. What about Tammy?"

"She can come with us," Suzanne offered. "You won't have room."

That was probably for the best. Until Jorie was very sure of shield integrity, she wasn't comfortable leaving Tamlynne alone in Theo's structure, even though physically she functioned well. She hadn't panicked when the zombie appeared, and she'd assisted Theo with removing the viewport draperies with no problems. In those ways, the lieutenant seemed to be healing.

Her conversations, however, were still disjointed. And there were no answers on the Tresh's appearance or Rordan's disappearance.

"Let's wrap this thing up." Theo nudged the dead zombie's shoulder with the toe of his boot. There was a gurgling sound, and another gush of yellow liquid ran through its jaws. "Zeke, give me a hand?"

But Martinez's hand was over his mouth. And he was moving as fast as he could out of the room.

20

"I told you before. We don't have that kind of time." Theo paced the back hallway of Suzanne's clinic. Zeke had hoisted himself up onto a metal grooming table and sat, palms planted against the top, keeping out of Theo's way in the narrow corridor.

Smart move. Theo'd had a feeling this conversation was coming and, on the drive over, had done a lot of thinking. His amusement over Zeke's reaction to the zombie had faded in light of the very real problems the creature portended. So he'd run through a few scenarios again, just as he had when he and Jorie returned to his house after the confrontation with the Tresh in Gulfview.

But this time, he caught the one big mistake. The downside to his answer to all their problems. He just hoped it wasn't too late to fix it.

He'd also made some very big decisions. And now

that he had, he wanted to act on them. Stalling was driving him crazy. There was too much at risk.

"Seeing that zombie thing will speed up the process, I think," Zeke said.

"Negative. The chief will want FDLE called in, and FDLE will want the feds. Then there'll be the usual fight over who heads the Zombie Task Force and who gets to staff it. Us? County? The National Guard?" He understood Jorie's objections so much more clearly now. "And where's the funding coming from? By that time the Tresh will have the whole herd in the 'new and improved' aisles and we'll be in really deep shit."

"We're already in deep shit, *amigo.* She said there could be three hundred of these things. There are only three of us. Those are not good odds."

"Yeah, I know." Theo stopped pacing and ran one hand through his hair. Okay, so he hadn't worked out all the kinks in his plan yet. "Plus, Tammy's not much help."

"Even if she could be, four is not good odds. We need to request at least a couple SWAT teams. For starters."

Theo shot a glance at Zeke. Yeah, he remembered thinking that was the answer. "I'm not dragging Jorie into the chief's office the day after Christmas."

"I don't think this can wait until tomorrow. You said yourself it'll take a couple days to set things up. Sooner the better. Besides, Brantley knows how to play the game. If anyone can cut through the bureaucratic bullshit the feds can generate, the chief can."

"That's not the point."

"Then what is? Face facts. We've got a potentially

catastrophic situation about to erupt here. Okay, there's going to be red tape, there's going to be politics. But do you really think they're going to drag their feet if hundreds of people could die? If nothing else, they'd be crucified by the news media. It'd be the Hurricane Katrina fiasco all over again."

"And what do you think," Theo asked quietly as his friend voiced the one downside he'd overlooked and now feared, "the news media will do to Jorie?"

Zeke's mouth opened, then closed quickly.

"A freak show, Ezequiel. It'd be a fucking freak show." Everyone would want a piece of Guardian Commander Jorie Mikkalah. The *National Enquirer.* *The Jerry Springer Show.* And worse. Bile rose in Theo's throat. How could he have been so stupid as not to realize what would happen? All this time he'd seen the Guardians' reluctance to reveal their presence as a selfish act. And he'd ignored what Jorie told them the Guardians learned from experience: niltech worlds routinely acted illogically—sometimes even violently—when faced with someone from another galaxy. "I'm not putting her through that."

"The feds will never let that happen. They'll put her under lock and key."

Another scenario he'd come up with and feared. "I'm not letting *that* happen either."

"Theophilus. I don't think you have a choice."

"Like hell I don't." Theo spun away from him and resumed pacing.

"What are you going to do, risk hundreds of people's lives because you don't want a bunch of scientists in some basement room of the Pentagon asking

Jorie questions? I think she can handle that. She's probably been trained to handle that."

Theo could see the tight, pained expression on Jorie's face as she told him about her captivity with the Tresh. He could feel her shivering against him. He could see her fingers trace the rough scar on her shoulder.

He could see her getting into a black government sedan with darkened windows, knowing he'd never see her again.

His breath shuddered out. This was the only scenario he'd agree to. And it too had flaws. "I'll give them the zombie, the weapons." They had both Guardian and Tresh now. "I'm not giving them Jorie."

"You can't hide her in your spare room the rest of her life. She has no Social Security number, no ID. She can't even get a job." Zeke raised his arms in an exasperated motion. "Talk about an illegal alien!"

"I'll get her an ID. A whole identity."

Zeke stared at him. "Be serious."

"I am."

"You know what that costs, a good fake identity?"

"I can take equity out of my house to pay for it."

Zeke barked out a harsh laugh. "Brilliant, Einstein. Traceable funds. There goes your career."

"I'm not going to write a fucking personal check." Theo glared at him. "I'm not that stupid."

"Then listen to yourself, damn it! You're talking felony jail time. Your life down the shitter. You *do* know what they do to cops in the Graybar Hotel, don't you?"

"You're assuming I'd get caught."

"No, *she'd* get caught, suddenly surfacing in all the databases." Zeke ticked the items off on his fingers. "She'd have to get a job, buy a car, rent an apartment—"

"Not if she's living with me, she won't."

"Living with—what're you going to do, Theophilus? Marry her?"

Theo raised his chin and met Zeke's question with a hard stare. This was one of the decisions he'd made driving through the bright Florida sunshine in the middle of Christmas Day with Jorie by his side. And a dead zombie behind them. "Yes."

"You're—*Ay, Jesucristo.*" Zeke dropped his head in his hands, then lifted his face slightly and peered up at Theo. "You got a thing for women with fake identities?"

The not-so-veiled reference to his disastrous marriage hit him like a sucker punch. Theo looked away, keeping his temper in check. But he couldn't keep the anger out of his voice when he turned back. "I'm sorely tempted to kick the shit out of you for saying that."

Zeke straightened slowly, eyes wide then narrowing. "You want to take it outside, Theo? We can take it outside."

Theo needed to hit something. He really did. But Zeke Martinez wasn't whom he needed to hit. It was Rordan and Lorik and Jorie's captain and all the Guardians who, by their reluctance to consider the threat of the Tresh, got him and Jorie to the point where they were now, backs against the wall and nowhere to go. And it was the Tresh and this guy

Prow. Oh, how he needed to hit Prow. Get him in a choke hold and watch the life drain from his iridescent eyes.

But Zeke wasn't Prow or Rordan or the Guardians. Zeke was his partner. His best detective. He ran his hand over his face.

"You got your fancy clothes on, *amigo*." He looked at Zeke out of the corner of his eye. "Suzanne will kill me if you get them dirty."

Zeke studied him for a few heartbeats, then snorted. "You 'fraid of my old lady?"

"Hell, yeah."

"Me too." Zeke brushed invisible dirt off his thighs. "I probably should have changed after Mass this morning, but when Barrington—we were talking in the parking lot after church—when he told me about these weird mummy bodies one of his deputies had found, all I could think of was getting to the SO to see what they had."

On Christmas. *The bad guys never take a holiday,* Uncle Stavros always said. Theo nodded. "Thanks. And, hey, I'm sorry. I shouldn't—"

"She's got you all wrapped up in knots, doesn't she?"

Actually, his feelings for Jorie were one of the few things he had no problems with. "This situation has me wrapped up in knots. It's not only Jorie. There's Tammy. Jorie's more worried about her than she says, and I know she feels responsible for what happened. Both of them are suffering in their own ways." He shook his head. "I keep thinking I'm going to wake up and it's all a bad dream." Except for Jorie. He wanted to wake up and find her beside him.

"There's only one way to end the bad dream, and you know it. We contact the lieutenant and he contacts the chief. Bring 'em here to see Big Butt-Ugly—"

"Baby Butt-Ugly," Theo corrected.

"—and we go in loaded for bear."

Theo's brain knew Zeke was right. But Theo's heart was afraid he'd lose Jorie in the process.

It was a damning discovery. One made possible, Jorie told Theo and Zeke as they stood in the doorway of the brightly lit examining room, only because Lorik's final report had pinpointed what she needed to do to find proof of the mutations. Doing that had taken Jorie and Suzanne almost two hours.

Theo listened intently as she went down the list: a zombie with an embedded personal shield. A zombie with an accelerated growth rate, a maturity beyond its stated numerical age. A zombie that not only took data and guidance from the C-Prime but was now able to regenerate a portion of what it used and send it back.

Making the C-Prime stronger. Making the C-Prime able to control a megaherd.

No longer a parasitic relationship, with the herd draining the C-Prime until the herd was forced to split, but almost trophobiosis: a feeding, a mutual protection.

Jorie put her scanner down on a nearby metal table. "Questions?"

From down the corridor, Theo could hear Suzanne's soft voice and a low squeal of excitement from Tammy. Suzanne had said she wanted to try something to help Tam focus, and judging from the glimpse of fluff a few moments ago, she'd brought a kitten out of the kennel and placed the creature in Tammy's arms.

Just as well. Tammy didn't need to hear about these new and improved zombies, anyway.

"How many are there, total?" Zeke was asking.

"Last count was three hundred eleven," Jorie told him, "but we terminated a few. If they've regenerated those, they're still in the egg stage."

Egg? Theo did not want to see what zombie eggs looked like.

Zeke nodded. "How long from egg to zombie?"

"In your planetary terms?" Jorie closed her eyes for a moment. "Two weeks, your time, egg to hatchling. They grow quickly after that. Three weeks to primary juvenile. Another four to six, depending on availability of foodstuffs, to full juvenile."

"But that's the old zombies," Theo said, remembering information she'd given him over the past few days. "Not the new and improved."

"I have no idea of the time line now, other than it would be faster. And I don't know if it accelerates all stages or just one. Egg to hatchling, maybe. Or juvenile to drone. I'd need time to determine that answer."

And time, Theo knew, they didn't have.

Zeke caught that as well. "In another two, three months there could be a hundred more of these things."

"At minimum. There are no sexes. All zombies can replicate and can do so every six days when needed to expand the herd or to populate out a new one." Jorie motioned toward an adjoining room, where the corpse of the zombie lay. "I can show you—"

"No thanks." Zeke closed his eyes and waved his hands in front of his face. "Pass."

Theo pushed away from the wall. There was something they were all missing here. Another factor. "The Tresh know we know this. They have to know we have the zombie."

"They also know I have no ship here, minimal weapons. They must know what I figured out—your projectile weapons can easily pierce their shields. This isn't a flaw they'll fix by tomorrow. But three, four days to design a correction?" She shrugged. "Another three or four to recalibrate their tech? I wouldn't discount it."

She'd been elated when she'd realized a Tresh shield couldn't stop a bullet. He had too, still thinking of some kind of small, private army. Nothing official. Nothing that would put Jorie's face in the news. Just cops he could trust. With the full understanding that if something went wrong—if the brass or the media found out about his band of zombie vigilantes—he would take the fall. No question. He accepted that.

But putting together his vigilantes would take time, with people being on different shifts and away for vacation. Two, three weeks, he could pull something together.

"So we have a small window in which to act, both on the zombies reproducing the mutation and on the Tresh shoring up their defenses," Theo said. "Do we have two weeks, at least? One?" New Year's Eve? Could he pull this off by New Year's Eve?

"The more we delay, the more we give the Tresh the chance to reconfigure for projectiles," Jorie said. "Two weeks from now there will be more zombies, and two weeks from now Tresh defenses will have improved. More people may die. My team and I have worked situations like that before, where we were brought in much later than we should have been. But it was only the zombies we fought, not the Tresh. And we fought them with full squadrons of gravrippers.

"Remind me someday," she told him with a nod as he paced to the other side of the room, "to tell you about Delos-Five. Three hundred fifty thousand people died before the Delos *pritus* agreed to let Guardian squadrons into their airspace."

He had no idea what a *pritus* was—some kind of head honcho or group, he assumed—but he clearly heard the pain in her voice at what she must have perceived as failing in her duty. A duty he knew he was asking her to delay.

"We have a chance to avoid that stupidity, the senseless waste of life here," she said as he paced back.

"Without a squadron of those gravrippers?" Zeke asked.

Jorie picked up her scanner and slid it into its holder under her sweater. "I don't intend to chase down the C-Prime. I'm going to trigger a craving and bring it to me."

Bring the C-Prime to her? Panic jolted Theo. He gripped the edge of the table. "That's suicide."

"I've done it before—"

"A C-Prime? Alone?"

"No, but—"

Theo leaned closer. "With insufficient tech and no emergency transport?"

"You never transit in close proximity to a zombie. It's too risky. Five maxmeters is the initial safe zone."

"I saw that feeding frenzy, Jorie. I got tagged by one, for Christ's sake. When you're surrounded by zombies, there is no safe zone."

"I just need one shot at the C-Prime."

"One shot? At the heart, right? And if you miss?"

She met his gaze squarely. "I'm not going to kill it. I'm going to reprogram it."

A vision of her climbing up the damned thing and shoving a DVD in its jaws jumped into his mind. Insanity. "Reprogram it?"

"I'm going to use the accelerated exchange rate at which the zombies now interact to spread a kind of virus among them. If I start with the C-Prime, then everyone—every *one*," she stressed, "will be infected. The C-Prime will give it to the juveniles, who'll give it to the drones, who'll bring it back—multiplied in strength, unless Lorik's calculations are in error—to the C-Prime." She paused. "They'll terminate themselves."

"The Tresh can't counteract that?" Zeke asked.

"They'll try. If they hadn't created a megaherd and instead worked in smaller herds with a number of C-Primes, they could isolate several of the herds and correct the problem, maybe only losing one or two herds in the process. But here, everything is tied to one zombie. Once the C-Prime's functions begin to fail, the herd will lose cohesiveness. It can't split for safety, because there's no strong, healthy secondary C-Prime rising in the ranks to give that order, no un-infected secondary C-Prime to keep things under control. Once the C-Prime terminates, the infected herd will feed on itself."

The sound of Suzanne's laughter filtered in. Theo glanced out the door as Zeke did, then he turned back to Jorie. "Couldn't you kill the C-Prime and have the same result?"

"That would disorient the herd, yes. But it wouldn't guarantee that a secondary C-Prime wouldn't develop, especially with the Tresh involved. We need them all sick and dying, the stronger feeding on the weaker, ingesting their virus, weakening and becoming prey themselves. That's the only way I can guarantee the Tresh will have nothing to work with."

Theo massaged the growing ache between his eyebrows with two fingers. "I cannot let you take on a C-Prime by yourself—"

"You do not hear my words." Jorie was shaking her head, as if she were chastising him for forgetting to pick his socks up off the floor, not discussing a suicidal attempt at bagging a giant zombie. "I never said I was doing this alone. I said I would be the one responsible for targeting the C-Prime. Anyone else who cares to help will have more than enough to keep themselves busy."

Anyone else who cares to help. Meaning more than just Zeke. Theo stared at her. "And your regulations that forbid contact with my people?"

"The regulations you kept demanding I break?"

She raised her arms, then let them fall to her sides. "I see no other possible way to solve this. And I have to. I'm a Guardian Force commander. It's my responsibility to protect all worlds from the problem we created. The fact that I'm the only functioning Guardian on this planet doesn't change that. I have to violate the no-contact rule. But I will not break the one demanding I follow my duty."

"No. Wait." Theo held up one hand.

"What do you mean, wait?" She put her hands on her hips. "You've been a one-note symphony since I arrived on your world, telling me we must get your people involved."

"And you gave me war stories of all the problems that happen when Guardians reveal themselves to nil-techs," he shot back.

"Yes. They want our ships, our jumpdrives, our tech, our weapons. Well, there's no ship for your people to have unless the Tresh offer theirs, and I doubt they will. I couldn't build a jumpdrive if you held a Hazer to my head. As for tech, I'm going to have to reconfigure much of what I have in your residence just to adapt my Hazer and create the reprogramming dart with the virus. I have my scanner, of course. And Tam's, though I may need to use that for parts as well." She shrugged. "I have the G-Ones and the two Tresh weapons. But there's nothing I can give your people that will bring them up to the technological level of the Guardians or help them get off this ball of dirt any faster. I can only tell them that, yes, other civilizations are out there and, yes, interstellar travel is possible. If they even believe me."

But they would believe her. Seeing the zombies

and dissecting the dead ones would convince even the staunchest of skeptics. Which meant only two things: the zombies and Jorie would be all over the news channels, or they wouldn't—they'd be in the deepest basement of the Pentagon.

Theo couldn't live with either outcome. He had to develop a third choice. A way to stop the zombies and the Tresh. A way to keep Jorie safe.

In less than a week.

He saw Zeke flip open his cell phone. Theo shot him a warning glance. "What do you think you're doing?"

"Just going to wish Lieutenant Stevens a Merry Christmas. And see if he wants to meet a zombie."

Theo closed his hand around the phone. "Give me a few hours."

"Theophilus—"

"A few hours."

"The clerk's office is closed. You can't apply for a marriage license until tomorrow."

He was aware of Jorie watching them and listening. He glanced over his shoulder at her while he hung on to Zeke's phone. "How long will it take you to make this reprogramming dart?"

"If the ship were here? Two sweeps. Now?" She blew an exasperated sigh through her lips. "Earliest, two days. Moonrise, day after tomorrow. Or sunwake of the next."

Well, it beat the hell out of two hours.

"Two days." He plucked Zeke's cell phone from his fingers, snapped it closed, then handed it back to him. "Two days."

"Providing we're not attacked by any more zombies," Jorie added.

"You know, the fun just never stops." Theo grabbed her hand and pulled her around the table toward him. "Go find Tammy. It's time to go home."

Jorie went in search of Tamlynne, very aware she had no idea of what was going on in Theo's head anymore. She thought he'd be bliss-infused to learn she was willing to work with his people. He was furious. She thought he'd want to attack the problem right away. He was hesitating.

Following the sound of Suzanne's voice, she found Tam in the clinic's small mess hall. It smelled of that coffee Theo so loved. Tam and Suzanne were sitting at a square table. Between them, a dancing and pouncing kitten—she was very sure that was the Vekran word—with bluish-gray fur attacked small balls of paper that Tam, laughing, flicked across the tabletop.

Suzanne looked up when Jorie entered. "This has helped," she said softly, motioning to the kitten.

"Look, sir! Isn't he wonderful?" Tam ran her hand over the small back.

A sentence. A full sentence in Alarsh. No hesitation. No singsong inflection. Jorie shot a quick glance at Suzanne, then back to Tam again. "He's very handsome," she answered, also in Alarsh.

"Suzanne say," Tam switched to Vekran, "cute. The cat is cute." She hesitated between each word, but it wasn't the hesitation Jorie had heard before but rather the normal one of someone learning a new language. Vekran. English.

"Yes?" Tam continued, looking at Suzanne. "Correct?"

"That's correct." Suzanne nodded. "The cat is cute."

Tam patted the table. "Table. Chair. Maga. Zine." She touched or pointed to the different items, naming them. "Ceelink. Vindow."

"I've been doing basic right-brain–left-brain exercises with her," Suzanne told Jorie. "You understand what I mean by that?"

Jorie nodded, her throat tight. Suzanne's compassion for Tam, a stranger, was a rare blessing. "So there's hope?" she managed after a moment.

"Her mind and her body need time to heal. Your doctors have machines to speed that up. We don't. All I can do is keep her exercising her brain, her senses. And hope whatever memories were repressed will surface."

Tam cradled the kitten and placed a soft kiss on its head.

Jorie pulled out a chair and sat. "Lieutenant," she said in Alarsh. "Guardian Force Field Regulation, Section Twelve, Paragraph Three, Subsection A."

Tam blinked. "If...if shielding malfunctions and cannot be repaired, the T...the T..." She frowned. "The T-MOD, yes! The T-MOD must be destroyed. Sir." She looked at Jorie and smiled.

Jorie smiled back, a small weight lifting from her heart.

"What was that?" Suzanne asked, one eyebrow lifting.

Jorie switched back to Vekran. "Something every green-as-*liaso*-hedges ensign would know. One of the most-quoted Guardian regulations. I gave her the cite. She replied with the regulation. She stumbled a bit, but she repeated it."

"Are you and Theo going to take her back to his house?" Suzanne asked as Jorie heard the sounds of footsteps approaching.

"He asked that I retrieve her."

Suzanne laid her hand on Jorie's arm. "A suggestion. Let her stay with Zeke and me for a day or two."

"Who's staying with us?" Zeke Martinez came up behind Suzanne.

The dark-haired woman turned. "I'd like Tamlynne to spend a few days at our house, Ezequiel. Hear me out." She raised one hand. "I am a doctor. Tam's been through a traumatic experience, one her brain associates with a certain location. I think the fact that she's improved since she came here—aside from the hour or so I've worked with her—is because she's no longer having flashbacks or reacting to an implanted autosuggestion triggered by being in Theo's house. I want to keep her out of the environment she associates with the attack."

"But—"

"We have the room. The guest room your mother uses when she visits."

"—it's Christmas," Martinez finished.

"Yes. And where's your generosity of spirit?"

"It could be dangerous, Suzy." Theo perched on the edge of the table. Jorie felt his hand rest on her shoulder. "The Tresh could come gunning for her."

"Then why haven't they?" Suzanne asked. "They haven't come to this clinic."

Theo looked down at Jorie, one eyebrow slightly arched.

"They follow tech and PMaT trails," Jorie said. "The Tresh knew about your residence because of the Guardian tech there. The same way I found the structure they were using."

"I know Zeke asked you this before, but are you sure there's no way they knew you were in my house when they sent the zombie?" Theo motioned to the corridor where the dead zombie's body now lay secured in a cold-storage unit.

"I can't tell you what they know," Jorie said. "But I can tell you that if I were working a nil world and saw Guardian shields over a structure and Guardian tech trails emanating from that same structure, I'd feel fairly sure a Guardian was in that vicinity."

Which was how they found Danjay Wain. She had no doubt of that now.

"And since I have Tamlynne's scanner and the Tresh implant has been removed," Jorie continued, "they have no way of tracking her specifically. If anything, they'd return to the implant's last signal, and that's Theo's residence. Not here and not your residence," she said with a nod to Martinez.

"It's not rocket science, Theo." Martinez punched Theo lightly on the arm. "Get it? Rocket science. Outer-space aliens."

Jorie frowned. "Starship propulsion has nothing—"

Theo ruffled her hair. "Don't encourage him. Please."

"So it's settled?" Suzanne asked, glancing from

Jorie to Zeke. "Tam comes home with us for a few days?"

"I think it's wise." Jorie reached over and stroked the kitten's soft head. "I'll tell her she has to help you care for the companion. The kitten. Her family had many when she was a child. It's a high honor on her world."

She translated everything to Alarsh and watched a light of happiness glow in Tam's eyes as she enthusiastically accepted her new "assignment."

Theo pulled Jorie to her feet. "Zeke, keep in touch with me."

"Yes, boss."

Jorie reached for Suzanne's hand and clasped it, trying to convey through touch what words could not.

Then it was just her and Theo in the white land vehicle, pulling away from Suzanne's clinic. And Tamlynne Herryck. The only other Guardian—the only other *person*—on this world who spoke Alarsh and who knew what it was like to travel between the stars.

Jorie had never felt so alone.

21

"Hungry?" Theo's voice broke into Jorie's troubled thoughts as the Essuvee rumbled away from Suzanne Martinez's companion facility.

She took her gaze away from her scanner, where she'd outlined the initial parameters for her reprogramming virus, and—after a short conversation with her stomach—nodded. "I need to get this transferred to my T-MOD. We have more peanut butter, yes?"

"Is three hours going to make a huge difference?"

She interpreted that to mean he wasn't intending to head back to his residence—and her tech—right now. "Overall, no." Everything was so uncertain without the tech and a team to compile needed facts. "But I can't afford any more mistakes here."

"You haven't—"

"I have." She recited the list of sins that were now emblazoned in her mind. "I should have alerted

Tamlynne and the ship when I picked up that dead zone. I don't know if Captain Pietr would have listened to me. Probably not, and, yes, I could have risked his questioning my competence. But Tamlynne would have listened. Acted. She would have been ready for Prow. And Rordan—"

His hand squeezing hers stopped her words. "You don't know for sure. Second-guessing yourself is going to create more mistakes, because you're not going to trust your instincts when you need them."

"My instincts say I need to get this program started."

With a sigh, Theo turned the vehicle around. "Okay, get it started. But my instincts say you need a break. You've immersed yourself in this for too long. We have an old saying about not being able to see the forest for the trees. You understand that?"

She did. "But—"

"We'll stop home. You get your computers working on this thing. Then I want to get you out of the forest for a while. Plus," he paused and glanced at her quickly, then back to the traffic ahead, "I've been thinking about how the Tresh hone in on your tech. The more we're there, the greater risk we have of a confrontation with them."

He had a point. Still... "You'd rather return to find a zombie has sliced up your main room?"

"Than confront it? Yes. Every confrontation distracts us—distracts *you*—from what needs to be done. Every confrontation risks lives. Something happens to you, Jorie, and we have no hope of stopping these things. You're the only one who understands how they function." He slowed the vehicle as the dangling lights changed to red. "If we could all go live at Zeke and Suzanne's for the next week until the zombies are stopped, I'd be a lot happier."

"The shields are secure," she argued.

"The shields tell the Tresh where you are," he countered.

But the shields were necessary to protect the tech, and the tech was necessary to stop the zombies. She understood his concerns but saw no options. She went back to her calculations on her scanner, not raising her head until Theo guided the land vehicle behind his structure.

Armed, they both exited the vehicle and—as she temporarily dropped the back sector shields—entered his residence. But nothing challenged them. She gave him an "I told you so" nod as she headed for his bedroom. Once on the floor, she segued her small scanner to the larger of the two MOD-tech units.

She was peripherally aware of Theo moving about his residence. At one point he changed his shirt, buttoning up a new one, then brought her a glass of water.

"Done yet?"

"Almost." She wondered how long she could keep saying "almost." Once the programming began running, it didn't need her input. But working with the familiar MOD-tech, speaking Alarsh into her oc-set's mike, was comforting.

Then Theo was kneeling behind her, hands on her shoulders. "Now, Jorie."

It wasn't a question. She sighed and stood. She had a feeling she knew where he wanted to go, and she fully understood. But it made her nervous—and not only because she'd be away from her tech. "Two, three sweeps," she told him as they entered his kitchen. "Then I must get back here." The back door clanked shut behind her. She sealed his residence's shields and followed him down the porch steps.

"I want to see my aunt and uncle. It's Christmas. You understand what that means?" he asked as he backed the vehicle out of his residence's narrow paved accessway.

"Only that it's a day of observation for you. An important one." She glanced at him. Moonrise was approaching, the world's natural light dimming. It was an experience that still struck her as odd. Shiplight was so much better. More consistent.

Plus, moonlight meant night, a time the Tresh preferred to move. She shook off her unease and went back to his question about his Christmas. "You're also thinking you might not see them again."

He looked over quickly. "You reading minds now?"

She'd known that's where he wanted to go because it's what she always did before she left on a dangerous mission: see the people most important to her. "I've spent most of my adult life either targeting a sentient or being a target. Every time I see Galin, I always treat it as if it's the last one."

"Galin?" Theo's voice had a strained note. "Don't tell me. Another concord?"

She frowned at him. "Not with my brother!"

"I didn't know you had a brother."

Sadness trickled past her heart. "Yes." It had been three galactic years since she'd seen him.

"Is he a Guardian too?"

She shook her head. "He designs starship jump-drives. The thing that makes—"

"I understand jumpdrives. Hyperspace." He lowered the pitch of his voice. "Warp Factor Ten, Mr. Data." He pointed one finger. "Engage."

Warp factor? How did he know the term? "Warp Factor Ten is fiction and, besides, denotes an infinite velocity and therefore is impossible."

They were stopped due to the edict of multicolored lights. Theo stared at her. She stared back. She felt that for some reason her comment had startled him. The vehicle moved forward again.

"What size do you wear?" he asked.

His question made so little sense in the current conversation about her brother and jumpdrives that she tried translating it in a few other galactic tongues. It still made no sense. She gave up. "Size?"

He plucked at his shirt. "Clothing size."

"What does that have to do with jumpdrives?"

"Nothing. But it has everything to do with Aunt Tootie and Uncle Stavros." He slowed the vehicle again, then turned left into a large paved area. "God bless Walgreens. They never close."

"Never clothes?"

Theo disengaged the vehicle's engine and twisted in his seat. "The shorts, sweater, boots"—he tapped her arm, then her leg—"won't pass muster with Tootie on Christmas. But I stopped here last week to get a soda. It amazed me what these places sell now."

"Soda?" Jorie was very lost.

That feral smile played over his lips. "You'll see."

What Jorie saw, as she followed Theo into the establishment, was a commissary. A decent-size one with a wide selection of items, most in brightly colored boxes. He threaded his fingers through hers and brought her to an aisle that contained...clothes. Not many. Most appeared to be shirts of the type Theo favored—short-sleeved and round-necked. But these were lettered: *Life's a Beach*. And *What Happens in Bahia Vista Beach Stays in Bahia Vista Beach*.

"Just some touristy stuff," Theo said. "But this might work."

It was a slender sleeveless dress, ankle length, deep green in color splashed with large white flowers. The material was very lightweight but soft. It looked like something worn in Paroo, and she said so.

"Hawaiian," he said.

Another nonsensical word.

"Flip-flops," he said, dropping a pair of white sandals dotted with lots of tiny gold beads on the floor next to her feet. "Women wear them everywhere these days."

Dress and shoes were chosen in the proper size. A colorful satchel with a shoulder strap was added, along with a soft, long-sleeved light-blue shirt—sweatshirt, Theo termed it—with *Bahia Vista, Florida* on the front and a matching pair of shorts. Jorie followed Theo to the front of the commissary and watched him hand greenish pieces of paper to a pale-skinned female with purple streaks in her short dark hair and a line of gold hoop earrings draped over the outside curve of her left ear.

"Wow, who does your hair?" the female asked her.

"She's not from around here." Theo draped one arm over Jorie's shoulder. "Somewhere she can change into this dress?"

"You guys going to a beach party? Customer restrooms are in the back. Go down the vitamin aisle and you'll see the door."

"Thanks." Theo nudged Jorie forward. "Merry Christmas."

Jorie felt silly changing her clothes, but she understood. In many civilizations, mode of dress was indicative of stature. Theo was taking her to see cherished elder family. When in Vekris...

She put her tracker clothes, socks, and boots into the plastic bag provided by the commissary and her scanner inside the satchel. She took a moment to scrub freshwater—so delightfully plentiful here—over her face and run wet fingers through her hair. Then she pulled the dress over her head. It was rather nice, narrow at the waist and flaring slightly over her hips. Slit up both sides. Good. If she had to run or kick out in battle, she could do so. She slipped her feet into the sandals—definitely not battleworthy.

Then she marched out of the small room.

Theo was leaning against the wall. His eyes widened. For reasons she couldn't quite explain, she blushed.

Theo stared at her as if she were the last morsel of peanut butter in the universe and he was starving. "Hot damn."

Hot? She did feel a little warm.

He slipped his hand into hers. "C'mon. Aunt Tootie can't wait to meet you."

"So nice to see you got dressed up, Theophilus," Aunt Tootie said in mock sternness as Theo opened the back door and stepped into her kitchen. Savory, mouthwatering aromas of meat juices and the yeasty tang of baking assaulted him immediately.

This was the house that he'd always thought of as home—a rambling pale-yellow stucco Florida ranch with the ubiquitous barrel-tile roof, on a corner lot filled with scrub palm, orange, and grapefruit trees. The house was within a few blocks of the bayou—a site of much boyhood mischief—but it was Aunt Tootie's kitchen that held the most memories.

He swept the small, silver-haired woman into his arms, chuckling. Tootie was laughing too. She'd been a cop's wife since she was twenty years old and was well used to her husband appearing in all manner of dress when he was working, and she believed Theo—in jeans and a black silk camp shirt that covered his gun on his hip—was working today.

Jorie's outfit, however, was another matter. The shorts and long sweater would have been an immediate negative in Tootie's eyes.

He kissed her cheek. *"Kala Christouyenna,"* he told her, wishing her a Merry Christmas.

Tootie stood on tiptoes to frame his face with her hands and kissed him soundly on both cheeks. *"Kala Christouyenna! S'agapo."*

Theo watched dark-brown eyes twinkle. "Love you too. Now . . ." And he turned her slightly. *Here it comes.* Tootie had hated Camille on sight. "Titania Petrakos, this is Jorie Mikkalah."

"Jorie." Tootie extended her hand, her face and tone completely unreadable. She would have made an excellent detective. "How nice to meet you. Welcome to our home."

Jorie took her hand. "Thank you, Theo said"—she glanced up at him, and he saw an unexpected sadness in her eyes—"this is a family time for you. I'm honored that you permit me to share it."

The first flicker of emotion crossed Tootie's round face. A softening? Theo wasn't sure. "It must be difficult for you to be away from your family. Theo said you're from—"

"Up north," Theo put in with a wave of one hand, delineating some distant place. Real distant. "Way up north."

Tootie patted Jorie's hand. "You'll get to experience your first Greek Christmas, then."

Thank God it was a Greek Christmas. Had it been one with a turkey and green beans on the table, there would have been a lot more explaining to do when Jorie didn't know what those dishes were.

But hungry people eat instead of talk. Theo and Jorie ate, and ate well. Jorie's fondness for peanut butter quickly extended to his aunt's cooking, and the obvious delight on her face as she tasted each offered dish and treasured each morsel gave a whole new meaning to the word *savoring*.

Still, Theo could tell she was nervous. The small macramé tote bag with her scanner and G-1 was never out of her reach, and several times he saw her touch it, as if for reassurance. And he suspected her trips to the bathroom were more to check her scanner than to powder her nose.

At the end of the meal, Theo helped Tootie and Jorie clear the table and put back the traditional wooden bowl of water with the basil-wrapped cross—a Greek tradition to keep the evil *Kalikantzri* at bay. He hadn't seen a zombie since this morning. Must be working.

Then he left the two women discussing Sophie Goldstein's honey puffs and headed for the living room. He was a bit concerned leaving Jorie with his aunt, but not overmuch. Jorie's mastery of English was—except for her accent, which was something of a cross between French and British—damned near perfect now.

Besides, if she blew it, it didn't matter. He hadn't been so insistent on seeing his aunt and uncle only because it was Christmas. He was going to tell Stavros the truth.

In case he was killed. He hadn't ruled out the possibility, because he knew Jorie was bound to try some wild scheme. And he knew he'd be there, right beside her.

Theo settled on the blue-and-yellow tropical-print couch in front of the television—a nice wide-screen plasma. Couple years old but still had a good picture. A basketball game was on. He watched disinterestedly for a few minutes while Uncle Stavros brought back his second plate of syrup-covered *melomakarana*.

Stavros Petrakos—a bear of a man with a full head of thick gray-streaked dark hair and eyebrows to match—sat down with a grunt. "Want one?"

"No room." Theo waved one hand. "Well, okay. One more."

Stavros snorted. "Cops and doughnuts."

"Pot calling the kettle . . ."

"How's things on the job?"

"Job's good." It was. Theo couldn't think of anything he wanted to do more than being a cop. "Got some budgetary wranglings coming up, but they've already approved the new MDTs."

"How did we ever do the job without computers in the cars? Ha!" Stavros licked his fingers. "Pretty gal you got there. How old is she?"

Theo knew the answer to that one now. "Thirty-nine."

"Doesn't look a day over thirty—*Skata!* You see that foul?" His uncle pointed to the television. "Illegal elbow if I ever saw one." He paused. "She divorced?"

Theo was ready with the recitation. "Never been married, though she was engaged once. Broke it off because the guy cheated on her. No kids. Has a lot of responsibility in her job—she's fairly high up the food chain. Well liked, well respected. Real team leader, you know? And, oh, she was in the marines."

A *melomakarana* stopped in midair. "Marines?"

"Flew combat."

"For Canada?"

"Multinational force, actually."

"You're pulling your old uncle's leg, right?"

"Nope." *And it's going to get worse.* "Remember that UFO sighting out over the Gulf when I was a kid? I was out with you and Dad night-fishing on the Tsavaris's boat?"

Stavros shot him a narrow-eyed glance, but nodded.

"You told me later you'd seen others but said the stories would have to wait until I was older. Well, I'm older." *Like thirty years older.* He wondered now—given his longtime dedication to sci-fi and things *Star*

Trek–ish—why he'd never asked his uncle for the rest of the stories before.

Stavros was silent for a moment, chewing his *melomakarana* and darting glances between Theo and the game on television. Then: "This is because your gal's a pilot, right? They see those things all the time. She saw one of those UFOs and no one believed her."

"No." Theo waited until Stavros swallowed the piece of cookie. "She *is* one of those UFOs."

"Theophilus, you're talking nonsense."

Theo rubbed one hand through his hair. "This is not going to make sense. But I want you to know what's going on, because I want you to understand if something...happens."

"Something—look, the job's stressful. No one knows that more than me. I did thirty years on the streets. But they have people who can help you." Stavros laid his hand on Theo's arm. "Counselors and such."

Theo ignored him. "Jorie's part of a group called the Guardian Force. They wouldn't have bothered with our planet except that these monster guard-dog things they created—they call them zombies—ended up here. Looks like another nasty outer-space group, the Tresh, are messing with these zombies' programming. But, unfortunately, these Tresh attacked Jorie's ship, and now it's just her and me and Zeke and maybe a few others to stop the bad guys."

He glanced at Stavros. His uncle was wiping one hand over his broad face. "I'll get you all the help you need," his uncle said. "If it takes every dime I have. It doesn't matter. You know Tootie and I love you."

"I love you too," Theo said, leaning forward and pulling his cell phone from his back pocket. He flipped it open and hit a number on speed dial. "*Yassou, amigo*. Listen, Uncle Stavros is about to Baker-Act me. Will you talk to him? Thanks." He handed the cell phone to Stavros. "It's Zeke."

His uncle took the cell phone gingerly, as if it might bite him. "Zeke? What kind of *skata* is my boy...Okay." Silence. Longer silence. "What?" he bellowed. "*Mou espasas ta arheedia!*"

Theo knew from experience that when he heard Stavros accuse someone of busting his balls, Stavros was not quite convinced but getting close.

Evidently, so did Tootie. "Stavros! Watch your language, please!" came from the kitchen.

Finally Stavros nodded, wished Zeke and Suzanne a Merry Christmas, and handed the phone back to Theo. "*Tis Panagias ta matia!*"

Now it was the Virgin Mary's eyes being invoked. "Yeah, I know," Theo said.

"If you're playing a game on the old man—"

"I'm not. We're not." He filled his uncle in on the rest of the details, including the problem with Jorie's lieutenant and the unknown status of the rest of her team and her ship. He could tell some of it simply didn't register with the old man. He'd seen too many Signal 20s in his day. But there had been those UFO sightings he'd been tight-lipped about for decades. Theo asked about them again now.

Stavros shook his head. "The one with your father and you wasn't the first, not by any means. But I'd stopped talking to anyone about them by that point. No one believes you, and you get a reputation—I had Tootie to think about. And you."

"You ever get taken on board, like I was?"

"*Skata*, it was enough just seeing these things zipping around the sky at night. If one grabbed me, I'd probably start shooting."

"That was my initial reaction too. But then you start thinking about where you are and who could get hurt, all the while telling yourself this is not really happening."

"But it did." His uncle studied him. He wasn't one hundred percent convinced. But Theo was family. "What do you need me to do?" Stavros asked.

Stavros Petrakos had been one damned fine shot in his day, but he was seventy-eight now. A robust seventy-eight who mowed his own lawn and trimmed his own fruit trees, but seventy-eight. "We're putting a task force together. But this is strictly under the radar. If anything should...happen, what the news media gets and what actually went down might be two different things. I just wanted you to know the truth."

Stavros's gaze didn't waver. "I still hope this is some kind of a joke."

"Wish it was too."

"When?"

"By New Year's, I'm thinking."

Stavros nodded. "The chief knows?"

"I'm trying to keep the brass and the news reporters out of it right now. I don't think they'll be able to move quickly enough. And I don't want to make a media spectacle out of Jorie."

"Poor kid. She's basically all alone in this."

Theo patted his uncle on the shoulder, then stood. "She's not alone. She has me."

He wandered back into the kitchen, which was empty, then, hearing a familiar tinkling sound, followed that to the spare bedroom in the back of the house, where his aunt kept her music-box collection. A thoroughly enthralled Jorie was holding a miniature palm tree in her hand as it played a tinny rendition of the Beach Boys' tune "Kokomo."

Yeah, that's what he needed to do. Run away with her to the Keys and a little place called Kokomo.

"Bliss!" she said when he stepped into the room.

He smiled. "Time to go."

"So soon?" Tootie plucked a music box in the shape of two intertwined cats from one of the shelves that ringed the small room. "Jorie's never seen these before. I guess there's not a lot of use for them in those Eskimo villages." She shook her head.

Theo took the palm tree from Jorie and put it back on the shelf where it belonged. He knew where each one belonged. He'd helped his uncle build the shelves as his aunt's collection grew over the years. "You know I'm working, *Thia*."

"I know, I know. But if I didn't make a fuss, I wouldn't be a good aunt." She shooed him and Jorie toward the living room, where Stavros was waiting. "Maybe around New Year's or after, you'll come for dinner, yes?"

His uncle's face didn't betray a thing. Man was a damned good cop.

"Sure." He hugged his uncle, then his aunt.

"She's a nice girl," Tootie whispered in his ear.

He bussed her cheek. "Told you so."

Stavros was holding Jorie's hand and patting it. Tootie pulled her away and gave her a hug, then put a bag of leftovers in Jorie's hand as they went through the kitchen. "Something to nibble on later," Tootie said.

Nothing like homemade Greek cooking to fuel a fight against zombies.

The bright moonlight and the glow of the porch light bathed Theo's back steps in a white glow. But Jorie let Theo handle the physical inspection of a structure he was more familiar with than she was. She studied her scanner. Residence shields were intact, with no attempted instrusions. Still, both she and Theo entered the back door with weapons out—and she kicked off her sandals as she came across the kitchen threshold. There was no way she could run in those things.

Only after they cleared the residence did Theo go back out into the warm night air to retrieve the bag with her clothes and Tootie's offerings from the vehicle's rear seat. Theo had a lovely family, Jorie realized as she leaned against the kitchen counter and slipped her sandals back on. It made her miss Galin all the more.

"Somebody left this on the back porch steps." Theo came though the kitchen door, bags and Tootie's containers bundled in his arms. And something else.

Jorie automatically reinstated the residence's rear shields as she stepped toward him. He put the food containers on the small table, the clothing bag on a chair, and turned as she approached, a squat silver cylinder in his hand.

Jorie froze, her throat closing, a tremor shaking her body so severely she almost dropped her scanner.

"This was tucked to the side, I almost missed— Jorie?"

"Where did you get that?" Her voice was a hard rasp.

"This?" He angled the metal cuplike object away from him. "It was on the steps."

Jorie sucked in a harsh breath and inched back.

"Babe, what's the matter? It's just some kind of capped soup mug with a built-in spoon thing—"

"A feeder. It's a feeder." She could make out the markings engraved on its side now: *Detention Compound 3 Ovzil*. Her heart pounded and she felt light-headed. She let the scanner slide from her hand to the tabletop, then gripped the back of the closest chair.

"A feeder?"

Vekran, English words fled. She had to close her eyes for a moment and focus, seeking the explanation in Alarsh, then in Vekran.

Theo's fingers curled around her arm. "Honey?"

The . . . thing was inches from her body, still in his hand. With a strangled cry she struck out at it, hard. It flew from his grasp and clattered to the floor, rolling back and forth a few times before it wobbled to a halt.

She watched in sick fascination. How many times had she thrown hers against the cell wall?

"Jorie!" Both hands were on her shoulders, and Theo's breath was warm on her cheek.

"A feeder." Her voice was rough. She raised her face to his. "It holds a liquid-and-powder protein mix. You slide the spoon down to stir," she pushed her thumb against nothing, yet she could feel the cold metal feeder in her hand, "then take a scoop and swivel it to eat. It's the only thing you get to eat when you're a prisoner of the Tresh." Foul-tasting. Even now, she wanted to gag.

"Fuck." Theo's face blanked, then hardened. "Shields are up?"

She knew they were. But she grabbed the scanner off the table, because her whole world suddenly tilted to one side. She nodded.

"You're sure that's what it is?"

Her gaze found the feeder on the floor. "Don't you see...?" But Theo couldn't read Supi, the Tresh language. "Those letters. Detention Compound 3 Ovzil." Ovzil Rok Por. A prison compound run by the Devastators at the base of the Ovzil Neha mountain range. The wind never stopped there. She could still hear its shrill moan through the ventilation system of her cell.

She shook her head, pushing away the memory. Theo released her shoulders and dug his weapon out from under his shirt.

Her own hand shook as she studied the scanner again. "No sign of any shield breach. They—someone left it here, knowing I'd find it." That someone had to be Prow. And he knew what finding it would do to her.

"Was Compound Three where you were?"

She swallowed. "Yes."

"With Prow?"

"Yes."

"They're playing mind games with you, Jorie. Psychological warfare. Because they can't get to you directly." He moved back to her, one large hand on her shoulder once again. Warm, reassuring, steady. "Don't let them win."

Jorie slid the scanner back into the small bag and palmed her G-1, forcing down the bile that threatened to surge up her throat. Forcing the memories away. Forcing herself to remember she was a Guardian Force commander.

By the time they'd checked every closet, every corner of the small residence, she was calmer. And Theo had spoken to Zeke Martinez. Nothing unusual there. Tamlynne was fine, the kitten sleeping in her lap. But they were alerted.

Jorie sagged down into a kitchen chair and rested her forehead against her fingertips.

There was the scrape of wood against tile, and Theo sat down next to her. "Why would Prow keep that feeder after all these years?"

"I doubt it's mine." The thing was still on the floor. Hers or not, she wouldn't pick it up. Could barely look at it. "There's likely a matter replicator on board his ship. Or ship's supply has some feeders and engraved it with the prison compound's name."

He pulled her hands away from her face and held them in his. "We can take it out in the backyard and fry it with your Hazer, if that will make you feel better."

Star's end, but he had a very good face and an

even better heart. "No. You're right. The vomit-brained bastard is playing games. He can't win unless I let him. I'm not going to let him." She drew a long breath. "He wants me to remember. I will remember. And I'll make him pay because I will not forget."

Jorie pulled her hands out of Theo's, strode to where the feeder lay on its side, and snatched it off the tile floor. Her stomach spasmed as her fingers touched the cool, slick metal, but she didn't drop it. Instead, she marched to Theo's bedroom and placed the feeder on the corner of his wooden dresser.

She would not forget.

Then cross-legged and teeth clenched, she went back to analyzing the reprogramming dart.

22

At some point during the late-evening hours, Theo dropped one of his light-green long-sleeved pullover shirts in her lap along with a pair of gray drawstring shorts, with the admonishment to "get comfortable."

And at some point even later that evening, Theo tugged her away from her screen and her worries and back into his arms—and his bed.

"Last night," she told him hesitantly as his hands slipped under the green shirt and massaged the aches along her spine, "we probably shouldn't have—"

His breath was soft in her ear. "Last night was wonderful. Perfect. Don't change that. Not everything happens according to plan."

"My only plan is reprogramming the C-Prime. Beyond that, I cannot even begin to speculate."

"Then don't speculate," he said, his voice husky

with emotion. "I told you. Take what's here and now."

Jorie turned in his embrace and saw the undisguised heat in his gaze. She couldn't remember Lorik ever looking at her like that. It thrilled her—and frightened her. There was so much at risk, so much at stake. So many unknowns.

And then there was Theo. Infuriating, obstinate, intelligent, compassionate, loyal, brave Theo. So she sought the heat of his skin as she had the night before, focusing everything on this one man right now, knowing full well this one man would haunt her dreams forever.

The next spate of bad news hit at about nine-fifteen local time the next morning. Significantly after sunwake and significantly after a morning meal of coffee—which Jorie was slowly acquiring a taste for when it was heavily sweetened—and peanut butter on toasted bread.

The scanner riding her hip under Theo's borrowed shirt screeched out a terrifying high–low warning that sent her careening out of the kitchen and into his bedroom. Structure shield failure. Her MOD-tech was gasping its last breath but still trying to run the calculations on the zombie reprogramming dart and still attempting to send signals to any Guardian ship that might be sweeping the sector.

She now understood Theo's panic at nakedness.

They were naked, exposed, vulnerable. If the Tresh saw the structure's energy pattern suddenly flattening, they were dead—and the terror the feeder cup symbolized would become real.

She grabbed her Hazers from under Theo's bed and tossed him the spare. "Hard-terminate!" She couldn't take any chances. A team of Devastators or a dozen zombies could appear at any moment.

"What happened?" Theo slung the strap over his shoulder, his projectile weapon already in hand.

"Shields are gone," she told him in English, then switched to Alarsh, forcing her MOD-tech units through a series of resets and reinstallations through commands given tersely into her mouth mike.

"Tresh?"

"My fault." She kept watch on her scanner. Anything could happen. In a way, she almost wished for another attack by the Tresh. She wanted this damned thing settled! "Overloaded the system."

He started for the door.

"Stay here. They'll zero in on the tech. I can't program and watch for them."

"I got your six, babe. Do your work."

She did, but there was no way she could resurrect full residence shields. Bliss luck it was daylight, the Tresh less likely to move easily then. But less likely hadn't helped Tam, Kip, or Jacare. Of course, she was the instigator, tracking down the Tresh first that day.

The zombies appeared in daylight or dark.

She worked feverishly to get the shield program to resurrect, aware of Theo pacing behind her, aware of every other noise in the residence, every land vehicle passing on the street, waiting for that cold draft that preceded a PMaT transit—or the green glow of a zombie portal forming.

None of her patches held. The unit was overtaxed. She was asking too much of it: shield the residence, design the zombie dart, parse the skies with a Guardian distress signal. Something had to go.

She gritted her teeth and deleted the distress signal, her heart sinking as she did so. The one chance, the only chance she'd have of being found, of going home again, lay in that signal. Even a seeker 'droid on mapping duties would have seen and reported it.

Now there was nothing.

With the deletion of that program, tech resources restructured, energy usage leveled. She had something to work with. She might not get home, but she could protect where she was.

She resurrected the roof shield first. "Overhead in place," she told Theo. Out of the corner of her eye she saw him glance up, and if she hadn't been so scared, aggravated, and under pressure, she might have grinned. So typical.

But the next datastream gave her nothing to smile about. There was insufficient power to re-create the wall shields. A core processor must have burned out in the shutdown. Capacity was under seventy percent of what she'd had last night. And she couldn't reduce functions any more. She couldn't stop the dart-program computations.

"Ass-faced demon's whore!" She hated no-choice situations.

Only when she caught Theo's raised eyebrow did she realize she'd sworn out loud and in Vekran. Alarsh epithets never translated well. "I can't shield your entire structure anymore. My tech took damage. I don't have time to chase down the problem, and even if I did, I've nothing to repair it with. So..." She keyed in changes to the shield program, shaking her head in frustration.

"What can you shield?"

"One room. This room, including your bathroom. That's all." She locked the shields in place, then flipped her oc-set over her right eye and glanced quickly around. Everything looked good. She pulled the band back down around her neck. "Perimeter secure. But anytime you go through that door, especially at night, you have to assume something you're not going to want to meet might be out there."

"You're sure the Tresh didn't cause this?"

"I checked once and am running a secondary check now." Best she could, with her tech's reduced capacity. "But I don't think so. It's just a basic overload on a unit that was never meant to do as much as it's been doing."

"I thought it was maintaining the shields and designing the zombie dart. Your scanners track the zombies and the Tresh, right?"

She'd never told him about the wide-beam distress signal. She'd convinced herself it was because there hadn't been time to discuss such things, but she knew it was really because of what she felt and what had happened the past two nights. Hesitantly, she told him now and saw the fleeting expression of disappointment on his face. Then it was gone, his features relaxing. She remembered his ability to subvert his emotions when they were in the cabin assigned to him on the *Sakanah*.

"We should be able to make a move on that C-Prime in a couple of days. Once that's done, you can put all your tech into contacting another Guardian ship." He reached down and tugged on a lock of her hair. "I know you want to go home, Jorie."

She also saw the darkening of his eyes every time he realized that.

"It's my duty to report what I've found out about the Tresh."

He hunkered down next to her, shoving his gun in his holster as he did so. "We had this conversation three days ago. Only I was telling you about my duty to be here. Do you remember what you told me? That you try to take what's bad and make it into bliss. Well, I've been trying to do that for you. Trying to let you know you're welcome here. More than welcome here. With me." He chucked her gently under the chin with two fingers. "It's not that I don't understand, babe. I do. I just don't know how to make things perfect for you."

He rose, then strode to the large viewport and stared out it without further comment.

"Nothing's ever perfect, Theo," she said after a while. Such were the problems of living in the here and now, she wanted to add but didn't. They were both adults. They both knew that.

He turned, shaking his head. "Ain't that the damned truth." He motioned to the door. "I need coffee. Drop the sizzle shields so I can go to the kitchen."

"I'll leave that door unshielded when you're here. Any PMaT transits in the area, or portal formations, will set off the alarms on my scanner. But at night or when I'm alone, we should keep all shields up." She keyed in the change and nodded at him.

Then she went back to her programs, very aware of the silver feeder cup off to her left. The threat still existed; there was still a lot of work to do. She brought up the log on the zombie dart and a cry strangled her throat. Her tech's failure had done more than crash the shield program. It had corrupted all her work to date on the dart. Almost twelve sweeps' worth, useless.

Heavy footsteps hurried her way. "Jorie?"

She waved one hand at her blinking screen with an abrupt motion, not bothering to hide her frustration. "Gone. All gone. I have to start all over again on the dart."

"Christ. Well." He huffed out a short sigh. "Just start over. It's the only thing we can do."

She thrust her hands through her hair and leaned forward for a moment, wondering if that was true. She straightened. "We need another plan. We're losing too much ground, Theo. I'm a tracker. I know survival programming and a bit more because I've made it my business to learn it. But I'm not part of a tech team. And this," she motioned to her T-MOD and its auxiliary units, "may not hold together long enough, even if I figure out exactly what to do. We may have to just try to terminate the C-Prime without the dart and hope the herd collapses in on itself from there. And that the Tresh don't take countermeasures."

The more she thought about it, the more she was convinced the feeder cup was a private message from

Prow. The Devastator team might well be unaware he sent it. It didn't fit their normal method of attack.

So that meant the Devastators had yet to make another move against her. She was sure they would before the next zombie germination cycle completed.

"Right now all we have is you, me, and Zeke." Theo didn't sound blissful. "A couple guys I talked to earlier this morning aren't interested or available to go on a private hunting expedition. I'm still waiting on callbacks from a few others."

A couple more people? With herself as the only experienced tracker, even ten people would be a tough fight. "What if I met with your security chief, your regional leaders?" She tried to remember the terms from Danjay's reports: major . . . mayor? And then some political figure over the larger populace. Meeting with a nil world's heads of state was forbidden by gen-pro regs. She no longer cared about gen-pro regs.

"It would have to go up through the chain of command, which could take weeks. And after that?" He shrugged. "You told me the horror stories, the governments fighting over access to the Guardians. It would all happen here. And you'd be at the center of it."

"We may not have a choice."

Theo's eyes narrowed. "I'm not opting for that as long as we still have some options." He pulled his cell phone—she'd finally learned the terminology for that thing—out of his pocket. "Let me try David Gray again." He wandered back to the main room.

Jorie returned to her programming, rebuilding the dart, very aware how outnumbered and ill-prepared they were. And even more aware there was nothing that could be done about it.

A few minutes later Theo returned, hunkering down again with a glimpse of that feral grin on his lips. "David's interested. I'll need to get him to Suzanne's to let him see the zombie. He knows—not what's going on, not yet, but FDLE has reports on mummified bodies—zombie attacks—that my department wasn't told about. The data wasn't considered relevant to our queries because the attacks weren't on people but on a whole herd of cows, up in Pasco County. Fifty or so."

"Cows." She ran the word though her mind. "Ah. Cattle?" When he nodded, she continued. "Juveniles in a feeding frenzy will often attack anything warm-blooded. And this Pasco is a location?" Another nod. "How far?"

"Twenty, thirty miles north—Wait, I'll show you." He left then returned with a fat paperbound book that had printed maps in the front.

"Where exactly in the region?"

"I don't know. I'll get the complete story from David when I meet with him at about three o'clock."

"He'll accept what you tell him is true?"

"He'll consider the facts and come to the only conclusion he can. He's a logical kind of guy—he worked SWAT at my department. Special Weapons and Tactics," he explained.

"Sniper?" She thought she understood the acronym.

"Damned good one. Like I said, very logical, very calm."

Sniper training was good. How Theo's friend

would react when confronted with a problem from another star system remained to be seen.

And she was still the only experienced tracker.

"I want to see Tamlynne before we meet up with him," she told Theo. She needed to hear a sentence in Alarsh. And she needed not to feel so alone.

Theo never thought he'd see the day he'd willingly say, *Hey, babe, let's go shopping for clothes.* But Jorie had to have something to wear besides her Guardian shorts and a Hawaiian print beach dress, and his T-shirts didn't cut it. They may yet have to face his lieutenant or Chief Brantley. They may yet have to do any number of other things to solve this zombie problem, which would require her fitting in visually in Bahia Vista, and she didn't.

Even the Tresh woman had worn white jeans and a touristy T-shirt.

Jorie, he knew, would look terrific in a pair of white jeans.

Plus, he sensed a growing unhappiness in her and had no trouble listing the reasons. Top of the list had to be the fact she was stuck on his world. He was acutely aware he could have exercised more control and not slept with her so soon. Okay, they were both adults. But in spite of her training and all that Guardian crap she did, she was a woman and she'd been abandoned. He'd played on that, shamelessly, because he couldn't stop wanting to touch her.

It had been a long time since he'd seduced a woman—Camille had been a practiced tease. No seduction necessary. But with Jorie, for all that he'd rushed it once he sensed there might be a mutual attraction, he'd taken his time with small caresses, light kisses. He wore her down in inches. And added to her problems.

So, hey, babe. Let's go clothes shopping, pick up something for Tammy, then we'll meet up with David Gray and talk about zombies covered by energyworms and Tresh Devastators with iridescent eyes.

Just your average couple out for an afternoon. And all women loved to shop for clothes, didn't they? Of course, going to T. J. Maxx the day after Christmas probably wasn't the brightest idea.

They managed to get her two pairs of jeans, a pair of black khakis, and some sweater and shirt combos that looked casual and covered her G-1. Tammy's size was more of a guess, so they went with an unstructured tracksuit, workout pants, and a sweatshirt.

"I didn't realize," she said, back in the SUV and buckling her seat belt, "that acquiring clothing was a body-contact sport here."

"We were amateurs up against professionals," he told her, and backed out of the space.

Her scanner was out. Anytime she was sure it wouldn't be seen, she had it out. Looking for another Tresh safe house. There had to be more than the one in Gulfview. But she'd found none.

He didn't know if that was good or bad news. He only knew it worried her.

Suzanne was home—her veterinary clinic operating on holiday hours this week—but Zeke was at the department. Theo would be too, in a couple of days. That worried him. If the zombie problem wasn't solved, he didn't discount that Jorie might go out on her own, find an abandoned house, work out of there. Not put him at risk.

All the more reason they had to solve the problem now. Meeting with David was one more positive step.

He left Jorie and Tammy alone in Suzanne's guest bedroom and found Zeke's wife in her home office at the other end of the house.

"Telecommuting," she said when he wandered in.

He immediately felt bad. "I'm keeping you from what you should be doing."

"Not at all. Robin handled the routine cases this morning." Robin was a bright, young veterinary intern that Suzanne hoped to groom as her partner. "No emergencies. No cats eating tinsel. Robin has off tomorrow and I'm handling the morning. We close at two all week."

Which was why he'd told David to meet him there at three.

"How's Tammy?"

"Tammy is quite a remarkable young woman. I have to pinch myself over the fact she's from another galaxy. She's regained a lot of spunk in the past twenty-four hours. But there's still amnesia over what happened at your house. Although Jorie says it could be artificially induced."

"Any nightmares last night?"

"Not that Zeke or I heard. But I have caught her just staring sometimes, and then she shivers. When I touch her, she snaps out of it."

He'd seen Jorie do that too and told Suzanne.

"Can you stop these people, Theo?" Suzanne's

eyes darkened. "I mean, here I am carrying on with my cats, dogs, parrots, and ducks as if nothing's changed in the world. But everything has. If you can't stop these Tresh and the zombies, what can we do?"

He squeezed her shoulder. "We'll stop them." But could they? With every passing hour, things looked bleaker; Jorie, less confident. And with every passing hour, he was more and more reminded—as with his talk with Suzanne—of all the reasons, the people he had to fight for.

He collected Jorie, accepted a surprise hug from Tammy, and, with Suzanne's spare keys in his pocket, headed off to meet the man whom he hoped would be his planet's newest recruit in the war.

"Shee-it." The former BVPD SWAT sniper and FDLE agent was from Texas and could draw that word out the way only a proper Texan could. Of medium height with dark-blond hair and blue-gray eyes, David Gray also looked like everyone's idea of the nice guy next door.

Theo had seen him in action during a few SWAT missions. Nice, unassuming David Gray was not a guy you'd want to piss off.

David pointed to the dead zombie in Suzanne's cold-storage locker. "You sure George Lucas didn't build that thing?"

"Yep. It was in my living room," Theo told him. "Alive. It's no special-effects puppet."

David's gaze moved to Jorie. "It's a baby zombie,"

she told him. "The adult drones can get," she closed her eyes briefly, "fifteen of your feet tall."

"Fifteen." David nodded, looked down at the zombie, and rocked back on his heels.

Theo tried to read his friend and failed.

"And you say these are from another galaxy?"

"Technically, no," Jorie put in before Theo could answer. "This was probably bred here. But the original zombie, yes, that's from the Chalvash System."

David wiped one hand over his face and turned to Theo. "If it was anyone but you, bud."

How often had he heard that in the past few days? "I wish it was anyone but me. This is not how I anticipated spending my vacation."

"And you shouldn't be. This is a bigger problem than a few of us can handle. You know that."

"How well is anyone going to handle it when the news trucks and the crew from *The Oprah Winfrey Show* arrive? And then the subsequent wild rumors? Stock market will crash, people will start shooting their neighbors and looting the grocery stores. Perfect opportunity for some of those nutcase terrorists to make a move. We can prevent all that with a small but effective operation here."

"What's to prevent these things from breeding more?"

"They'd need a C-Prime, a controller zombie," Jorie said. "If I can take that out with a reprogramming dart, the herd dies."

"I repeat. What's to prevent someone from bringing another C-Prime here?"

Theo looked at Jorie. He'd assumed their problems would be over with the death of this C-Prime. It

never occurred to him that someone—the Tresh—
might import others and that this was not a one-time
thing.

Jorie knotted her fingers together. "It would take
at least a year by your calendar, given the location of
the closest herd off-planet."

"A year." David didn't look happy. "And how do
we stop them a year from now?"

Jorie sucked in a deep breath. "If the *Sakanah*
wasn't destroyed, or if she managed to send a distress report, it's possible the Guardians already have
another ship on the way."

"And if they don't?"

"Then there's nothing you can do to stop the
Tresh or the zombies except what I'm doing now:
lure the C-Prime and terminate it."

"And who besides you knows how to do this?"
David asked Jorie.

Theo knew where he was going with this. He
knew, moreover, how valid it was. He just didn't like
it. Damn David for being so damned logical!

"At the moment, only me," Jorie said. "The problem isn't that I can't teach you what a tracker does; I
can. The problem is the MOD-tech that's a necessary
part of my job in tracking the zombies, in warning us
about the Tresh, communicates only in Alarsh. *My*
language. I can convert some to accept voice commands and basic displays in Vekran—English. But
much of it I can't."

David looked at Theo. "You try to do this alone,
it's a suicide mission."

"It is either way," Theo countered. "There's no
way the state or the feds could move on this in

four—max, six—days. You know that. We have to do something now. That means me, Jorie, and Martinez. If you feel you can't, I understand. But that's not going to stop the three of us from trying."

David paced over to the cold-storage locker and stared down at the zombie again. "Four," he said, turning around. "Four of us. I don't like it, Theo, but count me in."

23

It took Jorie two and a half more days to finish constructing the zombie-reprogramming-dart virus. Or at least, as she viewed it, to do all she knew how to do. Her abilities in that area were mostly self-taught, as she told Theo more than once. They had to work with the possibility that the dart would do nothing. Then hard-termination of the C-Prime would be their only option. That meant it would take longer for the herd to fall apart. And that meant—during that time—more zombies could be born.

It also gave the Tresh more time to counter their move. Which was why, when she wasn't working on the virus dart or nestled in Theo's arms, she put Theo through tracker training sessions. Gen-pro regs were history, as far as she was concerned. She told him—and trained him for—everything she could think of relative to the zombies and the Tresh.

They'd heard nothing from the Tresh or Prow

since the feeder cup appeared on Theo's back porch. The lack of interruptions was good, certainly, but it only made her more nervous.

"Like waiting for the other shoe to drop," Theo had said over dinner earlier that evening.

Jorie had never heard the expression before, but it was appropriate.

With the virus as complete as it was going to be, her next project was to modify one of the Hazers to carry the dart. "It's not a physical object," she explained to Theo when he sat beside her on the floor a few hours later, the spare Hazer's stock open to expose its core databoard. "We call it a dart because it's an encapsulated, self-executing program within the Hazer's data energy stream."

"You've done this before?" he asked, as she worked on lining up her scanner's infrared with the larger MOD-tech's.

"Not exactly."

"You've watched someone do it?"

"Only in a sim." Damn, damn! She couldn't get the scanner to synch with the main tech. She swore in Alarsh.

"I'm bothering you."

"No, I'm—" She wiped one hand over her face. Theo's presence was actually calming. She truly seemed to worry less when he was around. "I'm tired. I should be doing this in the morning, when my eyes can focus."

"Good idea." Theo brushed her bangs back from her face. "It's after midnight."

"You talked to Martinez? Tamlynne?" She knew

he did at least twice a day, but she needed the reassurance.

"Tammy's teaching the kitten to fetch balls of paper. Martinez has found two more incidents of what appear to be zombie attacks. No idea of when they occurred until we hear back from the ME's office."

If they were recent, her scanners had picked up neither of them.

"We'll get up early," Theo said. "We still have a couple days yet."

She knew they did. But she wanted to leave some time in case things went wrong. No, not *in case*. *For when* things went wrong.

She put the disassembled spare Hazer carefully on the low table Theo had brought in for her to work on and rechecked the residence shields. "I'm shielding the door. If you need anything from your kitchen, get it now."

"The only thing I need right now is you." Theo's voice was soft, his eyes smoky.

She sighed, set the shields fully around the bedroom, and turned back to him. A few hours' bliss. She lost herself and her troubles in him nightly now. Lost it all in his gentle yet expert touch, his fingers kneading, stroking. Mouths and tongues searching, touching. A few hours. And then another day of hard reality. And another day closer to hell.

The screech of an intruder alarm jolted Jorie out of a blissfully deep sleep. Theo's arms were tangled with hers at her waist, and there was some accidental bumping and shoving as she grasped for her Hazer and he—she assumed—for whatever weapon he kept tucked under his pillow.

Only as her skin rapidly chilled did she realize she was naked. She snatched her sweatshirt and shorts from the floor. Then, heart pounding and still naked, she knelt in front of her tech to check shield integrity. Theo had already pulled on a pair of sweatpants and stood at the doorway, flashlight in one hand, weapon in the other.

No breach. But someone or something had tried to. She yanked the sweatshirt over her head as she gave him the news.

"If that's one of my neighbors," he said when she looked at him, "we're going to have some explaining to do."

She rose quickly and stepped into her shorts. "At four-thirty in the morning?"

"Good point. They'll have some explaining to do too. What's out there?"

With half her tech in disarray? "A live entity. Not a zombie. That's all I know."

"One?"

"One."

"Armed?"

"We have to assume, yes." She knotted her shorts. "Ready?"

"On a count of three. You drop the door shield. I'll open the door, go out first. You follow, cover me."

"On three. One, two—" She keyed in the change from the scanner, now dangling from her hip belt. Theo yanked open the door, then, weapon out, moved quickly and quietly into the corridor. Jorie followed, Hazer primed and ready.

They swept into the main room, the glow from his flashlight moving left and right, then stopping at something—*someone*—sprawled awkwardly on the floor near Theo's couch.

She started to reach for her scanner but stopped. She didn't need it. Her heart skittered. She recognized him. "Kip!"

"Kip?" Theo asked.

"Kip. Commander Rordan." She knelt next to the still form, angling her rifle away as she felt for a pulse in his neck. Hope and fear clashed. "Alive, but I think my shield knocked him unconscious."

"Kip Rordan?" Theo's voice held a note of amazement.

She fully understood. How and why and *from where* Rordan had returned, she had no idea. She checked her scanner, keying in for the *Sakanah*'s resonance. Hoping, praying—nothing showed on her screen.

But Kip was here. And he was alive. Why? The surge of bliss she'd felt at finding him waned. Distrust raised its ugly head. The last thing left on her doorstep—so to speak—was the Tresh feeder cup. Now Kip. It was possible the two events weren't remotely connected. It was equally possible they were.

"Help me with him," she said to Theo.

"Jorie, wait." Theo hunkered down next to her. "Are you sure he's Rordan? Are you sure he's not working with the Tresh? Or the Tresh didn't send him?"

"I'm not sure of anything other than, yes, he's Kip Rordan. My scanner confirms his identity through his bioresonance and his palm print."

Rordan let out a low moan.

"We need to get him back behind the shields in the bedroom," she told Theo. "Help me lift him."

Theo was clearly not happy with her command, but whether it was because he'd disliked Rordan from the beginning or because he didn't trust which side Rordan was on now, Jorie didn't know. But she wasn't going to try for answers in an unshielded part of the residence. She might not know if she trusted Kip Rordan, but she knew for sure she didn't trust the Tresh.

Together they dragged Rordan back to Theo's bedroom and closed the door. Theo turned on a bedside lamp. She brought up the shields and checked her scanner one more time. "Nothing else; no one else is out there."

Rordan's eyelids fluttered open when she turned. "Jorie." His voice was raspy.

Theo was sitting on the edge of the bed and had his G-1 out, set for stun, Jorie noticed. Rordan was less than a maxmeter away, on the floor in front of the closet doors.

She pushed aside the fact she'd known him for years and grabbed for her professional personality. It was safer until she knew what in hell's fire was going on.

"Commander Rordan, what happened?" she asked, then, realizing she spoke in English, repeated herself in Alarsh. "What are you doing here?"

She studied him as she waited for him to answer.

He was in the green-and-black Guardian uniform—much as when she'd last seen him, several days ago. His dark hair was still pulled back but he was unshaven, his skin reddened and rough-looking. His uniform, she realized, looked rather worn as well.

Definitely not the usual impeccable Kip Rordan.

He was frowning, switching a glance from her to Theo and back to her again.

"Commander Rordan. Report."

Rordan levered himself up on his elbows. Theo stood quickly, pistol out. "Don't move."

"Tell that danker-brained nil to put the pistol away," Rordan snarled in Alarsh.

Well, that was definitely the Rordan Jorie knew and remembered. "Not until you answer my question," she replied. "The Tresh almost killed Tamlynne Herryck. You disappeared. Now you're back. I'm waiting to hear how and why."

"Not just the Tresh, Jorie. Devastators. There's a full contingent of Devastators here," Rordan said.

"Go on." She curled her fingers around the Hazer but didn't raise it. "What happened after Theo and I left in his land vehicle?"

The narrowing of Rordan's eyes told her he didn't miss the movement. "Herryck and I were receiving data from the ship. I told her to go back to the *Sakanah*. She insisted on staying a few sweeps longer. Some project." He shrugged slightly, as much as his near-prone position would allow. "I went to the galley to get a glass of water when I heard the alarms go off. By the time I got to the main room, the Tresh were everywhere. I fired on two but did little damage. They have some kind of shielding—"

"I know about that," Jorie said.

"So I backed up into the galley and transmitted a distress call to the ship, alerting them to the situation. I initiated an emergency PMaT for Herryck and myself, the ship acknowledged, then something went wrong."

"What's he saying?" Theo asked, when Rordan paused.

Theo couldn't understand Alarsh. And making Rordan use Vekran would slow them down and open too many chances for misinterpretation. "In a moment," she told Theo in English. "Continue," she said to Rordan.

"I felt the PMaT lock on, but I didn't end up on the ship. I ended up ..." He shook his head. "I'm not sure where, exactly. But it's taken me about four planetary days to walk back here."

Walk? Jorie's gaze raked over Rordan again. Hell's fire. It did look as if he'd been walking for four days.

"I haven't been able to contact the ship on my scanner," he continued. "I haven't been able to get a reading on you until about two sweeps ago. I saw the resonance of Guardian shields. But I couldn't make voice contact with you through the scanner. I thought it might have been damaged in the aborted PMaT."

"The ship's gone," Jorie said.

"Gone?" Rordan looked genuinely startled.

Jorie nodded. "Relay 'droids, seeker 'droids, all gone. Plus this planet's full of dead zones." Any one of those reasons would hamper scanner-to-scanner voice contact. But if Rordan was behind the destruction of the ship, he'd know that.

"Flashed out?"

"I don't know."

"And Herryck?"

"Alive, but they put an implant in her. I had to use a local med-tech to remove it. There's still residual damage."

"Ass-faced motherless whores!" Rordan sagged back, his eyes closing briefly.

Jorie agreed with his description of the Tresh.

He sat up again, this time completely but slowly, due to Theo's pistol following his movement. "Tell the dirt-sucker to—"

"Rordan." Jorie didn't keep the anger out of her voice.

He pulled his knees up and turned his beautiful unshaven face toward her.

"I'm going to get you a glass of water," Jorie said. "Then I'm going to brief Sergeant Petrakos on what you've told me. Understand we have no proof that what you've said is true—"

"Herryck can—"

"Herryck remembers nothing. So what would you do in my place, Commander? Gen-pro regs, now," she prodded, but her tone was anything but light. "Teammate returns from unauthorized absence after last being seen with enemy agents." She fixed him with a narrow-eyed gaze.

He nodded. "Teammate is to be treated with all courtesy but assumed to be working with the enemy until facts show otherwise."

"Then we understand each other."

"Completely."

"Then understand this as well: the people of this planet are not now or ever again to be referred to as nils, dirt-suckers, or any other creative disparaging epithet. They have ranks, they have names. You will refer to them with those ranks and names. Or you will find my courtesy toward you to be seriously lacking."

Jorie strode into the bathroom to retrieve a glass of water, wondering how much of Rordan's story was true. Wondering how she was going to prove it was—or wasn't. Any error in judgment here could be fatal.

"Oh, I could definitely tell you if he's lying. That's part of what I do as a Homicide detective," Theo said, half listening to the thrumming of the shower behind him. It was now almost six o'clock in the morning. He and Jorie had agreed letting Rordan get cleaned up didn't pose any immediate threat. If he tried to escape through the bathroom window, he'd get zapped again.

"But I'd need to speak Alarsh, and I don't," Theo continued. "So all I can do if you ask him about that Tresh feeder cup is watch his body language. But I suspect he's had training just like I have. It's not a foolproof method."

Jorie, with a pillow propped up behind her, was leaning back against her side—as Theo already thought of that half of his bed—of the wrought-iron headboard. He sat at her feet, the small G-1 pistol still in his hand, still set for stun.

As was Jorie's rifle. He noticed that too.

"All Guardians get interrogation training," Jorie confirmed. "We'll wait on that, then."

"Does he have an implant?" Theo asked, wondering what else might affect Rordan's responses if and when he decided to confront him, for Jorie's sake.

"None my scanner could find—and, yes, I checked, right after I took his palm print. But as Rordan noted, much of our tech is keyed to relay or booster through either our ship or the 'droids we put in your atmosphere for that purpose. With both of those gone, our range and capabilities are reduced."

It would be like having a cell phone with no cellphone towers. That had happened to him on vacation in the Virgin Islands. He understood her frustration.

"So you're saying he could have an implant and you wouldn't pick it up."

"I can't rule that out."

"How did he walk right into the house shields if he has a scanner?"

"That's easier. The scanner verifies that the shields exist but not their perimeters. I use my oc-set for that." She flipped the band up from around her neck and pushed the eyepiece down.

He'd noticed her doing that, never knew why. "Rordan doesn't have an oc-set?"

"He owns one, all trackers do." She pushed the band back down around her neck. "I haven't seen him wear one since this mission started, no. But he's also stayed in standard ship uniform, not tracker gear."

He'd noticed that too. He also knew cops on

patrol wore a lot more gear than detectives did. Evidently there were similarities with the Guardians.

"Have you ever heard of a beam-up go wrong and send someone elsewhere on the planet, like he said happened to him?"

She pursed her lips and blew out a small sigh. "Rare, but yes. If Ronna—our PMaT chief—knew the ship was under attack and knew Rordan and Tamlynne were in danger, she could have simply tried for an emergency relocate. If we have several field teams operating on a world, an emergency transport could take an agent from his location back to field base, rather than up to the ship. But there's no other base here that Ronna could have locked on to. To blindly send him somewhere—it's horribly risky."

"Because you don't know what's in the spot you're sending him to," Theo guessed, hearing Montgomery Scott's accented voice from various *Star Trek* episodes giving the warning about materializing inside solid rock.

She nodded.

"So—assuming that's what happened—why didn't this Ronna send Tammy?" Theo asked.

"She may have tried—assuming that's what happened. But if Prow already had a security field around Tamlynne, Ronna wouldn't have been able to get a lock on her bioresonance."

The sound of water ceased, the shower door slammed.

"What's your gut-level feeling?" he asked her, his voice low.

She sighed again. "He still hates you. If he was a

Tresh operative trying to ingratiate his way in, that's not the way to do it. He'd try to befriend you, find out what we were planning."

"Or he's been a Tresh operative and part of this zombie-breeding program all along and this is just a continuation of his usual, delightful personality."

"That would be hugely coincidental. We had no plans to come to your world. But, yes, it's something I will consider. The sad thing is, if none of this is true, we're hampering ourselves. Rordan's experience with reprogramming darts far exceeds mine. He's also an excellent tracker. I could use his help with this, desperately."

Theo knew that. He also knew he had to look past his personal dislike of the man and try—for Jorie's sake, for all their sakes—to figure out if Rordan was telling the truth.

He also knew one more thing: his private time with Jorie was over. Until they knew whose side Rordan was on, one of them would have to be awake and keeping an eye on the man at all times.

The bathroom door opened and Rordan padded out in a pair of Theo's gray sweatpants and a plain gray T-shirt. His long hair was unbound, hanging wet past his shoulders. He was scrubbing the towel over his face but stopped. Theo saw his eyes shift from Jorie with her rifle to himself with the G-1, sitting rather closely on the bed. Sooner or later—probably sooner—the man was going to figure it out, Theo knew. The only room in the house that was shielded was his bedroom. And there was only one bed in the room.

Rordan said something in Alarsh.

"Vekran," Jorie told him. "Become used to it. It's the language of the world where you live."

"As I learn for four days," Rordan said gruffly. He wiped the towel over his face one more time, then draped it over one shoulder. "So. I am not yet worthy of trust?"

"There's a lot at risk here," Jorie said.

"A long time you know me, Jorie Mikkalah."

"Yes."

Rordan said something in Alarsh that sounded unpleasant, then turned away. Jorie's gaze didn't waver. Theo could almost sense her anger and disappointment with one more problem she didn't need right now. He had to remind himself this was her teammate. He had to let her handle Rordan her way.

"You need food," Jorie said to Rordan, then looked at Theo. "Coffee?"

Theo nodded. "Drop the shield and I'll start a pot."

"We'll all go to the kitchen." Jorie tapped her scanner. "We all need food. And we need to talk."

"I do not work with Tresh," Rordan said as Jorie stood, adjusting her rifle.

Theo watched the man's eyes, watched his expressions, tried to read him as a detective should. Rordan was reacting as most innocent people would when accused. But Theo was also very aware Rordan was not "most people." He had military training. He was a Guardian. And he was from another galaxy.

But if there was a way to break him down and get at the truth, Theo would find it. He knew they were almost out of time to deal with the zombies. They couldn't afford any more mistakes now.

24

After a full day—and night—of trying to work around Kip Rordan and watch him at the same time, Jorie knew she had no choice. As much as it made her nervous to do so, she had to trust him. She pulled herself off Theo's bedroom floor, away from her blinking and humming and uncooperative tech, slipped her feet into the sandals Theo had bought for her, and headed back for the kitchen, where Theo and Rordan were finishing off midmeal—lunch, Theo called it. Probably giving each other a good case of indigestion.

Their mutual dislike was obvious. Worse after Rordan watched her get the into Theo's bed last night.

She'd "turned grounder." A derisive term for an agent or tracker—or any spacer, really—who'd chosen to be planet-bound. Dirt-locked. Forgotten what they were and adopted the ways and culture of a niltech world. Or worse, taken a grounder lover.

She hadn't forgotten she was a spacer. She never could—not even clad in the shorts and sweatshirt so indigenous to this locale. But she had taken a grounder lover. And now she was about to turn their only weapon against the zombies and the Tresh over to a man who might be a Tresh agent.

Life just became more blissful from one moment to the next.

She pulled out a chair across from Theo and sat. "I've come up against another technical problem," she said to Theo without any preliminaries. "One I can't solve alone."

He'd been leaning back in his chair, sipping that orange fizzy drink he so loved from a metal can. He let the front legs of the chair hit the floor with a thump. That was the only noise in the room. Neither he nor Rordan had bothered exchanging any meal-time pleasantries that she could hear.

"The dart?" Theo asked.

She nodded and noticed Rordan looking at her now. He knew about the dart. She'd brought him up to date over firstmeal—breakfast—but without too many specifics. And without letting him look at her tech.

Rordan's gaze was neutral, as if he sensed she'd come to a decision but didn't want to let any emotions play on his face.

She knew how that went. She'd worn the same expression herself many times with Captain Pietr.

She raised her chin slightly as she spoke to Rordan. "I am going to check everything you do. But I need your help. Or we're going to lose an effective time frame in which to confront the C-Prime."

"We'd be closer to a resolution if you'd let me work on it since yesterday," he told her in Alarsh. Rordan waved one hand before she could berate him for using their language and glanced at Theo: "I tell Jorie she wasted much time to come late to this decision."

"You'd be just as cautious if the situation were reversed," she shot back. They both knew damned well he was the one always spouting gen-pro regulations at every turn.

Rordan arched one eyebrow. "But also I would place traps," he said in Vekran. "So have you. Good." He stood. "I only hope, once you believe again that I'm with you, we still have enough time to stop the C-Prime."

So did Jorie, desperately.

She hunkered down in front of her main unit, with Rordan on her right, and showed him what she'd done. He nodded, asking very Rordan-like questions, then scrolled back through her work, making notations on his scanner. She watched him and listened to Theo pacing in his main room, talking on his cell phone to either Martinez or Gray. She wasn't sure which.

"Ah," Rordan said softly. "Here's your first problem. We're using a Hazer, yes?"

She nodded.

He pointed to a line of data. "This range parameter is too low."

"No, that's correct."

"No, it's not." He glanced at her, mouth pursed. "Where *are* you, Jorie?"

Hell and damn. She was on a planet aptly named after dirt. And she was working with regional atmospheric and environmental settings for Port Lraknal.

That corrected, he kept scrolling, now and then muttering, "Good, good." And on two occasions a short laugh and, "Excellent!"

After a while it ceased to register in her mind that neither she nor Rordan was in uniform, that the tech they worked on was cobbled together and limping at best, and that he'd been missing after last being seen confronting Tresh agents. It was as if this was just another Guardian field mission. She fell into an easy patter of exchanges with Rordan and so was surprised when Theo knelt down by her side.

"Will it work?" he asked in Vekran.

Vekran. She'd been speaking in Alarsh, and the words jarred her momentarily.

Not Vekran. English.

"Yes," she told him, feeling more confident than she had hours before. "If we get a clear shot at the C-Prime, yes."

He nodded and she saw his gaze flick toward Rordan, then back to her again, his expression unreadable. "David Gray has the reports on what might be zombie attacks in Pasco County, but I'd need to go to his office to view them." He hesitated. "He's in Tampa. That's at least thirty, forty minutes travel time each way."

He'd mentioned that information yesterday, showed her this Pasco County, north of their current location. Any expansion of zombie activity concerned her.

"I need that data," she told him.

"It would be risky to get you into his office. It's a secure facility and you don't have workable ID."

Yes, there was that. Jorie understood security requirements.

"And I definitely couldn't get you both in," Theo continued.

Jorie thought she saw what he was really asking: could he leave her alone with Rordan?

It was now late afternoon. If Rordan was allied with the Tresh, they'd had more than enough time to take some kind of action. Things at Theo's residence had been blissfully quiet.

"I need Gray's information," she repeated. "Commander Rordan still has work to do here. Bring back copies of whatever you can."

She could sense his indecision, his discomfort. He didn't want to leave her alone. Finally, he nodded. "I'm turning the answering machine off," he said, motioning to the small square object on his bedside table. "Phone rings, you answer. Every time. Got that?"

"I have acquired knowledge," she replied with a small smile. She couldn't remember the last time anyone—other than her brother—had worried about her. Jorie Mikkalah, ex-marine and Guardian Force commander, was well known for being able to take care of herself.

Yet Theo tried to take care of her, anyway. That amused her but warmed her at the same time.

"You don't answer, there's going to be a shitload

of trouble on your doorstep, quickly," he said, but he was looking at Rordan. "I can do that, no matter where I am."

"I have same interest in staying alive as you do," Rordan said with a quick glance away from his scanner.

"It's not your life I'm worried about."

"And same interest," Rordan continued as if Theo hadn't spoken, "in Jorie's life."

Theo pushed himself to his feet, grabbing Jorie's arm as he did so. She rose with him.

"Answer the phone every time," he said, his dark eyes serious. Then, taking her by surprise, he pulled her against him, his mouth on hers, one hand threading up into the back of her hair.

Her "Oof!" turned into a hard but quick kiss of passion and desperation that set her heart hammering. Theo pulled back slightly with a whispered, "No regrets," as he brushed his mouth over her ear. Then, in his normal tone: "I should be back no later than six-thirty or seven."

She waited until Theo disappeared into the main room before turning to look down at Rordan, expecting disapproval, and finding on his face what she expected. She knew she should be annoyed at Theo for staking his claim, as her brother would call it. Part of her recognized the childishness—or the very maleness—of his actions. But she also knew he cared, very much. And the kiss was not so much a message to Rordan as it was a message shared between themselves.

For if something were to happen, she knew that, yes, she would regret not having kissed him again.

She settled back down on the floor, aware of Rordan's gaze on her. She turned and awaited one of his usual remarks.

"Why?" was all he said, and that surprised her. Bothered her. She didn't understand and so gave him a perfunctory answer.

"What's between Theo Petrakos and myself is my personal business."

Rordan stared at his scanner. She could see his mouth thinning, she could see the tension in his fingers wrapping around the scanner's edge. Finally, he looked back at her. "You question my allegiance because I've been gone for four days. Now I'm wondering, should I question yours? This is not the Jorie Mikkalah I've worked with on the *Sakanah*. If Lorik were here, I'd understand. A revenge game. Stupid, but it might work. But he's not." Rordan shook his head, closing his eyes for a moment.

"This has nothing to do with Lorik."

"Then what does it have to do with?" His voice rose. "We call you the Ice Princess on board, you know that, don't you? We had bets years ago, when Lorik wanted you, how long it would take—"

Jorie shot to her feet and spun away from him, knowing if she didn't she'd smash her fist into his pretty face.

She was aware of the nickname a few of the men had bestowed on her. She'd heard the whispers, the snickers. She hadn't cared—it was almost a badge of honor on the *Sakanah*. Shipboard affairs fueled the long times between missions and filled the need for excitement.

When she was bored, she'd grab her Hazer and

pull up a zombie-attack sim in the ship's weapon's range. She'd never bed-hopped.

And then there was Lorik.

She didn't care to know if he'd won or lost the bet on how quickly he'd bed her.

"Jorie." The hard tone was gone from Rordan's voice. "Regrets. I spoke without thinking. It's just that I value you—"

"You value me?" She spun back to him. "So much that when Lorik was cheating on me, you said nothing? You even helped him in his duplicity! Tell me again how much you value me, Kip Rordan."

"Jorie—"

"Pietr offered you a captaincy too, didn't he?"

He studied her before answering. "I was aware of the offer, but that's not the only reason I took the assignment."

She bristled at his admission, but part of her anger, she knew, should be directed at Pietr. He'd deliberately made a difficult mission more difficult by pitting two teammates against each other—a method he'd been known to use before. And now look where they were.

She almost said as much, but it was useless. Pietr was gone, and the offered captaincy was a moot point.

"The assignment has changed," she said tersely. "I doubt it's one you would have signed up for originally. But it's what we have to do now: finish the dart, infect the C-Prime, and keep this world from being overrun by the Tresh."

"And Petrakos?"

She almost asked, "What about him?" but didn't

want to let the conversation get personal again. "Gen-pro regs no longer apply. It would be different if the Tresh weren't involved, if the zombies were dormant. We could stay covert, wait and see if a ship comes looking for us in a year. But that's not the case here. We need the locals' help if we're to have any chance of success."

"That's not what—"

The phone rang, interrupting Rordan's remark. She grabbed the handset and hit the button as Theo had showed her. Only as she opened her mouth did she remember to switch from Alarsh to English. "This is Jorie."

"Everything okay, babe?"

Theo's deep voice was like balm to her frayed soul. "As usual," she said, a small sigh accompanying her words.

"Rordan behaving?"

"That is as usual too."

"Being a pompous asshole, is he? If you zap him with your stunner, I won't complain."

She could almost see his feral, delicious grin. "Sadly, there's too much work to do yet."

"Well, keep it in mind. I'll check in with you later."

"Got it," she said, using his phrase.

"Very good!" He chuckled. "Later, babe." A click in her ear signaled the disconnect. She tapped the button again and replaced the handset in the holder.

Rordan had turned back to his calculations on the main unit. Jorie stared out the bedroom window for a moment, at the street bathed in late-afternoon sunlight, at the tall, thin trees with their long fronds, at the stouter trees with thick foliage draped in dangling gray mosses, and at the residences, neatly kept, that lined the street.

Two laughing children glided by on their wheeled shoes—Rollerblades. They spied Mrs. Goldstein arranging flowers in pots on her front porch and they waved. She waved back, calling out something that Jorie couldn't hear.

The children answered and continued on. A small blue land vehicle came into view from the opposite direction, moving slowly, aware of the children, no doubt. It went out of sight.

Mrs. Goldstein's front door slammed and her porch was empty.

But they were there, they were all there. In every street surrounding Theo's residence, the same scene was being enacted in a variety of ways. Bahia Vista. Florida. Earth. People living their lives. None of them knowing what lurked only a breath away.

Yet all depended on Jorie to stop it.

She stepped away from the window and resumed her place, cross-legged, in front of the MOD-tech. She concentrated on Rordan's work and tried very hard to keep all her worries at bay.

Theo telephoned three more times before Jorie was surprised by a rumbling sound outside the residence. Trotting quickly into the main room, her flip-flops slapping against her feet, she caught a glimpse of him in his large land vehicle moving past the window, heading around to the back.

Unexpectedly, her heart fluttered, and she felt silly

and stupid and girlish but couldn't keep the smile off her face. He was back early. Or else—knowing Theo as she was coming to know him—he'd always intended to return at this time but didn't want Rordan to know that.

And Rordan wouldn't know. Exhaustion after his four-day trek—or perhaps just from staring at the configurations on the screens since his return—had caught up with him. He was lying on the small couch in Theo's spare room, one arm slung over his eyes.

Still, taking no chances, Jorie had managed to adjust the security fields just enough that if Rordan left the room, she'd know. It wouldn't stop him, but he couldn't sneak up on her or out of the residence.

She waited for Theo in the kitchen, then stepped into the circle of his embrace as he held one arm out to her.

"Everything okay, babe?"

It was now. She nodded against his chest, then raised her face. "Program is complete. And it's a good one, I think. What did you find?"

"Something that will probably mean more to you than to me. Where's our friend Rordan?"

"Sleeping."

"Do we still need to keep him under guard?" He drew her away from his chest and nudged her toward the table, tossing a large tan envelope on its top. She pulled out a chair and sat, as he did.

"Only time will truly answer that question. I managed to set a motion-sensor field around the spare room, but my basic instinct is he told the truth. The emergency PMaT dumped him somewhere out of danger, either by accident or design. There have been any number of chances for him to contact the Tresh or for the Tresh to make a move on this residence after you left. Neither happened."

"Yet."

"Yet," she agreed. "You're back early."

He grinned. "I'm back right on time."

Ah! She'd been correct in her estimation of him. "And this?" She tapped the envelope.

He opened it and pushed a stack of papers her way. "All reports David and I could find that fit the zombie-attack profile. You need to go through them. Ask me anything you don't understand."

She thumbed quickly through the pages, nodding.

"You might want to turn off the field around Rordan," he told her. "We need to eat. I'll see what I can scare up for dinner for the three of us."

She frowned at him. "You need to frighten food?"

He stood and, reaching over, ruffled her hair. "More funny English."

"I prefer my food complacent, not frightened."

"How about complacent pizza?"

"Pizza?"

"You'll love it." He headed for the kitchen's cold-storage unit, then pulled out a can of his favorite beverage. She neutralized the sensor field around the spare room, turned back to the papers he'd brought, and began reading.

She was aware he left the kitchen after that, aware he was talking on his cell phone again. Aware even of Rordan's voice in the background, though only briefly.

The papers he brought her had her full attention. When he returned, she asked for explanations of some terms and odd acronyms. That solved, she went back to the papers again, her heart sinking with each page she turned.

A chime sounded, startling her. She grabbed her scanner, but it wasn't that. Theo was at his front door, talking to someone. The door closed with a thump. Then Theo came in with two large flat boxes that emitted a wonderful aroma, and for a moment her stomach overruled her troubled mind.

"Go tell Rordan dinner's ready," he said.

She stood but held up a handful of the papers. "This isn't good news."

"Eat first," he told her. "Bad news always goes better on a full stomach."

Yes, it did. Especially as it might be the last meal they'd have.

25

Pizza was wonderful—not as blissful as peanut butter, but definitely an experience Jorie would like to repeat.

The news Theo brought was much less so. Yet it was exactly what she needed, what her tech—without its interface with her ship—could no longer provide.

The northern area that Theo referred to as Pasco County wasn't the only site of expanded zombie activity. The zombies had struck south, in a region he called Manatee County. The expansion was worrisome but, as even Rordan agreed, predictable given the size of the herd.

"Big mission," Rordan noted in his halting Vekran as he perused the data. Theo's papers had replaced the pizza boxes and the delicious spicy food they'd contained. Jorie had arranged the papers chronologically. Theo was now aligning them to a crudely drawn map of the area.

Big mission, indeed. Not only what they had to do, but what the Tresh were evidently planning: a rapid zombie-breeding program that could provide them with the means to take control over a large number of the spacelane Hatches in a short period of time. What it had taken the Interplanetary Concord decades to put in place, the Tresh could accomplish in mere months.

"The key area," Jorie said, pointing to a small peninsula on the map, "is here."

Rordan agreed, nodding, confirming the location on his scanner.

"Fort Hernando Park," Theo said.

The name meant nothing to Jorie, but she vaguely remembered hearing it before and said so.

"Two bodies were found there a few days ago. Those were the pictures Martinez brought here."

She remembered fearing when she first saw them that one might have been Kip Rordan. She remembered also that Fort Hernando was a remote beach area, a T-shaped finger of land with very few residences and not accessible at night.

"That's the Skyway Bridge," Theo was saying, dragging his finger across a long line. "Fort Hernando is just west of that, jutting out into Tampa Bay. It's a county park and recreation area."

It was also—judging from the reports of attacks and *unknown disturbances* in the area, integrated with what Jorie could pull from her scanner—a hotbed of zombies.

"When do we do this?" Theo asked.

"We have to incorporate the virus program into

the Hazer's datastream," Jorie said. "That will take several sweeps—"

"Tomorrow, most early time," Rordan put in, and Jorie knew he was correct. Recalibrating the rifle was delicate work under the best of conditions and not something to be rushed. They didn't have the best of conditions—only some basic tech components on the floor of Theo's bedroom.

"Probably tomorrow," she agreed. "Which is still workable. We have a few days yet."

But what they didn't have was a sim. On missions like this, they'd always practice first in a sim on board. Work out all possible angles of attack.

That meant going into a mission blind with two operatives—Martinez and Gray—who'd never faced a zombie before and one—Theo—who had but had limited experience. The juvenile feeding frenzy Theo had encountered was mild compared to what a C-Prime could do. In spite of the training Jorie had put him through, things could go horribly wrong.

At the very least, they needed to draw up plans and contingency plans, she told Theo.

He understood. "That means we need a day where you, me, Rordan, Zeke, and David can all sit down and go over everything."

It wouldn't be a sim. She had serious doubts if it would even be enough. But it would have to do.

Bedtime, when it eventually happened, was as awkward as the night before. Jorie worked on the Hazer with Rordan until her eyes blurred, then—because she still wouldn't chance Rordan working alone—

ordered him to rest on the mattress Theo had taken
from the foldout in the spare room. The mattress,
along with a pillow and blanket, was shoved against
the bedroom wall near the bathroom.

"I'll sleep on the couch in the other room,"
Rordan said.

"I can't shield the entire house."

"You and Petrakos don't want your privacy?"
Rordan's voice held a petulant tone.

"I have one thread of patience left," Jorie
snapped, "and you're fraying it. Sleep here or sleep
standing in the shower, for all I care. But you're not
leaving this room."

She kicked off her sandals and—still wearing the
soft shorts and sweatshirt—climbed onto the larger
bed, plumping a pillow to put under her head.
Rordan eventually sat on his mattress, then, a few
minutes later, laid back, his arm thrown over his
eyes.

Jorie tucked her scanner and G-1 against her side
and dozed lightly until Theo came in. The bed jostled
as he crawled over next to her, his presence a welcome warmth in spite of the fact that Rordan was in
the room. She watched through lowered lashes as
Theo tapped on her scanner and sealed the bedroom,
just as she'd taught him.

If Rordan tried to leave the room, he'd be zapped,
as Theo was so fond of saying. If he tried for her
scanner, he'd have to pull it from between Theo and
herself.

Rordan tried neither, because when she woke,
sunlight filtering through the windows, he was still

on the floor—snoring lightly—and her scanner and G-1 were undisturbed.

Theo's hand brushed hers, sending flutters around her heart. She turned her face, lifting her chin so their lips met briefly.

"Coffee, *agapi mou*?" he asked.

"Blissful idea." She grabbed a pair of pants Theo called jeans and a short-sleeved green T-shirt on her way to the shower.

Things became less blissful as the morning progressed. The Hazer—evidently in as grouchy a mood as Rordan—refused to accept the virus-dart programming, in spite of all the tricks and tweaks Jorie and Rordan tried.

Frustrated and swearing in Alarsh, Rordan went to the kitchen for a glass of ice water. It was almost time for midmeal. Perhaps that would help. Jorie wandered into the spare room, where Theo—in jeans the same light blue as her own—had set up his own small computer. It was very rudimentary tech, but it accessed his world's databases—something Jorie's could not. She plopped down next to him on the small flowered couch.

"Are you sure it's not his programming that's screwing up?" Theo asked quietly.

"I'm double-checking everything he does," she told him. Which was also slowing down the process. It was hard to solve problems and watch for problems at the same time.

"But you can't rule it out."

"No," she admitted, a weariness enfolding her. She closed her eyes and let her head drop back against the couch. She was trying to do too much in too short a time, with too little resources.

Give up, a small voice prodded. *There's no shame in acknowledging your limitations. They're not even your limitations. If Pietr hadn't played games, if Lorik had listened, you wouldn't even be in this situation.*

It's no longer a Guardian problem. There aren't enough Guardians here to make a difference. Eventually, the security forces on this planet will recognize the zombies' existence and be forced to handle it their own way.

But there would be so many deaths before they did.

There already have been more deaths. You couldn't stop those. You didn't even know about them. Your tech is ineffectual now. The ship is gone, It's no longer a Guardian problem.

You can protect Theo. You can protect his family. You can protect your team. That's all you should be expected to do in this situation.

True. It was all true. Why couldn't she accept that?

Because you have to solve everything. You're the big important zombie tracker. Pietr even said it: there's not a zombie around that's a match for the intrepid Commander Jorie Mikkalah.

Lorik even said it: you're not a woman, you're a zombie-killing machine. It's all you care about. It's more important than anything else. Your kill record. A captaincy.

Ice Princess. Living in a castle of ice-cold corpses...

"Jorie? Jorie!"

Theo's voice in her ear, Theo's arms around her, holding her against him, against his warmth.

Jorie opened her eyes, shivering uncontrollably.

"Jorie?"

She stared into his dark eyes and tried to speak, but her mouth only made little gasping sounds. Where was she? What was happening?

"It's okay, babe. I'm here. I've got you."

"Theo?" she finally managed to croak. She wanted to reach up and touch his face, but her arms wouldn't obey. She clutched her spasming hands against her stomach.

"What—Jorie?" Rordan sat quickly on the other side of her. His fingers curled around her arm. "What's the matter?"

Alarsh. She recognized the language Rordan spoke. Alarsh. The language of her people, her ship. The ship where the intrepid Commander Jorie Mikkalah tallied her kills with notches in the wall of her ice castle. The ship where her bed was cold and vacant because Lorik had left to find a woman who was warm.

Not the Ice Princess. Killer of zombies.

She closed her eyes. A low, desperate moan filled her throat.

"I'm losing her."

Theo's voice. He'd leave too. No Ice Princess belonged with a man with a very good face. A nice family. He should be spoused. Loved. Surely all the females on his world weren't blind and unsexed. He would find love. But not with the Ice Princess.

"She...Lorik tells me of this. She dreams, cries. Cannot wake."

Vekran. Someone speaking very bad Vekran—ah. Kip Rordan, friend of Lorik's. Kip Rordan, beautiful man who knew she was cold, unloving. Lorik tells him this....

Ice Princess.

"She's come out of it before. Jorie. Babe."

Large hands, warm, against her face. She leaned into the warmth, but the keening cry started again. A thin wail. Pain. So much pain. And so cold. Shivering, shivering.

"C'mon, babe, c'mon." Hands moved rapidly up and down her arms. Another set massaged her shoulders, her back, through her thin T-shirt. "You're safe. I'm here. Nothing's going to hurt you."

More warmth. She was being pulled against someone, away from the hands at her back. Arms circled her, held her, rocked her. A low rumbling in her ear. A man's voice, singing softly.

She knew the voice. She knew the melody. Not Alarsh. Not the ship. Nothing cold, but warmth. A deep voice that sang to her before. Such bliss...

"Theo?" her voice cracked, her throat dry. But her face and Theo's neck were wet.

"It's me, babe. Easy. Take a deep breath."

She did as she was told, aching. But the shivering had stopped.

She was in Theo's lap, her face buried against his neck, her hands fisted into his chest. She could feel the tight bands of his arms around her legs and back. She took another deep breath. He was still rocking her, humming softly.

She tried to raise her face. He nudged her head back down. "Relax, *agapi mou*. It's over. I'm here. You're safe."

"Theo." She wrapped her arms around his neck, pulling herself more tightly against him, and fell into his warmth with a quiet sigh.

"She just needs to rest," Theo said, shifting Jorie slightly so his arms held her more securely. Rordan had reached for her two, three times during her nightmare or seizure or whatever it was. There was no way he was going to let the bastard touch her. He didn't discount that Rordan might have caused what happened.

He stood, intending to take her to the bedroom.

"I will—"

"No." He put the same force behind that single word as he had when he was on the streets in uniform. Rordan said nothing more. Theo angled around him, Jorie held tightly against his chest, and headed for the bedroom.

She murmured softly, her eyes fluttering open when he laid her on the bed. "Theo?"

"Naptime, *agapi mou*. Short nap."

"Mmm, yes." Her mouth curved in a small smile.

He kissed it lightly. "I'll be right here." He squeezed her hand. "Right nearby."

He straightened, then opened a drawer in his dresser and grabbed the Tresh feeder cup before confronting Rordan in the hallway, where he knew the man would be waiting.

"Kitchen," he told Rordan, holding the cup out of sight behind him. "Now."

When Rordan sat, Theo pulled back the chair catty-corner to Rordan's, sat down, and placed the cup with the unfamiliar inscription on the table. He watched Rordan's eyes and mouth and tried to keep the man's hands in sight as well. Some things didn't need a common language.

He'd done this before, placing a murder weapon or a bloodied scrap of clothing between himself and a suspect. Just put it there, watched and waited.

Rordan looked at him expectantly.

Theo sat, hands loosely on his thighs, as if Rordan's reaction mattered not at all.

Finally Rordan picked up the cup. When he turned it to the inscription, Theo saw him start slightly. Saw the minute widening of his eyes.

"Tresh," Rordan said. "You get this where?"

"You tell me."

"I . . . have no information."

"You know it's Tresh."

"These." Rordan ran his index fingers over the inscription. "Tresh words. Not my language." He put the cup back on the table.

"But you know they're Tresh words."

"Of course. Guardians know many things." Rordan's frown deepened and he looked away for a moment, muttering a long list of something nasty in Alarsh. His cursing, Theo noted, was more monotonous than Jorie's. Hers was melodious, even melodramatic. Rordan was obviously a rank amateur when it came to ass-faced vomit-brained demon's whores.

"You've known about the Tresh for a long time," Theo commented.

"Not like you want me to say, no. I learn of Tresh through study. We all learn through study. On my ship, on *Sakanah*, only few like Jorie learn Tresh through war."

Theo remembered her saying she was the only one on this team with direct combat experience.

"The war was over years ago. Yet the Tresh are here. So are you."

"I do not work with Tresh!"

Theo pushed the cup closer to Rordan. "Someone left this on my steps," he motioned toward the porch door. "Then you showed up."

Rordan shook his head. "No, no." He met Theo's hard stare without wavering.

"The Tresh are powerful," Theo continued, trying now to keep it simple enough that Rordan would understand. "They have this shielding. Better than the Guardians. I could understand someone wanting to be part of that. Part of their power. They even control zombies. Very powerful, the Tresh."

"Yes. Powerful. Dangerous—that is word? Dangerous."

Theo poked the cup again. "Why is this here?"

"Why? I don't have answer."

"You have power, Commander Rordan. You can be dangerous."

Rordan slammed one fist on the table. "I do not work with Tresh!"

Theo watched him, desperately wanting to see signs that the man was lying. But all words aside,

Rordan's body language and continued denials only proclaimed his innocence.

If he was reading Rordan correctly. There was no guarantee he was.

Rordan flexed his fingers, then clenched them again, his gaze hard and angry. He spat out a few Alarsh words, glanced past Theo toward the living room, then back to Theo again.

"Hear my words, nil." He pointed one finger at Theo, his voice lower now. "I tell you once so you understand and stop this stupid game. I do not work with Tresh. Not because I am Guardian. Forget Guardian. I do not ever hurt Jorie. You hear me? I do not *ever* hurt Jorie."

Rordan sat back, color rising on his face, and Theo saw clearly that the animosity he'd sensed from Rordan had nothing to do with Theo being a nil but with Theo being a male. And a male Jorie was interested in.

"I would never hurt her either," Theo told him.

Rordan crossed his arms over his chest. "You understand nothing of her. I understand. I live same life as Jorie. Same dreams. She is not for you."

Theo forced his anger down before answering. "I think that's Jorie's decision, not yours."

"Jorie has dream to be captain. You can give her this?"

"Your ship's gone."

"If—*when*—ship comes again, Jorie will be captain. And you say, no, Jorie? Stay and be nil with me? You love her, Petrakos?"

"I—"

"You love her and take away her dream?" Rordan

shoved his chair back and stood. "*I* do not ever hurt Jorie."

And he strode from the kitchen, leaving Theo alone with the Tresh feeder cup and an overwhelming urge to smash that cup against the wall.

He forced himself to go to the refrigerator instead. It was past lunchtime. A can of soda would suffice. He'd lost his appetite.

Rordan's words hit home. As much as he didn't want to admit it, it was something he had to face. Everything Jorie was, everything she'd lived, was something he'd never experienced. They'd found themselves thrust together because of emergency circumstances. But when normalcy returned—any kind of normalcy—they might find their lives didn't fit well together at all.

He knew that. He just didn't want to face that, because she'd made him feel alive again. She'd made him love again. She'd made him trust again.

That Rordan understood Jorie better than he did, he had no doubt. They had years of shared experiences.

Familiarity also breeds contempt.

He could only hope.

His cell phone trilled a familiar tune. He dug it out of his pocket and checked caller ID: Martinez.

"*Yassou, amigo.*"

"Theo, listen. Don't be mad at me. We got trouble. I'm doing all I can to help."

Theo's gut clenched. He did not like the sound of Zeke's voice. "What kind of trouble?"

"You and Jorie home?"

"Yeah." He was walking through his living room

and could see her sitting up in bed, talking to Rordan. He didn't like that either. Though she did appear to have some animation back in her face. "What—"

"We'll be there in about thirty minutes."

"We?"

"Trust me on this."

"Who's *we*?"

Zeke hesitated. "Chief Brantley."

"*Brantley?*" Theo stopped in his tracks.

"Just don't go anywhere, okay? I'm only trying to help. See you in thirty."

Theo flipped the cell phone closed. *Panagia mou!* The chief of the Bahia Vista Police Department was coming here to find out just what Detective Sergeant Theo Petrakos was doing harboring two illegal outer-space aliens in his city.

He could see the news-media trucks rolling in right behind him.

And then *The Jerry Springer Show*.

And then the feds' dark sedans with blackened windows.

Fuck.

26

Gerard Brantley was proof that brains were as important as brawn to a cop. That the slender, spectacled, pale-haired man was a scholar—with master's degrees in public administration and criminology—was well known. Even more well known was his impressive record as a detective in Special Investigations. Officers he worked with considered him persistent and thorough. Suspects he caught considered him relentless.

He was also often fair. At the moment, Theo was praying for fair.

"Sir," he said, stepping back to let the chief enter the front hallway. "Sir," he said a second time, to the taller, burly man behind Brantley whose tightly curled dark hair was sprinkled with silver. Jamont Sanders, head of BVPD's Forensic Services Unit. Like Brantley, he was in khaki pants and a short-sleeved white knit shirt with a green embroidered BVPD emblem. The department's casual uniform.

Behind Sanders, in jeans but the same knit shirt, was an uneasy-looking Zeke Martinez.

"Ezequiel," Theo said, with a nod.

Zeke had the good graces not to say anything. Theo wasn't sure what Zeke could say that he'd want to hear.

The only positive note was that Internal Affairs wasn't also part of the entourage. So he wasn't being stripped of rank—yet.

The four of them ended up in Theo's kitchen, because Sanders needed a table. When the broad-shouldered man pulled Jorie's battered T-MOD from his large briefcase, Theo knew he was in trouble.

"The lab tells me this is made of an unknown alloy," Sanders said without preamble, his deep voice laced with a Southern drawl. "Martinez tells me you can explain how we came into possession of it."

For a moment, Theo was shocked into silence. It never occurred to him that the laptoplike T-MOD would be analyzed for anything other than its data. He'd almost forgotten about the unit, what with zombies climbing out of green glowing portals and Tresh Devastators popping in and out surrounded by magic shields. Had Jorie's cover been blown by the firefight with the juvenile zombies in the park or after the encounter with the Tresh safe house in Gulfview, that would have made sense.

But the T-MOD...

"I can explain, sir," he told Sanders. "But I can't guarantee you'll believe everything I tell you."

"We might," Brantley said, pulling off his wire-rimmed glasses and buffing one lens with a cloth he pulled from his pants pocket. "We just came from Suzanne Martinez's veterinary clinic."

"Suzanne was busy with an emergency," Zeke said. "I had to get Baby out of cold storage myself."

No wonder Zeke looked a little green around the gills. Theo almost felt sorry for the man, but he still was disturbed by what he saw as a defection. Why did Zeke bring Sanders and Brantley into this? He knew how much Theo was opposed to any outside resources being brought in at this point—until he was sure Jorie was safe.

He no longer had a chance to do that, he realized grimly. While Brantley's involvement could result in a more effective attack on the C-Prime, it almost certainly guaranteed that Jorie—and Tam and Rordan—would become property of the media and the feds shortly thereafter.

"How much did Detective Martinez tell you about the zombie?" Theo asked Brantley.

It was Sanders who answered. "We limited his recounting to what he had experienced himself. He told us about Baby's appearance here." Sanders motioned to the wall behind him that separated the living room and kitchen. "But I understand you've had other encounters, not only with these creatures but with people who claim they're hunting them."

So Zeke had told them everything. His last small hope that he could keep Jorie out of this shivered and died.

"The biggest part of their proof—their ship—is gone," Theo told him. "It's a lot of hearsay at this point, a lot that will have to be taken on faith."

Chief Brantley leaned his hands on the back of the

kitchen chair, his shoulders hunching as if he was tired or annoyed. "Sergeant Petrakos, understand very clearly that the only reason we don't have FDLE here right now—not to mention Homeland Security—is because Detective Martinez insisted we have faith in *you*. I personally think what we have here is something far beyond our department's abilities. Far beyond even FDLE's. But Martinez refused to tell us anything more unless we first promised to give you a fair hearing." Brantley straightened and glanced at his watch. "You have forty-five minutes, Sergeant. Start talking. Or I'm getting on the phone to the governor's office and the Homeland Security task force."

Jamont Sanders had big hands for a cop who was also a forensic scientist, with fingers like brown sausages. But he was well known for his deft, sure handling of even the smallest bioswab or entomology needle probe. Sanders poked the air in front of him with that same controlled delicacy. "Force field, eh? Shit!" He jumped back as the invisible shield sizzled and a corresponding alarm erupted from Jorie's MOD-tech on the bedroom floor. "Feels like a damned Taser!"

"It could feel worse," Theo told him. "That's the low setting."

Brantley was silent, watching.

Next came the G-1 and the Hazer, both demonstrated in the backyard by an obviously condescending Rordan, who clearly didn't care that Brantley was chief of police in Bahia Vista. Theo could almost see NIL tattooed on all their foreheads.

Then the scanner, which of the three alien items

was the least convincing. Any twelve-year-old whiz kid could probably rig something like that, at least visually.

Sanders picked up the Hazer again, examining the touch pads on the stock closely. Rordan sauntered over and—with exaggerated motions, as if showing a child—went through the weapon's settings.

Theo knew language was a problem with Rordan, but not that big of one. He'd certainly made his intentions about Jorie clear enough.

He glanced at her standing on the bottom step of his back porch, hands locked loosely behind her back. They'd had little time to speak since Zeke's phone call and no time at all for anything private, other than a squeeze of her hand along with her reassurance that she'd recovered from her brief nightmare. He didn't tell her he was still worried—he wondered if the Guardians had something like post-traumatic stress syndrome.

Her gaze darted to him as if she felt his eyes on her. A corner of her mouth quirked briefly in a small smile, then faded. She was nervous, but whether it was because she was still drained from her nightmare or was picking up on his unease, Theo couldn't tell.

And couldn't ask. Not with Brantley next to him. Not with Rordan within earshot.

Minutes later they filed back into his kitchen. Sanders grabbed a chair and motioned Rordan, Jorie, and Theo to sit. The chief declined the offered chair and leaned against the counter, watching again. Zeke Martinez stood by the refrigerator, arms folded, looking decidedly anxious.

Theo was no longer immensely pissed at Zeke. He

had somewhat figured out the scenario in his mind—
the lab bringing their odd findings to Sanders, who
then cornered Zeke as primary on the Wayne case.
And Zeke had no answers other than the truth, as
bizarre as it was.

All he had was Baby, back in Suzanne's clinic. Any
twelve-year-old might be able to fabricate an "alien
scanner" and maybe even come up with some kind
of Taser-like force field. But no twelve-year-old whiz
kid could concoct Baby.

"So these zombies," Sanders was asking Jorie,
"progressed beyond their original programming?
And spread?"

She nodded. "They were designed to be defensive
but obedient. When the Mastermind Code was lost,
we could no longer control them or prevent the
adaptations from occurring. All we can do now is
terminate them as we find them."

"Killer bees," Sanders said softly.

Theo saw Jorie frown, not understanding the
analogy: a hybrid honeybee that was accidentally released in the late 1950s and became known for its vi-
cious and defensive behavior. It was never bred for
that—the bees were bred for better honey produc-
tion. But once in the wild, they became a force—and
a legend—all their own.

"Why do they mummify the people or animals
they kill?" Sanders asked.

"Again, a perversion of their original function.
They were constructed to take bodily fluid samples
from sentients they detained for analysis as protection against the spread of disease. They'd then se-
crete a chemical to seal the area where the sample

was taken—putting the probed area in isolation. Stasis." She looked at Sanders for confirmation that he understood her explanation.

He nodded. "Now they suck the entire body dry and then seal it."

Gave a whole new meaning to *overkill*, Theo noted silently.

"It wasn't always so," Jorie said. "The first attacks, a sentient might lose an arm, a leg. But now," and she shook her head, "it becomes worse as time passes. Worse with each new generation. The original program that initiated their testing function now goes out of control when stimulated by certain frequencies and the presence of a sentient. It's no longer sample and seal. It's drain, absorb, and kill—and crave more in a frenzied function to eradicate anything the zombie sees as capable of carrying an infection. Which is any warm-blooded living creature. That's why we call that their craving."

"Up until now you've stopped them." Brantley finally spoke.

"The zombies respond to frequencies emitted by tech," Jorie said. "That means they seek out—up until now—a ship, world, or station sufficiently advanced that we, that the Guardians, have no problems integrating with them. Or a low-tech world where the Guardians have established a small research colony or defensive outpost so that there are already resources in place we can use.

"Your world is different." Jorie waved one hand toward the porch door. "You don't house a Guardian outpost. And your tech is not yet at the level where the zombies would be drawn here—

which is why we ignored you, for the most part. But the Tresh didn't. I think the Tresh brought them here because they believed they could use your world and be undetected. It was happenstance that we found you. But because you are what you are—a low-tech world not capable of star travel, with no experience with other star systems—we're handicapped in solving the problem.

"Now, with my ship no longer here, we are handicapped even more. But, yes, up until now we have stopped the zombies. And, yes," Jorie said, raising her chin and meeting Brantley's skeptical gaze clearly, "even now I will try."

And that, Theo knew with a sinking heart, was why he cared so very deeply about her. It was something he'd seen in her from the very beginning: a sense of honor. Not blind duty. But a sense of honor because the lives she saved meant something to her.

It was a sense of honor—considering the odds—that could also get her killed.

Chief Brantley pushed himself away from the counter. "Sanders?"

"Sir?"

"I need to speak privately with you."

"Sir." Sanders stood, glancing around. "Sergeant, may we use your back porch?"

Theo doubted they were interested in his landscaping by zombie. "Please." He motioned toward the porch door. "We'll stay here." And sweat in the air-conditioning.

Sanders followed Brantley out. Zeke hesitated for a moment, then came and took Sanders's seat at the head of the table, opposite Theo, with Jorie and

Rordan flanking him. Rordan was poking at his scanner, ignoring the conversation.

"You still want to kick my ass, *amigo*?" Zeke asked quietly.

"Not as much as before. I can see where they had you—"

"By the *cojones*?" Zeke blew out an exasperated breath. "Like you wouldn't believe."

"I'm wondering if Brantley believes."

"You should have seen his face when I showed him Baby."

"I take it he's been tight-lipped about what he wants to do."

Zeke nodded. "You know Brantley."

"I do not," Jorie put in, fisting one hand on the tabletop. "Will he be a hindrance or a help?"

That brought a comment in Alarsh from Rordan, which received a quick, narrow-eyed look from Jorie. He decided Rordan wanted an argument. And Theo had no intention of giving Rordan anything he wanted.

"Chief Brantley could isolate the beach area, give us additional shooters, and pretty much insure innocents don't get hurt. That would be a help," Theo admitted. "But that help might come at a price." One that Theo didn't want to pay but one he couldn't refuse—unless he was willing to walk away from the job. An inconceivable thought two weeks ago. At the moment, this hour, with Jorie across from him and the memory of holding her while she shivered and cried in his arms still very real, it was no longer quite as inconceivable.

And that shocked him. Not Officer Theo Petrakos

who became Detective Theo Petrakos who was now Sergeant Theo Petrakos. Nephew of Stavros Petrakos, a thirty-year vet of the same job.

It was the only thing he'd ever wanted to do: be a cop. And he swore he'd never let a woman come between him and his career. Yet here he was with that possibility raising its ugly head.

And here he was—with Rordan's challenges echoing in his mind—capable of asking Jorie to do the same thing. What *would* he do if a Guardian ship returned?

An earsplitting sound halted his answer and doubled his heart rate.

Jorie was on her feet, lunging for the Hazer on the table. "Zombie!"

Rordan answered with a series of short commands in Alarsh that Theo ignored as he shoved away from the table. He grabbed his gun from under his shirt and was on Jorie's heels as she bolted through the porch door.

Theo was immediately aware of two things: Sanders and the chief rearing back and reaching for guns secured on their hip holsters as he and Jorie charged onto the porch, and—slightly to the left of the two men and about twenty feet behind them—a pale green glow starting to solidify into a circular shape.

Panagia mou!

"Behind you!" he shouted, praying both men trusted him enough to turn around and not perceive Jorie and himself—both armed—as the enemy.

Rordan bumped past Theo, laser pistol out, as Sanders glanced over his shoulder. "What in hell?"

The high whine of the Hazer punctuated Sanders's

question. Jorie fired, the head and upper arms of the zombie already in full view. This was no juvenile. It slithered through the portal, twisting as laser fire sizzled against the energyworms writhing frantically over its body.

Jorie's shouted exclamation drew Theo's attention. The zombie's lower arms slashed out in a wide arc. Jorie dropped to the ground as Theo flew down the porch steps toward her.

Eyes, he remembered. Opticals. Then go for the heart. He squared off, fired. Missed. *Fuck.*

The arms swung back. Theo dropped, rolled, came up again, and saw Rordan sprinting off to his left, trying to get behind the zombie. "Crossfire!" he called out. "Watch crossfire!" He didn't know if Rordan understood.

But there was no time. Razor-clawed arms were moving, reaching, grabbing, coming far too close to Jorie, who was—Theo realized with a surge of fear and anger—too close to this zombie.

Damn her!

The head dipped as he tried for the eyes again. Then one of Rordan's laser shots caught the zombie in the neck, and for a split second it reared back. Theo took aim with his Glock. Fired.

Pow-pang! An eye exploded with a hard crack, the impact from his bullet sending a chunk of zombie cheek flying in its wake.

The creature's head dipped, and when it raised it, Theo was ready. *Pow-pang!* Another eye. One more—

The zombie lunged as Jorie darted forward, Hazer raised, her concentration on the white heart and not on the clawed arm coming swiftly toward her. Theo damned the fact that he was in love with a woman who was constantly intent on bucking the odds.

"Jorie!" He jogged toward her, firing on a joint in the arm in an attempt to sever it. More zombie chunks flew, but the arm kept coming. "Jorie! Down!"

A stream of energy burst from her Hazer just as Theo reached her. There was a blinding green-white flash. He grabbed the waistband of her jeans, yanking her to the ground. She landed on her butt with a yelp and a sharp exclamation, cursing him, for all he knew. He didn't care. He threw himself on top of her as a rush of wind across his arms told him just how close they'd come to getting shredded like the roof of his car.

"Theo," she said into his neck as he was breathing in big gulps of grass and Jorie-scented air. "The zombie's gone."

He rolled off her, raising his gun as he did so. Everything was eerily quiet. And empty. Except for Rordan trotting toward them at a rapid clip, looking none too pleased at Theo's arms around Jorie. And Sanders, Brantley, and Martinez standing stiffly on his back porch.

The zombie *was* gone. Jorie must have hit its heart.

Theo shoved his gun back in his holster. Then he drew her to her feet and didn't let go of her hand, even though Rordan was a few steps to their left and Brantley and Sanders were now bearing down on them from their right.

"I thought I felt its arm swinging—"

"You felt the portal collapsing." She cocked her head at him, and it was all he could do not to plant a kiss on her smudgy, grass-streaked face. "Next time, retreat a few maxmeters from a portal before pushing me to the ground. Yes?"

"I'd like there to be no more next times," he murmured, because Rordan was approaching, spouting a stream of unintelligible Alarsh. "What now?" Theo added. He was tired of being left in the dark where Rordan was concerned. This was, damn it all, *his* planet. *His* chief was on the scene. Rordan needed to learn to speak English or—

"How many of those creatures did you say are here?" That was from Chief Brantley, his mouth set in a grim, determined line. Sanders, striding behind him, looked equally disturbed.

"About three hundred," he told Brantley, already seeing National Guard trucks rolling down Central Avenue. Followed by the media, of course. "But they're not all that big. Many are smaller, like Baby. And we really only need to deal with the main one, the C-Prime."

"Three hundred." Brantley gestured to where the zombie no longer stood. "Of those."

Now it was the black sedans with their darkened windows Theo could see in his mind. FBI. CIA. NASA. Some alphabet-soup agency that would take Jorie away from him.

As if sensing his fears, she pulled her hand from his and turned to Rordan.

Jorie said something low and short in Alarsh. Rordan was silent a moment, then answered.

Feeling lost in more ways than one, Theo turned

back to the chief. "I don't think this has to be a big operation, sir. I already have some volunteers. A smaller group would keep any wild rumors from causing problems."

"That's not your decision to make, Petrakos." The chief pulled out his cell phone and glanced up at Sanders. "I'm contacting Secretary Warren at the Homeland Security Task Force. And unless she has a better idea, the next call I'm making is to the governor."

Theo's gut clenched at Brantley's words. He didn't dare argue with the chief. But he had to. "Sir—"

"I hear you on the rumors, Sergeant. I know the problems we could face if the television stations got hold of this. But DHS is very experienced in dealing with exactly those kinds of situations. Let's let the experts do their jobs.

"In the meantime, I expect you and Commander Mikkalah to make yourselves available to anyone from DHS the minute they ask." He pinned Theo with a hard stare through his wire-rimmed glasses. "Your vacation is officially over." And with that, Brantley turned away and, cell phone to one ear, headed down Theo's driveway, Sanders in tow.

Theo waited until they'd rounded the corner of his house before letting his shoulders sag.

Zeke stepped back, his hands splayed in silent apology. "Theo—"

Theo waved away whatever his friend had to say. Words couldn't change things at this juncture. Only action could, and he wasn't sure what action to—

A blur of movement on his left and the sharp sound of a fist against flesh. Theo spun to see Rordan stumble backward, eyes wide, and land on his ass on the ground with a grunt. Jorie stood over him, eyes narrowed, rubbing her knuckles.

"What's going on?" Theo asked quickly, his right hand resting on his gun's grip as Zeke shouldered up next to him.

"Get up, Commander," Jorie ordered tersely. "In the residence. Now."

"What did he do?" Theo watched Rordan rise stiffly, a reddened patch on his jaw. When Jorie's hand shot out again, Theo thought she was moving in for a second punch, but, no, she was pointing to Rordan's scanner.

The man held on to it for a moment, then, with a brusque movement, yanked it from its holder on his belt and shoved it into Jorie's waiting hand.

She said something short and hard in Alarsh. Rordan answered, equally short. Then he strode off toward the rear door.

"What did he—" Theo repeated, but Jorie waggled the scanner in front of his face.

"That zombie," she said, "was not sent by the Tresh."

"*Rordan* did something to the scanner so the zombie would attack? But why?"

"How?" Zeke put in.

"That," Jorie answered as Theo fell into step with her, Zeke trailing behind, "is what we are now going to find out."

27

"What do you mean you did it for me?" Jorie hated questioning Rordan in Alarsh. She was all too aware of Theo's strained look as he sat at the head of the small galley table, arms folded and unable to follow the conversation. She was all too aware of Martinez's nervous, narrow-eyed stare from where he leaned against the refrigeration unit. But she couldn't afford any miscommunication right now between Kip Rordan and herself. His life, quite honestly, hung on what he said.

"We're surrounded by nils," Rordan replied easily. Her punch to his jaw didn't seem to hamper his speech, but then, for all his annoying qualities, Rordan had never been one to whine about physical discomfort. "Inexperienced, dirt-sucking nils who have no comprehension of the seriousness of the situation that faces them. I decided to show them."

"You decided." Jorie cut the rest of her sentence

short, reining in her temper because she knew she was tired and she knew she was stressed. She also knew—in a way she didn't want to face—Rordan was partially right.

But his method was so very wrong. "That zombie could have killed Theo's superior officer."

"With both you and me on the scene? The nil and his associate were also armed. I assume they've had the same training Petrakos has. And we've learned their projectile weapons can be somewhat effective. Given those factors, it was an acceptable risk."

"A risk you took without consulting me."

"I didn't foresee your cooperation." Rordan touched his jaw gingerly. Then, to her surprise, a wry grin played over his mouth. "You pack a good one for a lightweight."

"This isn't the time for levity, Commander."

A trilling noise came from Martinez's direction. Jorie angled around and saw him pull out the small communication cell phone, then place it against his ear. "Sir," Jorie heard him say. "Yes, I . . . yes, sir."

With a nod toward Theo, Martinez sidled out of the kitchen and into the main room, his conversation muffled.

Theo rose halfway, then settled back down. Jorie had a strong suspicion he didn't want to leave her alone with Rordan.

"Jorie." Rordan turned his hand toward her, palm open. "I'm trying to remind you I'm not the enemy here."

"Pulling that stunt—"

"We need to establish our dominance. I can see you allying with the nils. You're forgetting that *we* are the Guardians. This is *our* mission. If terrorizing the nils a little gains their cooperation, then it's worth it. They need to remember who and what we are." Rordan paused, then the hard edge dropped from his voice. "*You* need to remember who we are."

Jorie waited for him to say it—*you've turned grounder*—but he didn't. Perhaps he had no desire to experience another lightweight punch. Or perhaps, and more likely, he knew she already heard his condemnation.

"We," she told him, "are out of our element and outnumbered. Utilization of available resources is not only a recommended but a sane course of action."

Rordan leaned back in his chair. "Have you ever seen a nil society react to a Guardian—or to any what they call 'extraterrestrial presence' before?"

She knew what he was getting at. Rordan had been part of the rescue unit assigned to recover a Guardian research team from the nil-tech settlement on Borangari. She'd viewed the official reports and more than once listened to Rordan's stories over a pitcher of ale.

"No one's lashing us to boulders and pushing us off a cliff as a sacrifice to their god," she said.

"Goddess," he corrected. "No, they'll do things a bit differently here. But our presence will cause problems, and we will not be easily accepted."

"So you suggest what? Sit by and let the Tresh take over this world? Let them breed zombies so they can control the Hatches?"

"We risk that if you let Petrakos's people control

this mission. They might decide—and they will—that we are as much of an unknown as the zombies. I've been going over Wain's notes. Plus, Petrakos has a number of printed periodicals in his residence. You know I read Vekran better than I speak it. Everything points to a culture that is highly xenophobic. They classify as fiction the fact that sentients populate other star systems. We are the very things their nightmares are made of."

Jorie knew that. She'd read Wain's notes too. And she was trained in nil-tech contact procedures, almost all of which she'd violated in the past several days. Even since Sergeant Petrakos has ceased to be a nil and become Theo—colleague, friend, and lover—to her.

"So you add to their nightmares by dropping a live zombie in their midst." She shook her head. "And you add to mine by making me question your motives, your allegiance."

"I intended to warn you. It just appeared more quickly than I anticipated. I don't quite have your touch when it comes to that kind of thing." He hesitated, his eyes darkening. "You can't possibly still think I'm working with the Tresh?"

"I can think of a lot of different scenarios, Kip." She hefted his scanner. "For now, this stays with me. Your G-One too."

She saw the flash of anger in his eyes. So did Theo, apparently, because he shifted position, watching but very obviously coiled for action.

Not for the first time, Jorie felt torn between her upbringing, her training, and what experience was now teaching her. By all elements, Theo Petrakos was a nil. But he'd meshed so completely with her style, picked up so intuitively how Guardians operate, and she felt so comfortable with him.

But he was a nil.

Then why was she so much more attuned to him than to Rordan?

Because she loved him? Her silent admission shocked her, but even as she considered the truth behind the words, she knew what she and Theo had went far beyond the boundaries of the bedroom. She'd never felt so secure. And so afraid. And with so many larger problems looming over her.

Like Rordan's misguided loyalty—and ego. "The G-One," she repeated to Rordan, hand out. "Because, yes, I am a Guardian. And you know you'd do the same thing if the situation were reversed."

He slid the weapon across the table toward her, clearly not happy, but the tension that had surfaced in him was gone. Theo evidently sensed it too, relaxing somewhat. But not completely.

That was something else she'd noticed about Theo Petrakos. He never really relaxed. Even when she'd found him sleeping in his reclining chair, he'd lunged out of it, pinning her within seconds.

"But I will give you an assignment," she continued, pushing away the memory of Theo's body against hers. "We will be dealing with the local security force. And I fully believe their xenophobia will come into play. Finish that research. Build out from Wain's notes. I have no intention of sacrificing you, Tamlynne, or myself to their fears."

It took a moment before Rordan nodded. Then he

arched one eyebrow. "And I'm supposed to stop them when you take my weapon away?"

"We're going to deal with them with an even more powerful weapon. You can terminate ten, twenty sentients with this." Jorie raised the laser pistol. "But with knowledge, you can control thousands. And that, Commander Rordan, is what we have to use if we have any chance of survival."

She waited until Rordan left the kitchen and was several steps into the main room before she eased her forehead down on her arms, folded on the tabletop. Hell's wrath. She physically ached, though she knew part of that was the result of another nightmare episode she remembered only snatches of.

Snatches of feeling so safe with Theo's arms around her...the same arms that—after a short scrape of chair legs against the floor—encircled her now.

Jorie leaned against him for a moment, then let him pull her to her feet. She rested her face on his chest and listened to the sound of his heartbeat. Martinez's voice flowed into the room every few moments, a low exchange of sounds.

"So what's happening?" Theo asked quietly.

Too much, too fast, she thought. She pulled back slightly but kept her hands resting on his chest. She needed his warmth. "Rordan does not play subordinate well. He triggered the zombie's appearance, believing to do so would insure your chief's cooperation with us. With the Guardians," she amended. Theo was not "us."

"That was incredibly stupid." Theo's voice went hard.

"Not to Rordan's way of thinking."

"You're sure he didn't do it to help the Tresh?"

"One hundred percent? No," she admitted. "Ninety-nine percent? Yes."

"You took his gun away from him. And his scanner."

"Because I don't want him trying to play hero again. And he will. It's in his nature and—"

"He wants you."

Jorie raised her chin and blinked hard, not sure Theo had said what she thought he did.

"Rordan wants you. Wants in your pants. You understand the expression?" Theo asked, eyes narrowing for a moment as if he contemplated something unpleasant.

She nodded. She did understand.

"He's never told you?"

"He—not exactly, no." Their conversation in her office had held those overtones. But she'd tried hard since then to convince herself she was wrong. "He's Lorik's best friend."

"Goes after his buddy's girl, does he? Wonderful guy." Theo brushed her hair away from her face.

"But he was my friend too. For many years. I think you're misreading—"

"He warned me away from you. I'm not misreading anything, Jorie." He paused. "He knows I'm in love with you."

She stared at Theo, at that now-familiar face. Heat flared, blossomed. Fear spiked. Theo loved her. She wanted desperately to kiss him. She wanted desperately to push him away, so she could run and never have to face the consequences of loving him too.

"Theo—"

He covered her mouth with his, turning his name into a kiss that was heartbreaking in its gentleness.

"I know, *agapi mou*," he said after he pulled back slightly. His breath fanned her face. "My timing sucks. But I had to tell you in case something happens. I love you, Jorie. I don't care what planet you're from. I don't care who created the zombies or why. I don't care that I've never seen a gravripper and you didn't know peanut butter existed. I love you. I believe in you. And if need be, I will follow you into the jaws of hell, without question."

"Theo." Her voice wavered. She almost said it, almost told him she loved him. But fear kept the words from crossing her lips. Instead, she kissed him fiercely, far too aware that following her into the jaws of hell might be exactly what she'd have to ask him to do. Far too aware that loving Theo was also a hell of its own for her.

A noise made her suddenly pull back.

Martinez, clearing his throat. She sensed his disapproval and realized in some ways he wasn't unlike Kip Rordan. He was here to remind Theo who he was and what he was required to do.

"Sanders has scheduled a preliminary meeting for oh-eight-hundred tomorrow," Martinez said. "Information sharing, he calls it. Informal, but I take it DHS will be there."

Jorie tried to place the acronym and failed. But she guessed it was another government entity.

"I didn't tell anyone about Tammy," Martinez

continued quickly, with a slight nod to Jorie. "I thought you should know that. Suzanne and I discussed it. Tammy's vulnerable. Can't defend herself verbally. We thought..." Martinez shrugged and glanced at the floor for a moment. "You and Theo can protect yourselves. Commander Rordan's tough. But Tammy's not.

"If I'm wrong, boss, tell me," Martinez added, looking at Theo. "But we thought if Jorie knew Tammy was safe, it would be one less thing for her to worry about."

An unaccustomed tightness formed in Jorie's chest. Nils—Rordan's xenophobic nils—weren't supposed to act like this.

Theo seemed equally touched. "And if the brass finds out?"

Martinez shrugged, though a corner of his mouth quirked slightly. "Then we'll both be singing 'The Down-Home Unemployed-Cop Blues.' "

After Martinez left, Jorie returned to the floor of Theo's bedroom and the reassembled Hazer that still fought accepting the dart program. If they couldn't get the dart to infect the C-Prime, then the only choice they'd have would be to initiate a full-scale hunt. But how, on this world, with herself and Kip Rordan being the only trained Guardians?

Granted, Theo's projectile weapons were efficient for termination. Granted, it seemed as if Theo's government might be a workable problem—there would be questions, distrust, but there would be cooperation. Eventually.

But people would die while they tried to put all this together. And, worse, the Tresh would grow stronger, armed now with zombies capable of closing the Hatches. Those living in the outer colonies—like her brother—would be the first to be cut off. Trapped. Stranded.

Some colonies could survive off the planet's natural resources. But others could not. And the stations, like the one she was raised on, would be forced to evacuate to the nearest habitable world. If there was one.

Or worse—they'd be forced to bargain with the Tresh for their lives.

She went back to working on the Hazer with renewed determination.

"Jorie."

She started, turning at the sound of Theo's voice. Her back complained in wrenching spasms. She had no idea now long she'd been bent over the rifle. She stretched her legs out slowly, carefully. Painfully.

Theo folded himself down on the floor beside her and ran his hand down her leg. "It's past dinnertime. Cramp?" he asked, massaging a knot in her calf.

His ministrations hurt so much they actually felt wonderful. She locked her arms and leaned back, nodding.

"I brought David up to date," Theo said, dragging her other leg onto his lap and continuing his delicious massage. "Had a small talk with Uncle Stavros too. Both asked a lot of good questions, many of which I can't answer as well as you can."

She didn't want to answer any questions right now. She wanted to let Theo's fingers continue their exquisite torture and then reward him in kind. She sighed. Duty first, then pleasure. "What kind of questions?"

"Zombie breeding cycles, most vulnerable areas. Things like that. I told David about their heart and also the importance of hitting the eyes. But some of the details he wants I don't know. Like their life span."

"If David will be at tomorrow's meeting, I can answer everything then."

Theo shook his head. "At this point, no."

"Then why involve him now?"

"Because a good cop always appreciates backup. It has nothing to do with whether I think Chief Brantley is capable of handling this. He is. It's just that—"

Her scanner emitted three short, sharp trilling sounds that were duplicated by the T-MOD in front of her. Her heart stopped, then pounded a frenzied beat in her chest—a sound as loud as the thumping of Rordan's boots in the corridor.

She pulled her legs from Theo's lap and swung forward, her fingers flying to the T-MOD's screen. Rordan burst into the room.

Theo's "What? What is it?" was almost drowned out by Rordan's demands for coordinates and herd size.

She didn't answer either until she was absolutely sure.

"The C-Prime," she said, surprised at the calmness in her voice. "The C-Prime has scented a craving, a feeding frenzy."

"Where?" Theo asked.

She dragged over a paper map he'd used earlier and pointed to a T-shaped finger of land jutting out into the bay. The words—in Vekran or English—read *Fort Hernando*. "There. And we have less than one sweep, one *hour*, in which to get in position before it arrives."

Rordan pointed to the Hazer. "Working?"

She shook her head, anger and frustration suddenly roiling inside her. "I finally have the program loaded. But the Hazer is only recognizing half the command string—"

"It loaded?" Relief was obvious in Rordan's voice. "I think I can fix problem."

Theo was already standing. Jorie accepted his hand and let him pull her to her feet. "We'll handle the hardware," he said. "I want every weapon checked. We're not going to get a second chance."

No, they weren't. This was a mission riddled with errors, plagued with missteps. This one thing—infecting the C-Prime—had to unfold flawlessly. Because there was no option for an emergency transport if things went wrong.

This was it. Jorie raised her gaze from the line of weaponry on Theo's galley table that had been their sole focus for the past ten minutes, aware of time pushing them inexorably toward the most powerful zombie in the herd.

Do or die.

"Theo." She swallowed her fear and wrapped her fingers around his wrist.

He looked up from the projectile weapon he was

working on, a slight frown on his very good face. He was so focused on the mission now. So was she. But there was something else she had to do first, and it frightened her almost as much as the C-Prime.

"Theo," she said again, because the frown had turned into a questioning arched eyebrow. "You need to know. Before this happens tonight." She was fumbling, her Vekran failing her.

"Babe, what's the matter?"

She sucked in a breath. "Theo, I love you."

Both eyebrows arched. Then he released his hold on his weapon and dragged her into his arms.

Bliss.

28

"David? It's a go. Forty-five minutes. You in?" Theo
sat on the edge of his bed and kicked off his Top-
Siders, pinning the cell phone between his shoulder
and his ear. He pulled on his socks as he listened to
David Gray's exclamation of excitement. His own
heart pounded, but it wasn't solely due to the zombies.

"Shit, yeah. This is the big one?"

"The big one." He snagged his left boot and
shoved his foot inside. "Meet us at the 7-Eleven?"
Theo didn't have to say which one. There was only
one on the chain of finger islands leading to the state
park beach area. It was a notorious cop-stop-for-
coffee hangout.

"I'll be there in thirty."

Theo went over weapons and gear with David
one more time, feeling slightly foolish considering
David's expertise but not wanting his friend to forget
this was an unusual, high-risk circumstance.

Very high-risk. He hadn't contacted Chief Brantley. He didn't intend to.

He hoped he wasn't making the biggest mistake of his life. Because the best thing in his life had just happened five minutes before.

Jorie loved him. So he'd told her what *agapi mou* meant and answered her in Greek with *s'agapo*. I love you.

The love of his life walked in when he was sealing his tactical vest over his T-shirt. She wore the same funky shorts and half-sleeved outfit she had the first time he saw her. He knew what all the gizmos were now, even knew how she could power her weapons through the small ports in what she called her technosleeve. And how those same ports could transmit data to her ship.

If her ship was there. It wasn't, but he suspected she used the devices now to segue with Rordan.

Theo checked his Glock. "You give Rordan back his pistol?"

"He said to tell you thank you for your trust."

Theo doubted that. He glanced toward the corridor and lowered his voice. "You have a plan if he turns out *not* to be on our side?"

He saw the brief flash of pain in her eyes. It was never a pleasant course to contemplate—having to take down a partner, a colleague. A longtime friend. She'd admitted Rordan was one. That still made Theo pause and still made Theo hear Rordan's insistent challenge: *Jorie has dream to be captain. You can give her this?*

No, but he could love her. And she could love him. She'd been tinkering with something on her technosleeve. She looked up. "If he's working with the Tresh, we should know that very quickly."

"They'll react to the C-Prime?"

"They will probably note the onset of the craving. It seems to be a regular feed cycle, if somewhat early. But it wouldn't normally be something the Devastators would be concerned about, except they know I'm here."

That worried him. "Any chance they're using this C-Prime to draw you out?"

She shook her head. "I thought about that. If they didn't know where I was, yes. But they know. Prow was here."

Theo didn't miss the thinning of her mouth when she said the Devastator's name. He wondered if the man was dead or alive.

Evidently so did Jorie. "And if he still lives," she continued, "I cannot see him relinquishing to a zombie the chance to kill me. He likes, how do you say it here, the personal touch?"

She glanced at him again, head titled, eyes narrowed, looking defiant and confident and determined and saucy, all in one.

He knew that look well and brushed that saucy mouth with a kiss because he could. She was his. And he would do everything he could to keep that fact a fact.

He was rewarded with a small smile.

He draped one arm across her shoulders and pulled her tightly against him. "Let's go kick some zombie ass."

Rordan waited for Theo and Jorie in the kitchen, wearing borrowed jeans and sweatshirt but with his

Guardian weapons affixed to his belt. Theo noticed he didn't have the technosleeve that Jorie did. Tammy did—but Tammy was safe with Suzanne. Zeke would meet Theo, Jorie, and Rordan at the 7-Eleven, just like David Gray.

Theo called Zeke on the cell phone when he pulled out of his driveway. "I'm ten–fifty-one," he told him. En route.

"Ditto," Zeke said. "Fifteen minutes."

The chatter in his SUV was a mix of English, Vekran, and Alarsh, with Jorie doing double duty on translations. He was amazed at the calm tone of her voice but didn't miss her white-knuckled grip on her scanner.

He loosened his own tight grasp on the steering wheel and focused his mind into what he thought of as Code 3 mode: lights, sirens, and unknown trouble.

There were no lights flashing or sirens blaring on his vehicle. But there was unknown trouble. And known trouble. He'd faced a zombie before. He could extrapolate that experience to what it would mean to face a C-Prime.

Jorie checked the altered Hazer again, frowning. Rordan believed he'd corrected the problem, but Theo knew that the weapon and the program were untested. Things might have to be done the hard way, killing off the zombies as they appeared. Theo had no illusions they were going to eradicate the entire herd tonight.

That meant Brantley would be involved eventually. Like tomorrow. Theo ran through a list of possible excuses in his mind as to why he hadn't alerted the chief: he and Jorie were at Fort Hernando for a moonlight stroll. With Rordan. And an SUV full of weapons. Surprise! David Gray was there. Surprise! Zeke Martinez was there. Surprise! The zombies showed up.

Maybe a picnic. A sunset picnic. A few friends along. David. Zeke without Suzanne. The zombies showed up. . . .

He thought of ten more scenarios, but they all ended the same way: Brantley was pissed. And Theo would be lucky not to lose his job.

But he did not want the media here at this point. And he could see no way to keep the newshounds at bay if BVPD and DHS joined forces. It would leak, just as it always did. And Theo would lose Jorie.

As he crested the bridge leading to Tierra Grande, off to his right were the lighted caged pools and palm-tree-laced landscaping of the high-priced homes the island was known for. It was past seven-thirty; the sun had set more than an hour ago. The backs of the homes were dotted with squares of light: windows, sliding glass doors, and skylights. Other lights flickered from the small commercial buildings at the base of the bridge. The 7-Eleven sign was lit. He spotted David's red pickup on the southernmost corner of the parking lot.

His cell phone rang.

"*Yassou, amigo,*" Zeke said. "I got your six."

Theo glanced in his rearview mirror and saw headlights flash. Zeke in his black Ford Mustang.

Right on time.

The battle for Earth was about to begin.

Theo pulled his SUV next to David's pickup and motioned for Jorie and Rordan to stay put. Even though

David had found a darkened corner of the lot away from the glare of the convenience store's lights, they were all obviously armed. That could bring unwanted attention. At least Theo's vest said POLICE in large white letters across the back.

So did Zeke's. Theo leaned against David's door and unfolded the map with Jorie's notations on it. Zeke and David studied it in the light from the pickup's interior while Theo went over, again, what they needed to know about zombies: the heart, the eyes, and for God's sake watch those razor-edged arms!

"Leave the C-Prime to Jorie and Rordan," Theo said. "We need it alive to contaminate the rest of the herd. Our job is to take out any zombies protecting the C-Prime. Jorie needs a clear shot."

A loud bang and a staccato series of pops sounded behind him. Theo spun, reaching for his Glock. David jerked around in his seat.

Then out of the corner of his eye Theo saw the colors—red and blue—sparkling, streaking, falling. . . .

Fireworks. His heart slowed to a normal rhythm, then he shook his head. It was New Year's Eve.

"Concert on the beach in Pass Pointe," Zeke said. "There've been big ads for it in the newspaper all week."

Pass Pointe—a Gulf-front finger of land two blocks wide and thirty-one blocks long—was just across the channel from Tierra Grande and Fort Hernando. Theo briefly wondered if the noise from the fireworks and concert would affect the zombies but then hit on the real benefit: a big party in the

Pointe was bound to draw locals and tourists away from Fort Hernando's beaches tonight.

Satisfied everyone was on the same page, he climbed into the front seat of his SUV. Jorie was staring intently at her scanner.

"Visitors?" he asked, anxious to get his own party started yet very aware and more than a little nervous about what could happen.

She shook her head. "Not yet. But we won't have to wait long."

He cranked the engine. "Tresh?"

"No indication. But I discount nothing."

"So we go in loaded for bear."

She frowned. "Full, but with no clothes?"

It took Theo a moment—while pulling out of the parking lot and keeping an eye on Zeke's Mustang—to unscramble her misinterpretation. Bear. Bare. He grinned in spite of the fact that his adrenaline was threatening to race again.

Zombies loomed. A C-Prime. The Tresh. His career. And the foremost thought in his mind—even with Rordan no doubt glaring daggers at the back of his head—was Jorie naked.

Hopeless. He was sincerely, unequivocally hopeless.

"A bear," he said, then spelled the word, "is a large, fierce animal. It means we go in ready to fight anything."

Jorie hefted the Hazer. "If this doesn't work, anything is a good possibility."

Rordan's voice was a bearlike growl from the backseat. "It will work."

Theo had no means to judge that. He only sensed that Jorie was worried. And that worried him.

The road from Tierra Grande to Fort Hernando narrowed from four lanes to two, the palm-tree-dotted center median giving way to a plain tarmac road with rutted, sandy shoulders. Traffic disappeared as if someone had beamed the cars away. The state park didn't have any residences, and the gates to its overnight campground were locked at nine P.M. That meant another hour where people could yet come and go into the park.

Theo hoped they all went over to the Pointe for the concert. The fewer innocent civilians around to get munched on by a zombie, the better.

Headlights approached. Two boxy campers, a pickup towing a camper, and an old VW convertible with three teens inside bounced by as Theo headed over the small bridge and into the park. A few minutes later, the solitary road dead-ended at park headquarters. The old fort, fishing pier, and the popular north beach were to the right; the east beach to the left. No headlights twinkled from either direction. Theo had been out here dozens of times, but he was never more aware of its isolation than now.

And he had another cop, an FDLE sniper, and two Guardians with him.

"Which way?" he asked Jorie, mentally tallying the pros and cons of the smaller east beach area against the north beach and its picnic tables, shelters, restrooms, and playground. There was more cover on the north beach and it faced directly out into the Gulf of Mexico. The east beach faced the towering Skyway Bridge. He kept telling himself that both were too remote for there to be a concern about being seen, but the north beach had more advantages.

"That way," Jorie said, pointing out the window.

Theo's heart sank. East beach. Little cover once they passed the small picnic area. The majority of the beach faced the bridge and the channel. If there was night boat traffic—people fishing, partying, doing what people did on the water under cover of darkness—it might be an issue.

He headed east—the lights on the Skyway Bridge glowing in the distance—and filed the location away as one more thing he could do nothing about.

They parked almost at the end of the beach road, the three vehicles in a half circle. Theo leaned against the front fender, smelling the tang of salt in the air and listening to the wind whistle through the dune grass, while Jorie and Rordan had their heads together over her scanner.

Zeke and David—standing by David's pickup— were checking their weapons, including the Tresh rifle Jorie had given David. Theo let himself fixate on Jorie, on the tilt of her head, the curve of her shoulders, the soft short curtain of hair brushing her cheek. He saw her in patches of light and shadow from the vehicles' headlights and the full moon now rising overhead.

Some urge he couldn't identify forced him to memorize what he could see of her in this chiaroscuro landscape. It was as if he wanted to capture a prebattle picture so, when it was over, he could recall her satisfaction, her joy.

But something else said that wasn't it at all.

He couldn't let himself think about that. *You go*

home the end of each shift. It was something all rookies learned, a motto that was supposed to keep you alive through whatever came your way on the streets. Don't focus on what can go wrong. Focus on getting home.

They would. End of this mission, he and Jorie would go home.

"Theo!" Jorie straightened abruptly, swinging the scanner toward him. The screen swirled with colors, with data. Then it screeched.

His heart jolted accordingly and his gaze locked on movement behind her.

A faint greenish glow swirled twenty-five feet down the beach from where they stood. He drew his G-1 pistol as it became less translucent. It was easily three times as large as any he'd seen before.

"C-Prime," Jorie announced. "Hold fire."

"Holy shit," said David as four more green portals, smaller but solidifying quickly, suddenly popped into the air. Theo targeted the closest one and traced its edges with laser fire.

Then all hell broke loose.

Two of the smaller portals erupted, zombies slithering through them like oiled snakes going downhill. Laser fire spit from Rordan's weapon, slashing at the remaining expanding portal. David leveled his assault rifle and hit an emerging zombie with three quick, clean shots to the eyes.

But that only blinded it. It didn't stop it.

Zeke fired as a razor-edged arm raked too close to David's head.

"Get its heart, under the chin!" Theo dropped to one knee for a better angle and punched out three bursts. But the zombie—damn, the thing had to be more than fifteen feet tall!—took that moment to lunge sideways toward Rordan.

Theo fired again at the creature's jawline. *You owe me one,* he silently told Rordan as the zombie dissolved into a roiling cloud of green gas.

Rordan darted a narrow-eyed glance at Theo, as if he'd heard.

There was no time for a quick comeback or kudos. Two other zombies moved into the glare of the vehicles' headlights, lunging toward Theo yet staying close to the C-Prime. The C-Prime was fully through the portal, huge, almost bloated-looking, the worm-like creatures on its surface writhing so frantically that they flung themselves off in spinning clumps.

Theo saw Jorie nimbly sidestep a squirming clump and—*Cristos!*—suddenly realized how close, how too goddamned close, she was to the C-Prime.

Even though he knew better than to distract her, he couldn't help himself. Fear and possessiveness warred with practicality. He shouted her name but she didn't turn, didn't even glance his way. Rordan did, but only for a second. Then the Guardian commander was keeping pace with Jorie, covering her back per prearranged plan. Both moved too dangerously close to the biggest zombie he'd even seen.

The sharp, rapid crack of David's assault rifle brought Theo back to his own problems. Four large zombies—the one he'd killed had been replaced while he was watching Jorie—advanced across the sand toward Zeke. An upper arm lashed out, lengthening as if by magic before Theo's eyes. He fired at an arm joint as Zeke hit the sand, rolling to safety by a margin of inches.

"Extenders!" he called out to David and Zeke as he jogged toward them, his boots sinking in the soft sand. "The arms grow. Watch it!"

Another slash by a different zombie sent the tops of several medium-size palm trees flying. Theo ducked as fronds sailed past him, then straightened again, firing. He took out the zombie's topmost eye. The zombie reared back with a keening roar. Theo fired again. The laser's energy smashed into the creature's white heart, and in an almost blinding green flash it disappeared.

A larger one stepped up immediately in its place, its extenders filling the gap made by its missing partner. Behind it, Theo saw two more portals form. He swore harshly in Greek. He had to function for Jorie as Tamlynne had—destroying the portals before they could become zombies. David and Zeke would just have to handle the ones that got through.

He bounded for the pavement, trying to keep clear of the zombies as he headed for the forming portals. He heard David shout out a warning, followed immediately by the harsh sound of gunfire. He dropped to his knees behind a palm tree, cursing at the pain as stones cut through his jeans. A whining sound told him a razored claw had passed inches from his head.

"Clear!" Zeke called out. Theo sprang to his feet and ran. Three portals now glowed a sickly green, and, claws or not, he had to take out at least two of them, or Jorie wouldn't be able to get a clear shot to fire the dart.

These zombies were not like the juveniles he'd

fought in the park. These were full-grown, nasty-assed pieces of shit. And they were deadly as hell.

He sited the largest portal and ringed it with laser fire from his G-1, barely waiting to see what happened before moving to the next one. That odd *fooshing* noise a suddenly collapsing portal made was the only way he knew if he'd succeeded—or not.

One down...But the next two—*God damn it!*—weren't so cooperative. For every one he *fooshed,* another appeared. He felt as if he were inside a giant pinball machine with the damned things popping up left and right.

Fire! Jog left. Fire! Jog right. Duck, drop, roll, because a zombie noticed him again. Sweat ran down his face in spite of the cooling night air and the breeze off the bay.

He darted another glance at Jorie. Rordan was doing a good job of keeping the zombies away from her and hitting the few portals that formed nearby, but Jorie hadn't been able to get into position. Several times he saw her drop to one knee and prepare to fire, only to have to bolt out of the way of a clawed arm or worm-covered leg.

Seven zombies now guarded the C-Prime, with three directly in front of it. Jorie and Rordan hit them with a barrage. Zeke and David took on the other four, with David now using the Tresh laser rifle to very neatly drop two with nice shots under their chins. Theo laced two growing portals, going back and forth from one to the other, but he failed to see the third off to his left until a zombie was already halfway out of it.

He spun, fired, and missed. When he turned back,

claws were reaching through the two portals in front of him.

One closed with a hard *foosh!* A glance to his left showed Zeke taking on that zombie, yellow goo flying as bullets plowed into its face. Zeke wasn't going to eat for a week after this.

Theo peppered the remaining portal with laser fire, slicing across a zombie's extended arm. It fell to the sand, spasming as the portal snapped closed.

A harsh shout in Rordan's voice made him turn quickly. The spate of Alarsh words meant nothing, but they didn't have to. David's excellent marksmanship had eradicated all but two zombies—and one was reeling from Zeke's fire. Jorie surged between them, heading straight for the C-Prime.

Theo's heart stopped, but his brain and feet didn't. He bolted toward her, watching her focus on the towering monster as it seemed to focus on her, upper extenders uncoiling with an almost sinuous grace. She was too close. In the dark, cut by swaths of light from the cars' headlights, there was no way she'd see those upper arms bearing down on her.

The only reason he didn't shout her name was it would have required an expenditure of energy. And he needed every ounce if he was to reach her in time.

Rordan was too far away. She must have slipped past him as she had through Theo's grasp days ago.

She dropped to her knees a few yards from the C-Prime's feet, then shouldered her rifle. Theo heard Rordan's angry shouts to his left. He slowed, Glock out now, G-1 in his other hand, his gaze locked on that descending arm.

He had to let her fire first. If he fired and the

zombie jerked away, her shot would go wild. And they didn't have a second dart.

"I got your six, babe!" He shoved the G-1 into his waistband. The Glock was firmly in his right hand. "Hit 'im!"

Somewhere in the distance there was a high whine underscored by gunfire—David's laser rifle. Zeke's Glock. Rordan's G-1 flashing through it all. But Theo couldn't let his attention waver. There was the C-Prime. There was Jorie. The first threatened his world. The second was his whole world.

Nothing else mattered.

The Hazer jerked, a barely visible white-hot trail spitting upward—not at the C-Prime's heart but at another vulnerable spot under its jaw. A miss of inches would hit the white heart, killing it and the chance to infect the herd.

Teeth clenched, Theo waited for the flare of the laser against the zombie's charged skin. He fired the Glock at the arm, so close now he could see the worms twisting and turning. Three shots in rapid succession.

"Down!" he screamed at Jorie. "Get down!"

He lunged toward her, firing one last time as yellow goo exploded, splattering around him like pus-filled rain. He tackled her, covering her body with his as something slammed hard into his back. He tensed, waiting for the searing pain of claws ripping through his flesh, but whatever it was bounced off, leaving him gasping and groaning and very aware that he hurt like hell. But Jorie was alive.

Swearing a blue streak at him in Alarsh, but she was alive.

He glanced up. The C-Prime towered over them, seeming stunned, one arm missing, the others splaying outward slowly.

He didn't know what that meant. He didn't care. He pulled himself to his feet and her with him. "Go!" He took his gaze off the zombie just long enough to catch a wicked grin playing over Jorie's lips. It was the image he'd waited for. "Did you—"

Then someone shouted, "Move, now!" Theo grabbed Jorie's arm. They barreled back toward the vehicles, where Zeke and Rordan fought with the last zombie.

A piercing roar sounded behind them.

"It's working," Jorie huffed out as they ran. "The virus burns. The C-Prime feels it. It will return to the herd. Seek healing. Kill them—"

Theo saw it as she did, her voice halting abruptly. His boots dug into the sand. She raised her G-1 at the translucent milky square jutting out of the night darkness and shouted something in Alarsh.

Her words needed no translation.

The Tresh had arrived.

29

Theo dragged Jorie behind David's pickup, then shoved another clip into his gun. The sound of Rordan's laser filled the air. Theo edged around the front of the pickup, sighted one of the humanoid forms visible through the shimmering translucence, and fired.

No screams, no sounds of a body hitting the sand. Nothing.

Skata.

"Ass-faced demon's whores!" Jorie, beside him, poked frantically at her scanner.

"Their shielding," Theo guessed.

"Enhanced to counter projectile weapons." She said something in Alarsh as Rordan scrambled to their side of the truck. From the look on Rordan's face, Theo guessed Jorie had just delivered the bad news. *Nil weapons don't work.*

David—just off to Theo's left and using Zeke's

Mustang for cover—let loose with three shots from his assault rifle.

"No good," Theo called out to him. "Shields!"

"And that big one?" David shouted back.

The C-Prime hadn't created a portal and returned to the herd, as Jorie said it would. It stood in the moonlight swaying, serrated jaws grinding. Something was wrong.

"Are the Tresh controlling the C-Prime?" Theo asked her.

She was working her scanner and talking in soft but urgent tones to Rordan. "They're trying," she said, after a long moment during which Theo's nerves continued to fray down to the last strand. He did not want things to go wrong like this. He did not want to have to call for backup from Chief Brantley, who'd arrive with the media—and probably the end of Theo's career.

"They know we did something to the C-Prime but not what—yet," she said. "They can't risk it returning to the herd until they know. But they also can't terminate it—a herd that size would be insane without its C-Prime."

Suddenly Jorie barked out a short, mirthless laugh.

"They have an additional problem. They constructed their shields strong enough to prevent any incoming fire. But they also prevent outgoing. This is a blissful recurring problem with them."

Theo leaned around the edge of the pickup and eyed the three Tresh encased in the translucent haze. Definitely not happy. Like Jorie, they had handheld gizmos that two of them were furiously tapping. The third, armed with a rifle . . .

He ducked back. "Is that Prow?"

Jorie's gaze met his. "Yes. And I'm sure he knows I'm here."

Rordan said something, his voice low and urgent.

"My problem," Jorie answered him. "I will handle it."

Theo knew she meant Prow, and her answer didn't please him any more than it pleased Rordan. For once, he and Pompous Asshole were in agreement.

Movement near Zeke's Mustang caught Theo's attention. David and Zeke, motioning that they were coming over to the pickup. The two vehicles were almost dovetailed at the front, but there was a gap—a potentially dangerous gap—of a few open feet. "We'll cover you," Theo called out.

The rush of bodies made Prow jerk his head in their direction, but nothing more. Zeke hunkered next to Theo, his brows down, his mouth tight. Theo's cop senses went on overtime. Something was wrong—more than the obvious swaying of the C-Prime and the trio of Tresh.

Zeke shot a glance at Jorie, then back to Theo again. He patted the cell-phone case on his belt. "Suzanne text-messaged me. I..." He glanced at Jorie again. "Shit. Okay. Tammy's missing."

Theo saw the color drain from Jorie's face as he felt his own heart drop. "Tammy? When?" He draped his fingers over Jorie's wrist, trying to reassure her through his touch. *I'm here for you.*

"She leaves your residence?" Jorie's voice was strained.

"Yes—I mean, I don't know. About a half hour ago. They were folding laundry in the den. Suzanne went to the bathroom to put the towels away. When she came back, Tammy was gone. It was only seconds, she said. Not even half a minute. The doors were all locked. But she's not in the house, she's not in the yard, she's nowhere to be seen in the neighborhood. I'm...I'm sorry," Zeke stuttered, and Zeke never stuttered. "She's just...gone."

"The doors were locked," Theo repeated.

"Locked from the inside. There's no way she could leave and lock them behind her."

Theo knew that. That's why he asked. That meant there was only one other way out of Zeke's house.

"Tresh," Rordan said, spitting out the word. "The Tresh now take Tamlynne."

Jorie turned abruptly and glared at Prow. If looks could kill, Prow would be flattened, pulverized, and incinerated. Theo would gladly help, but he didn't think the takedown moves he'd learned in the police academy would be sufficient.

He was, he realized with a sinking feeling, out of his league. Killing zombies was one thing. Dealing with intergalactic politics and the kidnapping of a Guardian officer was far and away another. He didn't even know if Brantley and DHS could—

"Something's happening." David's voice held an urgent note.

Jorie was already rising, Rordan behind her. Theo glanced at her scanner, even though the swirls of colors and ASCII-like letters meant nothing to him. Then he looked at the C-Prime, because Jorie was.

A green glow encircled the monster's head, spilling over its shoulders and damaged upper-arm socket.

"It's returning to the herd?" Finally, something going right. He hoped.

"Trying," Jorie said, as Rordan carried on a monologue in Alarsh. "Perhaps I can help it." Her voice held a harsh note.

"*We,*" Theo said, but she was already ignoring him, tapping at her scanner. She brought her G-1 up to the unit. By the cascade of lights down the weapon's side, Theo guessed something had transferred between the two.

She flipped her eyepiece down and her mike up. "Cover me," she told Theo over her shoulder.

"Wait a minute, young lady," David drawled, inching forward.

"Jorie." Theo clamped his hand on her shoulder firmly enough to let her know he meant business. Just in case she missed the warning tone in David's voice.

She jerked her face toward him, brows down, golden eyes narrowed, and the intensity he saw there fairly sizzled the air between them. "Petrakos," she said. "They have Tamlynne. Now it's my turn."

"We work as a team—"

"My problem. My solution."

He'd heard that before. Didn't like it then, liked it even less now.

She shook off his hand. Then someone bumped him, moving past.

Rordan.

Jorie staggered. She regained her footing quickly. Rordan's name was the only thing Theo understood as she shouted after the man who'd already cleared the half circle of vehicles. Then she bolted. Theo's desperate grasp for her rewarded him with nothing but air.

Fuck!

The Tresh had Tamlynne. The only chance Jorie had of getting her back would be to force the Tresh to drop their shielding and try to kidnap Prow. A fact Rordan must have figured out seconds before Theo did.

Rordan, who wanted to play hero.

Damn him.

Theo tore after Jorie and Rordan, who were skirting the edge of the low dunes that lined the beach road. And who were arguing volubly if not understandably.

The Tresh turned, watching in their shielded space. Prow raised his weapon. He'd have to drop the shielding to fire, but that wasn't the only thing the Tresh could do.

Three greenish circles suddenly hovered over the sand. Theo had a feeling he would run out of ammo long before the Tresh ran out of zombies to send.

Jorie laced the closest zombie portal with her laser, then shouted at Rordan. He'd stopped, dropped to one knee, scanner out. Theo was only a few feet from Jorie when the C-Prime let out an eerie screech. It lurched toward Rordan, arms lengthening as it moved.

Jorie screamed Rordan's name, but Rordan was already racing to meet the zombie, scanner raised. A clawed arm shot out, clacking as it zeroed in on Rordan's head. The C-Prime's mouth opened, and, in a flash, Theo knew what had happened to Jorie's agent whose mummified head bore the indentations of a zombie's jaw: Guardian tech set to spur a reaction, and a Guardian agent who couldn't move fast enough.

So did Jorie, who put on a burst of speed just as Theo almost reached her.

"No!" he shouted, but she wasn't stopping and the arm was coming down. He heard gunfire. He didn't know if it was David or Zeke. It didn't matter. The zombie's claw struck Rordan's shoulder, sending him sprawling in the sand, the scanner spinning a few feet to his left. But a second claw was there, coming from the opposite direction.

If Theo stopped to aim and fire, he'd never reach Jorie. And she was already at Rordan's feet.

Theo's heart stuttered as Jorie reached up for the claw, his own cry of horror almost strangling him. Lungs burning, he lunged for her, intent on hanging on to her, no matter what. If he couldn't pull her away and the C-Prime took them both, so be it.

Cristos!

He tripped over Rordan's boots and grabbed her waist. She jerked up, the zombie lifting her. Her arms moved frantically, and only then did Theo realize the C-Prime didn't have her. *She* held on to the C-Prime.

"Theo! Loop this—"

The scanner's strap. She fumbled with the strap around one of the long bolts dotting the claw. With one arm still around her waist and his boots barely touching the sand, Theo reached past her and wrapped the strap once, twice around the bolt.

"Let go!" he bellowed at her.

"No. One more!" She hung on to the edge of the metallic arm and flipped the entire scanner over an adjoining bolt. "Now! Jump!"

She fell against him as they dropped to the sand. He dragged her to her feet. There was a third arm.

"Move!" He shoved her away.

"Rordan!" She spun, reaching for the man lying motionless behind them.

"I've got him. Now go!" He grabbed Rordan's wrists. As soon as he was clear of the C-Prime's arms, he'd throw the man over his shoulder, fireman style. But right now speed was critical.

He caught a fleeting glimpse of a grin on Jorie's lips. "Good work, *agapi mou*!"

Her Greek accent was lousy, but his heart swelled. "Move!" he said again. He didn't know why attaching the scanner to the C-Prime was important, but they'd done it. They were going to make it.

She darted past him as he dragged Rordan away from the zombie. Theo was aware of David shouting something. And Zeke—

"Down! Get down!" Zeke's command was clearer.

Another spate of gunfire. Then the high-pitched whine of a laser rifle. Theo jerked toward the sound. The Tresh shielding was gone. Prow raised his rifle and fired.

"Jorie, down!" Theo screamed as he released Rordan's wrists. He yanked his Glock from the holster and fired three shots at Prow, center mass. He pulled off two more as the Devastator lurched backward from the impact of the bullets, laser rifle sliding from his fingers.

Both Tresh on Prow's right fell too, but Theo didn't know if it was David or Zeke who took them out, because someone else was falling.

Jorie.

Jorie, twisting sideways, her G-1 slipping from her grasp, her eyes wide, her knees folding.

Theo bellowed out an anguished cry and raced toward her. She lay on the sand when he reached her, four neat holes puncturing her right shoulder, two more on her right side charring her skin, the edge of her uniform, and the top of her technosleeve. Her eyes were still wide, her breath coming in hard, rasping gasps.

"Th-Theo?"

Cristos. Cristos! "Babe." His own voice was as breathy as hers. "Don't move. Stay still. We'll get help." He reached instinctively for his police radio, but it wasn't on his hip, and for a long, agonizing moment, confusion flooded him. Then he remembered: he wasn't a cop now. He was Theo Petrakos, who'd acted without Chief Brantley's approval or help. Without the Bahia Vista PD as backup.

"Zeke!" Heart thudding painfully in his chest, he fumbled for the cell phone on his belt. The 911 dispatch would get an EMT unit here. There was a small fire station on the island, not far from the 7-Eleven. Three minutes, maybe five.

Jorie's eyelids fluttered, her gaze unfocused as Zeke and David knelt beside him in the sand.

"*Agapi mou.*" He took her cold fingers in his left hand, flipped open the cell phone with his right. "Stay with me, *agapi mou.*"

"David's got dispatch," Zeke said, closing his hand over Theo's phone. "We—"

Voices shouted something behind him. But not in English. Something...

"...Mikkalah! Mister Zeke!"

Theo looked quickly over his shoulder. Tamlynne Herryck and a team of Guardians sprinted toward him across the sand.

Tammy?

"Tammy!" Zeke thrust himself to his feet.

"Mister Zeke," she answered, then it was all Alarsh and hands shoving Theo away, scanners beeping and pinging and something that looked like a short Wookiee placing silvery pads on Jorie's wounds.

"Time is critical," a familiar voice said behind him.

Rordan, blood dripping down the side of his face and staining one arm of his uniform where the C-Prime's claw had ripped through. He leaned heavily on a shorter man's shoulder. Another Guardian in green and black. "Serious injury, she has," Rordan added.

The shorter Guardian said something. Rordan shrugged, then winced. "I go med-tech. Jorie go med-tech."

Med-tech. Theo's brain finally kicked into gear, overriding the panic that had encompassed him. Med-tech. "Your ship's here?"

"New ship," Rordan said. "Find Tamlynne. Search us. See Tresh. We go now." He hesitated. "Thank you, Theo Petrakos."

Something in the man's tone chilled Theo. "You go to the ship?" But he asked the question of thin, cold air. Rordan and his escort faded before his eyes. "No! Jorie!" Theo whipped around. Jorie, the Wookiee, and the medical team were gone. Only Tammy remained, hand on the transcomm unit on her belt.

Jorie. His Jorie was gone. Desperately, he motioned toward the night sky. "Beam me up there, Tammy."

"Regrets, Sergeant Petrakos." Tammy's voice was soft, her words uttered slowly. "Mission is over. It is good. The C-Prime is with herd."

Theo shot a glance to his right, only then realizing the towering zombie was gone.

"Virus spreads now," Tammy continued. "Tresh lose this herd."

"And Jorie?"

Tammy hesitated, drawing a breath. Then: "She, my commander, is strong. She hurts much, much serious. You..." and she stopped again, glancing first at Zeke, then at David. "You have deity? Faith? Yes? You pray. I pray very much now. For my commander."

Cristos, Cristos. Yes, he could pray. But he didn't believe anymore that his prayers would be answered.

Tammy splayed one hand outward. "Mister Zeke, tell Miss Suzanne much thanks. You are very bright stars in my sky of memory. You understand?"

"I'll tell her, Tamlynne," Zeke said quietly. "We'll miss you. And we'll pray for Jorie."

A tremulous smile played across Tammy's lips. She tapped her transcomm. Theo watched—his shoulders so stiff they hurt almost as much as his heart—as she faded into the darkness.

Jorie. A bright star in the sky of my memory.

A breeze kicked up, peppering his face with fine grains of sand. The air tasted of fish and salt. Lights twinkled on the Skyway Bridge across the water, which made a soft, shushing sound as it lapped invisibly against the sand.

In the distance, a siren wailed.

"Theo." David said his name.

Theo shook his head. He couldn't speak, because to speak he'd have to unclench his jaw, and if he did that, he wouldn't be able to contain the pained, anguished cry he knew would come out.

"Theo, the EMTs will be here shortly."

He'd never see her again. He'd never know if she lived or died.

"Guess we can give them those Tresh guys," Zeke intoned. "And the zombie arm. The ME might enjoy that. What do you think, *amigo*?"

The siren grew louder. Theo looked away from the lights on the bridge and toward the southern horizon, where the dark water met the dark sky. Flashes of light caught the corner of his eye. Fireworks off to the west, like shooting stars. He'd never be able to see them again without thinking of her.

"She's safe, Theo." Zeke's voice softened. "They have technology we don't. She'll be fine. She's back with her own people now."

Back with Rordan. *Jorie has dream to be captain. You can give her this?*

He had, he realized. If she lived, he had given her the chance for her captaincy. The C-Prime was infected, the herd would die soon. The Tresh were out of business. All because of one Commander Jorie Mikkalah.

Captain Jorie Mikkalah.

He held on to that thought, his prayer for her.

It was all he had.

30

"Captain Mikkalah, glad you're back with us. You've had us worried."

Jorie slowly opened her eyes at the sound of the unfamiliar female voice. The high-pitched tone with the clipped Gendari accent wasn't Marai, the med-tech on the *Sakanah*. The *Sakanah* was... She blinked from the room's bright lights. This wasn't the *Sakanah*, but she was in a sick bay. She'd been here for several days being poked and prodded and hooked up to tech because... because...

It came back to her in a rush: the C-Prime, Rordan's use of her program to lure it *and* stimulate the formation of a portal to send it back once it had been dealt with—a complicated little maneuver that had taken her years to create—and Rordan's failure to attach the altered tech to the zombie's arm.

She'd done it so many times to a normal zombie. Never before to a C-Prime.

Neither had Rordan. Thieving ass-faced demon's spawn. Try for *her* captaincy, would he?

Captaincy. Captain. *Captain* Mikkalah?

She blinked again. The unfamiliar female voice belonged to a familiar female face. She'd never met Admiral Nerzanya, but she recognized the thin, pale-eyed Gendari woman with the bright yellow hair. Who in the Guardian ranks wouldn't? And there was thieving ass-faced demon's spawn Kip Rordan behind her.

"Admiral, sir," she said, her voice sounding distinctly rusty. Her body felt correspondingly disused.

Of course. The C-Prime. The Tresh. And Theo—

Theo. The man with the very good face. The man who—She glanced quickly around the room. No Theo. The Tresh . . . no. She remembered him firing at Prow. Just after Prow fired at her. So Theo had to be alive. Where was he?

Her heart sank. Rordan. Thieving bastard. Rordan knew about the restrainer implant. Rordan knew Theo knew about the Guardians. Theo might already be on Paroo. Or worse. Admiral Nerzanya hated nils even more than Captain Pietr did.

Pietr. "The *Sakanah*?"

"The ship was rescued by a battle squadron that we diverted to this sector, based on new intelligence the Vekrans provided. They tracked one of their missionary ships missing for over half a century now . . ."

Missionary ship? Theo's misquote sounded in Jorie's mind: *The needs of the many outweigh the needs of the one.* Is that how he, his people, knew Vekran sacred text? And starship warp factors?

". . . to this system, and they alerted us to Tresh energy trails," the admiral was saying. "My flagship was part of that squadron. The *Sakanah* took damage, but casualties were light. And my cruisers destroyed the Tresh ship that attacked her. So rest easy, Captain."

Captain. Nerzanya said it again. "My rank is commander," Jorie chanced, knowing that correcting Nerzanya wasn't something one did if one wanted to stay a Guardian.

The woman smiled. "I'm aware of Pietr's offer. You have more than earned the promotion."

Jorie held herself very still, while every fiber in her body wanted to dance with blissful glee. Captain. Captain Jorie Mikkalah! She did it! She—

Theo.

"We're establishing an outpost in this sector," Nerzanya was saying. "This nil world is a useless ball of dirt, but the Tresh want it. We need to find out if it's for more than to breed zombies. Plus, as we expand the Hatches, it might become useful. This sector, if you accept the commission, would be under your command, Mikkalah."

This sector. Earth, the planet aptly named after dirt. The planet that was Theo's home.

Theo. She couldn't ask yet.

"Earth's planetary governments are aware of this?"

"I don't think the nils are yet ready for us, though that is something that will be considered at a later date. We've deleted all traces of our visit by reclaiming Agent Wain's body and the zombie corpses."

Jorie hesitated, not sure she wanted to know the

answer. "And Th—Sergeant Petrakos and his people?"

"Unfortunate casualties but not unexpected, knowing the Tresh," the admiral said with a slight nod to Rordan. "Full details are in the commander's report. Fortunately, he neutralized the nil sergeant's implant, so there will be no record of it if the bodies are autopsied."

The bodies . . . Theo. Theo, Zeke and David Gray.

Theo. Her breath caught painfully. Please, *please,* no . . .

She stared at Rordan, her body rigid. He stared back at her.

The admiral—who'd made her a captain, who had little respect for nils—waited.

"Thank you, Commander Rordan," Jorie said evenly.

Nerzanya smiled. "Congratulations on your promotion, Captain." With a nod, she turned and left the small room.

Rordan stayed, with only the sound of voices in the main sick bay and then the muted thump of the large doors closing behind the admiral filling the silence between them.

"*I* neutralized Theo's restrainer," Jorie said finally.

"I know. You have a knack for those kinds of things. I'm still learning." He pulled his scanner from his belt and held it out toward her. "Here's the report. What do you think?"

She almost couldn't look at it. Zeke Martinez. David Gray. Theo . . .

She changed screens, looked at the coding behind

the images, looked at time-date stamps, looked at everything, even though her heart was breaking and the tears filling her eyes sometimes made it damned near impossible to see.

And then Tamlynne's report on Suzanne's death . . .

Tamlynne . . .

Tamlynne wasn't nearly as skilled as Rordan in forgeries. But she was good enough to put this one by Nerzanya's scrutiny.

"You slut-bucket bastard," Jorie whispered, but she was smiling.

Rordan smiled too.

"The admiral's shuttle departs within the sweep," he said. "I told her you weren't one for any kind of captain's ceremony. You'd want to get right to work. She's leaving us this ship—a rather decent Red Star Class Seven. Not as big as the *Sakanah,* but it has an upgraded PMaT. Much less disconcerting. I thought—once Nerzanya was gone—you'd want to test it. Until then, as your first officer, I suggest you take a relaxing cleanser and find something to eat. Captain." He inclined his head in a gesture of respect. "I'll be on the bridge if you need me."

Jorie watched him leave, tears of gratitude and amazement spilling down her cheeks.

"I've always loved a man in uniform."

Theo closed the door of his marked patrol car and turned at the sound of Sophie Goldstein's voice. She strode up his driveway, a veritable rainbow of colors, from her red shoes to her blue-and-red polka-dot pants to her yellow-and-blue shirt with a green-and-blue polka-dot vest. She held some kind of covered dish in her arms. Again. He couldn't imagine what it was this afternoon. So far this week he'd been treated to brisket, cheese blintzes, noodle kugel, potato pancakes, and more honey puffs.

"Kasha varnishkes." She shoved the dish at him. "It's got rice, noodles, and mushrooms. It's good for you. Have you heard from your lady friend?"

His "lady friend" had returned to northern Canada to be with her family for some kind of emergency. It was somewhat the truth. And it kept Sophie from poking further into his obvious blue mood.

A mood that had little to do with his return to uniform.

That early-morning meeting almost a week ago with Chief Brantley and DHS hadn't gone so well. The zombie corpses—including Baby—had disappeared, giving DHS little to put into their top-secret file on the matter other than the Paroo cube, his G-1, and his, Brantley's, and his team's accounts. And sworn statements by all involved to reveal nothing without explicit permission from the feds. But at least Internal Affairs hadn't been there, and Theo hadn't lost his job. Nor his rank. He was still a sergeant. He was just a sergeant in uniform working street patrol.

It was a way to keep his mind off Jorie. And to do his penance to Saint Brantley.

He was damned lucky to still have a job.

He transferred his duty duffel bag to his left hand and took the covered dish. "You're spoiling me, Sophie." The dish was still warm, and the aroma, as always, was tantalizing. But in truth he'd found it hard to enjoy much of anything since New Year's Eve.

"So what's the news from Jorie?"

"Still tied up with family." He tried to smile and failed.

Sophie Goldstein made the *tsk-tsk* noise that some women had down to a fine art. She patted his arm. "Things will work out."

Juggling the dish and his duffel, Theo unlocked his back door, then dropped the duffel on the floor. He slid the dish onto the counter. A cold orange soda waited for him in the fridge.

He took a swig, then plodded through his living room, stripping off his uniform shirt as he went. A wry grin played over his mouth at Sophie's comment about a "man in uniform." There was nothing remotely sexy about a white polyester shirt and green polyester pants. And a bulky tac vest. Though Aunt Tootie might not agree. She always said Uncle Stavros—

"Theo?"

He stopped dead in his tracks in his bedroom doorway, shirt halfway down one arm, and stared at the woman in the green-and-black jumpsuit rising from the edge of his bed. His heart thumped so loudly in his chest that it momentarily trapped the name he was trying to say.

She looked like...

"Jorie?" His voice rasped with emotion. He unglued his feet from the floor and sent the command to his legs to move, now! "Jorie!"

Then she was against his chest and in his arms,

and warm and real, and, *Cristos, Cristos,* she was alive. She was alive and he was holding her, touching her, kissing her. He tasted the salt of the tears on her face as they mixed with his own.

Jorie.

He yanked the shirt off his arm, then thrust his hands in her hair, giving her mouth no escape from his. But she leaned into him, her arms locked around his neck. He had no escape either. And this was a wonderful, beautiful prison.

Only when his hands roamed down her body and up again did he remember the ugly charred wounds on her skin. "Are you okay?" He ran his fingers lightly over her shoulder.

"Now, yes." She tilted her head slightly, her eyes half-closed, her smile incredibly enticing.

"What happened? Can you—" A hundred questions raced through his mind, but as desperately as he wanted answers, he had to kiss her again.

"Please tell me you're not here to say good-bye," he murmured as he released her mouth.

Keeping her hands linked around his neck, she leaned back and looked up at him. "Actually, I'm here to offer you a job."

A job? With the Guardians? Relief flooded him— and a surge of excitement. There'd be problems if he left, but somehow, some way, he'd handle them. "Do I have time to see Tootie and Stavros?"

She grinned broadly. "No good-byes, Theo Petrakos. *We're* staying here." Her expression turned more serious, in direct contrast to the seductive way her fingers were playing with his hair at the nape of his neck. "The C-Prime and the herd are dead. But we believe the Tresh have the code and will be back. Your world—especially your Florida—is too perfect for what they want to do with the zombies. We also suspect they're here for other reasons and may still have operatives on your world. We need to know where they are. And stop whatever else they try to do."

She nodded upward. "My ship will guard your world. But the Tresh appear to be able to manipulate the zombie portals in ways we cannot. Yet. So we need someone on the surface, someone who knows this locale and knows zombies. Someone"—and her voice turned throaty and soft—"I can work closely with. As head of the mission. As *captain* of the ship."

Captain. Her dreams had come true. And his prayers had been answered.

He pulled her closer, weapons—his and hers—and bodies—soft and hard—merging. "That calls for a special celebration. Your place or mine?"

She touched her lips to his. "Yours," she whispered, her fingers already working to undo his tac vest. "You have glorious peanut butter."

About the Author

A former news reporter and retired private detective, Linnea Sinclair writes award-winning, fast-paced science-fiction romance for Bantam Spectra, including *Finders Keepers*, *Gabriel's Ghost*, *An Accidental Goddess*, *Games of Command*, and *The Down Home Zombie Blues*. Her books have won or been finalists for the RITA, Sapphire, Pearl, and Prism and in various regional RWA contests. Sinclair is also a John W Campbell Award nominee. When not on duty with some intergalactic fleet—or playing human slave to her two spoiled felines—she can be visited at *www.linneasinclair.com*.

If you enjoyed

The Down Home Zombie Blues

be sure not to miss

SHADES OF DARK

the next exciting novel from

Linnea Sinclair

—and the long-awaited sequel to her
RITA Award-winning novel

Gabriel's Ghost

Court-martialed captain Chasidah Bergren, once the pride of the Sixth Fleet, races against time to stop the powerful Hayden Burke from inciting a civil war in the empire, and placing blame for the atrocities on the man Chaz loves: Gabriel Sullivan—poet, mercenary, and hated shape-shifting telepath. But Chaz's world collapses around her when corruption surfaces among her crew, her friends, and even her family, pushing Chaz and Sully to their limits. Everyone has a price. Everyone can make a choice. But when Sully makes his, Chaz must choose between what Sully has become—and what her heart demands she must do.

Coming in summer 2008, from Bantam Books